THE GIRL WITH THE CREEL

Doris Davidson is a retired primary school teacher who still lives in her native city of Aberdeen. She has been writing novels since 1984 and the first to be published was *The Brow of the Gallowgate*, in 1990. Her married daughter is a civil servant and lives in Surrey, but her son, an art teacher, also lives in Aberdeen and presented her with a grandson in 1987.

DORIS DAVIDSON

The Girl with the Creel

HarperCollins*Publishers*

HarperCollins*Publishers*
77–85 Fulham Palace Road,
Hammersmith, London w6 8jb

A Paperback Original 1997
3 5 7 9 8 6 4 2

Copyright © Doris Davidson 1997

The Author asserts the moral right to
be identified as the author of this work

A catalogue record for this book
is available from the British Library

Set in Sabon by
Rowland Phototypesetting Ltd, Bury St Edmunds, Suffolk

Printed in Great Britain

For Isabel Harrison
whose enthusiasm for the heritage of her home town
inspired me to write this novel, with gratitude for the
help she gave, especially for correcting me on
various points.

My thanks to:

Doreen, who, as usual, read through my manuscript for typing and other errors. Sheila, Debra, Alan and Carol, for letting me bounce ideas off them, and for giving me some suggestions.

Isabel (again), Hugh and Margaret, for the help given me in the Buckie Heritage Cottage, which is run voluntarily.

All concerned in the *Buckie Drifter*, run by the Fishing Heritage Society.

Bertha and Bill, for taking Jimmy and me up the coast road, for going down into Pennan (home of 'Local Hero') and Gardenstown, and for finding the Heritage Cottage once we reached Buckie.

Jimmy himself, for driving me back there more than once.

Lillias and Ted, for telling us about the Heritage Cottage in the first place.

Last but by no means least, the lady (I very much regret not asking her name, but she lives in No. 19 the Yardie) who was hanging out clothes on the sea front when I asked if she could spare me a few minutes. Born and brought up in the Yardie (although not in No. 19), she and her husband spent a full twenty minutes with us, and she gave me a good description of life there in the thirties.

Apologies to the good folk of Buckie for not using their dialect in my novel.

PART ONE
1928–1938

Chapter One

❦

Excitement pounded through Lizann Jappy as she took her new dress out of the cupboard. It was absolutely beautiful, the ribbons slotted through the holes at the neck in a slightly darker shade of pink, and a dainty pearl button to fasten it at the back. The tiny sleeves just capped her shoulders, and although it wasn't fitted at the waist, the sash would pull it in to any size. Her father had never allowed her to go dancing before, and he had only agreed, after much pleading, on condition that her brother looked after her and saw her home. At sixteen and a half she didn't fancy being chaperoned, and, slipping the taffeta creation over her head, she hoped that Mick would be too involved with his own affairs to watch what she was doing. She intended to dance with as many different boys as she possibly could; she was determined that she would find romance tonight!

Smoothing the ends of the sash over her right hip, she went downstairs slowly and came to a halt in the doorway of the kitchen. She had planned to make a grand entrance, but the other three members of her family were in a huddle over the fire and were totally unaware of her. Waiting to be noticed, she studied them critically. People often told her that she took after her mother and she could see it for herself now. They both had fair skins – surprising with such black hair and dark brown eyes – were small-boned and quite short. The only difference was that her mother bordered on the delicate, whereas she was wiry and had hardly had a day's illness in her life.

3

Lizann compared the two men now. Mick, at twenty-one, bore a striking resemblance to their father, with bushy eyebrows and light brown hair that waved at the front. They, too, had brown eyes, but their years at sea had made their complexions ruddy and weatherbeaten, and, at just under six feet, their height camouflaged their breadth.

As if sensing her scrutiny, Willie Alec turned round. His admiring gasp let her know that the effort she had put into making herself look her best had been worth every minute, and Mick looked thunderstruck at her improved appearance. Her mother, who had bought her the dress last week in McKay's, was smiling at their reactions and nodding her head.

Recovering from his astonishment, Willie Alec spoke first. 'You'll draw lads to you like a magnet looking like that, lass. You see now, Mick? You'll have to make sure she doesn't come to any ill.'

Mick had been objecting to being told to look after his young sister, but he could understand his father's concern for her now. She was bound to be swamped with partners, and she was too young to know how to sort the chaff from the grain. She could easily be led astray by some sweet-talking rogue. 'I'll watch her like a hawk,' he promised.

'And mind you take her home,' Willie Alec grunted.

The Jappys lived in a fishing hamlet called the Yardie, consisting of sixty-five variously-sized cottages tightly packed into an unbelievably small area. Perched on the Moray Firth, it was made up of a rectangle of dwellings with several tiny, pavement-edged closes (not wide enough to be called streets), each holding perhaps five or six domiciles, filling the interior. The main road north – to Elgin and Inverness – ran close past one of the long sides of the oblong, but it was quite obvious that the houses facing it had been there first. The opposite side ran parallel with the sea, facing what had once been a small harbour but which had silted up so often that it had fallen out of use and been dismantled.

A stranger chancing on the Yardie and interested enough to investigate beyond its façade would be forgiven for thinking, probably correctly, that the original inhabitants, those who had built their homes by the grey North Sea over a century ago, had wanted to keep completely apart from the communities on either side of them and had thus packed as many houses as possible on to their piece of land. Being men who earned their living from the sea, whose whole lives were bound by the sea, they had made no provision for gardens, only minuscule backyards where nets could be spread out to dry. Sadly for those who followed on, the Yardie had eventually been swallowed by the expanding port of Buckie – although it still seemed to present an aura, an identity, of its own.

As soon as they left their house, one of those bordering the road, Lizann said indignantly, 'You don't have to look after me, Mick, I'm not a bairn now.'

'You don't know anything about lads.'

'And I'll never get a chance to learn if you keep spying on me,' she declared hotly.

They walked the rest of the way without speaking – Lizann hoping he wouldn't spoil her evening, and Mick wondering if Jenny Cowie would let him see her home when they'd have his sister with them. After delivering Lizann, of course, he and Jenny would be alone, but her house was hardly any distance along from his.

When they arrived at the Town Hall, Mick waited for Lizann to come out of the cloakroom, and was surprised when Peter Tait, his closest friend, showed up. Like Jenny, Peter lived in Main Street, Buckpool, originally another village in its own right but, practically rubbing shoulders with the Yardie, now integrated as the most westerly part of Buckie. He and Mick had been in the same class right through school, and Peter had been as often in the Jappys' house as in his own until Mick started working seven years before – he was engineer on the *Silver Star*, the drifter on which his father was mate. Peter had carried on his education in order to become an apprentice draughtsman in Jones's shipyard, but he still popped into the Yardie at least once every time Mick was ashore.

'I didn't expect to see you here,' Mick smiled. 'I thought you weren't all that keen on dancing.'

Peter pulled a face. 'Neither I am, but I went to ask if you'd come out for a walk, and your mother told me you were here.'

'I'd to take Lizann with me, worse luck.' It occurred to Mick that his friend could share his burden. 'Peter, I don't want to tie you down,' he said, hopefully, 'but ... um ... would you mind giving her a dance or two?'

'No bother.'

Lizann appearing at that moment, Peter's expression changed to stunned amazement at the butterfly which had emerged from the chrysalis. 'I'll leave you to it,' Mick grinned, and made a beeline for Jenny Cowie, the slender, chestnut-haired girl he had fancied for quite a while.

For the next twenty minutes or so, he did take a few looks to check on his sister, but when he saw that she was still being partnered by Peter, he relaxed to enjoy himself.

Proudly displaying the steps Mick had taught her over the past week, Lizann wondered why Peter didn't dance with any other girls, and then guessed that he was too shy. He'd always treated her like a sister, so he would feel as easy with her as she felt with him, but she wished he'd give some of the other boys a chance to take her up.

Peter stood awkwardly beside her during the interval, and she hoped that he would look for another partner for the second half, yet she was quite glad when he led her on to the floor as the band struck up again. The waltz had scarcely begun when he murmured, 'I hope you don't think I'm being too personal, Lizann, but that dress makes your cheeks pinker, and your mouth . . .' He stopped, colour suffusing his face, and swallowed before he went on, diffidently, 'Your lips are like cherries.'

'It's lipstick,' she laughed, 'and if my mother knew I'd bought some, she'd have a fit. I put it on in the cloakroom.'

'It suits you. You're . . . very pretty tonight. I never noticed before.'

Something in his hazel eyes made her heart flutter, and when he added, 'You're the prettiest girl here,' she didn't know what to say. She was seeing him in a different light, too, and instead of the old familiar Peter, it was a tall, handsome, blond stranger who was holding her in his arms.

For the next hour, they were acutely conscious of each other, and she felt confused each time their eyes met. His hold was firmer than it had been earlier, as if he were afraid she would turn and run, which was the last thing she would have done. She didn't know what was happening to her, but whatever it was, it felt good.

'Can I walk you home?' Peter asked suddenly, begging almost.

'If . . . you want,' she whispered, doubting if her quivering legs would carry her that far.

His grip on her tightened even more. 'There's always a mad rush at the end, so we'd best go now, before the last dance starts.'

'I'll have to tell Mick . . .'

'Go and get your coat. I'll tell him.'

In the empty cloakroom, she looked at herself in the mirror above the wash-hand basin. She had brushed her short springy hair so many times when she was getting ready that it seemed as though her face was framed by dozens of shiny black bubbles, and her dark eyes sparkled above her flushed cheeks. Her lipstick had worn off, but her lips weren't as pale as they usually were. She did look different, not pretty exactly, but certainly more attractive. Was it only the effect of the new dress, or was it because Peter had paid her those compliments? Surely it wasn't just being with him? She felt timid now at the thought of him taking her home. What if he tried to kiss her? After considering this, she decided that it might be quite nice . . . but he likely wouldn't.

When she went into the passage again, Peter was waiting for her. 'Mick says it's fine by him.'

His voice sounded odd, trembly, making her suspect that he felt just as strange as she did, but he followed her out into the darkness of the November night. The cold air made her shiver, and he put his arm round her waist and pulled her close. They walked slowly for some distance before he muttered, 'It's funny. I've always thought of you as Mick's wee sister, and now . . .' His voice trailed off, and when he spoke again it appeared to be with difficulty. 'Lizann, you don't know what you've done to me.'

Not conscious of having done anything, she wished he would explain, but he said nothing more, and when they came to the small cluster of old houses that made up the Yardie, she said, 'Goodnight, Peter, and thanks for seeing me home.'

His brief hesitation made her hope he was going to kiss her, but he dropped his arm. 'Will you come out with me tomorrow night?'

'Yes, if you like.' She didn't think her father would object; Peter had always been like one of the family.

'I'll come for you about seven, then. Goodnight, Lizann.'

When she went into the house, Willie Alec said, sharply, 'Is Mick not with you?'

'No, Peter Tait took me home.'

8

He frowned. 'Mick likely had other fish to fry.'

'She'd been safe wi' Peter, though,' Hannah smiled. 'D'you want a cup o' tea, Lizann, before you go to your bed?'

'No thanks.' Climbing the stairs, she reflected that all she wanted was peace to recall the wonderful evening.

Practically sure that Peter had wanted to kiss her good-night but had been afraid to, Lizann wondered if Mick was kissing Jenny. He probably was, for he'd had eyes for nobody else. He obviously liked her, maybe loved her? Did she love Peter? This happy yet oddly disturbing churning inside her, was that love? And did he feel the same?

At breakfast, Mick teased her about Peter. 'Anybody'd have thought it was the first time you'd met, the way you looked at each other.'

Willie Alec's scowl made Hannah step in before he could say anything. 'You'd likely been neglecting her, Mick, and Peter had danced wi' her because nobody else asked her.'

Lizann's heart cramped. Had he felt sorry for her? Was that all?

Mick dispelled her fears. 'He didn't give anybody else a chance, he stuck to her like glue.'

Hannah poured herself another cup of tea. 'It's a good thing somebody looked after her. Eat up now, or you'll be late for the kirk.'

Winking at Lizann, Mick did as he was told. Despite pressure from the American evangelists who targeted the area at intervals, Willie Alec had staunchly clung to his own beliefs, and, although Mick had quite enjoyed the catchy tunes of the hymns sung at the few Gospel meetings he had attended on the quiet, and the modern approach to the teaching of the scriptures, he hadn't been brave enough to go against his father and break away from the Church of Scotland. So he still went with Lizann

9

to the morning services in the North Church in East Church Street, while their parents attended in the evening because Willie Alec preferred the shorter sermons.

'I wish you hadn't said that about Peter,' Lizann observed, as they walked along the road. 'You wouldn't have liked if I'd told them about you and Jenny Cowie.'

Her brother grinned. 'It was just a bit of fun.'

'I'm supposed to be going out with him tonight, and Father'll likely not let me go now.'

Mick looked surprised. 'Don't tell me you and Peter ... I never thought. I'm sorry, little sister, trust me to open my big mouth and put my foot in it. But you don't need to say it's him you're going out with. Say it's one of your chums. Father wouldn't be any the wiser.'

'I'm not telling him any lies.'

'Well, I'll stick up for you if he tries to stop you seeing Peter.'

'Will you?' Lizann sounded more optimistic. 'Thanks, Mick. Um, are you to be going steady with Jenny Cowie?'

'I hope so, but she doesn't get out much. Her mother's an invalid, and her father's not fit to work, so she has to look after them. She can't have a proper job, either, just taking in sewing for other folk.'

'Oh, poor Jenny, and she's such a nice girl.'

'Aye, she is that.'

Entering the church, they walked sedately to their pew, for which Willie Alec paid half-a-crown per year and which was marked by a card reserving it for 'William Alexander Jappy and Family'. The first two hymns were each followed by a prayer and then the Reverend Crawford gathered his loins to deliver his sermon. Coming to the end of a long ministry, he sometimes did not have the energy to prepare anything new, and as soon as he launched into his oft-repeated dissertation on the Ten Commandments – so oft, indeed, that his regular listeners could have prompted him if he stuck and many of the young fry cheekily mouthed along with him – Lizann settled back to think about Peter.

It took her some time to imagine him actually kissing her, and when she succeeded, it was so pleasurable that she opened her eyes guiltily in case something of it showed in her face. All eyes were turned towards the pulpit, however, some of them glassily unaware of what the preacher fondly imagined he was getting across to them with his thumps on the large Bible, some of them even closed in sleep. Relieved, she slid back into her daydream, and she was savouring a particularly tender kiss when the raising of the minister's voice disrupted her well-being. 'Thou shalt not covet thy neighbour's house,' he roared, 'thou shalt not covet thy neighbour's wife, nor his manservant, nor his maid-servant, nor his ox, nor his ass, nor anything that is thy neighbour's.'

The gnome-like white-headed figure let his burning eyes circle round his now wide-awake congregation, searching for the nervous, give-away signs of those who had sinned during the week, or were contemplating sinning in the week to come. 'Yes, my friends!' he thundered. 'The Lord can see right into the wicked hearts of those who do not heed His laws, and He has a long memory. They will be punished – if not at the time, at some time in the future – in a way befitting the nature of their sin.'

His eyes lit upon Lizann at this point, and for the first time in her life she felt herself shrivelling under his concentrated gaze. Had she sinned without knowing it? Was it wrong to dream of being kissed? No, it couldn't be. What would be the harm in just dreaming? But she'd been praying that the dreams would come true tonight, that Peter really would kiss her.

The slamming of the big Bible made her jump, and she was glad that the minister had turned his eyes to heaven away from her. 'Amen,' he chanted, 'and may the Lord add His blessings to these readings from His holy word!'

He lowered his head then, revealing a small bald circle at his crown, and the two elders whose duty it was that day sent the collection plates (wooden handled and lined with red velvet) off along the pews, starting at the front rows – more expensive and cushioned with leather – where the most affluent townspeople sat.

During the uncomfortable silence which lasted throughout this ritual, Lizann took a surreptitious glance around her, unwilling to believe that the Reverend Crawford could suspect any of the people sitting within her range of vision to be in need of saving. None of them could ever have sinned nor would sin in the future, not even Mick . . . or would he? He was a bit of a lad amongst the girls, or so he made out to her.

The minister had descended from the pulpit to stand behind the altar, where the elders now laid their heavy burdens. Most parishioners could afford only a silver coin, few as much as a half crown, but there was a sprinkling of paper money, brown ten-shilling notes, pound notes in the different colours of the various Scottish banks, and reclining regally on top – dug up from underneath and strategically placed in full view by the elder on his way down the aisle – one large white English fiver. This, as everyone knew, had been donated by the frail widow of a long deceased skipper of a whaler whose fortune, as everyone also knew, would come to the church when she passed on.

Lizann often puzzled over this. How could the poor woman believe God was good when He had taken her husband from her as still quite a young man? Not only her husband. According to the huge black marble headstone in the kirkyard, their three sons had been 'taken to God's bosom on the same day', which was a fancy way of saying they'd all gone to the bottom of the sea with their sailing ship.

The Reverend Crawford let his eyes skim over the

money before giving thanks for the bounteous goodness of his flock, and after the last hymn he held his arms aloft to give the benediction. According to their age and ability, the men, women and children stood up quickly, or slowly, or painfully, and remained standing until the blessing was over and he had walked past them on his way to the door.

The shuffling queue waiting to shake his hand took a long time to reach the heavy portal, but, anxious as she was to find out, Lizann didn't dare to ask her brother anything until they were clear of the church. 'Mick, why is it only Thou-Shalt-Nots he goes on about? Surely somewhere in the Bible there must be some Thou-Shalts?'

Mick cocked his head to the side for a moment and then grinned. 'Thou shalt have no other gods before me, how does that suit you?'

'Och you! It still means something we shouldn't do.'

His face sobered. 'Did you do something you shouldn't with Peter last night? Is that what's got you so worried?'

'I'm not worried,' she protested. 'I never did anything, and neither did he.' Hoping that Peter wouldn't be so backward tonight, she wished she knew whether or not kissing was a sin. 'Have you ever broken any of the Commandments, Mick?'

He roared with laughter at this. 'All ten, I'd think, at some time or other.'

'You never stole anything?' she gasped.

'I once took a thruppenny bit off the collection plate when I was a wee laddie, instead of putting in the penny Mother gave me to put in.'

She was relieved that that was all, but something else had occurred to her. 'You never coveted anybody's wife, did you?'

'Many's the time, and his ox and his ass . . . well, at any rate, his cat and his dog.'

13

He was making fun of her, but she had to laugh with him. 'I suppose you've kissed lots of girls, and all,' she said, wistfully, after a while. 'Is that a Shalt-Not?'

'No, kissing's all right, thank God, or I'd have been struck down years ago.'

Lizann felt much happier knowing there was no law against it, but back home, she waited until dinner was over before she said, very cautiously, 'Peter asked me to go out with him tonight.'

Hannah cast an anxious glance at her husband, who barked, 'If you're thinking on going steady wi' him, you can put it right out o' your head. For one thing, he's ower old for you.'

Keeping his promise, Mick stepped in. 'Five years is nothing, Father, and it's not like he's a stranger.'

'She's just a bairn!'

'I am not a bairn!' Lizann cried. 'I'll be seventeen in April!'

'That's still a bairn!' her father insisted.

Mick stuck doggedly to his guns. 'She's old enough, and if you stop her seeing Peter, she could take up with some scoundrel and . . .'

'That's enough!' his father thundered. 'It's nothing to do wi' you. I'm her father, and I'm not letting her go wi' anybody yet!'

'But I've promised,' Lizann wailed.

'You'd no right to promise anything without asking me first!'

'You weren't there to ask,' she ventured.

'Peter should have had the sense not to . . .'

'God Almighty!' Mick said, vehemently. 'Anybody would think it was still the Dark Ages to hear you. Lassies of fifteen, never mind sixteen, have lads nowadays, and . . .'

'Not my lassie!' Willie Alec's eyes were glittering dangerously.

'It's no use, Mick,' Lizann said, her voice breaking, and bursting into tears she ran upstairs.

Giving his father a venomous glare, Mick charged out, slamming the outside door behind him, and Hannah, who had made no contribution to the argument, rose to clear the table, her lips gripped tightly together.

Gathering that his wife was also outraged by his decision, Willie Alec shifted himself to his armchair by the fire, but after a few minutes, he said, as if in defence, 'I'm feared for her, Hannah.' Getting no answer, he added, 'She's innocent as a babe.' A reply still not forthcoming, he fell silent, but when she was laying the dishes back in the dresser, he muttered, 'She might take up wi' the first lad that makes eyes at her, a rotter, maybe, like Mick said, and we ken Peter wouldna . . .' Rising, he went purposefully to the foot of the stairs and called his daughter down.

It wasn't in him to apologize or admit he'd been wrong, so when Lizann made her reluctant appearance, her eyes still red and puffy, he mumbled, 'Your mother . . . we think . . . ach! You can go out wi' Peter the night.'

Her heart leaping, she said, 'What if he wants us to go steady?'

After a slight hesitation, her father nodded. 'But not every night. I just saw your mother once a week when we was courting.'

Lizann was appalled at this. 'I've only to see him once a week?'

Her fallen face made him relent. 'Twice then, but that's plenty.' He stood up. 'I think I'll take a walk to let my dinner go down.'

Lizann looked gratefully at her mother when he went out. 'How did you get him to change his mind?'

'I never said a word to him, it was what Mick said, that and his own conscience. You'll need to mind, though, just twice a week if Peter asks you to go steady, or your father'll put a stop to it.'

They sat quietly for the rest of the afternoon – Mick had brought home a wireless set some time ago, but Hannah never allowed anyone to listen to it on Sundays. As Lizann gazed idly at the fireplace, she couldn't help admiring the shining range, always kept spotless despite being the only means of cooking food and heating water. Since she left school she had been responsible for buffing the steel parts with emery paper until she could see her face in them, using a dampened rag to coat the larger areas with blacklead, then burnishing them with a curved brush with a handle on top. It was hard work, but worth it. And of course, after every meal, the pots – having been set directly on top of the hot coals – had to have the soot scraped off them with the old knife kept for the purpose, before they were washed and laid past in the corner press; the outside of the big black kettle was cleaned with a wire brush every night. There was an oven on each side of the range, one being utilized to dry the sticks one or other of them gathered from the shore for kindling, the other, being hotter and more dependable, produced perfectly baked puddings and roast meat.

Her eyes moved idly round the room now, to the mantelpiece, crammed with ornaments and fancy shells and edged by a strip of scalloped lace, changed every wash-day; to the lace-screened window that had a geranium on the wide sill; to the little stool she had upturned and pretended was a boat when she was small; to the couch, obviously bought at a different time from the two leather armchairs, whose sagging, cracked seats were covered with lumpy cushions; to the lace antimacassar on the back of her father's chair – her mother had been a great one for crocheting at one time; returning to the fireplace and the heavy poker resting on a trivet inside the iron fender.

Willie Alec came home just after quarter to five, had a quick shave, the second that day, and was changing into his Sunday suit in his room when Mick walked in, so Lizann was able to tell him what had happened. 'And it was thanks to you he changed his mind.'

'Well, well,' he grinned, 'wonders'll never cease. I thought I'd made things worse, sticking my oar in.'

When their mother and father went to church, Mick put on his jacket. 'I'm going to see if Jenny'll get out. When are you meeting Peter?'

'He's coming for me about seven.'

'Don't do anything I wouldn't do,' he teased as he went out.

After washing her face, she went up to her room to brush her hair, then, remembering the papier poudre she had bought at the same time as the lipstick, she took the small packet out of a drawer and removed one leaf. She hadn't had the courage to use any before the dance, but she found it put a velvety bloom on her face, enhancing the effect of the thin layer of lipstick she applied last. Back in the kitchen, she sat down by the fire to wait for Peter, her insides wobbling like jelly. When the knock came, she was glad he was prompt, for she wanted to be out of the house before her parents came home.

As they walked westward along the street there was a reserve between them that hadn't been there the night before, making Lizann sure that he regretted having asked her out, but, once they were clear of Buckpool, he said, 'I've been looking forward to this all day.'

Relieved, she whispered, 'So've I.'

'Honest?'

'Honest.'

'Did Mick say anything about ... about us?' He sounded anxious.

'He teased me a bit. He said you stuck to me like glue.'

'I couldn't bear to let anybody else ... were you angry?'

'No, I liked dancing with you.'

'I never cared much for it before, but it was different with you.'

They strolled along the open road, with the golf course on their left and the sea on their right, and had almost reached the first houses in Portgordon, about a mile beyond Buckpool and completely independent of Buckie, when he burst out, 'I'd things I wanted to say, but I can't.'

'Why not?'

'It's too soon, and you'd think I was off my head.'

'I wouldn't.'

He drew to a halt and turned to face her. 'You're the first girl I've ever gone out with, Lizann, and I'm not used to saying what I feel. You'll have to let me take my own time.'

Wishing that he wasn't so shy, Lizann said, 'My father thinks I'm too young to be going out with a lad.'

'And he likely thinks I'm too old for you.'

'He did say that, and all, and Mick argued with him.'

'Mick stuck up for you? I thought he might be annoyed at me for taking possession of his sister.'

Thinking she was getting somewhere with him, Lizann was disappointed when Peter made an about turn. 'We'd better go back. I don't want to keep you out in the cold too long.'

The return journey was made in the same restrained manner until they were passing his house in Main Street. 'My Mam and Dad were pleased when I said I was going out with somebody,' he observed. 'I think they've been a bit worried that I'm twenty-one and never had a girl-friend.'

She couldn't understand why this had worried the Taits; her parents worried because her brother had so many. 'D'you think Mick's going to stick to Jenny Cowie?' she asked.

Peter laughed. 'Goodness knows. He never sticks long

with any of them, but it did look last night as though he was serious about her. I hope he is, for she'd be a good wife to him, she'd steady him.'

When they arrived at the Yardie again, they stood up outside her door, and she thought that nothing that had gone on tonight would have upset her father. 'Goodnight, Peter,' she said, a little regretfully.

'Will you ... come out with me tomorrow again?'

He hadn't asked her to go steady, but her father's rule had still to be observed. 'Not tomorrow. Wednesday, maybe?'

'Oh.' His voice was flat. 'That's a long time away ... but Wednesday it is. Goodnight, Lizann.'

Willie Alec looked surprised when she went inside. 'You're back early, it's not half past eight yet.'

'Peter didn't want to keep me out in the cold.'

'Aye,' Hannah smiled, 'he's a sensible laddie.'

Willie Alec nodded. 'Are you to be seeing him again?'

'He asked me out tomorrow, but I said not till Wednesday.'

'It's the best way, lass. Now sit down at the fire and get a heat.'

It had gone half past nine when Mick came in. 'Is my seabag ready for morning?' he asked his mother.

Accustomed to both her men depending on her to do everything for them, Hannah smiled. 'Your gear's all in, washed and ready. Your ganzy's on its last legs, but I'll have your new one finished for your next trip.' She knitted all the heavy jerseys for her son and her husband, but only Willie Alec let her knit wheeling wool drawers for him; Mick said they made him scratch and besides, he wasn't an old mannie yet.

Yawning, Lizann stood up. 'The sea air's made me sleepy.'

The coldness of her room made her undress quickly, and she was glad of the 'hot pig' her mother had put in to take the chill off the linen sheets. But the little warm spot soon cooled down when she shifted the earthenware hot-water bottle down to heat her numb feet, so she took it in her arms and curled round it to try to get warm. She'd had such high expectations for tonight, and Peter hadn't kissed her yet.

When the men left in the morning, Hannah wrote out a list of things she needed from the town, and Lizann, having done most of the shopping since she left school two years earlier, set off willingly. She would have loved to have a job of some kind, but her father wouldn't hear of her going out to work. 'Mick and me take in enough to keep the house going,' he said, any time she brought up the subject. 'A woman's place is in the home, and your mother'll learn you everything you need to ken so you'll be as good a wife to some man as she's been to me.'

And so Lizann had been taught how to knit the long seaboot stockings and heavy jerseys, to patch and darn, and she was now as proficient as Hannah at cooking and baking. She had learned how to gut the fish her father and brother took home, and how to salt the large haddocks and dry them on wire grids until they were bone hard. They kept for a long time, and before being used they were soaked in water to soften them, then boiled and mixed with mashed potatoes and a mustard sauce to make what was known as 'hairy tatties', a great favourite with the men.

Despite these accomplishments, Lizann often wished she could earn some money for herself instead of getting a little pocket money to buy odds and ends, and having to depend on her parents for everything else she needed. This morning, however, as she walked to West Church Street – where there was a better selection than in the small shops in Buckpool – she had something different on her mind. She was convinced that Peter felt more than liking for her, and she could hardly wait till Wednesday when, surely to goodness, he'd have got over being shy with her. Nobody could say it was love at first sight for them, she had known him as long as she could remember, but their eyes had been shuttered until Saturday night.

She was smiling to herself when she met Peggy May Cordiner, a friend from her schooldays who lived a few doors along Main Street from Jenny Cowie, on the opposite side from the Taits. 'What are you looking so happy about?' Peggy May asked. 'Have you found a lad?' Lizann's blush made her go on, eagerly, 'Who is he? Do I ken him?'

'It's Peter Tait,' Lizann told her, rather proudly.

Peggy May's green eyes widened. 'But he's a lot older than you!'

'Just five year, and he danced every dance with me on Saturday night.'

Tossing her long blond hair, Peggy May said, 'Och, is that all you're on about? I thought . . .'

'And he saw me home.'

'Oh!' This obviously put a new aspect on it for the other girl, but she sneered, 'He'd to pass your house, any road, and I bet he didna even kiss you.'

Lizann couldn't say he had, but she did have an ace up her sleeve. 'I was with him last night, and all, and we're going out on Wednesday.'

Peggy May looked impressed now. 'So he is your lad?'

'I don't know,' Lizann said, deciding to be perfectly honest, 'but I hope so.' She changed the subject. 'Are you not working just now?'

'I start tomorrow at the yard again. We get a few days off when we get back from Yarmouth, you see. You should come next year, Lizann. I've told you before, it's great fun, and you'd meet dozens o' nice lads.'

Several of the girls who had been at school with them now followed the herring fleet, some from the beginning of the season in March, when the fish were landed at Lerwick, and some, like Peggy May, working in one of the fish houses for most of the time and just going to Yarmouth to gut and pack the last catches of the year. Lizann had asked her father last summer if she could go, but he'd been horrified. 'God kens what some o' they lassies get up to when they're down there away from their mothers and naebody looking after them.'

Lizann had tried to sidetrack him. 'I can gut as fast as any of them,' but he had said, with decisive finality, 'Your mother needs you here.'

That was why she hadn't asked him this summer, and she didn't think she would ask him ever again. She had Peter now, so she wasn't jealous of Peggy May getting away from Buckie for a while. She was likely hoping to find a lad.

'I'd better get on,' Lizann said now. 'I've a lot of things to get.'

'See you some time,' Peggy May smiled.

It wasn't quite so cold on Wednesday night, so Peter suggested walking in the other direction this time. They didn't say much as they ambled along, but when they came to Portessie, the moon was playing over the stretch of sand, turning it to shimmering silver. Stopping to admire it, Lizann turned to him, her eyes shining. 'It's really lovely, isn't it? The sea's so calm, not like it was on Sunday.'

The dream she had nurtured since Saturday night suddenly came true. Peter's arms enfolded her, and his tender kiss left her longing for more. 'I never knew it could be like this,' he said, softly.

'Neither did I,' she whispered, but another kiss proved that it was.

They made slow progress now, stopping every few yards to savour the wonder of blossoming love, until

Lizann's throat was tight with emotion and she thought her heart would burst with happiness.

'We'd better turn back,' Peter said at last. 'You look cold.'

She was unwilling to put an end to the rapture, but she was grateful that he was considering her well-being, for she hadn't realized before that her feet were freezing.

When they returned to the Yardie, Peter took her round to the seaward side of the houses so they wouldn't be seen from the street, and with the icy wind which had sprung up howling around them and the crashing of the waves on the shore in their ears, he kissed her so fervently that her frozen toes thawed out and curled up. Then he stepped back with a sigh. 'You'll have to go in, Lizann, it's getting late.'

'Oh, Peter, I don't want to go in yet.'

'Your mother'll blame me for keeping you out. Um . . . Lizann will you . . . go steady with me?'

It had come at last. 'I'd like that,' she whispered, 'but it'll have to be just twice a week.'

'You haven't another lad, have you?'

'No, there's nobody else.'

'Thank God for that, for . . . I love you, Lizann.'

Her legs were in danger of giving way, but she whispered, 'And I love you, Peter,' before turning to let him kiss her once more. This time, new thrills started deep inside her, something she had never experienced before and hoped was part of being in love.

He let her go so soon that she said, anxiously, 'What's wrong?'

'Nothing's wrong, but you'd better go in. I can't stand any more.'

Too innocent to know what he meant by this, or to recognize her own jagged emotions as frustration, she felt as if he'd rejected her. What had she done that he couldn't stand? Her spirits sank even lower when, instead of giving her another loving kiss, he gave her a peck on the cheek. 'We'd best make it Saturday and we can go dancing again ... if you want to.'

'Yes, I want to.'

'Goodnight, then ... my darling.'

He walked away and she went inside where Hannah eyed her knowingly. 'I can tell he's kissed you.'

Blushing, Lizann nodded. 'And he's asked me to go steady with him.'

'Och well, your father said as long as it was Peter ... Be careful, though, for if he loses his head, he could land you in trouble.'

Snippets Lizann had uncomprehendingly overheard as a schoolgirl came back to her mind, yet she still didn't fully understand the kind of trouble she could land in. She knew she should be thankful that Peter had put an end to the kissing before he lost his head, but she wasn't. She would have preferred to find out what came after – she could have stopped him if he did anything she didn't like.

In bed she snuggled round the hot water bottle. It had never crossed her mind before Saturday to think of Peter as anything other than Mick's pal. She had always liked him, and looked up to him because he was so much older, but five years didn't seem such a big difference now. What she couldn't get over was how quickly the liking had turned to love ... in a flash. Was that how it always happened? A removal of blinkers? A sudden blinding revelation?

She called up an image of him in her mind. Before she danced with him, she hadn't noticed that his blond hair was so silky, nor that his hazel eyes were so tender ... but maybe they hadn't looked at her so tenderly before. He was taller than Mick, and though he wasn't so broad, he still made her feel daintily fragile. Oh, it was good to be loved!

*　　*　　*

Having lain awake into the early hours of Thursday morning thinking of Lizann, Peter's mind was not on the blueprints in front of him that day. He could remember how, at five years old, he had admired the new baby girl who had appeared in Mick's house. He had seen her progressing from toddler to schoolgirl; he'd played all kinds of board games with her; he had always been fond of her ... as the sister he didn't have. But he had never, ever, thought he would feel like this about her. Love hadn't just crept up on him, it had exploded over him, knocked him senseless – he hardly knew what he was doing any more.

Mick had been making love to girls since he was sixteen and had often told him he didn't know what he was missing, but he had never felt the urge before. He'd even wondered if he was one of the pansies folk made fun of, and it was a great relief to know he wasn't ... anything but!

Having banished his latent fear, he allowed his thoughts to proceed a little further. Lizann was still too young for him to think of defiling her. Well, maybe he would dream about it, but he would wait till they were married before he touched her in that way. He'd have to ask her father for her hand, but he was sure Willie Alec would agree, though he'd probably make them wait till she was eighteen.

Peter's thoughts wavered here. Would he manage to keep his hands off Lizann for a whole year and a half? It would be difficult, but if he slipped, bang would go any chance of making her his wife. He would have to be damned careful every time they were alone together.

On Saturday night, Mick being home every weekend, the four young people walked back together from the dance, Mick carrying on to Main Street with Jenny when Peter stopped at the Yardie with Lizann. He led her round to the sea side again, where he kissed her circumspectly for ten minutes until she flung her arms round his neck and pressed herself against him. For a few moments, he forgot his resolve and kissed her so passionately that a savage need arose in him and he had to thrust her from him. He could see that she was hurt by this, but he couldn't explain. He would be far too embarrassed to tell her about the birds and the bees, and in any case, it would likely disgust her.

Holding himself so that his body did not come into contact with hers at any point, he took her face in his hands. 'Don't ever forget I love you, my darling,' he murmured, huskily, 'but you'd best go in.' Brushing her lips gently with his, he walked off.

He looked across at the Cowies' house before going into his own, but there was no sign of Mick or Jenny. Remembering that her mother was a chronic invalid and her father nearly as bad, he guessed they would be in bed, and Mick would likely be making love to Jenny in the kitchen – the lucky blighter!

Peter was not entirely wrong in his supposition. Mr and Mrs Cowie were in bed, Mick was alone with Jenny in the kitchen, but she was not one of his easy conquests. She had let him take the hairpins out of her long, chestnut hair and run his fingers through it; she had let him kiss her, had even been kissing him back quite ardently ... until he tried to open her blouse. 'No,' she said, firmly, shoving his hands away.

Other girls had refused his first advances and he had always persisted until he got his way, but he liked Jenny far too much to go against her wishes. He would bide his time; she had promised to be his steady girl, and she'd give in eventually. 'Sorry, Jen,' he said, nuzzling her neck.

She showed her forgiveness by kissing him again, then

said, 'Maybe I shouldn't have let you come in. I should have known what would happen.'

'I won't do it again,' he murmured, 'not unless you want me to.'

'I do want you to,' she whispered, 'but I can't risk it. I don't want to land with a bairn – I've my mother and father to think on.'

Mick could see her point. Her parents depended on her, and her mother especially was so frail that the shock of being presented with a bastard grandchild could kill her. It did not occur to him that, if Jenny were to fall pregnant, he could make the baby legitimate by marrying her. He wasn't ready to be tied down to marriage . . . not yet.

Over the winter, Peter's kisses came no closer to meeting Lizann's expectations, but his declarations of love seemed genuine, so she blamed the cold weather for his lack of passion. Besides, because of the rain or snow, many of their evenings together had to be spent in the Yardie under her mother's watchful eye, which, she supposed, would be enough to dampen any suitor's ardour.

When spring arrived, Lizann suggested going farther afield on their Wednesday walks, hoping to find a secluded spot where they could sit down for a while, but even though they found several, Peter got edgy after a few minutes and wanted to move on. She longed for him to kiss her as a man should kiss the girl he loves – he had done it once, so she knew he could – but he didn't do it again. Her love for him had grown even deeper, and she occasionally tried to show him that she had a woman's feelings now, but he always pulled away from her, his face scarlet.

She said nothing at first, believing that he was afraid to go on in case he went too far, but she was sure that he would have to give way to his feelings some time. After some weeks of waiting for the miracle to happen, she made up her mind to force him into it.

The next Wednesday, therefore, she pulled him down to lie beside her on a mossy bank they had found behind some trees, and when he drew away uneasily, she put her arms round his neck to hold him there. 'You don't have to stop, Peter.'

His lips came down on hers in a way she had only dreamed of. Was she about to find out what came next? Pulling her hair back, he nibbled her ears then began to kiss all over her face and neck. She could hardly breathe with the thrill of it, and his breathing was harsh and erratic, but suddenly, he gave a hoarse cry and sprang back.

'What's wrong?' she wailed.

'You know what's wrong,' he muttered. 'Lizann, I can't touch you.'

She couldn't shame herself by confessing that she had been longing for him to touch her, to do more than touch her, and she sat up, frustrated.

Throughout the summer she tried unsuccessfully to make him respond to her as she wanted, bewildered by the reserve she could sense in him, and at last, one night in August, she asked, plaintively, 'Have you stopped loving me, Peter?'

'Oh, don't think that, my darling,' he groaned. 'I love you too much, that's what's wrong. I can't trust myself when you kiss me like that.'

She was desperate to experience what she believed to be the ultimate pleasure, but she could see that he was determined not to be tempted into it. When he took her home that night, his last kiss was so brief that she went inside upset as well as frustrated, and couldn't get rid of the suspicion that he was tired of her.

She was in a despondent mood next morning, and Hannah, sensing that something was wrong, despatched

28

her to the shops to take her mind off whatever was bothering her. Lizann was going up High Street when she spotted Peggy May Cordiner coming out of West Church Street. Not feeling like talking, she wished she could hide in a doorway out of sight, but her friend had already seen her.

'You're looking down in the dumps,' Peggy May observed. 'Have you fell out wi' Peter Tait?'

'Not really, but . . . ach, it's nothing.'

'Dinna tell me, if that's how you feel. I've other things to think on. They're leaving for Yarmouth the morrow, six crews of three from our yard – that's two gutters and a packer – but Janet Reid's expecting so my crew's one short, and we canna go unless we find another gutter the day.' Peggy May's round face brightened. 'I just minded. You can gut, can't you? You could come . . . or do you nae want to leave Peter Tait?'

The hint of sarcasm made Lizann say, impulsively, 'It might do us good to be away from each other for a while. All right, Peggy May. I'll come . . . if my mother lets me.'

'Tell her my Dad'll be there to look after us and she'll maybe agree. You'll need to let me ken by dinnertime, though.'

On her way home again, Lizann wondered if she had been too hasty. What would Peter say? He'd likely be angry at her for going away, but there was always the chance that he'd miss her so much that when she came back he'd . . . She gave her head a shake. She should stop worrying about it, for she couldn't really see her mother letting her go.

Sure that Peter had done something to upset her daughter, Hannah wished she could separate them for a while. Lizann was getting far too serious, and Peter was a man, after all, with a man's inclination to lust. Willie Alec had been the same, though she'd never let him touch her till they were man and wife. But Lizann might give in to Peter and land in the family way, and her father would go off his head.

Hannah let out a deep sigh. She would have to speak to Lizann again, to make her understand how Peter could be tempted by her slender body and blossoming bosom. It was strange how a man was always fascinated by a woman's breasts – handling hers still fired Willie Alec – and Lizann was only seventeen; she shouldn't be subjected to that kind of thing.

Looking up when her daughter came in, Hannah saw that she seemed much happier and thought it would be a good time to get the lecture over, but before she could say anything, Lizann burst out, 'Peggy May Cordiner was saying they're one short in her crew this year, and she asked me to go.'

'To Yarmouth?'

'Can I, Mother? They're leaving the morrow morning.'

Hannah felt at a loss. Her husband always made all the decisions and he wasn't at home to discuss this. She knew he wouldn't agree to it, but it would give Lizann and Peter time to cool down . . . or would their love build up so they wouldn't be able to control themselves when she came home? It was a risk Hannah decided she would have to take, and Willie Alec would surely let them get married . . . if they had to.

'Peggy May's father's going,' Lizann urged. 'He's a cooper.'

Trusting that this would satisfy her husband, Hannah muttered, 'All right. You can go . . . this once.'

Lizann's anxious face lit up. 'I'll have to let her know.'

Hannah watched her skipping out, then rose to sort out some clothes for her. God knew what her father would say, but it was done now.

* * *

As Lizann had known, Peter was not pleased at her news. He had been surprised to see her on a Thursday night, and had looked at her warily when she asked him to come out for a few minutes so she could tell him something. 'Yarmouth?' he gasped, in dismay, as they walked from his house to hers. 'I'm surprised your mother didn't stop you, and what'll your father say?'

'I'll be away before he's home. We're leaving in the morning.'

'As soon as that? Oh, God, Lizann, what am I going to do without you?' He grabbed her, and when his lips came down with all the passion she had been longing for, she clung to him and wouldn't let go. His hands slid down and pressed her against him so hard that, for the first time, she felt his need grow, then he thrust her away from him abruptly. 'I can't, Lizann! No, don't touch me. You'll have to let me be for a minute.'

He wheeled away and she waited resentfully until he turned back to her. 'Please don't go, Lizann.'

'I can't back out now. I've told Peggy May.'

'Well . . . will you promise to marry me when you come home?'

This took her by surprise. 'If you'd asked me that before . . .'

'I was waiting . . . I thought your father wouldn't let us get wed before you were eighteen, but we could be engaged now.'

'I'll have to think about it. I'll tell you when I get back.'

His last kiss made her go inside wishing she hadn't been so childish. She had kept him dangling to punish him for not giving way to his feelings, and she'd ended up punishing herself as well. She loved him with all her heart, and now he had actually asked her to marry him, she wished she hadn't agreed to go with Peggy May. Two months was an awful long time to be away from him. Anything could happen.

Chapter Two

'When the ro-o-oll is called up yo-onder,
When the ro-o-oll is called up yo-onder,
When the ro-o-oll is called up yo-onder,
When the roll is called up yonder I'll be there.'

The last chorus ended in breathless laughter, and Dozy
Cordiner hoped the girls weren't going to stop altogether.
The long journey passed much quicker when they were
singing the Sankey and Moodie hymns. 'What about
"Will Your Anchor Hold?"' he asked.

Exuberant because they were free of their drab exist-
ences for a few weeks, they needed no further encour-
agement.

'Will your anchor hold in the storms of life?
When the clouds unfold the-ir wings of strife . . .'

Lizann Jappy had joined in as lustily as any of them, but
she leaned back now to have a breather. She had woken
up at the crack of dawn telling herself that eight weeks
would soon pass and looking forward to the adventure
in front of her, though she hadn't thought the travelling
would be so much fun. The early-morning stir in the
station at Aberdeen had been an eye-opener to her, and
special trains had been laid on there to transport the
fisher quines from all round the Moray Firth – and even
Fraserburgh and Peterhead, judging by the tongues she
had heard around her. Thankfully, they hadn't had their

32

kists to worry about, for the wooden chests containing their clothes – covered with sacking lashed down with ropes – had been loaded last night on to carts that went as cargo on the drifters also bound for Great Yarmouth.

Most of the gutters and packers were seasoned travellers who knew how long the journey took, and when their train was in motion the Buckie contingent had come to Dozy's compartment to have a sing-song to pass the time. Others from farther along soon joined them, until the whole corridor was filled with women and girls singing the well-known hymns, and Lizann thought joyfully that if this stage of her first time away from her mother was anything to go by, she would never feel homesick.

The voices soaring into the final refrain, she took part again.

> 'We have an anchor that keeps the soul
> Steadfast and free while the billows roll,
> Fastened to the Rock which cannot move,
> Grounded firm and deep in the Saviour's love!'

Long before the journey's end, the fishergirls were too hoarse to sing any more, and gradually they returned to their own compartments to eat the sandwiches they had taken with them and have a much-needed rest. Peggy May looked at Lizann with her eyebrows raised. 'What d'you think? Will you be happy working with us?'

'Oh, yes,' Lizann smiled. 'I'm going to have a great time.'

'Not too great,' Dozy warned, from his corner by the window. 'You'll be kept at it, it's nae a holiday.'

'I know it'll be hard work, but that doesn't worry me.'

After about an hour, Dozy went to check on the other girls from his yard and Peggy May took the chance to say, 'Never mind him. We'll have some good times, and all. A lot o' romances start in Yarmouth.'

'I don't need a romance there,' Lizann protested, 'I've got Peter.'

'He'll never ken if you've a wee fling.'

Too tired to argue, Lizann lay back and closed her eyes. She wouldn't like to think Peter was having a 'wee fling' while she was away, and it wouldn't be fair to him if she had one.

At last, the train steamed into Yarmouth, empty now of holiday-makers, and the gutters, packers and coopers spilled on to the platform. 'I'll take you to my landlady,' Peggy May announced, as they made their way into the street. 'We buy our own food, but Mrs Marks cooks it for us.'

'What happens about washing our clothes?' Lizann enquired.

'We send our dirty washing home every week.'

When they arrived at their lodgings, Peggy May asked the landlady if she and Lizann could be together. 'It's her first time away from home, you see, and she's a bit shy of strangers.'

Having had a profitable summer, Mrs Marks relaxed her three-to-a-bed, six-to-a-room rule, on condition that they just used one of the two double beds, and that agreed upon, Peggy May took Lizann to the Denes to show her the farlans – the troughs which would soon be filled with herring to be gutted – where they would be working. 'Some days,' she explained, 'if there's nae a lot o' boats in, we can finish early, but I've seen us working till near midnight.'

They waved to Dozy, who was checking that everything would be ready for the next day when the vanguard of the herring fleet was expected, and then bought some food on the way back to their digs, patronizing only those shops Peggy May knew to be cheap and reliable.

'I couldn't understand a word they were saying in

there,' Lizann observed as they left a small but crowded butcher's. 'It was like double Dutch to me.'

'I was the same the first time I came,' Peggy May grinned, 'and they couldn't understand me, but you soon get used to it.'

'How d'you find your way about? This is a lot bigger than Buckie.'

'Somebody asked Mrs Marks about that last year, and she looked it up in her Pears Cyclopaedia. It said Buckie had a population of . . . och, I canna mind, but Yarmouth was near seven times bigger. You can look it up yourself, for the book's still lying on a shelf beside her umbrella stand.'

When they returned to their lodgings, the first thing they did was to check the encyclopedia. 'Buckie,' Lizann read out. 'Fishing town, co . . . that would be county . . . Banff, Scotland. P . . . that must be population . . . eight thousand, nine hundred and twenty.' She turned the pages slowly, her finger moving snail-like down the small print. 'Ah, here it is. Great Yarmouth, co bor . . . county something . . . Norfolk, England, noted herring fishery, population sixty thousand, seven hundred and ten.'

'It's nae seven times bigger than Buckie, then!' Peggy May exclaimed.

'It's nearer seven times than six times,' Lizann pointed out.

The population of Great Yarmouth was increased by thousands in the herring season, perhaps surpassing the number of summer visitors who were more profitable to the landladies. For more than six months of each year, therefore, the town was probably more than seven times the size of Buckie, if the girls had but known.

Their voices brought Mrs Marks out of her kitchen. 'What do you want me to cook for you tonight?'

Peggy May handed over the paper carrier bag. 'Sausages and eggs.'

'That won't take long, you'd better eat before you unpack.'

'Oh, have the kists come?'

'The lorry delivered them all at lunchtime, and I asked the driver to put them in the proper rooms.'

After washing and having supper, the two girls went upstairs. 'At least this is a decent place,' Peggy May smiled, as she struggled with the knots in the ropes holding the sacking in place.

Giving a quick glance around the small but clean room, and even though it just had two double beds, two odd chairs and a cupboard for their clothes, Lizann nodded. 'Aye, this is real nice.'

'Them that go to Lerwick get put in huts wi' nae heating . . . and it's freezing cold up there in March. That's why I've never went. It's bad enough here by November, but Mrs Marks is real good. She lets us sit at her fire in the evenings, if we're not out.'

'Where do you go, if you do go out?'

'It depends. If it's dry, we walk round the town – we're always coming across new places, it's so big – or along the prom, the Parade, or up and down King Street, then if we click, they pay us into the pictures if it's wet. And you can meet some real nice lads at the dances.'

'I told you! I don't want to get a lad.'

'Suit yourself, but I'm nae biding in wi' you if I meet somebody.'

Finished unpacking first, Lizann undressed and stretched out on the double bed by the window. Would it be so wrong to go dancing? Peter wouldn't expect her to stay in every night, and she could tell all her partners she had a boyfriend at home.

'That's me done.' Peggy May shed her clothes quickly, hauled on her nightdress and plumped down beside Lizann. 'We'd better get some sleep, for we've an early morning.'

It had been a very long, exhausting day, and despite having to share a bed for the first time in her life, Lizann fell asleep almost as quickly as Peggy May.

They rose early the next morning and were on the Denes by six, but it was coming on for eleven before the first catch was in the farlans. The women and girls passed the time by knitting where they stood – Peggy May having warned Lizann about this, she had come prepared with a set of short knitting needles and wool to make socks for Mick. Her mother had taught her how to shape the legs with sections of rib, and how to turn the heels, so he would have no complaint about the fit.

Once they started work it was a different story. Their fingers, bound with rags to shield them from the razor-sharp knives, slit each herring and removed the innards so fast that the blink of an eye could have made an onlooker miss it.

Lizann hadn't realized how hard the work would be, nor that they would have to stand on the open quayside in all weathers. Some days, however, between one and two if they could get away, lorries took them to the White Lion for something to eat, a welcome break.

They had to work until eight to clear the farlans on Saturday night, because the herring would go bad if left uncleaned and unsalted, but that didn't stop most of the girls rushing back to their lodgings to get ready to go dancing. In spite of washing thoroughly and changing into their best clothes, there was still the smell of fish about both men and girls, and there was a recklessness about them as if they were forced to make the most of every minute. The young fishermen came from all over – Lerwick, Buckie, Scottish east and west coast ports, Shields, Newcastle, Yarmouth itself, and Lizann meticulously told each of her partners about Peter. Most of them heeded her unspoken warning. A few tried to kiss her but didn't persist when she shoved them away, and only one was a pest. He had been drinking heavily and, short of screaming, she hadn't been able to prevent him taking her outside. She put up a desperate struggle, but he would have forced her to the ground if Peggy May's father hadn't come out for a smoke.

Dozy Cordiner – his heavy-lidded eyes had given rise to the nickname when he was just a boy – was quite short, but he had muscles as hard as steel and was more than a match for her would-be seducer. One punch was enough to send the drunk reeling away. 'You'd better nae touch none o' my lassies again,' Dozy yelled after him, 'or you'll have a mouthful of nae teeth!' He put his arm round Lizann. 'Did he hurt you, m'quine?'

The concerned last word – fisher for 'my girl' – made her say, 'No, I'm fine.' Her legs were still shaking, but just with relief.

'There's aye one out to make trouble,' Dozy laughed. 'I was watching that ane a' night, but he'd seen his chance when I went to the lavvy.'

It wasn't funny at the time, but Lizann couldn't help smiling about it when she was in bed. Dozy had been a comic figure to her at home, but not any longer. She would always be grateful to him.

Sunday was a day of rest. No fish were landed, and, accompanied by the overseers, coopers and driftermen – all in dark ganzies and cloth caps, almost like a uniform – the fishergirls went to church or to a mission hall, their pure sweet voices bringing tears to the eyes of the usual congregations.

Both afternoon and evening, Lizann and May joined the parade of bodies meandering about the town, some in gangs, some like them in pairs, a few already arm in arm with a young man. 'I tell't you a lot o' romances started here,' Peggy May reminded Lizann. 'Mind you, some o' the lads are married, so a lot o' lassies go hame wi' sore hearts.'

38

A complete contrast, since one had long, straight blond hair and the other had short black curls, they drew quite a few admiring glances, but they were chattering too much to notice.

On Wednesday, Peggy May took Lizann to the Windmill. She had never seen a film before and was fascinated by the moving pictures and the words that came on the big screen to let people know what the actors were saying. 'I wish we could see one of the speaking films they're making now,' Peggy May whispered.

Lizann didn't care. She was more than happy with what she was seeing, and she wouldn't have missed all these new experiences for anything – not even for Peter. She didn't grudge the sixpence admission fee, though their pay was just fifteen shillings a week, and seven of that had to go to the landlady for their rent. Everything else, including food, had to be bought out of what was left.

The time flew past for Lizann, each weekday fully occupied in keeping up with the other members of her crew – who did their utmost to beat the crews standing nearest to them – each Saturday evening taken up by dancing or going to a concert organized by the fisher people themselves, each Sunday gloriously free. Peggy May had gone out with three or four different boys – 'None o' them worth a damn,' as she said – but Lizann had kept faith with herself and hadn't accepted any of the invitations made to her.

She had written to Peter every Sunday, telling him about their working conditions, their living quarters, the friends she had made, the films she had seen with Peggy May, and how much she was longing to see him again. His replies had been disappointingly short and stilted, though he always wrote at the end, 'PS. I am missing you.' Maybe he was paying her back for going away, or maybe he just wasn't good at writing love letters. She hadn't mentioned the dances because she didn't want to worry him or make him jealous, but she meant to tell him when she went home. It would be easier to make him understand, face to face.

When Dozy said that the season was nearly finished, Lizann felt quite glad that she would soon be on her way home. She would miss the company, the friends she had made, the money in her pocket, but she was missing Peter more, and she would accept his proposal – if he still wanted her.

Hard at work one forenoon, she sensed that someone was watching her and curiosity made her raise her head. Her eyes met those of a young man who was staring at her intently and, flustered, she concentrated on her job again. When she looked up minutes later, he had vanished, and she wondered who he was and why he'd been studying her. He wasn't carrying a camera, so he couldn't be one of the photographers who sometimes came to take shots of the Scottish fisher lassies, and anyway he was dressed in seaman's garb. He'd looked really nice, though.

At last the farlans were empty for the day, and Lizann straightened up and rubbed her aching back before joining the throng of girls who were making for their lodgings, still laughing and talking although their faces were drawn with fatigue. She was listening to someone's account of a tussle with a boy the previous night, when Peggy May nudged her. 'I think there's a lad after you, Lizann.'

Looking round and seeing that it was the young man she had noticed earlier, she smiled shyly and, seemingly encouraged, he put out his hand and drew her to a halt. 'Lizann?' he said. 'That's a bonnie name. Mine's plain George.'

He looked so solid and dependable that she murmured, 'It suits you.'

Her friends were well ahead now, but she was still

taken aback when he asked diffidently, 'Will you come out with me the night?'

The resolution she had previously made didn't enter her head, but when she was telling Peggy May in their room later, she finished, sheepishly, 'I shouldn't have said I'd go . . . oh, I'd better not.'

'Don't be daft! Go and enjoy yourself, it's maybe your last chance.'

'What if Peter finds out?'

'Who's going to tell him? I'll not say anything.'

While she washed, dressed and had her supper, Lizann continued to feel guilty about deceiving Peter, but the minute she saw George again she knew why she had agreed to meet him. He was tall and broad, with untidy brown hair slightly lighter than Mick's and the same brown eyes, but above all, he had something about him that played havoc with her heart.

As she walked by his side, she contemplated telling him about Peter – it wasn't fair to let him think she was free – and she was on the point of confessing when George said, 'Lizann, I'd better tell you . . . I've got a lass at home in Cullen.'

Relieved in one way, she said, 'I've a lad in Buckie.'

'Are you promised to him?'

'Not exactly, not yet. Are you promised to her?'

'Not yet.'

Nothing else was said for several minutes, then George told her a bit about the other members of his ship's crew and asked her about the girls she worked with. Wanting to learn more about each other, they discussed their relatives, their homes, their likes and dislikes, and they kept walking and talking until it was time for Lizann to go back to her lodgings.

Before she went in, George slid his arms round her. 'A first and last kiss, Lizann?' he coaxed.

She wouldn't have refused even if he'd given her the

chance, and she was sorry when he stopped at one. 'That's it, then,' he sighed as he released her. 'I hope you and Peter make a go of it. Goodbye, Lizann.'

Peggy May was waiting eagerly to find out what had happened. 'Did he kiss you?'

'Just once.'

'What's his name? Did you like him? Is he as nice as he looks?'

'His name's George, and yes I like him, and yes he's nice, but he said he'd a girl in Cullen and I told him about Peter.'

'Will you be seeing him again?'

'No, he's sailing home tomorrow.'

'So that's it?' Peggy May was disappointed. 'I was looking forward to you telling me what you and him got up to, the juicy bits, but there's nothing for it but go to sleep.'

Lizann's thoughts kept her from sleeping for some time. She shouldn't have gone out with George but she had, and she wished he hadn't waited so long to kiss her. If he'd been quicker, he'd have had time to do it again ... and again? Imagining it, she could actually feel the thrill of it and her heartbeats quickened at an alarming rate. His hands would have run over her, gently at first, then more insistently until ... Oh, God, what had got into her? She should be thinking of Peter, of his kisses, of his arms around her. It wouldn't be long now.

Late the following forenoon, when she stopped working momentarily to wipe her brow, she had a pleasant surprise. 'Oh, here's George,' she whispered to Peggy May, who said, somewhat accusingly, 'I thought you said he was going back to Cullen the day.'

'That's what he told me.' Lizann gave George a warm smile when he reached them.

'We've been held up for repairs,' he explained, 'so we'll

have a few more days here. Can I see you tonight again? Please, Lizann?'

She knew she shouldn't go out with him again, not after the things she'd thought last night, but she couldn't say no and was glad that Peggy May didn't say anything sarcastic, neither then nor later when she was making ready to meet George.

During their first hour together they made light conversation and teased each other a little, and then – she didn't know what sparked it off – he pulled her into his arms and kissed her hungrily. 'I shouldn't be doing this,' he muttered in a few minutes.

Thrusting aside the thought that she shouldn't be letting him, she whispered, 'I like it, George,' a gross understatement, for every inch of her was responding to the stimulus – responding in a way that, in her naivety, she did not understand could have only one possible outcome.

George, however, was cautious. 'But what about Peter, and Katie?'

Propelled on to find out what Peter had always held back from, she looked at George now and said, 'They'll never know,' adding with an embarrassed half-smile, '. . . whatever we do.'

Straightaway, it came to her that saying this might put him off her, make him think she was cheap, and she wished she hadn't been so bold, but when George murmured, 'Do you mean what I think you mean?', she didn't correct him.

Obviously taking her silence as agreement, he pulled her to the ground. She had been afraid that the reality wouldn't measure up to her dreams, but, carried away with the rapture of it, she lost track of everything except a mounting, spiralling need. Being so innocent, it did not dawn on her that she was being guided by an expert, an expert who had gentled her past the initial pain and soothed her with kisses before taking her on a soaring flight which came to the wildest, most wonderful conclusion. Only then did she become conscious that the wetness from the soggy grass was seeping right into her clothes, that a dense fog which had descended unnoticed was lying over them like a blanket.

Silently, George helped her up and turned his back so that she could make herself presentable. She was quite relieved that he kept quiet, but disappointed when he took her to her lodgings and left her still without saying a word. When she went upstairs, she excused her flushed face and damp clothing to Peggy May by saying that he had lain on the grass with her and kissed her an awful lot, and if her friend suspected he'd done more than that, she didn't say so.

Lizann's dreams were predictable that night, but in the morning she wondered if George had been disgusted when she offered herself to him, for that's what it had amounted to. She was thankful, therefore, when he appeared on the Denes in the forenoon, and there was no hesitation in the nod she gave in answer to the question in his eyes. Time couldn't pass quickly enough for her now, and when work was finished for the day she set off for their digs at a pace that had Peggy May complaining, 'Slow down, Lizann, for ony sake. I ken you're desperate for his kisses, but there's nae need to rush me off my feet.'

Unhappily for Lizann, George did not kiss her once that night, nor the following night. She couldn't understand it. Why was he acting as if nothing had happened between them? But when he said, at Mrs Marks's door, that tomorrow would be their last night together, she still agreed to meet him.

Her thoughts were confused when she went inside. She'd been attracted to him the first time she saw him, but her feelings for him went much deeper now. She should really steer clear of him tomorrow, for they were both committed, almost, to somebody else, but . . .

She met him as promised, praying that he would stop being so distant, but again he talked only about trivialities. Lapsing into a dejected silence, she wished he would speak about things that mattered. If he didn't want to see her again, why didn't he just tell her, bid her goodbye and leave her? Short and sharp, it would still be better than dragging it out like this.

Hearing a change in the tone of his voice, she turned to look at him. 'Lizann,' he said, 'are you angry about what I did the other night?'

'No, I'm not angry,' she replied, honestly, 'and I'm not sorry we did it.' She was more to blame than he was, after all.

'What's wrong, then?'

'What are we going to do, George? After this, I mean.'

'When I go back to Cullen and you go back to Buckie?'

'I still love Peter, and I can't tell him.'

'No.' After a pause, he said, slowly, 'I'm still going to marry Katie, and you'll marry Peter. What we did hasn't changed that, but I'd better get you back . . .'

'Not yet. If I'm never going to see you again, give me a last night to remember.' It was out before she knew what she was saying.

'Are you sure?'

A twinge of conscience made her say, 'D'you think I'm awful?'

'No, I want it as much as you.'

Now it was as if nothing of the outside world existed for them; they were conscious only of their rising passions, of the shared thrills and heart-stopping ecstasies, then, stealthily intruding, the awful thought that their time together was coming to an end. They were reluctant to break away from each other, but the parting had to come some time, and at last they walked slowly, morosely, to the door of Lizann's lodgings. George's final kiss was long and tender, and her spirits leapt when he groaned, 'Oh, God, Lizann, I think I love you.'

'I think I love you and all, George.' She looked at him in awe for some seconds, as if trying to find some way they could have a future together, then suddenly said, 'No, I can't let Peter down now.' With a strangled sob, she ran inside.

Peggy May eyed her in concern but, to Lizann's great relief, asked no questions – she didn't want to speak about it. Nobody could understand how she felt; she didn't understand it herself.

Lizann lay in torment that night. She had been unfaithful to Peter, she had let her mother down, and she could imagine how angry her father would be if he ever found out what she had done; but she wasn't sorry for having done it. What she did regret was that she would never see George again.

Would Peter notice anything different about her when she went home, and what would she tell him if he did? But she didn't need to tell him anything; it was natural that she'd be different after being away from home for the very first time. Nothing had really changed between them, and if he asked her again to get engaged, she would say yes.

Chapter Three

❧

On the train, in spite of the singing and joviality going on around her, Lizann Jappy remained silent, as she had been since they set off in the morning. Normally her cheeks shone with rosy good health, her mouth was turned up in a smile, but today her face was peaky and her dark eyes had lost their radiance. Slumped in her seat, she seemed to have no interest in anything, but when the singers started up again, the first few words penetrated her consciousness.

> 'What a friend we have in Jesus,
> All our sins and griefs to bear,
> What a privilege to carry
> Everything to God in prayer!'

Parting with George was the worst grief she'd ever had to bear, she thought wretchedly, and not even God could help her. How could she pray after the awful sin she'd committed? It had started off with her wanting to satisfy her curiosity because Peter . . . no, she couldn't blame Peter, and he was such a decent man that she couldn't hurt him by telling him. Besides, as George had said, what they did hadn't changed anything. When she went home she would accept Peter's proposal and put George right out of her mind.

'What's wrong, Lizann?'

The voice in her ear made her jump. 'Nothing.'

Her friend was not to be fobbed off. 'Why are you nae

singing? Are you thinking about that Cullen man? That George Buchan?'

'I love him.'

Peggy May's eyes widened. 'Does he love you?'

'He said he did.'

'Well, he'll come and see you, won't he?'

'He said he'd a girl at home, and I told him about Peter, so we're not going to see each other again.'

Peggy May was astonished. 'But you're nae promised to Peter?'

'He asked me to marry him before I came away, and I said I'd give him my answer when I got back.'

'You could tell him you've fell in love wi' somebody else.'

'What's the use? George is going to marry his Katie. He still loves her, the same as I still love Peter.'

'I canna understand you. Who d'you really love, Peter or George?'

'I know it sounds silly, but I love them both. I really do.'

After some thought, Peggy May said, 'You'll soon forget George once you're married to Peter.'

'I suppose so.'

Peggy May clicked her tongue in exasperation. 'You will, Lizann. You only ken't him for a wee while, and you've ken't Peter your whole life. You've went steady wi' him for months.'

Gathering that Peggy May had grown impatient with her for being lovesick over a boy she hardly knew, Lizann came to the conclusion that her friend was right. 'Aye, I'm being daft, amn't I? George and me had just been ships that pass in the night.'

Peggy May grinned, 'That's right, so tell Peter you'll marry him.'

Her own decision now being endorsed, Lizann smiled and joined in the singing, but exhaustion had finally caught up with the other girls, and when they came to the end of this hymn they dispersed to their own compartments. Those who were left settled back with their eyes closed and Lizann was the only one not to doze off.

Two years ago, when she asked if she could go to Yarmouth, her father had said, amongst other things, 'The English are different from us, and you never know what kind of queer folk you could meet.' She gave a faint smile at the memory. She hadn't met any of the queer English folk, only George – tall and broad, with untidy hair and soft, loving eyes. Could she ever forget him?

Hannah was still up when Lizann arrived home just after midnight. 'It's awful late,' she said, accusingly. 'I was beginning to think something had happened to your train.'

'It's an awful long way. It took us over seventeen hours.'

'You must be wore out.'

'I'm ready to drop, and I'm going straight to my bed.'

It was late afternoon before she woke, refreshed by her long sleep, and when she went down to the kitchen, Hannah said, 'That's better. You was like death warmed up when you come in last night. Did you tell Peter when you'd be back?'

'I wrote to him the same time I wrote to you.'

'He'll likely come after he's had his supper, then.'

He came at seven on the dot, and Lizann was astonished at the way her heart jolted at the sight of his dear face. 'You got home all right?' he asked, unnecessarily, as he waited for her to put on her coat.

Out in the street, he put his arm round her and observed, 'You're a lot thinner. Was it awful hard work?'

'Aye, it was, and I'm glad to be back.'

Because it was November again, cold and dreich, he took her along the road instead of the shore, asking questions which she'd already covered in her letters, but at last he said hesitantly, 'Have you made your mind up now, Lizann?'

She had been waiting for this, but she still wasn't absolutely sure.

'Lizann?' he urged, anxiously.

She hadn't the heart to keep him waiting any longer. 'Yes, Peter.'

'D'you mean yes your mind's made up, or yes you'll get engaged?'

Burning her boats, she smiled shyly. 'Yes, I'll get engaged.'

His hug nearly squeezed the breath out of her, and when he let her go, he fished in the breast pocket of his jacket and produced a small velvet box. 'I bought the ring last week after I spoke to your father.'

Feeling a niggle of irritation that he'd taken her answer for granted, she nevertheless opened the box as if it contained the crown jewels. It wasn't an expensive ring, she could see that even in the feeble rays of the moon – just one tiny diamond on a raised shank – but it was likely all he could afford. 'Oh, Peter, it's right bonnie,' she assured him.

'Let me put it on,' he said, lifting her hand. 'The jeweller said he'd change it if you didn't like it, or if it didn't fit.'

She did like it, and when he slid the ring down her finger it fitted as if it had been made for her. His arms came round her again, and his kisses were all a young girl could have desired – if she hadn't been comparing them with another man's. 'My dearest darling,' Peter muttered hoarsely, 'you'll never regret this.'

Already half regretting it, she could only say, 'I know I won't.'

'I love you, Lizann. I love you with my heart, my soul and my body. I'd wed you tomorrow if I could.'

'My mother'll want me to fill my bottom drawer first, so it'll be a year or so yet.'

'A year or so yet?' He grabbed her again. 'What if I say I can't wait another year? Will you let me . . . ?'

His heavy breathing alarmed her. She wasn't ready for this. It did seem like a sin when it was Peter. 'No! I'll not let you, not till you put the wedding ring on.'

'Is the engagement ring not enough?'

She pulled away from him. 'No it's not, and if you're going to carry on like this, Peter Tait, you'd better take it back.'

He took a deep breath. 'I'm sorry, Lizann. It's just that I haven't held you for so long . . . I didn't mean it, and I'll not do it again.'

'You'd better not!' She was on the point of saying she wasn't a girl like that when she remembered that it would be a downright untruth. Less than a week ago, she had . . . No! She mustn't think of that! 'It's better to wait,' she said, gently.

'Aye, and as long as I know you love me . . .' He broke off and gazed earnestly into her eyes. 'You do still love me?'

'Yes, Peter, I still love you.'

His breath came out in a long contented sigh. 'That's all I wanted to know.' Slipping his arm around her waist, he pulled her forward. 'We'd better move; we'll be frozen to the spot if we stand here much longer.'

Just before they reached Portgordon, Peter swivelled her round to make the return journey. 'I wish there was a place we could sit down and have a real cuddle . . . and I just mean a cuddle,' he added, hastily.

'There'll be plenty time for cuddling once the better nights come in,' Lizann murmured, already apprehensive as to where cuddling might lead. She didn't want to spoil their marriage by giving in to him beforehand.

'It's funny,' Peter reflected, 'a couple of years ago, if

anybody had said you'd be my wife some day, I'd have laughed in their face.'

'Was I so ugly?'

'That's not what I ... you were Mick's wee sister, always there.'

'Like the furniture?' She couldn't resist teasing him.

'You know what I mean. I didn't realize you were growing up till I saw you in that pink frock.'

She was seventeen and a half now, but it was still difficult for her to accept a compliment. 'You fell in love with the frock?'

He stopped and pulled her against him. 'I fell in love with the lovely young girl inside the frock. Your lips were quivering like you weren't sure whether to come right into the hall or turn and leave, and when I took you up to dance and felt the curves I'd never noticed before, my heart galloped like it's galloping right now.'

His long searching kiss started her heart galloping, too. 'Peter,' she gasped, when he drew back. 'I wish we'd got engaged before I went away.' If she'd been fully committed to him, she thought wryly, she wouldn't have done what she did, and there wouldn't be this little voice in her head now, telling her she was making a terrible mistake.

When they went into her house, her parents were waiting to celebrate the engagement, and the slap on the back Willie Alec gave Peter was so hearty that it made him stagger. Hannah tutted at her husband. 'You near knocked him flat on his face. You dinna ken your own strength.'

Laughing gustily, Willie Alec broke open the bottle of Drambuie he had bought for the occasion. The *Silver Star* had landed two hours earlier, and he'd been waiting to toast the betrothed couple. 'You've a nose like a bloodhound,' he joked to Mick, who came in at that moment.

'You can smell drink a mile away.' But he filled a third glass. The two women, not being whisky lovers, especially not the sweet liqueur, made do with some of the Hall's Wine Hannah bought to fortify herself every winter.

Willie Alec held his glass aloft. 'Here's to Lizann and Peter,' he boomed. 'May they have health, wealth and happiness, and be blessed wi' as fine healthy bairns as me and Hannah.'

'Ach, Willie Alec,' she reprimanded, 'you shouldna be speaking about bairns and them just new engaged. And I think they shouldna set the date till Lizann's nineteen.'

'That's a year and a half yet,' her husband protested. 'It'll gi'e them time to be sure o' their feelings.'

'Aye, well, maybe that's best.'

When the laughing and joking began, Lizann couldn't help thinking how lucky she was in her parents. Hannah, slim and dainty, with only a few silver hairs shining through the black, did voice her opinion sometimes, but let her man have his own way over most things. Peter's mother was a big fat lump who domineered her husband. Bowfer was a puny little man who hardly ever opened his mouth when his wife was anywhere near. He was a joiner to trade, working in the same shipyard as his son, and his evenings were spent swilling beer down his throat. He likely needed Dutch courage to go home and share a bed with Bella Jeannie, Lizann reflected in some amusement. Not that he would get much room, for she must take up about three-quarters of it. Willie Alec, on the other hand, was master in his house when he was not at sea. He never bullied his family, but he could be real strict if he thought it was necessary.

'Come on, Lizann,' Mick called, breaking into her reverie. 'Why are you sitting there dreaming? It's your engagement we're celebrating.'

Her father refilled her glass, wrinkling his nose at the

smell of the wine. 'You're not having second thoughts about it, are you?'

She laughed along with him, and looking at Peter she said firmly, 'No, I'm quite sure.'

Her fiancé walked across the room and pulled her to her feet. 'I'm the happiest man in Buckie the night,' he grinned, sliding his arm round her waist and drawing her close. 'And I'll be happier still on the day the minister makes her my wife.'

Mick nudged him in the ribs. 'It's the wedding night that'll make you happiest, though, eh, Peter?'

The three men laughed uproariously at that, but Hannah frowned at her son for touching on so delicate a subject, and Lizann turned crimson.

'Ach, Mother,' Mick cried, 'stop glowering at me. It's only natural to enjoy the first night, isn't it? I'm sure you and Father enjoyed yours.'

The last remark involving him, Willie Alec considered that his son had overstepped the bounds of decency. 'That's not the kind of talk I like in my house, Mick,' he said, sharply.

'Ach, I was just joking, Father.'

'It's not a joking matter.'

'Don't quarrel,' Lizann pleaded. 'It was only a bit of fun.'

'You're right, lass.' Willie Alec's expression changed as he lifted the whisky bottle again. 'You'll have another dram, Peter?' he grinned.

'I don't think I should.'

'If you're worried about going home drunk, I'll tell Bella Jeannie the morrow it was my fault.'

Sure that Lizann's father would be a match for his mother, Peter held out his glass, and after topping it up, Willie Alec turned to Mick. 'I was ower hasty, son, and we'll forget about it, eh?'

With harmony restored, the jollifications continued,

and by the time Lizann was undressing for bed, she was sure she had done the right thing in promising to marry Peter.

'Mam wants you to come for your supper the morrow,' Peter told Lizann on Thursday, 'though she says it'll not be anything special.'

'That doesn't matter,' she exclaimed, pleased that Bella Jeannie was being friendly. She wasn't to know that Peter had pressurized his mother into asking her.

When Hannah was told about the invitation she said, 'I'm surprised Bella Jeannie hasna kicked up a fuss about this engagement. I'd have said she wouldna think there was a lassie in the whole o' Scotland good enough for her Peter. She's for ever telling folk about him learning to be a draughtsman.'

Lizann smiled proudly. 'She likely thinks he could do a lot worse than marry into a good family like the Jappys.'

Nevertheless she was apprehensive when she was taken into the Taits' kitchen on Friday. Bella Jeannie was dozing by the fire, her vast body jammed into an armchair, still in a stained wrap-around overall, her sleeves rolled up, revealing the wobbling blubber of her upper arms. Giving a start, she opened her eyes. 'I didna expect you yet,' she said accusingly. With many grunts and groans, she succeeded in separating herself from her chair, but when Lizann asked if there was anything she could do to help, she snapped, 'I'll manage.'

'Let her see the ring, Lizann,' Peter said, nerves making his voice rise in pitch a little.

Shyly, she went forward and held out her left hand, but the woman gave it only a cursory glance and snorted, 'Have you tell't Willie Alec yet? The bride's father's to pay for the wedding, you ken.'

Lizann looked helplessly at Peter, who said, still a trifle

nervously, 'He gave me his blessing when I asked him, and Hannah was pleased about it, and all.'

'Hannah's never been able to see past Willie Alec. Naebody understood why he chose her, for she was a plain wee moose, and dozens o' lassies had their eye on him. He was a right handsome man in his young days . . . still is.'

Suspecting that Bella Jeannie had been one of the girls whose eye had been on him, Lizann let the slur on her mother pass, but she still felt a bit rattled that Peter had spoken to her father before she came home.

Taking her frosty expression as dismay at his mother's reaction, he prompted, 'Are you not going to congratulate us, Mam?'

Waddling across, she put her fleshy arms round him. 'Congratulations, son, but I hope you ken what you're doing.' Then she turned to Lizann. 'You're getting the finest man in the land. I've done everything for him from the day he was born, and I hope you'll look after him right.'

Peter stepped in before Lizann could answer. 'We'll look after each other, for she loves me as much as I love her.'

Lizann expected her to sneer at this, but she said, 'Ach well, it'll maybe work out. Now, for ony sake, sit yourself down.'

Taking the chair the man pulled out for her, Lizann watched the woman as she filled the plates and set them down at each place, puffing with even the slight exertion of stretching across the table. Her face was bright red from the heat of the stove, and her iron-grey hair was damp and straggly. Hoping that the stew would be less offensive than the cook, Lizann was relieved to find it very palatable.

'So Willie Alec's happy about this engagement?' Bella Jeannie barked suddenly, a few more greasy wisps escaping from the hairpins. 'Well so he should be, for my son's a fine catch for ony lassie.'

'Mam!' Peter protested, embarrassed.

'It's true,' she declared. 'I aye hoped you'd pick somebody from your office, maybe, or a lassie ... ach well, I'll say no more.'

Bowfer Tait – so nicknamed because his chronic bronchitis made him bark like a dog – spoke for the first time. 'She's a right bonnie lass.' His leg brushed Lizann's – by accident, she hoped.

'Are you going out tonight, Dad?' Peter asked.

'I aye go to the Harbour Bar for an hour or so,' Bowfer told Lizann, 'but seeing you're here ...'

'Don't stay in for me,' she interrupted.

'No, Dad,' Peter smiled. 'Go out for your pint as usual.'

'One pint?' Bella Jeannie sneered. 'Half a dozen, more like.'

'It's the only enjoyment I get,' her husband complained.

Lizann could well believe that; Bella Jeannie must wear on him. They were an ill-matched couple, the woman big in every sense of the word and the man insignificantly small and weedy. Even his sparse hair seemed to be receding to get away from her.

When the meal was over, he stood up. 'Well, if naebody objects, I'll away out.' He addressed all three of the others, but it was his wife's permission he sought with his eyes.

'Aye, away you go!' she ordered, and as he scuttled off, she said to Lizann, 'He's better boozing wi' his cronies than sitting here snoring.'

Lizann's offer to help with the dishes was taken up, but little was said during the operation. When everything was washed and laid past, Bella Jeannie bundled up the tablecloth, shook it out at the back door and, with not one dirty spot to be seen on it, put it in the washing basket to be washed the next day. Then she swept the floor, remarking, 'I like everything to be spick and span, and it's best to clean up as you go along.'

With this evidence of pride in her house, Lizann expected her to take off her filthy overall before she sat down, but she settled herself into her armchair oblivious of her own appearance, her eyes closing almost as soon as her huge rear end came in contact with the seat.

Afraid to speak now, Lizann looked at Peter, who grinned. 'That's her till Dad comes in again, and she's as bad as him for snoring. We'd be as well leaving her to it.' Getting up, he went over to his mother and gave her arm a poke. 'We're going out for a walk, Mam, and then I'll just take Lizann home.'

'Thank you for having me, Mrs Tait,' Lizann murmured, deeming it best not to address her by her Christian names, although it was how she was commonly known.

'You'll have to come back some time,' Bella Jeannie mumbled vaguely, before her eyelids drooped again.

'I don't think she's pleased about the engagement,' Lizann remarked when they were outside.

Slipping an arm round her waist, Peter said, 'It wasn't that. She was annoyed I'd spoken to your father and never said anything to her, but she'll get over it. She'll be a good mother-in-law to you when the time comes, I'm sure.'

Lizann shuddered at the prospect of having Bella Jeannie Tait as a mother-in-law – something that had slipped her mind until then – but Peter couldn't choose his relations any more than anybody else could.

'We're not going to live there when we're married?' she asked.

'God no! She'd never stop interfering. We'll look for a house . . . up the town, not in Buckpool, but there's plenty of time.'

Before she went to sleep that night it crossed Lizann's mind that she hadn't thought of George the whole day. She could hardly believe it, but it was surely a good sign. She'd had the feeling, on their last night, that if she'd

given him the slightest hint that she might not marry Peter
he'd have thrown over his girlfriend and come to Buckie
to court her. But he probably wouldn't have, and he'd be
engaged to his Katie by now, so it was best to forget him.

If she married Peter ... when she married Peter, she
corrected herself, she would be ecstatically happy. She
hadn't told him a lie when she said she still loved him,
for she did ... didn't she?

Chapter Four

'It's time I tidied out the foot o' the lobby press,' Hannah observed, one dull morning, after Willie Alec and Mick had left. 'Your father just chucks everything in there.'

'I'll do it if you like.' Lizann was glad of a change from polishing the brasses and washing and ironing clothes, and there was always a possibility that she would come across something interesting.

She smiled ruefully when she opened the door. The two shelves where her mother kept articles only needed for occasional use were neat and tidy, but the bottom of the cupboard was in a proper mess. She lifted everything out and laid it on the linoleum behind her, then scrubbed out the wooden floor and, waiting for it to dry, looked to see what could be thrown out. There were tins of nails and screws, a box of the tools her father used for the jobs around the house and a cardboard box with old door handles and lots of other items he obviously thought might come in handy. She sifted out the things she thought were past being useful, and put the rest into the carton neatly before she returned boxes and tin to the cupboard.

Next she set an old storm lantern in its original place, also two old rolls of wallpaper her mother used for lining drawers. Lastly she came to a thick bundle of old newspapers dated 1908 and tied with a piece of string. Wondering what was so interesting in them that they'd been kept twenty-two years, she undid the knot and felt something hard and flat inside. Carefully opening out the yellowing pages, she uncovered a gold-framed picture of a fishergirl with a creel on her back, standing on the shore looking out to sea.

It was a sketch, not a photograph, but it fascinated her because she could see a likeness to her mother in the girl's face and the way she was standing. She could be a sister, but Auntie Lou was Hannah's only sister and she had never mentioned going round with a creel when she was young. Maybe this was a younger sister who had died . . . or got into some kind of trouble that had made her run away in disgrace?

Intrigued, Lizann took the picture through to the kitchen, but when Hannah saw it she let out a horrified gasp. 'Ach, I forgot I'd hid that thing in there.'

This increased Lizann's curiosity. 'It's not a thing, Mother, it's a lovely picture. Why did you hide it away?'

'Never you mind. Put it back and leave it.'

But Lizann couldn't drop the subject. 'Who is she?'

'It's me!' Hannah snapped. 'So now you know.'

This was a great surprise to her daughter. 'I didn't know you'd ever sold fish. Were you ashamed of it? Was that why you hid the picture?'

'Aye, I was ashamed. I wasna brought up to earn my living. My father was like Willie Alec; he didna believe in lassies going out to work. But he was a terrible drinker and he died wi' some disease on his liver when I was sixteen, and Mother pined that much, she passed on less than three weeks after him. Lou got the house in Rannas Place and I was to get the money, but there was hardly nothing left when the funerals was paid for. Lou'd been going steady wi' Jockie Flett, so they got wed, but they couldna afford to keep me for nothing, and . . . well, Mother's old creel was still in the loft, and Lou said I could easy sell fish round the doors like Mother did when she was single. I didna argue, for Lou was aye a lot stronger than me.'

'Selling fish round the doors wasn't a disgrace,' Lizann said, gently.

'I was just a hawker, and the country folk looked down on me.'

'You just imagined that.'

'Then Willie Alec ... well, he took a fancy to me, and after we got wed, he got ... a man he ken't to draw that picture of me.'

Detecting a faint unease in her mother now, Lizann asked, 'Who was he, the man that drew you?'

Hannah's eyes darted away. 'He was ... ach ... he was just somebody your father ken't.'

'Did you not know him?'

'Not till Willie Alec took him to the house after we was married.'

Her mother's patent reluctance to talk about it only made Lizann want to hear more. 'You must have got to know him when you posed for him.'

Clearly embarrassed, Hannah refused to be drawn out any further. 'Your father hung it up above the fireplace, but I didna like being reminded of ... of things, so when he was at sea one time, I put it away.'

Sensing a mystery here, Lizann said, 'But he must have noticed ... ?'

'He ken't why.'

Lizann gave up. 'Can I take it and hang it up in my room?'

'Ach, do what you want wi' it!'

When Lizann had placed the picture to her satisfaction, she stood back to admire it. It looked as if the artist had thought a lot of her mother ... maybe loved her, but it would have been all on his side, for she had never looked at any man but Willie Alec, everybody said that. She would have sent this other man packing and had hidden the picture because it reminded her of him ... or had she been drawn to him in spite of herself?

Wishing she knew the truth, Lizann reflected that whatever the story behind the picture, she would treasure it for ever.

When she returned to the kitchen her mother tutted irritably. 'Ach, I should have got another bag o' flour yesterday, though I'd have had plenty for this pie if your father hadna wanted scones last night.'

'I'll go and get some.' Putting on her coat, Lizann opened the door and stepped out into the frosty January air. The new year of 1930 had started very cold.

'Lizann!'

Her heart started palpitating at the sound of the familiar voice, and, praying that her ears hadn't deceived her, she spun round. 'George!' she exclaimed in wonder. 'What are you doing here?'

'I've come to see you.'

'What about Katie? Does she know?'

'I broke off with her. What about you and Peter?'

The bubble burst. 'I've promised to marry him.' She couldn't back out now, not when all their friends and relations knew they were engaged.

There was a pause before he said, 'Congratulations! And I hope you'll be very happy together.'

Although it was heartily said, Lizann could tell he was downcast, and when he made to walk away, she grabbed at his arm. 'You can't go just like that.'

'I think I'd better, before I forget myself and kiss you.'

'George, I'm sorry,' she whispered.

'Don't be. I'm pleased for you.'

'But I still love you, and all.'

'Don't say it, Lizann,' he groaned.

'It's true, and I wish you could kiss me.' She also wished with all her heart that she wasn't wearing Peter's ring. If she had known George would come back to her, she would never have got engaged.

They gazed at each other, the same pain stamped

plainly across both faces, then a voice from inside the house broke the spell. 'Who's that you're speaking to, Lizann?'

Startled, she whispered, 'It's my mother,' and called in answer, 'It's a man asking how to get to Portessie. I've been trying to tell him, but it would be easier if I took him up and showed him.'

'Aye, that would be best, and you're going up the town, ony road.'

Over aware of each other and unable to let even their hands touch, they walked along the street. 'My mother's waiting for flour. I'll have to hurry. I'm sorry, George.'

He looked at her sadly. 'I should never have come. We said all that had to be said in Yarmouth.'

'I'm awful glad to see you.'

'Forget about me, Lizann. Marry your lad and be happy.'

'Will you marry Katie now?'

He shook his head. 'I don't think so. I said things to her that . . . maybe I expected too much.'

They had come to a junction – where Low Street leads to the harbour and the seafront, and High Street, to the right, goes up to the central shopping and housing area – when Lizann whispered, in alarm, 'Oh, here's my auntie. You'd better go down that way.' She pointed to the low road, and raised her voice. 'Straight along there. You'll see all the big houses up on the brae, that's Portessie.'

'Thank you,' he said, politely, walking off.

With her aunt's inquisitive eyes fixed on her, Lizann had to drag hers away from George, but his slumping shoulders had told her that he was as miserable as she was at their being riven apart with no chance to say goodbye. 'He wanted to go to Portessie, Auntie Lou,' she explained, 'and Mother said I could show him. She needed me to get flour.'

Louise Flett nodded. 'I'll come to the grocer wi' you,

64

then, and walk back wi' you. I was going to see her, ony road.'

Sore at heart, Lizann had to listen to a long diatribe about her Uncle Jockie's shortcomings, thankful that Lou didn't expect any comments from her. Back home, she offered to make the pastry to let the sisters chat, and at last her mind could deal with her own troubled thoughts. Seeing George again had made her realize that she loved him much more than she had ever loved Peter. For the five minutes they'd been together it was as if the sun had come out from behind a cloud to light up her world; as if she had been sexually stimulated. Every nerve end in her body was raw and tingling, waiting for some miraculous wand to be waved so that she and George could make love again.

Feeling the fire burning inside her and wondering if it showed on her face, she glanced across at her mother and aunt, but they were totally absorbed in their gossip and wouldn't have noticed if there had been a chimney on top of her head sending up great puffs of smoke. Smiling at this inane thought, she picked up the rolled-out pastry with trembling hands and laid it over the meat in the pie dish. After flaking the edges and decorating the top, she asked, 'Will I put this in the oven now?'

Hannah tore herself away from Lou's graphic account of what Jockie had done when he came home drunk the night before. 'What's that, Lizann? Oh, the pie! No, just leave it. It doesna need to go in for a while.' She turned to her sister again. 'Now, Lou, you was saying . . . ?'

Their supper taken care of, Lizann went upstairs and lay down on her bed. No matter how loving Peter was, he had never made her feel the way George had done today without as much as touching her. And she should be ashamed of the sinful thoughts she'd had downstairs, things that should never enter the mind of an unmarried girl . . . but she was married . . . to George, if not by vows made in front of a minister, by the bonds they had forged, the bonds of love, of physical fulfilment. She shouldn't have let him go a second time. She wouldn't get a third chance.

Despite being sure that he would go back to Katie, whatever he'd said, she knew that her heart would always belong to him. Right to her dying day, she would remember how his twinkling eyes had grown serious and tender when he looked at her; how his work-roughened fingers had gently traced the outline of her cheekbones; how their bodies had fused ... She shook her head to stop the pain-filled thoughts, and then realized that they all added up to one thing. She couldn't marry Peter now, and the sooner she broke the engagement, the better.

She went out in answer to his knock that night so tense that her stomach churned and knotted, even threatened to disgorge its contents, but her resolve remained unshaken.

'I'm taking you home with me,' he said, linking arms with her. 'My granny's not well, and Mam and Dad are away to Fochabers to see her.'

There was an underlying excitement in his voice, and she wondered if he was hoping she would let him have his way when they were on their own. If he was, he was in for a rude awakening.

He took her coat when they went inside, laid it over a seat and then flopped down on one of the easy chairs, holding out his arms to her as an invitation to sit on his knee.

'No, Peter,' she said, quietly, perching on the edge of the chair at the other side of the fire. 'There's something ... oh, how am I going to tell you?'

'Tell me what?' he asked, warily.

A pulse was beating in her throat, and she knew that if she didn't get this over quickly, she would never do it. 'I can't marry you, Peter.'

'Don't make jokes, Lizann.'

'It's not a joke. I can't marry you. I . . . love somebody else.'

'But . . . but . . .' He was stuttering in confusion. 'You've never had a chance to meet anybody else. You're always with me.'

'I met him in Yarmouth.'

His eyes narrowed. 'And you still came back and got engaged to me?'

'I thought I could forget him, but . . . he came to see me today, and I . . . I knew he was the only man for me.'

Peter's white cheeks had taken on red spots of anger. 'Who is he? Some fancy Englishman that turned your head?'

'No, he's from Cullen.'

'I don't suppose you told him you were engaged to me?'

'I did tell him, and I let him go, though I wish now I hadn't.'

'But . . . you said you still loved me.'

'I do love you, Peter,' she said, gently, 'but not enough.'

'Now he knows you're engaged, he'll not come back.' Another painful thought coming into his mind, he burst out anxiously, 'You didn't tell him you were going to finish with me?'

'No I didn't. He's going to marry the girl he's been going with, but it doesn't make any difference. I love him too much to marry you.'

After a moment's silence, he gave a harsh snort. 'I know what it is! You and him . . . you let him . . . do it, didn't you?'

Hoping that the truth would make him accept the situation, she nodded, her cheeks scarlet with embarrassment.

'Why?' he said, mournfully. 'Why didn't you stop him?'

'I didn't want to stop him. There was something between us, a kind of . . . oh, I can't explain.'

'He didn't take you by force?'

67

'George Buchan's not like that. It was my fault, and I'm not ashamed of it.' She stood up, removed the ring and laid it on the table, then walked out, leaving her ex-fiancé speechless.

Her mother was surprised to see her back so soon. 'Have you and Peter fell out?'

'I've given him back the ring.'

The cup halfway to Hannah's mouth was laid down with such a thump that some tea slopped into the saucer. 'What made you do that?'

Lizann had intended telling her everything, but facing her like this and knowing her mother's strict morals, it was impossible. 'I . . . I've been thinking about it for a while.'

'But you and him aye looked so happy. What went wrong? I thought you loved him.'

'Not enough.'

'You were lucky having a man like him. Once his time's out, he'll have a good, steady job. Why couldn't you . . . ?'

'My mind's made up.'

Remembering her tea, Hannah took a mouthful to steady her nerves. 'I dinna ken what Bella Jeannie'll say.'

'It's my life. You loved the man you married.'

'Aye, lass, your father was the only one I ever loved.' Hannah's smile faded. 'Is there another man? Is that why you . . . ?'

Unable to take the risk, Lizann shook her head. Besides, there was no other man . . . not now. George had gone for ever.

Hannah took another sip of tea. 'Your father'll not be pleased.'

When her husband and son came home some days later, Willie Alec took the broken engagement better than she had thought. 'Hold your whisht,' he cautioned Hannah, who had been lamenting about what people would say.

'There has to be love on both sides to make a marriage work.'

He took a slice of bread off the plate and continued his homily as he spread it thickly with butter. 'Thank God Peter didna take advantage o' you the time you were engaged, lass. Some men think the first ring gives them the right, and if he'd bairned you, you'd have had to marry him. As it is, seeing there's nae other man involved, you'll maybe get back wi' him again some day.'

Feeling the heat coming into her cheeks – she'd never thought at the time that George might land her in the family way – and uncomfortably aware of Mick's speculative eyes fixed on her, she muttered, 'No, I'm finished with him for good, Father.'

'Aye, well,' he nodded, taking a huge bite and chewing for a moment, 'you were right to gi'e him his ring back if you were as sure as that.'

The meal over, Willie Alec stood up. 'It's been a long hard day, so I think I'll just turn in now. Are you coming, Hannah?'

'When I've done the dishes.'

'Mick and Lizann can do them.'

Her face pink, Hannah went out with her husband, and Mick grinned at his sister. 'We know what he's got on his mind, eh?'

Lizann collected the dirty crockery. 'What a thing to say about your own father.'

'It's true. He's a horny old devil when he likes.'

As he dried what Lizann washed, Mick changed the subject. 'You didn't tell them,' he accused.

A prickle of fear touched her. 'Tell them what?' she gasped.

'I ran into Peter when I was coming past the yard. He's right cut up about you carrying on with that lad when you were away.'

'He'd no business saying anything to you about that.'

69

'We've told each other all our secrets since we were in short breeks.'

'It was my secret, not his!' She looked at Mick anxiously. 'You won't tell Father?'

'I won't tell a soul, and I'm not condemning you – I've taken quite a few girls myself – but surely . . . if you're not to be seeing this Cullen man again, couldn't you just have married Peter and said nothing?'

'Is that what you'd have done?'

'It's what I'd have done, but I don't know how girls think.'

'I can't marry Peter – I love George a lot more than I love him.'

Mick eyed her keenly. 'Are you sure this George wasn't . . . I mean, some men can turn a girl's head till she doesn't know what she's doing.'

'He wasn't like that!' she retorted, hotly. 'He loved me!'

Mick smiled. 'All right, I believe you. Any road, you're still young, and you'll fall in love with somebody else.' He held up his hand to stop any protest. 'I'd better wash and shave. I'm seeing Jenny at half nine.'

'You've been going with her for a good while. Is this the real thing?'

Lifting the kettle from the stove, he said, more serious than she had ever seen him, 'Aye, I think it is, and I think she feels the same.'

In Main Street, Peter Tait was wishing that he hadn't said anything to Mick. It was bad enough to have it constantly buzzing round in his brain that the girl he loved had given herself to somebody else, but to have it buzzing round the whole town would be worse. And now he'd had time to think about it, he was sure Lizann had expected him to forgive her. She hadn't really meant to break their engagement. Her affair with the other man couldn't have lasted long, and she'd have forgotten all about him if he hadn't come upsetting her.

Peter's spirits lifted. The fisherman – George Buchan, she'd called him – would think she was still going to marry her fiancé, and he was getting married himself, so he was out of the running. All he, Peter, had to do was wait until she got over it and propose to her again. She'd sworn she still loved him, so there shouldn't be any problem, and his mother didn't know that Lizann had given him back the ring; he had just said they'd had a wee tiff.

'You're looking better the day,' Bella Jeannie smiled, the following morning. 'Have you and Lizann made it up?'

'We're not going to see each other for a while, so we can sort things out in our minds.'

His mother hesitated. 'Maybe she's nae the right lass for you, and if you dinna want her, m'loon, there's plenty would jump at the chance of marrying a fine man like you.'

Basking in the compliment, Peter didn't dream of saying that his heart was set on Lizann, nor that he was determined to marry her however long he had to wait.

Chapter Five

❧

Lizann was resigned to being at Hannah's beck and call all day. She had only been expected to do the heavy cleaning before, but it was quite a while now since her mother had said she wasn't fit to do much housework and had left more and more of it to her daughter. She'd ended up by having to do everything. Not that she minded. It was better to be kept busy.

Going out to the cart to have the flagon filled one morning in June 1931 she was dismayed to see Peter Tait speaking to the milkman. She would have turned back if he hadn't noticed her, but she was forced to go up to him with a smile. 'Hello, Peter, I haven't seen you for ages.'

She had seen him several times since she gave him back his ring – it was inevitable when he passed her door on his way to and from work – but usually she just remarked on the weather and gave him no chance to speak. Today, though, he hung back until she was served and it was quite clear that he wanted to say something.

Taking care not to jog the hand carrying the milk, he steered her away from the other women. 'Lizann,' he murmured, 'I wanted to ask you . . . it's nearly a year and a half since . . . have you changed your mind yet?'

Also keeping her voice low, she said, 'I'll never change it, Peter.'

'Are you still hoping that George Buchan'll come back?'

'He'll not come back – he's married now.'

A hint of triumph crossed his face. 'Stop fretting about him, Lizann. Come back to me, I still love you. We could have a quiet wedding if you like, and set up house anywhere you want . . .'

'I told you, Peter – no! Now, you'd better go, or you'll be late for your work.'

'My apprenticeship's finished, and I won't take long to save up enough to buy a house.'

She clicked her tongue testily. 'Can you not take a telling? You can keep on at me till you're blue in the face, but you'll not get me to marry you!'

She walked away and left him standing, but as she reached her door she glanced round and saw him trailing off dejectedly. She was sorry she had hurt him by being so blunt, but he'd get over it and it was his own fault. He shouldn't be so persistent.

Later, thinking it over, she wondered if she had been stupid to turn him down again. Why should she make a martyr of herself because of a man who didn't want her? Peggy May Cordiner had told her she'd heard George saying he was getting married when he went home last November, so there wasn't the faintest hope that she'd ever see him again. But a girl had to love with all her heart to make a marriage work, and she couldn't consider Peter as a husband. As a friend, yes, if he'd let her, but that was all.

Three more months dragged past with Lizann's only excursions outside the house being to go shopping. Setting off one day she was alarmed to meet Peter's mother. She tried to walk past, but Bella Jeannie grabbed her arm. 'I want to speak to you.'

'What about?' Lizann asked, apprehensively.

'My son deserves better than you, Lizann Jappy, and there's more than one lass would wed him if he asked.'

Stung, Lizann snapped, 'They're welcome to him.' She regretted it at once and said hastily, 'I'm sorry, I shouldn't have said that. Peter's a fine man.'

73

Mollified, Bella Jeannie muttered, 'Naebody kens that better than me. I've never took nothing from him for his board, and he was saving every penny o' his wages to buy a house for you, but you've kept him hanging on for near two year. It wouldna surprise me if you'd never had ony intentions o' wedding him.'

Unwilling to go into any explanations, Lizann said stiffly, 'I told him at the time I wouldn't marry him, and I thought you'd have been pleased. You don't really want him to marry at all, do you? You want to keep him all to yourself.'

Looking uncomfortable, Bella Jeannie blustered, 'I wasna pleased when he got engaged to you, but it was you he wanted and I'd have . . .'

'You'd have put up with me?' Lizann butted in, smiling in spite of the fury boiling up inside her. 'You've no need to worry, Mrs Tait. I gave Peter back his ring when we split up, and I'll never be your daughter-in-law.' She nearly added, 'Thank heaven,' but managed to hold it back.

Bella Jeannie was obviously shaken. 'Oh? I didna ken you'd gi'en him back the ring.'

'So your son doesn't tell you everything?' Lizann couldn't resist the dig as she made her escape; the nasty besom deserved it.

She didn't tell Hannah of the encounter when she went home, for she still felt angry that Peter had let his mother believe the engagement was still on, though he'd likely been too proud to admit that it wasn't. In a few minutes, however, after a cup of tea, she saw the funny side of it. Bella Jeannie had been on her high horse, sure she was getting rid of the fiancée who was trifling with her son's affections, and her face had been a picture when she learned the truth – fancy any girl turning down her Peter!

* * *

Lizann had almost succeeded in pushing George to the back of her mind as a wonderful yet painful memory, but as another November came round, the memory flared up again and she pined silently for the only man she would ever want. When she learned that the gutting crews had arrived home once again, she pocketed her pride and ran along Main Street to ask if Peggy May had any news of him.

'He wasna there this time,' Peggy May told her, 'and I heard he'd got his own boat and was landing fish at Peterhead. And to save you asking, he is married. I'm awful sorry, Lizann, but you'll have to put him right out o' your head.'

'I suppose so.'

'I shouldna tell you this when you're so down, but I canna keep it to myself. I met a Buckie lad down there, and we're going steady now.'

'I'm pleased for you.' She really was, and had to find out more. 'Did you know him before? What's his name?'

'Ned Yule, and I didna ken him afore. He's near three year older than me, and he said he's had a lot o' girls, but I'm the only one he's ever really loved.'

'And d'you love him?'

'Oh, aye, Lizann ... I hope you're nae jealous o' me being so happy?'

'No, I'm not. I just wish things had worked out for me and George, that's all.'

'Are you still determined nae to go back to Peter?'

'Bella Jeannie would have a fit if I did.'

'You dinna need to worry about her.'

'I wouldn't, but I don't want to go back to Peter. I'd never be able to love him as much as I loved George.'

'But you still love him a bit?'

'Who, Peter?' Lizann considered this for a moment. 'Yes, I suppose I do,' she said, at last. 'A bit, but not enough.'

'A bit could be plenty,' Peggy May said, triumphantly. 'Think about it, Lizann. You loved him more than a bit at one time.'

'Peter's aye been a real nice lad,' Lizann said, thoughtfully.

Suspecting that she was weakening, Peggy May wisely did not press the matter any further.

Polishing the stairs one afternoon the following spring, Lizann was seriously contemplating going back to Peter, having given it much thought over the winter, but Hannah's plaintive voice broke into her train of thought. 'Lizann, I need some corn plasters. My little toe's throbbing that bad, I'm sure we're in for rain.'

'I'll go in a minute, Mother, when I'm finished this last step.'

Getting up off her knees, she laid the dusters and tin of polish past in the lobby cupboard and took her coat off the row of pegs on the opposite wall. 'Here's a ten-shilling note,' Hannah said. 'Get me this week's *Friend*, and all.'

Lizann was at the door when another order came. 'And something fine out o' Mrs Campbell's . . . maybe a quarter o' chocolate gingers.'

'Corn plasters, the *People's Friend* and chocolate gingers,' the girl repeated dutifully.

She had gone only about a hundred yards when she met Babsie Berry, one of their neighbours, who stood up to speak. Only half-listening to the woman's account of things her grandchildren said, Lizann's eye was caught by the familiar gait of a man walking towards them. It couldn't be, she thought, but when he came nearer her stomach turned over. 'I'm sorry, Babsie,' she said, tremulously, breaking into Mrs Berry's flow, 'but I'd like to have a wee word with this man coming along. I haven't seen him for a long time.'

The woman gave a quick glance round. 'An old flame,

is he?' Her house being next door to the Jappys', she went on chuckling to herself.

Wanting to run to George, to tell him how much she had missed him, to kiss him till her lips were swollen and sore, Lizann had to keep telling herself that he was another girl's husband. The trouble was, he looked the same, his hair still stuck up in the same places, his clothes were still untidy . . . he couldn't have a wife looking after him. Peggy May must have got hold of the wrong end of the stick! This last thought gave her the power to move, but her trembling legs refused to hurry, which was maybe just as well, for she could be taking things for granted that weren't really so.

He too was walking slowly, as if unsure about what he was doing, and she felt like shouting to him that she loved him more than ever, but all that came out when she opened her mouth was a weak, 'I didn't think I'd ever see you again, George.'

He gripped her hands and she was sure that his eyes were telling her what she wanted to know, but she needed him to say it and they couldn't talk properly here. 'I'm on my way to the shops if you want to . . .'

Letting her go, he turned and walked alongside her, both seemingly struck dumb, but very soon she knew she couldn't wait much longer to find out, and tried to think how to phrase her question. At last, giving up all pretence, she whispered, 'I was told you married Katie.' His quiet, 'I did,' drained the colour from her face. Why had he tortured her by coming back?

Obviously anxious not to prolong her agony, he said quickly, 'But I found her out in something I can't forgive her for.'

She was ashamed of how her heart had started to pound in what she could only describe as excited anticipation; what he was saying really made no difference to anything, Katie was still his wife when all was said and done, and nothing either of them could do would change that. Nevertheless, she murmured, 'I didn't marry Peter.'

'Oh, thank God!' He looked at her beseechingly now. 'I wish I hadn't ... but I'm going to ask her to divorce me. The thing is, I'll have to give her grounds.'

Too ecstatic about his marriage being over to take in the meaning of what he was saying, she asked idly, 'Grounds?'

He looked embarrassed. 'I'm going to book a room in a hotel for you and me to ...'

This shocked her out of her euphoria. 'George Buchan!'

'It's the only way. I'd never have married her if I'd known the awful things she'd done, and when she divorces me ...'

'Divorce?' Her horror made the word come out louder than she meant, and she looked around her in agitation, but thankfully no one was near enough to have heard. 'I never thought ... oh, George, you can't let her divorce you.'

'It's the only way I'll get free of her,' he protested.

'I can't help it. Divorce isn't something that happens to nice men ...' Realizing that he might take this as a slur on him, she said, quickly, 'I didn't mean that like it sounded. You're the nicest man I know, but ... I can't sleep with you. I couldn't get away, even for one night ...'

'It doesn't need to be at night,' he urged, 'and we don't actually need to ... to sleep together. It's just ... I have to get a hotel receipt to prove I've been unfaithful to her. We could go some afternoon.'

She could feel her face flaming. 'No, I couldn't! I couldn't!'

'We don't have to do anything, Lizann. All I need is just for you to be there.'

'I couldn't come to some room ...' She stopped, utterly woebegone. 'I couldn't, not like that! Besides, somebody might see me, and it could get back to my mother . . . Oh, I just couldn't!'

They had left all the shops and houses behind and were now out of town on the road to Arradoul. Her senses reeling, she let him pull her to a halt and slide his arms round her. 'I shouldn't have asked,' he said. 'I didn't really think you would . . . I don't know if I even wanted you to. Don't cry, Lizann, I'll think of another way.'

It felt so good to have him holding her again that it was some time before she whispered, 'I'm sorry. I suppose you hate me now for not . . . ?'

'Hate you? I could never hate you, whatever you did. It was a terrible thing to ask any girl, never mind the girl I love. Look, I'd better take you home . . .'

She gasped. 'Oh, I forgot! I'm supposed to be buying some things for my mother. She'll wonder why I've been so long.'

George accompanied her to the various shops, then walked most of the way to the Yardie with her. He would have taken her to her door but she said he'd better not. 'My mother's got some funny ideas. She wouldn't be pleased if she saw me with a married man.' It didn't occur to her that Hannah didn't know George existed, let alone that he was married.

'Will you meet me tonight, Lizann?'

'Are you not going back to Cullen?'

'I need some time to myself so I can work out what to do. I'll take lodgings here for a week, so we could see each other every night.'

'Not at your lodgings,' she said, hastily.

'We could walk out into the country again, for an hour or two.'

The prospect of being with him for an hour or two every night for a week was too great a temptation. 'I'll see you here at seven.'

'What took you so long?' Hannah asked when she went home.

Lizann had already thought of an excuse. 'I was speaking to a boy that was in my class at school, and he's asked me out after suppertime.'

'So you're definitely nae going back to Peter?'

'That was finished long ago.'

'I thought you might . . . oh, well. It'll do you good to start seeing another laddie.'

With her mother deep in the *People's Friend*, Lizann prepared the supper, though she knew she wouldn't feel like eating anything herself. She could hardly believe that George had really come back to her, but this divorce business . . . ! She had been about ten at the time, but she could still remember the furore there had been when Cassie Duthie from Main Street married a Buckie man whose wife had divorced him. It had been the talk of the place – the poor things had been more or less driven out of their home and never seen since. Lizann had always considered it a tragedy, but it came to her now that it was no such thing. The young couple had been truly in love, and they were likely living happily together somewhere else. What did it matter what other folk thought? She loved George and if the only way he could marry her was to ask his wife to divorce him, that's how it would have to be.

When she met him that night, he said, 'I got lodgings in East Church Street with a Mrs Clark, she's a real nice body. Her man was a skipper and his boat went down fourteen years ago. He'd left her comfortable, but they didn't have any family and she likes company.'

'I'm glad you found somewhere nice,' Lizann smiled.

'It's great! I'd a plate of tattie soup, and enough stew and veggies to feed two, then sponge pudding with about half a pound of bramble jam on top. I'll be putting on weight if she goes on like that.' Laughing, he patted his flat stomach, then asked, 'What did your mother say about you coming out with me?'

'She said it would do me good to have another lad.'

They were on the Arradoul road again, but this time, when they came to a gate into a field enclosed by a dry-stone dyke, George turned her in. 'We'll have a seat here for a while – nobody'll see us.'

She sat down on the grass, somewhat uneasy, but he pulled up his legs and clasped his hands round his knees. 'I'm going to write to Katie. She knows about you already, and I'm going to tell her I want to marry you.'

'Will she not come here and fight to get you back?'

'No, not Katie. She knows it's all over between her and me.'

'All right,' Lizann sighed, 'if you're sure.' She went into his arms glad that he wasn't going to tell any lies, and his kisses gradually dispelled the vague pity that she felt for his wife.

'I love you, Lizann,' he whispered against her ear. 'I'll never stop loving you till the day I die.'

'And I'll love you till the day I die and all, George,' she said, twisting so that their lips met once more, and she was glad that there was no fiery passion this time. It made their love seem all the purer.

As if reading her thoughts, George murmured, 'We'll wait till we're man and wife to love each other properly again, my darling.'

Her throat constricted, she could only nod blissfully.

It was much later when George looked at his watch. 'It's well after ten. What time do you have to be home?'

'Before this,' she gasped, struggling to her feet.

Although they went as fast as they could, it was nearly a quarter to eleven when they came in sight of the Yardie, and George left her with a breathless, 'Tomorrow same time?'

'Aye, tomorrow.'

She was panting when she went inside, and it didn't surprise her when her mother said, 'What kind of time's this to be coming in? Does your lad not have a watch?'

'He forgot to look at it.'

Hannah's eyes narrowed. 'You're awful carfuffled. I hope you havena been doing anything?'

'George and me were just walking and speaking ... about old times, but we'd to hurry all the way back.'

'George? Which George would that be?'

'You wouldn't know him, Mother. His name's Buchan, and he bides ... out Arradoul way.' It was the only place to come to her mind.

'I never heard you speaking about a laddie from Arradoul when you was at the school.'

'He wasn't there all the time,' Lizann said, desperately, trapped in a web of her own lies. 'Only about ... six months.'

'Where does he work?'

'He works ... on his father's farm.'

'His father's got a farm?' Hannah seemed pleased about this. 'He'll be a real steady lad, then?'

Sensing that her mother had already married her off in her mind to the fictitious farm boy with prospects, Lizann forced a smile. 'We're going out together, that's all.'

'You like him, though?' Hannah asked, archly.

'Aye, I like him.' That was putting it mildly, Lizann thought, for she loved him more every time she was with him. She wasn't that happy about his wife divorcing him, but if it was the only way he could marry her ...

Her mother and father would be horrified when they found out he'd been married already – like all fisherfolk, they considered divorce an awful disgrace that reflected on a whole family – but she didn't need to tell the truth about him till he actually was free.

There was bound to be trouble then, but she'd be

prepared for it, and wasn't there an old saying, 'Love conquers everything?' Surely she and George would win through.

Chapter Six

In a well-furnished, very comfortable room in East Church Street, George Buchan was deliberating on what he should do. He had loved Katie once – he had given Lizann up because of that love – but he had been utterly disillusioned and couldn't trust her any more. It wasn't so much the discovery of what she had done – the men she'd been with – it was her not telling him before their wedding that he couldn't forgive. Worse, she wouldn't have told him at all if old chickens hadn't come home to roost and it had been forced out of her, bit by gut-twisting bit.

Remembering that last sickening revelation, and how it had come about, George felt the same disgust that had made him tell her, as he stormed out, that the next time she heard from him would be through a solicitor. It had been said in the throes of a white-hot anger, but even after two weeks spent trying to cool down in his mother's house, he still hadn't changed his mind. He had come to Buckie on an impulse, purely to satisfy himself that Lizann was happily married and never dreaming that she was still single; now all it needed was for Katie to divorce him and he could marry the girl he should have married in the first place. Only . . . could he be sure that Katie would agree to divorce him if he just asked politely? If Lizann had only . . . maybe he should look for a girl who'd be willing to go to a hotel so he could give his wife grounds?

After racking his brain half the night for another way out, he could think of nothing, and went down to breakfast still preoccupied.

'Is something bothering you, m'loon?' his landlady asked in concern when he pushed back his chair. 'You've hardly eaten a thing.'

He hadn't meant to confide in anybody, but, even though she'd never had any children, she was such a motherly person that he found himself telling her. He had expected her to condemn him, but she bobbed her head knowingly. 'You've loved this other lassie for a while? Maybe before you married your wife? Maybe you were torn between them?'

Amazed at her perception, he mumbled, 'I suppose I was.'

'And you chose the wrong one?'

'It turned out that way.'

He told her now how he had met Lizann and how they had fallen in love, and Mrs Clark – a small, jolly woman with white hair in a softly-styled bun at the nape of her neck – listened with an occasional nod and one slightly disapproving shake of her head. Then he told her shame-facedly what he had asked Lizann to do, adding, 'But she wouldn't.'

'Nor would any decent girl!' his landlady declared. 'And you should be right pleased she wouldn't. So . . . what are you planning to do now?'

'Goodness knows!' George said, morosely. 'I was going to tell Katie I wanted to marry Lizann, then I wondered if I should find some girl that would come to a hotel with me and . . .'

The old woman clicked her tongue disapprovingly. 'No, that wouldn't be very wise. You'd maybe find you've started something.'

George lifted his shoulders expressively and let them sag again. 'I didn't really like the idea, anyway.'

Her brow wrinkling in thought, Mrs Clark poured his cold tea into a slop bowl and filled his cup again, and her own. 'You know, George,' she observed after a quick sip, 'maybe you'll not believe this, but I wed the wrong man, and all.'

'You?' he gasped, taking an absent-minded mouthful himself.

She smiled a little sadly. 'It's too long a story, but I know what it feels like to be parted from the one you love. Now, if you're sure you don't want anything to eat...?'

He shook his head and watched her piling the dirty crockery on to a tray then disappearing into her tiny scullery. His mind returned to his problem. If Lizann wasn't such a ... no, he was glad she had strong morals ... but if she hadn't, he could maybe have rented a furnished room and persuaded her to move in with him.

His pain-laden heart gave a tentative jump. Lizann would definitely turn down the idea, but if he told Katie they were living together, she might believe it. Surely that would make her give him up ... and if he could make the correspondence official, a letter from a law firm, say, it would give even more weight to the lie.

When Mrs Clark appeared again he asked if there were any solicitors in Buckie, and she gave him the name and address of the man who had conducted her late husband's business.

George was very much taken aback when he was ushered in to see the solicitor. Mr Sandison was a thin, balding Englishman, who looked, and talked, as if he had a marble in his mouth, but he could not have been more helpful. After hearing what George had to say, he put the tips of his long thin fingers together. 'You refuse to name the girl you are living with?' At George's stubborn nod, he continued, 'That will make it rather more difficult, but ... hmm ... can you supply any proof?'

This was what George had feared. 'I'm afraid not.'

Mr Sandison thought for a moment, then said, 'Would anyone else be prepared to swear to it?'

Knowing that Lizann would refuse, George remembered how sympathetic Mrs Clark had been, and, thankful that he hadn't told the solicitor where and when the 'adultery' had taken place, he decided to jump in with both feet. 'Would my landlady do?'

'I would require her to sign an affidavit to the effect that the girl is sleeping in the same room as you.'

George's heart sank. He knew that Mrs Clark was a staunch member of the kirk, so it would be against her principles to perjure herself, but she was his only hope. 'I'll ask her and see what she says.'

'The sooner you get that done, the sooner I can set things in motion.' Mr Sandison smiled reassuringly.

George hurried back to East Church Street with little hope. 'It's the only way I'll be able to marry Lizann,' he said, sadly, after telling Mrs Clark what he required of her.

'You're asking me to sin my soul?' she asked, looking at him with her eyebrows raised. 'I'm not saying I won't do it,' she continued, hastily, when his face fell, 'but I'll need to know all the outs and ins. For a start, you didn't tell me exactly why you left your wife.'

George heaved a long sigh. 'I found her out in something . . .'

'What something?' she persisted.

He hadn't wanted to blacken Katie's character, but he owed Mrs Clark some explanation and gave her only a watered-down version of the truth.

'She'd been taking up with . . . other men . . . she even got rid of a baby . . .'

'Did she try to make you think it was yours?'

'No, no! It all happened long before we were even keeping company.'

'And you couldn't forgive her?' she asked in surprise. 'You likely hadn't been lily-white yourself.'

Having made love to several girls in the years before

Lizann, George blustered. 'It's different for a man.' As soon as he said it, he was sure it would set his landlady against him, but he needn't have worried. In Mrs Clark's world, it had always been different for a man.

'And what about Lizann?' she asked. 'How do you know she's not keeping secrets from you? She could have had men before, and all.'

'No!' George burst out. 'She was a virgin when I . . .' He stopped, his face scarlet.

Mrs Clark's mouth lifted slightly at the corners. 'And did you tell Katie about that?'

'I did tell her . . . after a while, but she wouldn't have told me a thing if I hadn't found out she'd given all our savings to somebody that was blackmailing her. That's why I got so angry . . . the underhandedness . . .'

'Aye, I can understand that.' She got to her feet purposefully. 'Now, what's this thing Mr Sandison wants me to sign?'

George was astounded that she was agreeing after what he had told her. 'You've to make a statement that I've been sleeping with Lizann in your house. That's to get proof of adultery.'

'Just one thing, George. Wouldn't it be easier if you divorced Katie?'

'I don't know if I could, seeing she wasn't my wife when she . . . anyway, I couldn't shame her like that.'

'Well, I'll give you credit for that. I'll get my coat and hat.'

On the way to the solicitor's office, Mrs Clark said, 'How long are you and your Lizann supposed to have been . . . ?'

'We'd better make it . . . two weeks?'

The affidavit drawn up and duly signed, Mr Sandison said, 'I shall post this to your wife, Mr Buchan, and she can take it to her solicitor and ask him to instigate divorce proceedings against you. The Court of Session in

Edinburgh will then serve you with a notice detailing your misdemeanours and giving you the date on which the case will be held and you and your witness will have to appear in court.'

Mrs Clark looked alarmed. 'Oh my, don't tell me I'll have to stand up in a court in front of . . . ?'

'You may not have to. They may consider your affidavit sufficient.'

'What if Katie won't divorce me?' George asked.

'Then I'm afraid there is nothing more you can do . . . unless you can find her out in something?'

George's face tightened. He had already found her out in too much. 'No, there's nothing like that.'

Outside, Mrs Clark said, 'I hope I don't have to go. I don't think I could tell a barefaced lie to a judge.'

'Mr Sandison didn't seem to think they'd need you,' George muttered, uncertain now if he had done the right thing. Maybe he should have got hold of some girl who would be willing to do the needful. Sordid it might have been, but it would have been above board.

Having brooded about it all day, it was the first thing Lizann asked George when she met him that evening. 'Did you write to Katie?'

Positive that she would be annoyed if he admitted what he had really done, he nodded. 'I posted it this afternoon.'

'Did you say . . . what you said you were going to say?'

'I just said I wanted to marry you and asked her to divorce me.'

'Will that be enough?'

'We'll have to wait and see.'

Wanting to avoid the temptation that could arise if they went out along the Arradoul road again, Lizann took him back past the Yardie and through one of the lanes which led down to the old Buckpool harbour and the shore. They would be in full view of the rear windows of all the houses on that side of Main Street, but it couldn't be helped. She grew uneasy when George stopped to kiss her and hurried him past the back of the Taits' house, praying that Peter wouldn't be looking out of his bedroom.

'Have you told your mother about me?' George asked, after a while.

'I said I was going out with a boy I knew at school.'

'You'll have to tell her the truth some time.'

'We'll tell her together, when Katie divorces you.'

'What if she doesn't?'

'Would you go back to her?' This was Lizann's main fear.

'Never! You're the only one I love now.'

After a thoughtful silence, Lizann murmured, 'I couldn't let you go again. If she doesn't let you free, would you . . . would you take me away somewhere with you?'

Pulling her closely against him, he said, 'You'd leave your mother and father . . . for me?'

'If I have to, but . . . I hope it doesn't come to that.'

'No, it'll never come to that,' he declared. 'Katie knows I'm through with her, and she'll not be difficult.'

'I wish I'd met you before I was going with Peter.'

'Aye,' he said, ruefully. 'I'd never have got married if you hadn't been promised to him . . . though I did love Katie. I can't deny that.'

'I loved Peter and all. Oh, George, what a mess we're in.'

'It'll sort itself out, and when we're married we can look back and laugh about all this.'

'I don't feel like laughing right now.'

'Neither do I. I'd like to let everybody know how much I love you, and I can't even kiss you the way I want to.'

'How long will it be till Katie tells you, one way or the other?'

'Not long, I shouldn't think.'

They stopped again to kiss, then Lizann whispered, 'You said you'd taken lodgings for a week. Will you go back to Cullen after that?'

'I can't hang about here. I need to earn some money, so I'll have to find a berth, and I've more chance of that where they all know me.'

'Peggy May said you'd a boat of your own?'

'It was needing repairs I couldn't afford, so I sold it for scrap.' He didn't tell her, as he had told Mrs Clark, that his wife had cleared out their bank account. Katie had been too scared to let him know she was being blackmailed, though if she had confessed her past to him before, that evil devil wouldn't have had anything to hold over her.

Watching the expressions on George's face, Lizann guessed that there was something he wasn't telling her but, presuming he had bought a boat that wasn't seaworthy and was ashamed to admit how gullible he'd been, she didn't ask. Instead, she turned her questions again to the chances of their getting married.

Approaching the Yardie, George said, 'We've only four nights left, so we should stop worrying about things we can do nothing about.'

'You'll tell me when you hear from Katie, though?'

'The minute I get a letter.'

'What if it's not good news?'

'It has to be good!' He squeezed her arm, thinking she wouldn't want him to kiss her so near to her house. 'Tomorrow, same time?'

'Same time.' She waited until he was out of sight before she went in, and when her mother asked if she'd been out with George Buchan again she tried to sound happier than she felt. 'Aye, we walked along the shore.'

Her spirits lifted when she was in bed. George had sounded so sure that Katie would let him go, and though she would miss him when he went home, it wouldn't be long till he came back . . . to marry her!

Peter lay back against his pillow, the muscles of his stomach taut with jealousy. Lizann had been with another man! He hadn't been sure it was her at first, hadn't wanted to believe it was her, and it wasn't until they were level with his bedroom window that his gut had twisted with recognition. Despite this, he had watched them stopping as lovers do to kiss occasionally and walk on, craning his neck until he could see them no longer and then waiting until they came past again on their way back. But who had she been with? The Cullen man was safely married now, so it couldn't be him. It must be somebody local . . . but who?

Peter spent a restless night. He had been positive that it would just be a matter of time before he got Lizann back, and the thought that she had transferred her affections so quickly from him to George Buchan and now to somebody else had cut the feet from under him, but he wasn't going to give up on her.

That morning being Sunday, when he knew Lizann would be at church, he slipped along to the Yardie at five past eleven. Hannah looked surprised to see him. 'If it's Lizann you're wanting . . .' she began, but he interrupted. 'No, it's you I want.'

She invited him in and offered him a cup of tea. 'Now,' she smiled, when they were both seated, 'what can I do for you?'

'Nothing, really,' he said, wondering how to go about discovering what he wanted to know. 'I saw Lizann last night . . .'

'Ah!' Hannah sat up a little straighter. 'You saw her wi' George?'

'George?' he echoed, hollowly, a sickness at the pit of his stomach. 'George who?'

'George Buchan. He was at the school wi' her.'

'He was not!' Peter exclaimed. 'She met him down in Yarmouth!'

Hannah looked puzzled. 'She never said nothing about meeting . . .'

'That's why she broke our engagement. She said she loved him more than she loved me.'

'But she . . .'

Driven by jealousy, and not thinking of the consequences, he blurted out, 'She even let him . . . and she wouldn't let me . . .'

Jumping to the correct interpretation of this cryptic statement, she shook her head. 'Oh, I canna believe that! Nae my Lizann?'

'That's not the worst of it. He's married!'

'Oh, my dear Lord!' Hannah's hand went to her breast. 'You canna mean . . . she let a married man . . . ? And she tell't you that?'

'Not willingly,' he admitted, 'but I got it out of her, though I'm near sure she'd have forgotten about him if he hadn't come to see her. He went away when she told him she was engaged to me, but he'd unsettled her, for that was the day she gave me back the ring.'

'Oh, my dear Lord!' Hannah exclaimed again. 'You're sure it was him she was wi' last night?'

'If his name's George Buchan, it's him. He must have come back.'

After wringing her hands for a few moments, Hannah's tortured face changed. 'She tell't me a parcel o' lies!' she said, angrily. 'My own daughter! Wait till she comes in, I'll . . .' She halted, then muttered uncertainly, 'Oh, I dinna ken what I'll do. I wish Willie Alec was here, he would stop her nonsense. I hope nothing's happened to him, for he was due in yesterday.'

'Something's likely held him up.' Peter stood up, nervously pulling down his cuffs. 'I'm sorry, Hannah. I shouldn't have said anything. I never dreamt it was him she was with.'

'You've nothing to be sorry for, Peter, it wasna your fault.'

At the door, he said, 'You'll not tell Lizann I've been here?'

'You have my word on that.'

Peter returned to his own house with mixed feelings. He had been as shocked at learning it was George Buchan as Hannah had been at what he told her, but he was pleased she thought Willie Alec would stop it.

'Where have you been?' Bella Jeannie demanded, when he went home.

'Just out for a wee breath of air.' If his mother knew what Lizann had been up to, it would be the end of any hope he had of marrying her. And there was every hope, he assured himself, happy in his relief at how things had turned out. When she was forbidden to see George Buchan she would turn to her first love for comfort.

Agonizing over Lizann's misconduct, Hannah looked up in relief when Willie Alec came in some twenty minutes later. 'That damned idiot!' he stormed. 'I said we'd miss the tide yesterday, but would he listen? So now we're in and we canna land the fish till the morrow.'

'Forget about your fish!' Hannah cried. 'Peter Tait's not long away, and you'd best sit down and listen to what he was telling me.'

When she finished, her husband had forgotten his anger at his skipper, but he was apoplectic with fury at his daughter. 'Good God, Hannah!' he roared. 'Did you never tell her not to let a man touch her?'

Knowing that she had neglected her duty as a mother, Hannah let her husband's wrath envelop her without saying a word.

'But I suppose you couldna bring yourself to speak

94

about things like that,' he went on, sarcastically. 'Well, it's no thanks to you she didna land in the family way, and I'm thankful it's over and done wi'.'

'She's still seeing him,' Hannah ventured. 'He's come to Buckie . . . and she was out wi' him last night . . . and the night before.'

'D'you mean to tell me you ken't she was . . . ?'

'I didna ken a thing, till Peter tell't me.'

'That's it, then! She'll not go out wi' him again . . . supposing I've to tie her to her bed.' Taking deep rasping breaths, Willie Alec sat down heavily on his chair, gripping the arms as if clutching at a lifeline.

'Are you all right?' Hannah asked, anxiously.

It was some time before he could answer. 'To think she's carrying on wi' a married man. I've a good mind to leather her backside till it's black and blue.'

Practically sure he wouldn't, Hannah murmured, 'And a lot of good that would do.'

'Aye, you're right. Keeping her from seeing him again'll be the best punishment for her.' His chin sinking and coming to rest on his chest, he lapsed into a stony silence.

As the minutes passed, Hannah grew increasingly agitated. She hated rows, but there was no way out of this one. Willie Alec was building up for it, and it would explode the minute Lizann came through the door. If only his son was here to support him. 'Where's Mick?' she asked.

'He's away wi' Bluey Barclay,' Willie Alec mumbled. 'I think he said they were going to Strathlene.'

The swimming pool was a favourite meeting place for all the young blood round about, and Hannah knew they would be lucky if they saw Mick before suppertime. Hearing Lizann's step outside, she cautioned, 'Take it easy, Willie Alec.'

'Easy?' he grunted. 'How the devil can I take it easy?'

Looking very smart in her grey Sunday costume with

its matching floppy beret, their daughter came in smiling. 'D'you know what the minister's sermon was the day?'

'Never mind the damned sermon!' Willie Alec barked. 'Sit down.'

'Let me take off my tammy and my jacket,' she said, apprehensive at his tone of voice, and wondering why he looked so angry.

He began with no preamble. 'Who's this man you've been seeing?'

An icy tremor ran through her. 'George? He's a boy I knew at school.'

'That's enough o' your lies!' Willie Alec thundered. 'We ken all about him. We ken you met him in Yarmouth. We ken he's married . . .'

'Who told you that?' she quavered.

'Never mind who told us. Is it true?'

'Aye,' she whispered, giving up all pretence. 'He wasn't married when I met him though he is now, but he's getting divorced . . .'

His rage making him forget that he was amongst women, he shouted, 'And you think it was all right to let him fuck you . . . ?'

'Willie Alec!' Hannah exclaimed, horrified at the word she had never heard him utter before.

'What's that mean?' Lizann asked, screwing up her face.

He had the grace to look ashamed. 'You let him have his way with you.'

'Oh!' Deep crimson, she wondered how he had found that out.

'You did, didn't you?'

'Yes, but we couldn't help it, Father, we loved each other. I still love him, and he's going to marry me when his wife divorces him.'

Hannah, who had been watching her husband closely,

was alarmed at the purplish tinge creeping up his cheeks. 'Willie Alec,' she warned, 'let it go till you calm down.'

It was as if he hadn't heard her. 'You'll not see him again! Do you hear me, Lizann?'

Shaking from head to toe, she said defiantly, 'I'm seeing him the night.'

'You're nothing of the kind! You'll go to your room after your supper and you'll bide there till I say you can come down!'

Hot tears stung her eyelids. 'But George'll wonder why I . . .'

'Let him wonder. I'm not giving him a chance to take you again.'

This was a side of her father, a hard unforgiving side, she had never seen before, and the tears edged down her cheeks. 'I can't let him stand and wait . . .'

'It'll cool him down,' Willie Alec said, callously.

'It's for your own good,' Hannah put in. 'You were lucky in Yarmouth – he could have bairned you – and he could yet, if you dinna steer clear o' him. Just think on the disgrace there would be if . . .'

'He's promised we won't do . . . it again till we're man and wife,' Lizann gulped.

'Promised?' her father growled, his voice rising again. 'A man that carries on wi' somebody else when his wife's waiting at hame for him? A decent man wouldna do that! D'you think a man like him would keep his promise when he's fired up wi' lust? Nothing would stop him!'

'If you met him, Father,' Lizann sobbed, 'you'd know he wouldn't . . .'

The dark patches on Willie Alec's face faded slightly. 'Lassie,' he groaned, 'you've no idea what men'll do when a lassie's body's driving them wild. They can be like beasts . . .'

'No, no! George isn't like that. He'd have stopped the first time if I hadn't made him do it.'

'You what?' her father roared, his whole face a deep magenta as he jumped up and grabbed her by the shoulders. 'You *made* him? You *made* him?' Every stressed word was accompanied by a shake that rocked her head and made her teeth rattle.

Aghast, Hannah rose and took a step forward, but discretion kept her from interfering.

'Let me go, Father,' Lizann beseeched, tears dripping off her chin. 'You're hurting me.'

'I havena started yet,' he shouted, his face only an inch from hers. 'It's a good hiding you need, you little ... you little whore!'

Hannah was rendered speechless by his coarseness, though she would not have dared to say anything anyway, with him in such a temper. Her legs trembling, she rammed her knuckles in her mouth when her husband took his open hand across the girl's cheek.

'Aye, a whore!' he repeated, letting her go. 'That's what you are!'

'No ... Father ... I ... loved ... George.' Her words were punctuated by harsh sobs. 'I ... still ... love ... him!'

'Love?' he sneered. 'What do you know about love? I thought you loved Peter, and now I hear you've let ... no, *made* another man take you.'

'I ... couldn't ... help ... it.'

'Well, I can help it!' he roared. 'You'll not see him again!'

Free of his hold and still weeping hysterically, Lizann spun round and ran out, her feet hardly touching the stairs as she went up to her own room.

Collapsing in her chair, Hannah tried desperately to stop her husband from following the girl. 'That's enough, Willie Alec,' she pleaded. 'Let her be. She kens you mean it, and she'll nae go against you.'

He sat down with his head in his hands. 'I canna get

ower what she's done,' he said, sorrowfully, 'and standing there defying me. Where did she learn that?'

She could have told him that Lizann got her headstrong nature from him, but she had never been able to say anything against him – not to him nor to anyone else. 'She likely thinks the world's come to an end the now, but she'll get ower him.'

'But I canna understand how she let him...' Willie Alec stopped and raised his head, pain spreading across his lined face. 'She didna let him, though, she made him. Our Lizann, Hannah! My wee lassie! I thought it was Mick we'd have trouble wi', he's aye been after the lassies. I thought she was different, and she tells me she's nae better than the harlots that walk the streets o' Aberdeen.'

'She said she loved the man,' his wife reminded him.

'That doesna excuse her. Oh God, I can hardly bear to think on it.'

Hannah knew that he would keep thinking about it, just as she would, and there was no point in trying to sweep it under the rug. 'We canna keep her in for ever,' she murmured.

'You said he's from Cullen? He'll surely be going back there some time? If we could find out how long he'll be here...'

'I'll ask her.' Hannah went upstairs and poked her head round their daughter's door. 'You'd best come down for your dinner, Lizann, for the broth must be stuck to the bottom o' the pot by this time.'

The girl didn't even look round. 'I'm not hungry!'

'Please yourself, then, but your father wants to know how long that George'll be in Buckie.'

Turning her swollen face hopefully, Lizann said, 'He'll be going back to Cullen on Wednesday. Is Father going to let me go to...'

'No, he'll not let you out till the lad's away.'

Lizann's tears began to flow again, and Hannah went

back downstairs. 'She's not coming down,' she told Willie Alec, 'and she says he'll only be here till Wednesday, that's just three days after the day.'

'Thank the Lord for that. Now, we'd best take our dinner, though it'll stick in my gullet.'

It was lucky that neither of them felt like eating, because the whole pot of broth was singed and Hannah poured it down the outside drain then made a pot of tea to steady their nerves. Not another word was said, and after tidying the kitchen she sat down opposite her brooding husband. The afternoon passed in silence, both upstairs and downstairs.

Lizann was so exhausted after her bouts of weeping that she fell into an uneasy sleep, and it was only when she woke that she began to wonder how her father had found out about George. Peter was the only person she had told and even if he'd seen them together last night he wouldn't have known who she was with. In any case, surely he wouldn't have shamed her – and hurt his own pride – by telling her father she'd made love with another man.

She was still puzzling when her mother came in again. 'Supper's near ready,' Hannah said brusquely, and even at the sight of her daughter's ravaged face she didn't question what Willie Alec was doing to her.

'Mother,' Lizann begged, 'who told on me?'

'That's between me and the body that tell't me, and if you think your father'll let you wed a divorced man, if he ever gets divorced, you can put it right out o' your head. We've aye been able to hold our heads up, and what would folk say if . . . ?'

'It's yourselves you're thinking about, not me,' Lizann muttered, her misery so great that the only thing that stopped her from pummelling her fists into her mother's sanctimonious face was knowing it would only make things worse. 'If you'd just let me see George tonight I'd tell him I can't see him again till he's free, and when he is we could go somewhere else to get married, so nobody would know and you could still hold your heads up.'

Hannah sighed. 'Face up to things, lass. You're coming between a man and his wife, a wife that he must have loved as much as she likely still loves him. You'll fall in love wi' another man some day, so forget him.'

'I'll never forget him, and I'll never love anybody else.'

'Have it your own way then!' Hannah snapped, her patience stretched too far. 'Now, are you coming down for your supper or are you going to starve yourself to death ower a man you canna have?'

Recognizing the futility of further argument, Lizann watched her mother stamping out. She couldn't hate her parents for judging her by their own straitlaced standards, but it was awful to think of George standing out in the cold till it dawned on him she wasn't going to turn up. He'd think she didn't want to see him again, and . . . oh God, surely he wouldn't go back to Katie? She had no way of letting him know that she still loved him, that her parents wouldn't let her marry him, wouldn't even let her out. If only she could speak to him, ask him to wait the few months till she was twenty-one and could do what she liked . . . but she knew full well that she didn't have the courage to defy her father like that, and he would never let her do what she wanted.

A flurry of raised voices downstairs told her that Mick had come home and was being told about the disgrace she had brought on the family, but despite listening intently, she couldn't make out what was being said. She wasn't surprised, however, when her brother walked into her room.

He sat down on the bed and pulled her round to face him. 'You haven't half stirred up a hornets' nest, little sister. Mother's flapping about like a demented hen, and Father's beside himself. Don't get your hackles up, for I think he's wrong in what he's doing, and I'm on your side.'

'Are you really, Mick?'

'Do you think I care who I get for a brother-in-law? I'm not as old-fashioned as they are. I wouldn't care if you married one of the French onion Johnnies that come round on their bikes, as long as I was sure he wouldn't let you down.'

'If you met him, you'd know George wouldn't . . .' She halted, her eyes brightening with hope. 'Mick, will you go and tell him what's happened? That's if you're not going to Jenny's?'

'She's got sewing she wants to finish for the morrow, but I promised to see the lads in the Square . . . ach, where were you to be meeting him?'

'Just along the road at seven. Tell him to write and let me know what his wife says. I always take in the post, so Mother wouldn't see it. Oh, and get an address for me to write to him.'

Mick grinned. 'Any further orders, madam?'

She didn't rise to his teasing. 'No, that's all.'

'Right. Are you coming down for your supper?'

She was hungry now, but after considering she said, 'I'd better not. They'll maybe see by my face I'm up to something.'

With neither Hannah nor Willie Alec feeling in the mood to go to church and face people, supper was later than usual, and at five minutes to seven, glad to leave the strained atmosphere in which the meal had been eaten, Mick lifted his jacket. 'I'm going up the town to meet some of the lads,' he told his mother, 'but I won't be late.'

He had not gone far when he saw a stranger kicking idly at the stones at the side of the road. 'Are you George Buchan?' he asked.

The other man looked up, startled. 'Yes?'

'I'm Lizann's brother Mick. Father found out what's been going on and there's been a helluva row. He's not letting her see you again.'

'Oh God, no!' George exclaimed, in dismay. 'What'll we do?'

Mick passed on his sister's messages, and wrote down George's address in Buckie and his mother's in Cullen, then he said, 'We can't go for a pint on a Sunday, but what about coming for a walk? I'd nothing special on, and it would be a chance to get to know each other.'

They went eastwards out of Buckie by the lower road, passing Cluny Harbour on their left, then the houses of Portessie on their right, the opposite direction from where Lizann had taken George the previous night. While they strode along, Mick repeated what he knew of the trouble there had been, George swore that he would always love Lizann no matter what happened, and Mick grew more convinced with every passing minute that his sister's faith in this man was not misplaced.

They had gone through Findochty and were halfway to Portknockie when George gave a low laugh. 'We'll soon be in Cullen, at this rate.'

'Good God!' Mick laughed. 'I didn't notice how far we'd come.'

'Mick,' George said, some time after they turned to go back, 'how did your father find out?'

'I've been wondering that myself. From what they were saying, somebody passed it on to my mother, and as far as I know, Peter Tait was the only one Lizann told.'

'The lad she was engaged to? D'you think it was him? Is he the kind to try to get back at her for throwing him over?'

'I hardly think so, and I know him as well as I know myself, for we've been pals for years. It must have been somebody else.'

'Maybe somebody Peter let it slip to,' George suggested.

'He was real cut up when he told me, but he likely felt I was the only one he could confide in. He wouldn't have told anybody else.'

'Oh well,' George sighed, 'the damage is done. Lizann must be feeling terrible, and I'm grateful to you for coming to tell me. If you hadn't, I'd still be waiting for her.'

Mick laughed this off, but he felt quite close to George now. There was nothing secretive about him, and he was clearly just as distressed by what had happened as Lizann was.

Back at their starting place, George held out his hand. 'She's lucky having you for a brother, Mick. I can't thank you enough for helping us like this.'

With a brief but firm handclasp, Mick said, 'She's lucky having you, but what's your plans now?'

'I'd be as well going back to my mother's. There's no point in staying on here if Lizann can't get out. I don't suppose there's any chance of your father changing his mind?'

'No chance! The sky could fall on his head and he'd not change it. Um, maybe I shouldn't give you false hope, but when you get your divorce . . .'

'If I get it,' George interrupted ruefully.

'When you get it,' Mick repeated, 'I'd advise you to come and tell him – him, mind, before you even tell Lizann. That'll let him see you're an honourable man and he might come round to you. But you'll have to play by his rules the now. No trying to get Lizann to meet you in secret here or in Cullen, and it might be best if you didn't write to her at all.'

George looked glum. 'I understand what you're getting at, Mick, and I'll not rock the boat. I love your sister too much to spoil what little chance I have. The thing is, I promised to let her know what Katie says, so can I write that one letter?'

Mick gave a gurgling laugh. 'You make me sound like I've been laying down the law. I've just told you what I think, but it's up to you, and you can't break a promise. I'll have to go, though, for Lizann'll be desperate to know what's happened. Good luck, George.'

When he went home, he spoke to his parents for a few minutes then said he was going to bed, but when he went upstairs – to what had once been a loft where wives of different generations had mended the nets but Willie Alec had made into two rooms for his children – he went in to report to Lizann. As he had known, she was waiting anxiously and he told her as much as he thought she should know.

'Maybe I'm not the right one to be dishing out advice to anybody,' he chuckled, 'when I can't get things worked out with my own girl.'

Too concerned with her own problems to worry about any trouble Mick was having with Jenny Cowie, Lizann said, 'You'd tell me if you knew who told Father about George and me, wouldn't you? Peter was the only one I told, and you said he told you, and I know it wasn't you.'

'It was Mother that was told, and I'm sure it wasn't Peter. Did you tell any of the lassies you worked with in Yarmouth?'

'Peggy May Cordiner knew I went out with him, and it was her that told me he was married. Maybe she saw us together last night?'

'I doubt it. She bides on the other side of Main Street, doesn't she?'

'She didn't know everything, any road, so it couldn't be her.'

'It's a mystery.' Mick ruffled her hair and went into his own room pensively. However much he hated to admit it, Peter appeared to be the only one who had known the whole truth, and by God, if it did turn out to be him that spilt the beans, Mick Jappy would make him pay for the trouble he had caused Lizann, old pal or no old pal.

Chapter Seven

❧

As soon as Peter saw the glowering figure standing outside the shipyard gates at stopping time on Monday, he knew he was in for a telling-off, if not worse, but thought he'd be as well getting it over. 'I know what you're going to say . . .' he began but got no further.

'So it was you, you sneaking bugger!' Mick roared, his right fist cracking against his old chum's jawbone and splattering his spotless white collar with blood. 'What the hell did you think you were doing?'

'I'm sorry,' Peter quavered, casting his eyes around in the hope that nobody had seen, but several oil-streaked men, some in dungarees, some in boiler suits, had already gathered, curious to know why one of 'they office loons' was being assaulted by a rough fisherman.

'You're sorry?' Mick growled. 'Is that all you can say?'

Rubbing his throbbing face, Peter looked imploringly at him. 'Come on, Mick, we can't fight here.'

They broke through the disappointed onlookers and walked off, an ill-matched couple, one in a well-pressed navy suit, shiny on the seat from sitting so much, and the other in a finely-knitted navy ganzy with a high neck and pearl buttons down one shoulder. They kept going until they turned a corner and were out of sight, then Mick grabbed Peter by the collar. 'What the hell did you think you were doing?' he repeated. 'I'd have sworn you thought more of Lizann than go telling on her.'

Not so sure now that it had been a good idea to face up to it, Peter babbled, 'I couldn't think more of her, you know that, and I didn't mean to tell your mother. I saw

Lizann out with a man, and I was only trying to find out who he was. It was Hannah saying it was George Buchan that made me come out with everything, I was that jealous.'

Having been reluctant to think ill of his friend in the first place, Mick was inclined to believe this, but it still didn't excuse him. 'For God's sake, man, didn't you think what it would do to Lizann?'

'I didn't think, I just saw red, and I'm truly sorry, Mick.'

'Aye, well, maybe you are, but you near finished her.'

'Finished her?' Peter looked alarmed. 'She didn't try to . . . ?'

'She's more sense than do away with herself, but if I hadn't helped her out she could easy have tried.'

'Helped her out? What did you do for her?'

'Never you mind,' Mick said sharply. 'You've done enough harm.'

'I wouldn't tell anything again, honest! I love her, Mick.'

Mick shook his head sadly. 'You've a funny way of showing it, that's all I can say. Come on, man, we'd better get home.'

As they walked back along the road, Peter said, 'I thought you'd have sailed this morning? You usually go on Mondays.'

Mick gave a slight frown at this attempt to take his mind off the more important subject. 'We were late coming in so we're not sailing till the morrow, but never mind that, just listen. I know you love Lizann, Peter, and nobody would've been more pleased than me if she'd married you, but it's George Buchan she wants and you'll have to let her go.'

'But . . . he's married already . . . isn't he?'

'He's getting divorced . . .'

'Willie Alec would never let her wed a divorced man.'

'I wouldn't be so sure about that. George is a real decent lad.'

'You've met him?' Peter was astonished.

'Aye, I've met him, and that's all I'm telling you. The best thing you can do, Peter, is find another girl.'

'I'll never stop loving Lizann.'

'That's up to you, but you haven't a hope in hell of getting her.'

Offended as well as discouraged, Peter was dourly silent for the rest of the way, but as they parted company at the Yardie, he looked at his old friend in deep entreaty. 'Mick, let her know I didn't mean her any harm . . . please.'

'I'll tell her, but I can't see her ever forgiving you.' Mick went inside wishing that he had found out the whys and wherefores before he lashed out . . . but Peter should have kept his big mouth shut.

Mick had to wait until their parents went to bed before he could tell Lizann what had happened, and when she found out that Peter actually was the culprit, she said mournfully, 'I knew he was the only one it could have been, but I didn't want to think it was him.'

'I was that mad, I thumped him before he'd a chance to say anything,' Mick muttered, sheepishly. 'He said he saw red when Mother told him it was George you were out with. He wasn't trying to make trouble for you.'

'He did, though,' Lizann gulped. 'And George'll be back in Cullen now, and goodness knows how long it'll be till I see him again.'

Mick pulled a face. 'For any sake, don't tell Father he's gone home already or he'll wonder how you know. If he thought I'd poked my nose in, I'd be for it. As it is, he'll likely tell Mother to let you out in three days and maybe you'll have heard from George by that time.'

*   *   *

It was a week later, when Lizann had almost given up hope of hearing, before the letter arrived, and it took all her courage to lift it off the mat. She was desperate to know what Katie had said, but she was afraid it might be bad news. Stuffing the envelope inside her cardigan in case her mother saw it, she went up to her room and slit the top with trembling fingers.

All it said was, 'She's agreed to it,' and she was disappointed that George had taken Mick's advice so much to heart. Surely he could have written a proper letter, telling her he loved her and what Katie had actually said? But at least she knew that everything was going to be all right . . . and she wasn't confined to the house any longer.

'You're awful chirpy the day,' Hannah observed that forenoon. 'I hope you've forgotten all your nonsense now.'

Lizann nearly told her it wasn't nonsense, but deemed it best to let her mother think she had got over George . . . until he came back to claim her. The fat would be in the fire then with a vengeance, but as it said in the Bible, 'Sufficient unto the day is the evil thereof.' She wasn't going to worry about it until the time came.

Peter still had not got over his confrontation with Mick. He had told his mother he had walked into a door, and thanks to the cold compress she'd put on the swelling on his jaw was almost gone, but it was more than flesh and blood could stand to think that Lizann might one day be George Buchan's wife. He honestly hadn't meant to cause trouble for her, but he was glad now that he had told Hannah. Surely Willie Alec wouldn't let his daughter waste her life on a divorced man . . . and anyway, maybe he wouldn't get divorced. Maybe his wife wouldn't agree to it.

The more Peter thought about that, the more likely it seemed, and he turned his mind to planning how to console

Lizann when the time came. He would be sympathetic, and he wouldn't scare her off by rushing her, but gradually, as she got over her disappointment, he would let her see that he still loved her, had never stopped loving her and never would. He could imagine himself stroking her black curls, taking her in his arms and kissing her, but nothing more than that, for Hannah would have told her to keep herself pure until her wedding night.

With the impact of a blow from a sledge-hammer in his solar plexus, he remembered that Lizann wasn't pure. She had already given herself to the man she hoped to marry. Swallowing the bitter, brackish liquid rising in his throat, Peter wondered what George Buchan looked like. All he'd been able to make out when he saw them was that he was fairly tall and quite well built. Maybe Lizann preferred broad men to skinnies like himself? Maybe he should try to build up his body? He could send for one of those chest expanders advertised in the American detective magazines he bought occasionally, or a pair of Indian clubs. Or even apply to Charles Atlas for information on how to have a body like his, bulging with muscles though he had once been a ten-stone weakling ... or so he claimed. Of course, Peter mused, that could be a downright lie to entice fools like him to pay through the nose for some kind of course that wouldn't have any effect. A chest expander would be best. He'd heard that it could be months, maybe years, till a divorce came through, so he'd have plenty time to make himself into the kind of man Lizann seemed to prefer.

Having made his decision, Peter took a pile of old magazines out of his wardrobe and started leafing through them.

With the coming of summer, Hannah was easier in her mind about Willie Alec being at sea. Every winter she was on edge from the time he sailed on Monday till he came back on Friday or Saturday, and near out of her senses with worry when there were gales. He never told her what it was like to battle against the elements, but she knew it must be dangerous. The boats never went out in a storm, but storms could spring up out of nowhere, and when Willie Alec was away she listened every night to the trawler waveband on the wireless, to the skippers speaking to each other or to their wives. Not the Buckie skippers, worse luck, for none of the drifters had wirelesses, but they must get the same weather – the wild nor'easters that tossed the boats around like matchboxes, and the anticyclones, whatever they were. A lot of Buckie women had been left widows quite young, with little bairns to bring up, so she could count herself lucky to have her man so long ... but ...

Hannah's mind, never completely free of worries, jumped to Lizann. She had got over that awful row real quick ... too quick, maybe. If she loved that George Buchan as much as she said she did, she'd still be moping for him, but apart from the first week or so, she'd been going about as happy as a lark. But just lately something was obviously bothering her again, for she was that jumpy and short-tempered even her father had noticed it.

'It'll have taken her a while to realize she'll never see the man again,' he had said before he went away on Monday. 'She was strung up that tight about me keeping her in, she likely didna think further than that at the time. She'd calmed down by the next day, so maybe she hoped he'd try to see her. I'm real surprised he didna, but it showed he didna really care about her. Ach well, she's bound to forget him come time.'

But it was six months already, Hannah reflected, and if Lizann hadn't forgotten him by now, maybe she never would. Maybe it was a true saying that a woman never forgets her first love ... but Peter had been her first love. George had been ... her first lover, that could be what the saying meant. Hannah couldn't tell, one way or the other, for Willie Alec had been both to her – though there had once been a time . . .

Breaking into her mother's wavering thoughts, Lizann trailed in as if all the troubles of the world were on her shoulders, and watching the effort it took her to lift the bulging shopping bag on to the table, Hannah felt a touch of pity for her. 'Was that load ower heavy for you?' she asked, in some concern.

'No, I was tired anyway.'

'Aye, you're looking a bit run down. I'll get out the Hall's Wine, it aye picks me up.'

'I don't want it. I'll be fine.'

Lizann had no peace to think until she went up to her room at night. She wasn't run down, she was miserable. She'd been expecting George to come any day to tell her he was free, and instead . . . Mick had knocked the bottom out of her world, though he'd just been trying to explain why she was having to wait so long.

'Mancie Will was telling me his cousin in Glasgow divorced her man last year,' he had said when he was home the weekend before last, 'and it was three years from the time he walked out on her till she got free of him. Apparently, the divorce judges or whatever they're called have to be sure a couple are really . . . irreconcilable. That means they'd never even think of getting back together again.'

'Three years?' she had gasped, her senses swimming with shock.

'Oh, I'm sorry, little sister, I didn't . . . I thought if you knew that, it would stop you wondering why George hadn't written to you, and he's been away from his wife since the end of February, so that's only two and a half . . . are you all right?'

She had assured her brother that she was fine, but every night since, she had been haunted by thoughts of what could happen in two and a half years, of what could have happened already in the time he had been back in Cullen. George might have got together with Katie again, been . . . what was it? . . . reconciled with her. What if they'd only had a tiff and he'd been amusing himself with her till it blew over? But surely he could have written to let her know, one way or the other, even though it meant breaking his promise to Mick? He must know she would be worrying.

Dash it all! She was tired of waiting, and more tired of being kept in the dark. Maybe she should have stuck to Peter? She hadn't seen him for weeks after the row he had caused, and she'd felt like walking past him when she did, but he had stopped her.

'Lizann, I'm truly sorry,' he'd said. 'You're the last person in the world I wanted to hurt, but it was out before I thought.'

His sorrowful look made her say, 'I'm sorry Mick punched you.'

His eyes had brightened. 'I suppose I asked for it.'

She had caught sight of him going past the window occasionally since then and had thought there was something different about him, but she couldn't make up her mind what. It was only this morning, when she had seen him coming and had a better chance to study him from behind the curtain, that she realized what it was. His face had filled out, his body not so boyish, and he looked all the better for it.

George had been a man the first time she saw him, broad but without an ounce of superfluous fat on him. He was completely different from Peter, whose blond hair was brushed back neatly, clothes always spick and span. George's brown head, on the other hand, looked as if he'd hacked at it without looking in a mirror, and his clothes – there was nothing to say for them except they'd seen better days. But just thinking about him like this, with his dear face fresh in her mind, she could feel the love she had for him gaining strength once more, and she knew she could never go back to Peter. It was George she wanted, and if he didn't come back to marry her, she was prepared to remain an old maid.

When Peggy May Cordiner returned from Yarmouth that November she had news for Lizann. 'Me and Ned's getting married when we find a house,' she announced, almost breathless with excitement. 'And you ken old Mrs Dey next door to us? Well, her Norrie's trying to get her to go and bide wi' him in Lossie, and if she does, he's promised to let us have it as cheap as he can, so I'll maybe be Mrs Edward Yule by Christmas.'

'That's good,' Lizann murmured, happy for her friend, yet envious that she wasn't having to do any waiting.

Her lack of enthusiasm communicated itself to Peggy May. 'Have you still nae had nae word from George?'

'I'm beginning to think I'll never get word,' Lizann said, dejectedly. 'It's near eight months since he sent the note about Katie agreeing.'

'But your Mick said divorces took three years, didn't he? Dinna lose heart, Lizann. Time flies, as the man said when his wife threw the alarm clock at him.'

Nevertheless, time did not fly for either of them. First 1933 inched into 1934, which dragged on into 1935, and all the while, along with her own fear that George had never meant to marry her, Lizann couldn't help feeling sorry for her friend; if Ned Yule wanted to make Peggy May his wife he could surely find another house and not have to wait for old Mrs Dey to move out. And Peggy May, beginning to wonder if her fiancé was not as keen as she thought, was almost sure that George Buchan was going to let Lizann down.

Chapter Eight

❧

'I sometimes feel like giving that Mrs Dey a good shake,' Peggy May confided the evening before she left for Yarmouth, 'but poor soul, she doesna want to give up her house, and you canna really blame her, now can you?'

Every bit as downhearted as her friend, Lizann shook her head, her thoughts not actually on the old woman. 'I wish George would write and let me know how the divorce is going . . .'

'He'll just be waiting, the same as you.'

'But . . . he must realize what this not knowing's doing to me.'

Peggy May eyed her sympathetically. 'You should write to him. Mick got his mother's address for you, didn't he?'

'George and me both promised Mick we wouldn't write.'

'Well, then, you can't do nothing!' Unsure of her own romance, Peggy May's patience was wearing dangerously thin, but the tears which had sprung to Lizann's eyes made her hasten to say, 'I tell you what! I'll look for him down there, and if I see him I'll . . .'

'Don't tell him to write,' Lizann begged, afraid that this would bring bad luck. 'Just ask if he still feels the same about me.'

Lizann was on edge when it was time for the fisher quines to come home.

'What's the matter wi' you?' Hannah demanded one forenoon.

'I'm waiting for Peggy May,' Lizann answered, honestly.

'I wanted to ask if Mrs Dey's given up her house yet.'

Believing that her daughter had got over the man from Cullen, Hannah took this reply at its face value. 'I dinna ken why you canna be like her and find a lad.' She paused and eyed the girl slyly. 'You wouldna have far to look, for Peter Tait would . . .'

Lizann decided to ignore this. Her mother's mind was like a butterfly these days, flitting from one thing to another and never lingering long.

It was 2 December – a freezing fog blotting everything out – when Peggy May tapped and popped her head round the door. 'Have you a minute, Lizann? I've something to tell you.'

She waited until her friend got her coat from the lobby and threw a shawl round her head, then they walked round the corner into one of the posies – the tiny alleyways between the houses where even the weather had trouble reaching. 'Yes?' Lizann asked, breathlessly, her legs almost buckling under her with apprehension of what she was about to hear.

Peggy May did not prolong her agony. 'He wasna there, but I got Ned to ask some of the Cullen men, and they said George was still biding wi' his mother. He's waiting there till he gets his divorce, and he's on a boat fishing cod round about Iceland.'

Relief made Lizann feel faint and she was glad there was no room for her to collapse. Peggy May gave her a little time to digest the news, then said gently, 'So you've been worrying yourself sick over nothing. It's all going to be all right, and by the looks of things, you and George'll be wed afore me and Ned.'

Lizann was ashamed for not having asked before. 'Oh, I'm sorry. Is Mrs Dey still . . . ?'

'I havena been hame yet, but in her last letter Ma said nothing had changed.'

When Lizann returned to her house, not even Hannah's

accusing, 'Where have you been? You ken I dinna like being left by myself,' dampened her spirits. George and Katie hadn't got reconciled, and there were just three months to wait now.

Having been adamant for so long that she would never give up her home, Mrs Dey surprised her son just before Christmas. 'I can see I'll get nae peace till I shift to Lossie,' she sighed, 'but I want one last Hogmanay in my ain hoose.'

And so, on the day after New Year's Day, Peggy May was given the key to what was to be her marital home. When Norrie Dey apologized for leaving it in a mess, she laughed, 'Me and Ned'll easy clean it up.'

The wedding was arranged for 1 February, which did not give Jess Cordiner much time to arrange everything, but Dozy had been saving for years to give his only child a big wedding. Most of her friends were green with envy when Peggy May entered the church on her father's arm wearing a lovely creation of white tulle and lace, dotted with pearls. Her maid of honour, the daughter of her mother's sister, was dressed in pale pink taffeta with a long spray of pink roses fastened to the skirt to allow her hands free to bear the bridal train.

Lizann wasn't jealous of anything – she wouldn't have been jealous if the bridal gown had been topped by a diamond-studded tiara instead of a wired head-dress edged with looped lace caught up with pearls – but she couldn't stifle her resentment that Peggy May had got the man she loved, while she herself didn't know if the man she loved still loved her.

Then she told herself not to be pessimistic. Of course George still loved her, and the only reason he had never written to tell her so was her father. Like Mick had said, if George played by Willie Alec's rules it would be easier to win him round, but it was awful having been left up in the air, not sure of anything, for what felt like half a lifetime. Still, in another month, maybe a few days more, George would be coming to claim her. She was old enough by now not to need her parents' permission ... but there could be trouble. Would George manage to hold out against any fierce opposition from her father? More to the point, would she?

In his mother's house in Cullen, George too was sitting in a brown study. When the divorce papers had come, he had thought it would be all over in a week or two, then, realizing that there was no letter telling him when the case was to be heard, he had resigned himself to wait until the solicitors or whoever gave him a date when he had to appear. And there hadn't been a letter from anybody.

Then he'd heard it took three years, and only Mick's old advice to keep away from her had stopped him from going to tell Lizann. His mother had said somebody had likely told her, but if nobody had, she could be thinking he'd made it up with Katie when he hadn't set eyes on her since he left her. Probably she could tell him what was going on, but it would be damned awkward facing her; he would remember the vile things she had done and kept secret from him. He did feel ashamed now and then for walking out on her. Those things had happened before they began going steady and he should have forgiven her, but he couldn't, though she had been a damned good wife to him apart from that. Maybe he would have forgiven her if he hadn't already met Lizann ... who knows?

His mother – who always kept her eyes and ears open – had heard that Katie had boarded the south train one day three weeks ago and come back the same night, but nobody knew where she'd been. Shopping in Aberdeen, George supposed ... but Katie had never been one for gallivanting, and in any case, where had she got the money?

His mother came bursting in at that moment. 'Ach, George!' she puffed. 'Here's you sitting like the bells that never rung, and me wi' something to tell you.'

'Go on, then,' he sighed, knowing that she would, whatever he said.

'Lizzie Fenton says your Katie's speaking about leaving Cullen, and she says she'll be a lot happier where she's going.'

This made him feel less guilty at leaving his wife. He'd been afraid she might go into a decline, and instead she would be making a new life for herself somewhere else. 'I'm glad to hear that,' he smiled, 'but I wish I knew what was happening about the divorce.'

'Oh, that's another thing.' Ina Buchan took a long brown envelope from the top of her shopping bag. 'I met the postie when I was going out and he gi'ed me this.'

She laid it down on the table beside him and he said, 'It's from Edinburgh, so I suppose it's to tell me when I've to go.'

The news was even better than that. In effect, it told him that Katie Buchan, née Mair, had been granted a full and final divorce from George Buchan 'as from the second instant'. He shook his head in a kind of stupor. 'But I was never asked to appear.'

'They surely didna need you.' Ina thought for a moment, then an idea struck her. 'I bet it was Edinburgh Katie went to yon day.'

When the meaning of this sank in, he jumped up and enveloped her in a bear hug. 'I'm free! At last! Buckie, here I come!'

'You're nae going right now?'

'I'm not waiting a minute longer.' As he put on his jacket, he said, 'You'll like Lizann, Ma.'

Ina gave a disdainful sniff. 'I dinna understand you.

The minute you get clear o' one woman, you canna wait to tie yourself to another.'

Mick grinned when he opened the door to George's timid knock. 'This is it, is it?'

'Aye, at last. Is your father in?'

'He's in, and I'll just tell him somebody wants to see him. If I say it's you, Lizann'll build her hopes up, but he might put his foot down with a heavy hand again.'

George's confidence began to waver, and before he had time to think of a way to boost it Willie Alec came to the door in his slippers, his face mottled red from sitting too close to the fire. Even with his shirtsleeves rolled up and a pair of braces supporting his shapeless trousers, he was a commanding figure. 'You want to see me?' he barked, his brows down.

George felt his courage draining away, but he had to face up to this man if he was to stand any chance of marrying the girl he loved. 'Mr Jappy,' he began, hesitantly, 'I've something important to ask you, but not here on the doorstep. Could we take a wee walk?'

'I'm taking no walk till you tell me who you are.'

'I don't want Lizann to hear.'

'Lizann? What's she got to do with it?'

'Please, Mr Jappy, I'll tell you when we're clear of the house.'

Puzzled, Willie Alec said, 'Wait till I put my shoes on, and get my jacket and my bonnet.'

George had primed himself for this meeting, but his nerves were in shreds as they walked along the street. In spite of his gruff manner, Lizann's father gave the impression of being a fair man, a man with a sense of humour, yet he had imprisoned his daughter simply because she was seeing a man he disapproved of. Would he come round now?

'Well?' Willie Alec asked, coming to a sudden standstill.

'What's this important thing you wanted to ask me?'

'Hear me out before you say anything, Mr Jappy.' George's voice gained strength as he went on, 'I love Lizann with all my heart...'

'You're George Buchan?'

There was accusation in the three gasped words, but George wasn't to be put off now. 'Please let me finish. I've done nothing behind your back. I kept away from her till I was free, and now I've got my divorce I'm asking your permission to marry her.'

'By God, you've got some nerve! Did you think I'd welcome you wi' open arms after what you and her did down in Great Yarmouth?'

'I swear to you, Mr Jappy, I've regretted that ever since.'

Willie Alec's dark scowl eased a little. 'I believe you there, for she said you'd have stopped if she hadna made you go on.'

'I'm not blaming Lizann,' George said, staunchly. 'She was seventeen and I was twenty-one. I knew what I was doing.'

'Did you make a habit o' breaking lassies' maiden-heads?'

George's hopes were sinking fast, but he was still determined to tell the truth, however condemning. 'I had a few lassies, but hers was the only maidenhead I ever broke. The rest had been broken before.'

'Well, now!' Willie Alec murmured, his rough hand tugging at the lobe of his ear. 'At least you're honest. I like that in a man. So you sowed your wild oats? I can hardly blame you for that, for I did the same ... before I met Hannah. But that's between me and you, mind.'

'Of course.'

After a moment's pause, Willie Alec said, 'You say you love Lizann, but you wed another lassie after you'd been wi' her.'

'I'd half asked Katie before that, but I wouldn't have married her ... I came to see Lizann first, and she said she was engaged.'

'So you married this Katie because you couldna have Lizann? You didna love your wife?'

'You'll maybe not believe this, Mr Jappy, but I loved both of them at that time. It was a while after I married Katie till I found out she ... wasn't the girl I thought she was.'

'She'd had other men?'

Reluctantly, George told him everything, in the same way he had told Mrs Clark. 'It was her not telling me before I married her,' he ended, 'that's what I couldn't forgive.'

'Aye, there shouldna be secrets between a man and his wife. Now, you said you were free ... ?'

Willie Alec was obviously thawing, and George's spirits took an upward swing. 'Aye, Katie divorced me. I was notified the day.'

'She divorced you? Had she grounds for that?'

Hell-bent on being scrupulously honest, George described the deception he had carried out, and was amazed when Willie Alec let out a rumbling laugh. 'By God, lad, you took a chance there!' His smile fading, he went on, 'You blackened Lizann's character, though.'

'Her name wasn't mentioned in the affidavit,' George defended himself. 'It was an unknown girl, that's what Mrs Clark signed to.'

'You ken this, George? I canna help admiring you for the way you've fought to get my lassie.'

Hardly daring to presume he had won, George murmured, 'You'll let her marry me?'

'I think we'd best go back and see what her mother says.'

Hannah got little opportunity to say anything, because Lizann jumped up and flung herself at George when he went in, and Willie Alec looked at his wife and shrugged.

'You can see how it is,' he told her. 'He's free now, and we'd best just give them our blessing.'

'You're not letting her marry a divorced man?' she gasped, aghast at how quickly he had changed his tune.

'What does that matter when you can see for yourself he's the one she wants?' Willie Alec was already at the dresser, bringing out a bottle.

Mick pumped George's hand gleefully, but Hannah remained tight-lipped throughout the short celebration that followed. Then Willie Alec turned to George again. 'Take Lizann for a walk, I can see she's desperate to ken what's been going on. And tell her everything, mind. Everything.'

When they went out, he looked at his wife. 'You needna say what you're thinking, Hannah. I can see you're not pleased.'

Never having questioned her husband's decisions before, she felt bound to do so now. 'I have to say what's in my mind, Willie Alec. I thought you was as against him as I was.'

'I was, but not now. He's a decent man, Hannah. He told me things I'd never have found out myself, and for all he ken't they could have set me more against him than ever. But I like a man wi' spirit, a man that's not afraid to fight for what he wants, and he wants our Lizann. He loves her and he'll make her happy. Besides, he's one o' us ... a fisherman.'

'Hmmm!' Hannah grunted, knowing that his mind was made up.

'Are you not happy for Lizann, Mother?' Mick asked.

'I'll not be happy till I see for myself he takes care o' her right.'

Mick looked at his father with his face screwed up, but Willie Alec only smiled. 'We'll drink to that, then. Eh, son?'

* * *

Lizann was rapturously happy when she went to bed. After all the months of worry, George had come for her, had even persuaded her father to let them marry. He had promised to see the minister with her in the morning, to arrange for the ceremony to be held in the manse, although they would have to wait at least three weeks for the banns to be cried. He had done wrong in making his landlady put her name to a false statement, but only to make Katie divorce him ... and it had worked. She turned when Mick came into her room, smiling because he was slightly unsteady on his feet.

'Well, that's it, little sister,' he said. 'I knew George could talk Father round.'

'It's all thanks to you,' she admitted.

'I'm pleased he took my advice, but he pulled it off himself. Mother's not pleased, though.'

'I don't care. Father's given us his blessing, that's all we need.' Her own future settled, Lizann wondered about her brother's. 'What about you and Jenny Cowie, Mick?'

'I can't get past the kissing stage,' he sighed. 'I doubt I'll have to marry her first.'

'Would that be so bad?'

'I'd not say no to it, but the thing is ... her folk need her.'

'You should ask her. Maybe she'd say yes.'

'Maybe she would, but I'll wait a while. One wedding in the family's enough at a time. Now I'd better let you get to sleep, so you can dream about your George.' Dropping a quick kiss on her head – which surprised them both, for they were not in the habit of showing the affection they had for each other – he went to his own room.

Lizann snuggled down to think of being George's wife, of having his children, of scrimping and saving so that he could have a boat of his own again, though she wouldn't tell him that's what she had in mind till she could put the money into his hand.

While Lizann – and George, in Mrs Clark's front bedroom again – slept peacefully, Mick was wondering if he should ask Jenny to marry him. What she earned from the sewing she took in was all that went into the house; if she left, Mr and Mrs Cowie would be destitute. He couldn't even suggest moving in as her husband because, from what he had gathered, she slept in what was little more than a boxroom. Besides, living in the same house as two invalids wasn't his idea of marriage. If he ever did manage to get her away he would be expected to pay for the wedding, the furniture, the bedding and dishes, as well as the rent of wherever they found, and to provide for her mother and father. He had started to save, but it was a slow business and it would take him years to get enough to let them set up house. He just hoped that Jenny wouldn't meet a man who could afford to buy a house big enough for her parents, too.

In Main Street, Peter Tait was still trying to get over the shock of seeing Lizann, his Lizann, strolling past his house with George Buchan again. It had been just by chance that he'd looked out of his bedroom window before closing the curtains, and there they'd been, gazing into each other's eyes as if they were the only two people in the world. His heart aching, he had watched them kissing, long kisses with their bodies rubbing together, which had driven him mad with jealousy.

He wondered if her parents knew and contemplated going to tell them in the morning, but Mick would punch him in the face again if he did. And it looked like Lizann didn't care who saw them. George Buchan must have got his divorce, after three whole years, and, though it was hard to believe, her father must have given permission for them to marry.

His head pounding and his insides whirling, Peter paced the floor. His chest-expanding exercises had gained him nothing. He was going to lose the only girl he would ever love . . . but wait! He had a sort of ally in Hannah, hadn't he? She wouldn't be happy about Lizann marrying George. She would make them wait – give him enough time to do something.

Sitting down on his bed, Peter tried to think what he could do.

'Did you tell Mr Lawrie you'd been divorced?' Hannah asked, when George and Lizann returned from arranging a date for their wedding.

'I did that, Mrs Jappy,' George answered, knowing she had thought the minister would refuse to marry them – he had thought that himself. 'He said the Church of Scotland left it up to individual ministers, and he didn't mind, seeing we were happy for it to be in the manse.'

'Old Mr Crawford wouldna have agreed,' Hannah muttered, 'but this new man's . . . ach! It's nae right that a man can throw off his wife when he wants somebody else.' Her voice turned sepulchral as she misquoted, 'Them that the good Lord hath joined together, let nobody pull asunder.'

'Nobody's going to pull George and me asunder.' Lizann looked at her husband-to-be adoringly.

Hannah tutted impatiently. 'I meant him and his real wife.'

'Katie's not my wife now,' George pointed out quietly.

Hannah couldn't resist one last hit. 'You must have promised to love, honour and keep her . . . but I'd better hold my tongue seeing I'm odd man out. I'll be ashamed to walk down the street after this, though.'

George shook his head at Lizann to prevent her arguing any more. It was clear that his future mother-in-law resented him, but he would show her. This marriage would endure till long after Hannah herself was dead and buried.

When Willie Alec returned from visiting an old friend who, in his opinion, 'wouldn't see the winter out', and Lizann told him that the ceremony would take place in four weeks, he looked more down-hearted than ever. 'I'd have liked to give my only daughter a big do,' he said, sadly, then shrugged off his melancholia to avoid spoiling things for the radiant girl. 'Ach well, there's other things to consider and it canna be helped.'

Lizann didn't care. A big wedding was a waste of money, and marrying George was all that mattered to her.

Her father looked at his soon-to-be son-in-law. 'Will you be biding here after you've tied the knot?'

George coloured. 'If it's all right with you . . . just till I can afford to furnish a rented house.'

'There's no hurry.' Willie Alec smiled expansively. 'You're welcome here for as long as you want.'

'The first thing I'll have to do is find a berth in Buckie.'

Willie Alec looked smug. 'I was speaking to Heck Lindsay of the *Dawn Rose* when I was out, and he says old Johnnie Ledingham retired this trip, so that would be a deckie's job for you, if you want it.'

'But George has his skipper's ticket,' Lizann protested.

Her father nodded. 'Aye, he tell't me he'd had his own boat. It'll be a come-down for you, lad, but it'll do till something else turns up, will it nae?'

George had worked as mate on a Cullen boat since he sold his own for scrap, so a deckhand's job was not what he was after, but, as Willie Alec said, it would do till he found something better. 'Thanks for letting me know, Mr Jappy,' he smiled. 'Where do I go to see about it?'

Willie Alec grinned mischievously. 'Heck's expecting you to turn up on Monday. He aye leaves the same time as the *Silver Star*. Have you got your gear wi' you?'

'It's at my mother's, but I'll go and get it the morrow. I'll have to tell her about the wedding, any road.'

George took Lizann with him on the bus the following morning, though she was dreading meeting his mother. He was another only son, and Mrs Buchan might be another Bella Jeannie Tait. George himself wasn't relishing the thought of making the introduction. His mother hadn't been pleased about his first marriage, but that was because there had been a mystery about Katie's birth and there was no mystery about Lizann's. Surely it would be different this time?

They didn't talk much on the short journey, but when they came off the bus and were walking towards the house, Lizann whispered, 'I'm scared.'

George squeezed her arm. 'Ma'll not bite you.'

She discovered that George's mother was the exact opposite of Bella Jeannie in appearance – very thin, pure white hair drawn neatly back, black dress spotless. 'So you're Lizann?' she smiled. 'I've heard plenty about you.'

Unaware of how two-faced she was, Lizann warmed to her. 'I'm pleased to meet you, Mrs Buchan.'

'We've set the wedding,' George grinned. 'Four weeks from yesterday. There'll just be the four of us at the manse – Lizann's brother's going to be best man, and his girl's going to be bridesmaid – but you'll come to the Jappys' house for the wee do after, eh, Ma?'

'There'll be plenty there without me,' Ina said carefully, 'and I'm not a one for mixing wi' strangers.'

George did not press her. He was quite glad that she wouldn't be there – she'd a habit of speaking out of turn. 'Lizann's father got me a berth in Buckie, so I'll need my seabag.'

'It's packed ready.' His mother looked at Lizann when he went out of the room. 'You'll be used to driftermen?'

'My father and my brother are both on the *Silver Star*.'

'So you'll ken about the big washings you'll have to do for George?'

'I do all the washing anyway. My mother's not very strong.'

'George never went away without his things being washed and ironed and mended, so you'd better look after him right.'

'I'll do my best,' Lizann murmured.

'I suppose you canna do better than that.'

George's return stopped Ina from saying more on the subject, but as she made a pot of tea for them she said, 'I'm sorry I canna offer you any dinner. If you'd let me ken you was coming, I'd have . . .'

'That's all right, Mrs Buchan,' Lizann assured her. 'We'll get dinner when we go home.'

Ina looked at her son with a sad smile. 'Aye, of course Buckie'll be your home now.'

'We'll come and visit you,' George said, hastily. 'And when we get a house, you can come to see us.'

She pursed her lips briefly. 'I like my own house best, so I'll not promise anything.'

When they were leaving, she said, 'I'll send on a present . . . sheets, maybe, or something for your house when you get it?'

'We don't need any presents, Mrs Buchan,' Lizann said shyly.

'I canna let my son's wedding go by without giving him something.'

George laughed now. 'Whatever you think, then. Well, cheerio, Ma. The next time you see us we'll be man and wife.'

Ina's natural sarcasm came to the fore now. 'I hope this marriage'll last longer than your first.'

Frowning, he muttered, 'This one's for ever, be sure of that.'

'I forgot to tell you, Katie went away yesterday.'

He made no answer to this and pulled Lizann through the door, saying as they went along the street, 'I thought it was too good to last. She likes causing trouble.'

'Don't worry, George. It's not as if I didn't know about Katie.' She wasn't jealous of his first wife – a part of his life that was over and done with. 'Do you know where she was going?'

'I know nothing about it,' he said, uneasily.

'Well, wherever it is, I hope she finds somebody to make her happy.'

He hesitated for only a second. 'So do I. She's had a hard life.'

When they were on the bus he took her hand. 'I meant what I said to Ma, Lizann. Our marriage will last for ever.'

'Till we're old and grey and wrinkled like prunes?'

'You'll never look like a prune,' he smiled.

'I might, and you'll wonder what you ever saw in me.'

'I'll still see you like you are now.'

With George away on the *Dawn Rose*, Lizann took the opportunity to buy her trousseau – her father had been very generous in the money he gave her for the purpose. She spent a long time trying on dresses before settling on a powder blue crêpe de chine with tucks down the bodice. After a search through the hat department of McKay's she found a pillbox in the same shade, with a slightly darker veil. Knowing it would be impossible to find accessories to match, she plumped for navy courts and handbag. In the lingerie department she bought three petticoats, three pairs of French knickers, and three nighties, one blue, one pink and one white – all Courtauld's celanese. She was on her way out of the shop when she remembered that she would also need silk stockings, suspender belts and brassieres – no bride in the fishing community shamed herself by going to her groom in anything old – and had to go back in.

It was closing time when she eventually reached the street, loaded with bags of all sizes, but exhilaration kept her from feeling tired. She had gone down High Street and was into Bank Street when a voice said, 'Let me carry some of that for you.'

She turned round feeling she had been caught redhanded in something she shouldn't be doing. 'I'll manage myself, Peter.'

'No, no, let me help.'

After disentangling the bundle in her arms into individual bags, Peter took all but two. 'You've fairly been lashing out. Did you come into a fortune?'

'Father gave me the money,' she murmured, then, thinking that she may as well tell him, she added, 'for my trousseau.'

'Your trousseau?' he gasped.

'Yes, the wedding's a week on Saturday ... in the manse.'

Although she had known he would be upset, she was not expecting what happened next. Throwing down what he was carrying, and knocking her two parcels out of her hands, he grabbed her by the shoulders. 'I'll not let you wed George Buchan! You're mine, Lizann! Mine!'

'Let go of me!' She struggled, but couldn't break his grip.

'I'll never let you go,' he cried. 'I love you, Lizann! Tell him to go away, and come back to me.'

She felt sorry for him now, but she had to let him know how he stood. 'No, Peter. I still like you, and I hope we'll always be friends, but I love George ... with all my heart. Now, will you please let me go so I can pick up my things?'

He looked at her for a short time in disbelief, then

released her and stepped back. 'I'll give you a hand,' he mumbled.

Their hands were trembling so much that one of the paper bags burst and spilt its contents on to the road in a glistening shower of white, pink and blue. Peter bent to retrieve the articles, but when he saw what they were, his face twisted. 'Nightgowns? To wear in bed with him?'

Crimson with embarrassment, she snatched them from him and stuffed them back into the bag while he bent down again and opened another bag deliberately. He held up a pair of flimsy open-legged knickers, then, with a tortured groan, he thrust them at her and strode away. She had never felt so humiliated in her life, but she could sympathize with him as she sorted out the rest of her belongings. It must have been awful for him to look at the things she had wanted only George to see, things she thought would excite him but was ashamed of buying now.

When she arrived home she didn't mention the incident to her mother, and showed her only the dress and hat before taking all the bags up to her room. She wasn't angry at Peter, but she wished he hadn't ridiculed her trousseau, for he had spoiled her pleasure in it. With a sigh she folded up the underwear and laid it in her chest of drawers, hung the dress in her wardrobe and put the hat, handbag and shoes on the top shelf. Then she collected all the paper bags and screwed them into a ball to burn in the kitchen fire.

His whole body shaking with the bitter jealousy that was eating into him like acid, Peter stamped blindly along Main Street, carrying straight on past his house. When Lizann told him her wedding was so near he hadn't been able to control himself, but discovering what she'd be wearing on her wedding night had been ten times worse. He had wanted to strangle her so George Buchan would never see her in the transparent nightgowns with only thin straps at the shoulders and necks so low that her breasts would be almost completely on show, but he had kept his hands from going round her neck. The frilly knickers, their legs so wide and inviting, had nearly been his undoing; if he hadn't walked away, he *would* have throttled her.

How could she buy things like that? His subconscious told him why, but he didn't want to think about her parading herself half-naked in front of George Buchan. He couldn't shut it out of his mind and found himself picturing a faceless man slipping down the straps of the nightdress and fondling her, stroking her, kissing her, mounting her. Groaning aloud, he tortured himself further by remembering that she would have been his wife if the man from Cullen hadn't interfered. Until today there had always been hope that he would get her back, but now there was nothing but a void inside him that only she could fill.

Stopping to take a deep, shuddery breath, he realized that his mother would be wondering why he hadn't come home for his supper and made his way back, slowly and wretchedly.

Bella Jeannie Tait was really worried about her son. He had been in a queer mood for over a week, and he'd been sitting staring into the fire since dinnertime ... not that he'd eaten anything. He wouldn't tell her what was wrong, but she knew there was something.

'I'm going next door to see Mary Kate,' she told him now. 'She's got her phlebitis again, and I promised I'd take her some o' my scones. I'll not be long.'

He turned his head listlessly. 'You don't need to hurry.'

Mary Kate was pleased to see her neighbour, and not just because of the scones; she had some gossip to pass on. 'I'd Ruby Strachan in this forenoon,' she said, her pain-filled eyes momentarily gleaming. 'She was saying Lizann Jappy's getting wed the day. Your Peter was engaged to her at one time, wasn't he?'

Bella Jeannie understood now why her son was so down in the dumps. 'He broke it off. She wasna the right lass for him, ony road.'

'Oh?' The older woman seemed surprised. 'I aye thought she was a real nice wee thing.'

'I suppose she was nice enough, but . . .' Bella Jeannie shrugged as if she knew something she wouldn't tell about Lizann Jappy.

'Oh, well, it takes all kinds,' the other woman said, philosophically. 'Mind, I got a right shock when Ruby tell't me they'd to wait till the man's first wife divorced him.'

This was also a shock to Bella Jeannie. 'Well!' she exclaimed, quite pleased to have something concrete against Lizann at last. 'That shows what kind o' lassie she is. Hannah'll nae be so high and mighty now, but I'm surprised Willie Alec didna stop it.'

'It's a wonder your Peter didna say onything about it. He musta ken't. Him and Mick Jappy were aye great pals.'

'I dinna think they're so pally these days. Mick's been going steady wi' Jenny ower the road for a good while now.'

As Bella Jeannie had hoped, this took Mary Kate's mind off Peter, and for the rest of her stay, they discussed how the Cowies would manage if Mick married Jenny and set up house away from Main Street.

As soon as she went into her own home again, she said, 'Did Mick tell you their Lizann was getting wed the day?'

'She told me herself,' Peter muttered.

'And you didna let on? I aye said she wasna right for you, and she's proved it now. Taking up wi' a man that had a wife already!'

'That's her business!' he snarled.

'Ach, Peter, you're nae still hankering after her, are you? She didna want you, m'loon. Get yourself another lass.'

About to say he only wanted Lizann, it struck him that seeing him with somebody else might make her jealous. She would realize, too late, that it was him she loved after all. But it wasn't too late! He wouldn't ask her to divorce George, he would just take her away. He would easily get a job in a shipyard where nobody would know they weren't married. His lack-lustre eyes brightened. 'You know this, Mam? I think I will look for another girl.'

When the wedding party returned from the manse, the kitchen was packed with people. 'I wanted this to be a day you'd never forget,' Willie Alec crowed to his daughter, letting his eyes sweep round the people he had invited for a 'wee dram' to celebrate.

During the issuing of presents and congratulations, Lizann saw that the guests were all her father's friends – fishermen and their wives – some of whom she had never met before, and she presumed, correctly, that her mother had not invited any of hers. Hurt that she was still holding George's dissolved marriage against him, Lizann told herself that this was the happiest day of her life and nobody was going to spoil it – not even her mother.

At Willie Alec's behest – and with the help of Peggy May Yule, who had popped in with a gift and offered her services, which had included going to the baker for boxes of fancy cakes – Hannah had made platefuls of various kinds of sandwiches. No one noticed that she sat with her mouth pursed through all the light-hearted chaffing, not even Lizann, who was delighted to see her friend there, though she didn't stay long. Willie Alec was happily dispensing liquor from the battery of bottles on the dresser, and wouldn't take no for an answer when George put his hand over his glass to stop it being topped up again.

Lizann wondered how her husband would stand up to the amount that he was pouring down his throat – she had never seen him drinking before – and she wasn't surprised when his eyes glazed over just after half past eight. She was thankful when Mick said, about twenty minutes later, 'I think it's about time we let Mr and Mrs Buchan get to their bed. Come on, Jenny, I'll see you along the road.'

With many knowing winks and nods, the visitors dispersed to their own homes, and Willie Alec said, slurring his words, 'Never mind the dishes, Lizann, I'll help your mother to tidy up.'

When George got to his feet he grabbed at the back of the chair to steady himself, and Lizann had to help him up to their room. She made him sit on the bed so that she could remove his shoes, socks and shirt, but she felt shy about taking off his trousers, and while she swithered about how to manage, her bridegroom toppled back with his mouth gaping, out for the count.

It wasn't her mother who had spoiled their wedding night, she thought, mournfully, as she undressed herself, it was her father. He'd certainly given them a day she would never forget, though she doubted if George would remember much about the last few hours. With a sigh, she lifted her lovely white nightdress and slipped it over her head. It didn't matter now that Peter had seen it first, for George wouldn't notice if she went to bed in a sack; he was snoring like an old man. Heaving him over to make room, she lay down beside him.

Mick, who had purposely sipped his drinks slowly and hadn't taken nearly as much as George, was sitting in the Cowies' kitchen with Jenny on his knee. 'A wedding's a wonderful thing, isn't it?' she sighed, laying her head on his shoulder. 'Lizann looked really happy.'

'I doubt if she'll be so happy now,' he smiled. 'George'll not be much use to her the night.'

'Ach, Mick,' she scolded, giving him a playful slap on the side, 'you say some terrible things.'

'Nothing terrible about that,' he retorted. 'It's natural when a man and woman love each other.'

'It's natural once they're wed.'

He knew what she wanted him to say, and he would, but not yet. 'Some folk don't bother about getting married,' he muttered.

'Some folk,' she said, disdainfully, sitting up, 'but not me. So you needn't think you'll get round me like that, Mick Jappy.'

'I wasn't trying to get round you,' he sighed. 'I love you, Jenny, and I want you, but I'll never take you by force.' To prove that he wasn't putting any pressure on her, he gave her a tender kiss, and she snuggled against him once more.

Earlier that same evening, to stop him wondering what Lizann and George might be doing, Peter Tait went to the dance in Buckie, and took a full thirty minutes to pick out a girl suitable for his purpose. Elsie Slater wasn't as beautiful as Lizann; in fact, she looked real common with her bleached hair, plucked eyebrows and scarlet lips. She was an awful flirt, but so much the better – it wouldn't bother her much when he dumped her. She seemed pleased that he claimed her for every dance, and he found he quite liked the feel of her in his arms. Elsie was clearly attracted to him and, even better, he was getting envious glances from other young men. Showing off, he pulled her closer, letting his hand slide slowly down her back.

'Oooh, Peter,' she giggled, 'you dinna ken what that does to me.'

When he took her home he kissed her at her door in North Pringle Street, the way she opened her mouth to him letting him know she was no novice. He was also sure that she would have let him go further if he tried. 'It's getting late,' he said, breathily, after a while, 'but I'll see you again?'

'You bet,' she laughed.

He arranged to meet her on Monday evening, and walked home wondering if he had been stupid to let the opportunity pass. The thing was, he had never made love to a girl before and was afraid she would laugh at him if he didn't put up a good show. But surely nature would tell him what to do and when to do it? Hopefully, Elsie wouldn't know he was just a beginner, however experienced she was.

He was almost at the Jappys' house when he realized where he was and his eyes went up to Lizann's window. The room was in darkness, and his stomach jolted nastily as he remembered that it wasn't her first time with George Buchan. She would be in bed with him now in one of those revealing nightgowns, or, more likely, with nothing on at all, letting him explore her body. Feeling like kicking the door in and screaming that she should have been his, Peter forced himself to move on.

His torture was so great that it was a relief to hear footsteps coming towards him. Whoever it was, he would stop and speak, to get his mind off Lizann. Unfortunately for him it was Mick, on his way home from Jenny's. Pulling himself together and striving to sound as if it didn't mean a thing to him, Peter said, 'How did the wedding go?'

Mick looked at him in amazement. 'You knew Lizann got married today?'

'I bumped into her over a week ago. Why didn't you say anything the last time I saw you?'

'Well, I thought . . . with you and her being engaged at one time . . .'

Peter had to swallow before he said, 'It was somebody else she wanted, and that's it.'

'You'll not . . . try anything to . . . ?'

'If she's happy, that's enough for me.'

'Thank God for that! And you'll likely find somebody else.'

Trying to prove that he wasn't the heart-broken wreck Mick thought he was, the heart-broken wreck he truly was, Peter boasted, 'I think I've found her already.'

'Good for you. Well, I'd better be going in. See you again, Peter.'

'Aye, cheerio.'

If Mick only knew, Peter thought, as he carried on to his own house.

Lizann was awake in the morning almost ten minutes before George opened his bleary eyes. 'You've come round, have you?' she asked, with just a hint of sarcasm.

'Oh, God!' he groaned, his hands going to his head. 'What time is it?'

'Nearly eight o'clock.'

'In the morning?'

She couldn't help laughing at him now. 'Aye, in the morning.'

'But . . . how did I get . . . was I drunk?'

'Paralytic!'

'Oh, Lizann. I'm sorry.'

'It wasn't your fault.'

'But . . . our wedding night . . . and I . . . ?'

'I hope you've learned your lesson.'

'I'll never drink again, I swear. It's like a traction engine's going full blast inside my skull.'

'Poor George.' She stroked his brow and his arm came round her.

'Lizann, my darling . . .' he said thickly.

'We haven't time for that. We should be up.'

'But we haven't . . .'

'There's always tonight.'

'I'm sorry,' he said again, watching her get up, but the sight of her in her nightdress sent the blood pounding through his veins. 'Come back to bed . . . please, my darling.'

She steeled herself to withstand his entreaty. 'No, my mother'll have the breakfast ready in a minute, and you'll have to rise and all.'

He got out at her side of the bed and grabbed her round the waist. 'Give me a kiss, then.'

The kiss would probably have had the desired effect if Mick had not knocked at the door. 'Come on you two lovebirds,' he called. 'You can't lie there all day.'

Lizann jumped away from her husband. 'I told you. We'd better hurry.'

When they went into the kitchen, Hannah fixed George with a glare of disapproval. 'You were in a fine state last night.'

'Ach now, Hannah,' Willie Alec said, 'you ken fine it was my fault.'

'He didna need to drink what you gi'ed him.'

'I'm sorry, Mrs Jappy,' George put in. 'It'll never happen again.'

'I hope no'.'

Sighing, Lizann said, 'I'd like for us to be kirked this morning.'

Her father beamed. 'Aye, it would make you feel right married.'

She wouldn't feel that until the marriage had been consummated, but it was the custom for manse ceremonies to be blessed in the church and she didn't want to flout convention. She turned to her brother. 'Will you and

Jenny come with us?' That, too, was part of the custom.

He nodded. 'She was saying last night we'd likely have to go.'

Breakfast over, he went to collect Jenny, and the four of them walked to church together.

Left alone with his wife, Willie Alec looked reprovingly at her. 'You could have been a bit friendlier to George, Hannah.'

'And him that drunk last night Lizann had to help him up the stair?'

'Ach, surely you could excuse him that once.'

'I've never seen you as drunk as that. You were aye able to walk, even on our own wedding night.'

'I was able to do a lot more than walk,' he chuckled.

Blushing at the memory of what he had done that night, she muttered, 'I'll never take to him. I canna forget he's had a wife already.'

'Ach, woman! There's nothing wrong wi' that. He's a good man, and you should be glad he got free, for if he hadna, Lizann would maybe've left us and went to bide in sin wi' him.'

'Oh, I hardly think that.'

'Hannah, it's time you broadened your ideas a bit. He's Lizann's man now, our son-in-law, and I for one welcome him into my family. In fact, I'm going to buy a boat and take him on as skipper.'

Her chin dropped. 'Can you afford to buy a boat?'

'That's why I couldna give them a big wedding. I've got enough to put down, and I could pay the rest bit by bit.'

'You'd buy it on tick?' She was even more appalled by this.

'It's not buying on tick, it's what everybody does now-adays, so stop your arguing.'

Hannah closed her mouth, but she was now harbouring another grievance against George, for Willie Alec would never have dreamt of buying a boat if it hadn't been for him.

George wanted to take Lizann to their room in the afternoon, but he knew that, although Willie Alec and Mick might just make a coarse remark, Hannah would be utterly disgusted that he couldn't wait, so it was after ten before they went upstairs.

In the act of slackening his tie, George suddenly said, 'That's a real bonnie picture you've got, Lizann.'

She was pleased that he was admiring her most treasured possession; it was good that they liked the same kind of things. 'It's my mother.'

Scarcely able to credit that staid, disapproving Hannah had ever gone round with a creel on her back, he hid his astonishment. 'It's really good ... lifelike.'

'Father got a man he knew to do it, but don't say anything to Mother. She doesn't like being reminded she once sold fish at folk's doors.'

He could well believe that. 'I'll not say a word, though it's nothing to be ashamed of.' Hauling off the tie, he looked at his wife again and was struck anew by her beauty, her appearance of innocence. He had made love to her before, yet he couldn't banish the feeling that he was on the brink of defiling her. Desire suddenly raged through him, and he turned his back to take off his trousers, so that she wouldn't see how rampant he had grown.

'George,' she whispered, 'you don't need to be shy with me.'

Turning round, he wished that he could make a picture of her in her filmy nightdress. She held out her arms to him, and without being aware of crossing the few feet between them, he was holding her loveliness against him and the warmth of her body was driving him frantic. Unable to speak, he lifted her and took her over to the bed, panting as he laid her down.

'You've made yourself breathless lifting me,' she chided him.

He couldn't tell her that it wasn't lifting her that was making him breathless, for he couldn't wait a minute longer.

When morning came, their marriage had been well and truly consummated, and George had to drag himself away from his wife. He had to leave at the same time as Mick and Willie Alec – he couldn't afford a honeymoon – and the door had barely closed behind them when Hannah muttered, 'You'll be thinking there's nae another man in the whole world like him?'

Determined not to be needled, Lizann smiled. 'There isn't.'

'That'll nae last long,' Hannah said, grimly.

Why did her mother have to spoil things? Lizann thought angrily. Her marriage had lasted, so why wouldn't her daughter's?

Chapter Nine

Willie Alec had ordered the drifter against his wife's wishes, and by the time the *Hannah* was fitted out he was as excited as a small boy with a new, expensive toy. 'It's nae worth me sitting for a skipper's ticket at my age,' he had added, noticing his son-in-law's hesitation at the offer of the job, 'and you're nae getting the good o' yours. You're family now, and Mick and you'll get a share of the nets.'

That had been the deciding factor for George. It wasn't as good as having a boat of his own, but the *Hannah* was much grander than his *Mary Ann* had been. He did sometimes feel guilty that Willie Alec had put himself in debt to give him a job, as Hannah was fond of reminding him when her husband wasn't within earshot, but it was the man's own business and he'd sworn it was something he had dreamt about for years.

The extra money was very welcome, for George was saving every penny he could to buy furniture for the house he hoped to rent. He was grateful to Willie Alec for letting them live at the Yardie, but he had to get away from Hannah's constant carping. When she was alone with him, she kept going on about folk saying Lizann had wed a second-hand man, and though they'd only been married for three months, it was getting under his skin. Much more of it and he'd be at her throat.

By July, George had had enough, and after only two months of being a skipper he knew he'd have to make a move. 'I think we could chance it,' he told Lizann.

'Chance what?'

'Looking for a house. If we got two rooms, we wouldn't need to buy so much furniture, though it would likely clean us right out.'

Lizann looked at him doubtfully. 'What's the rush, George? Are you not happy here?'

He didn't like to tell her that her mother had the knack of making him feel like an interloper without saying a word, as if he were only there on sufferance. 'I'd be a lot happier if I had you to myself every time I came home. The only time we can speak properly here is when we come to bed, and you're aye so scared your folk'll hear us you hardly let me . . .'

'I can't help it,' she murmured, nestling against him.

'Willie Alec wouldn't think anything about it . . . or Mick.'

'Maybe no', but you know what my mother's like.'

'Aye,' he sighed, grimly, 'that's why I want to get away. Oh, Lizann, darling, I want us to be free to do what we want, make as much love as we want . . . in an afternoon if we feel like it.' He slipped her nightdress straps from her shoulders to cup her breasts.

Giving a soft moan, she whispered, 'That's what I want and all.'

He let his hands glide slowly down and down, but even his passionate kisses couldn't make her forget her fear of being overheard.

'Go on, Peter,' Elsie urged. 'What are you waiting for? Better days?'

Having sampled the delights of her body many times since his first fumbling attempt, Peter grinned at her haste. He liked teasing her, for the leading up to it gave him nearly as big a thrill as the act itself, but there came a point . . .

When it was over, Elsie lay back with her hands behind

her head, her peroxided hair fanning out on the grass. 'That was great, Peter,' she said, languidly.

This gave his ego a tremendous boost, but he had been wondering for weeks if it was time to tell her it was over. His original reason for going out with her had backfired. She lived too far from the Yardie for Lizann ever to see them together and be jealous, and it would be better if he found a girl in Buckpool. 'Erm, Elsie,' he began, nervously, 'maybe we should stop seeing so much of each other . . .'

Her baby blue eyes clouded. 'Are you tired o' me?'

'No, it's not that. It's . . . well . . .'

Sitting up, she snapped, 'It doesna matter if you are, ony road. It's too late.'

'Too late?' he asked, perplexed.

'You didna think you could carry on like that for months and get away wi' it, did you?'

Fear gripped him now. 'What are you saying?'

'I'm saying you've put me up the spout.'

'Up the . . . ? You're not . . . expecting?'

'Aye, I'm two month gone.'

His stomach heaved sickeningly. 'Two months?' he gasped, drawing in deep gulps of air.

'It must've been yon night we'd been to Cathy's and we stopped on the road hame. I can mind thinking – that's it! He's done it this time.'

In a rush of shame, he recalled how the unaccustomed drink he had consumed in her friend's house that night had driven him wild with lust for her, and he had got her out as quickly as he could. At the first suitable spot he had pushed her to the ground and taken her forcefully, insistently – and, it seemed, fruitfully. 'God!' he groaned. 'Do your folk know?'

'Nae yet, but they'll see for themselves in a wee while.'

So this was it, Peter thought, self-pity flooding through him. He should have known – nothing ever worked out the way he wanted. Instead of getting Lizann back, he'd landed this . . . this fast, painted piece in the family way, and there was nothing for it but to marry her. 'I'll come home with you and speak to your father.'

'You'd better nae say there's a bairn on the road,' Elsie warned, 'or he'll go for you. When it's born, we can say it's come early, and he'll never ken.'

This did nothing to relieve Peter's worry. Even if they could fool her father, her mother would know the reason for the hasty marriage. Women could always tell when a girl was expecting, or so his mother said.

Only twenty-five minutes later, Peter was making his thoughtful way to his own house, wondering why Nell and Chae Slater had been so ready to agree to a wedding? Did they know the kind of girl their daughter was? Were they glad to get her off their hands? It had looked very much like it to him, and he'd felt like lapping up the whisky Chae had produced, but thank heaven he'd only taken one dram. He had still to tell his own mother and he would need all his wits about him for that.

He had half hoped that she would be in bed, but she was still sitting by the fire when he went in. 'Mary Kate died the night,' she told him, mournfully.

'Oh, I'm sorry to hear that.' He really was sorry, for Mary Kate had given him sweets and cakes when he was a boy, and had fed him when his mother was laid low with a terrible flu one winter.

'It was awful sudden, for I was in seeing her yesterday and she was just the same as she aye was.'

'You'll miss her,' Peter observed, for the two women had been friends for years.

'I will that.' Bella Jeannie wiped her eyes with the heel of her hand. 'But when the grim reaper comes, nobody can do nothing about it.'

Peter wondered if he should wait until morning to tell her his news, but it wasn't anything that could wait. 'I've something to tell you and all, Mam,' he said, looking everywhere but directly at her.

'What's that?' she sniffed.

'I've been going with a girl from up the town for a while, and . . .' he hesitated, then ended in a rush, '. . . we're getting married.'

'Married?' Mary Kate's death was brushed aside in Bella Jeannie's shock at this. Losing her only son to some ill-brought-up lassie was far worse than losing her friend. One hand clutching at her huge bosom, she demanded, 'Who is she? I dinna even ken her name.'

'Her name's Elsie Slater, and . . .' Peter stopped. He had been about to say she would like the girl, but he knew perfectly well she wouldn't, so he said instead, '. . . and she works in Pozzi's.'

'A shop lassie?' Bella Jeannie sounded happier. 'Oh, well, she'll have good manners, for they're trained to be polite to folk. You'll be taking her here to bide?'

'We haven't discussed it yet.' The thought of Elsie and his mother in the same house was not a pleasant one, and he could foresee the ructions there would be.

'Invite her for her supper on Saturday, so I can meet her.'

Knowing that they'd have to meet some time, he said, 'I'll ask her.'

Peter's remorse at what he had done in order to get Lizann back kept him from sleeping, and as the night wore on he was hit by apprehension at how his mother would react to Elsie – and vice versa – plus the dread of what people would say when the baby was born just six months after the wedding. No, not people, just his mother; his father wouldn't give two hoots, he was an easy-going man, and it was nobody else's business.

The winds were fierce for October, Hannah reflected, as she set the table, her thoughts turning to Willie Alec and

Mick. 'Did you hear if there was gales at sea when you were out?' she asked Lizann.

'I met Auntie Lou in the post office and she said she listened to the trawlers on the wireless last night, and one of the skippers said it was hurricane force gales where he was.'

'Oh, no!' Hannah wrung her hands in her distress. 'I couldna make out what they were saying for all the crackling. I hope it's nae in the same place as your father.'

'I hope no'!' Lizann could not reassure her mother because she herself was worrying about George. If anything happened to the *Hannah* she'd lose not only her father and her brother, but her husband as well.

The two women said little while they had their meal, and sat silently by the fire in the afternoon and evening, but each knew that the other was praying for their men at sea.

At nine o'clock, Hannah switched on the wireless and tuned it to the trawler waveband. At first atmospherics distorted the intermittent snatches of voices, then four words came through as clear as a bell: '. . . the *Hannah*'s gone down . . .'

'Oh, my dear Lord!' Hannah exclaimed, looking at her daughter in deep anguish. 'I ken't it. I've had a funny feeling the whole day.'

Torn between mourning along with her mother and telling her not to worry, Lizann plumped for the latter. 'Maybe it didn't mean . . . maybe it was too rough for them to get to Buckie, and they've had to go down to the Broch or Peterhead.'

Her mother eyed her doubtfully. 'I suppose it could be that.'

'It must be that!'

Neither of them went to bed that Saturday night, and the teapot was filled, emptied and refilled a dozen times as they huddled over the fire with aching hearts. Lizann was slightly more optimistic than Hannah, but when it occurred to her that her mother must have endured many ordeals similar to this – if not quite so bad – in the thirty years she had been married, she wondered if she herself would have to go through it again or if George was lost to her already. Her little gulp made Hannah look up.

'Aye, m'quine,' she said, gently, 'it's hard on the wives.'

In North Pringle Street, Elsie Slater went to bed in a temper. Her visit to Buckpool had been a disaster. She had thought Peter's mother would make her welcome, but the fat lump hadn't liked her and hadn't tried to hide it. Peter had been on heckle pins all the time, and if she'd had any sense she'd have walked out. But she wanted Peter. Not that she had to marry him, for she wasn't expecting at all, but he was the best catch she'd ever get. She quite fancied being a draughtsman's wife and she didn't want him to get away.

When he was seeing her home he'd said his mother would be the same to any girl he took into the house, and she could well believe that. She'd seen that the woman thought the sun shone out of his backside, so she wouldn't think anybody was good enough for him. His father hadn't been so bad; a wee pasty-faced man with a boozer's red nose, he'd eyed her like she was a side of beef he wanted to buy, but she was accustomed to men looking at her like that. He'd hardly got the chance to say a word and he'd likely have been a lot happier sitting in a pub. Well, maybe he didn't mind being henpecked, but his wife wouldn't have it all her own way when Elsie Slater moved in as Mrs Tait Junior. And when Peter found out she'd tricked him into marrying her, she would easily get round him.

Bella Jeannie rounded on Peter when he arrived home. 'You've surely lost your senses to think o' marrying a trollop like that! Painted up to the eyeballs, and sitting wi' her skirts up so you could see her bare hips! And your father was as bad as you, gawking at them, and likely getting himself all worked up. He's away to his bed, but if he tries it on wi' me when I go up, I'll knock him into the middle o' next week.'

The thought of his father trying anything on with her made Peter grin, and she glared at him suspiciously. 'Maybe you've been at it wi' her already? Is she in the family way?'

Peter's smile vanished and he felt as if his tongue was fixed to the roof of his mouth. His mother had always been able to put her finger on the truth, no matter what lies he told when he was younger, and she had done it again.

'Is her father forcing you to wed her?' Bella Jeannie persisted.

He was on safer ground here. 'No, it's nothing to do with her father.'

'Maybe I'm wrong then, but I'd rather you married Lizann Japy than that one.'

And so would he, Peter longed to shout, but it would have been as good as admitting that he had been forced into marriage by Elsie herself, not her father. In any case it would all come out when she began to show, and his mother would half kill him for not telling her before. He was between the devil and the deep blue sea, and it was hard to tell which of the two women was more of a devil. His life would be one long hell after Elsie came here to live, with the two of them going on at him day in, day out.

'Speaking about Lizann Japy,' Bella Jeannie said, suddenly, 'Rosie Mac was in when you was seeing your fancy piece hame, and she tell't me Willie Alec's boat's went down.'

'Who told her that?'

'She was listening to the trawlers. It'll be an awful shock to Hannah, her man and her son both lost, and it wouldna surprise me if she went out o' her mind, for Willie Alec's been her whole life since the day she met him. It's a good thing she'll have Lizann there to help her get ower it. Well, your father should be sleeping by this time, and it's time all good folk was in their beds.'

Waiting until she closed the door, Peter sprawled down in his chair, his legs stretched out and his toes pointed at the fire. Poor Lizann, he thought, losing her father and her brother at the same time; she must be devastated. Should he call on her tomorrow to express his sympathy? It would be natural with him being a close friend of Mick's, but it would be awkward if George Buchan was there. He had seen them together several times since their wedding, and the happiness shining from her eyes had made a knife twist in his heart. He'd better keep away; her man would be the only one she'd want at a time like this.

He sat up abruptly. George Buchan had been skipper of the *Hannah*! He'd nearly forgotten that, and it meant Lizann was a widow! She would be heartbroken right now, but once she got over it ... Dear God! When she got over it he could have made her love him again, but he'd be married to Elsie Slater by that time! With an infant on the way to weld them even more firmly together.

If only he'd waited. If only he hadn't rushed into taking Elsie as a substitute – taken in every sense of the word, not once, but three or four times a week for about seven months, with no precautions. He should have known better. He'd been asking for trouble, and he'd bloody well got it! Well, he mused wryly, it was no use crying over spilt milk, so he'd be as well going to bed. He would never get Lizann now, and he'd have to make the best of things. At least Elsie could satisfy him, could more than satisfy him, so he'd have no complaints on that score, and he might enjoy being a family man with a toddler or two running around his feet.

Hannah had dozed off, but Lizann was still sitting hunched up, her eyes bone dry. She couldn't believe that the *Hannah* had gone down, that she would never see George again. It couldn't be true! They'd had so little time together, they had not even made a child – though it could have been time if she had let herself go like George asked her to. What would it have mattered if her mother had heard them? They were man and wife. But . . . if the *Hannah* had gone down, she wouldn't be his wife any more. She and her mother would both be widows!

Chapter Ten

❧

Daylight was shining through the curtains when Lizann heard quick footsteps outside and leapt up, but before she reached the door her aunt burst in and barged past her, her grey hair untidy, her coat fastened askew.

'I've just heard,' Lou gasped, striding over to the fireside, 'and I come as fast as I could. I see you ken already, though. Who tell't you?'

Startled out of a doze, Hannah gave her head a slight shake as if to clear her brain. 'It was on the wireless last night.' Her voice broke and, grabbing her sister's hand, she burst into tears.

Determined not to believe the worst until they were told officially, Lizann said, 'Who told you, Auntie Lou?'

'I saw a boorach o' women in the street, and I went out to see what they were speaking about, and that's what it was. So I went back inside for my coat and I've run near the whole road here.' She laid her hand on her heaving chest.

But Lizann wanted to hear more. 'Who told them?'

'Isie Stewart had been listening to the trawlers last night, and all, and she said she near fainted when she heard about the *Hannah*, for she ken't it was Willie Alec's boat.'

'Did she tell you what she heard . . . the exact words?'

'She said she'd an awful job making onything out, and she just heard somebody saying the *Hannah* had went down.' Lou turned again to her sister, whose sobbing had increased in volume. 'Dinna let it get to you, m'dear. I'm sure they hadna ken't what happened.'

'What do you know about it?' Lizann's nerves, coiled spring-tight, were ready to snap. 'A boat would take a long time to sink . . .'

'Oh, well, they'd have ken't they were going to drown,' Lou protested, looking slightly abashed, 'but driftermen must aye have that at the back o' their minds.'

Hannah's sobs had reached a crescendo of hysterics, and Lizann wished that she hadn't argued with her aunt. She had only made things worse for her mother. She herself was still convinced that Hannah had jumped to the wrong conclusion after hearing the fateful four words. 'I'll make a fresh pot of tea,' she muttered, pushing Lou aside to reach the teapot.

It was just after nine, Lou still being more of a Job's comforter to her sister than a solace although Hannah seemed to benefit from it, when someone knocked on the door. Lizann went to answer it and stepped back in surprise. Peter was the last person she had expected to see.

'I had to come,' he murmured, 'to say how sorry I am about . . . George.'

She hadn't wanted to believe it, but a second person calling to tender condolences was too much for her, and without knowing how, she was in his arms, weeping on his chest while he stroked her hair. 'That's right, my dear,' he nodded, 'let it out. It's the best way.'

'Oh, Peter,' she sobbed, 'I did love him.'

'I know that, my dearest girl.' After a short pause, he said, softly, 'This isn't the right time to tell you, but I'm getting wed myself, so you'll not need to feel guilty about me any longer.'

Her tears tailing off, she gasped, 'You're getting married? Who to?'

'Her name's Elsie Slater and I met her at a dance a while back, and . . . well, I couldn't have you, and I started going steady with her, though I wish now . . .'

'No, Peter,' she said, breaking away from him. 'There could never be anything between us again, and I'm happy for you, really I am.'

'Who's there?' came Hannah's quavering voice.

'It's Peter,' Lizann called, adding in an undertone to him, 'You'd better come in.'

'No, I'm not coming in. Tell her I'm sorry about Willie Alec and Mick, and remember, Lizann, if I can help at all, just let me know.'

She closed the door and returned to the kitchen. 'He came to say how sorry he was, Mother.'

'Peter's aye been a nice laddie. You should have stuck to him instead o' that Cullen . . .'

'Mother! That's a horrible thing to say, when George . . .' Lizann broke off, too distressed to go on. She knew her mother didn't like him, but she wouldn't have believed she could be so callous at a time like this.

Lou butted in now. 'You shouldna speak to your ma like that, Lizann. Think what she's suffering already.'

'Do you not think I'm suffering? I've lost my man, as well as her.'

'Aye, but you havena been wed near as long as her, and she's lost her son, and all.'

'Mick's my brother,' Lizann shouted, 'so I've lost three men I love and she's only lost two. She couldn't stand the sight of George.' She was so overwrought that she didn't care what she said, though Hannah had gone into another paroxysm of tears. 'I just had George for a few months and she's had Father nearly thirty years.'

Recognizing that she had two distraught women on her hands, Lou tried to repair the damage she had done. 'I'm sorry, lass, it must be just as bad for you. I shouldna have said that.'

Taking in a long deep breath to calm herself, Lizann

murmured, 'I'm sorry and all, Auntie Lou. I shouldn't have lost my temper.'

'Well, we'll say no more about it. If you tell me what you was to be having for your dinner, I'll cook it for you.'

Totally confused, Peter took a walk before he went home. He had thought he could cope with saying a few words to Lizann, but he hadn't counted on her throwing herself into his arms – he hadn't expected to hold her like that ever again. She had turned to him for comfort, as he had known she would . . . and he'd had to tell her he was marrying another girl. There was no way out of that, for he couldn't let Elsie bring up his child on her own. He would have to make the best of his marriage and put Lizann out of his mind.

When he returned to Main Street, more than an hour after he left, his mother said, 'You've been an awful long time at the Yardie. How's Hannah . . . and Lizann?'

'Bearing up.' What else could he say?

'I hope you're nae thinking on trying to take up wi' Lizann again? She didna want you before, and she'll not want you now.'

'I'm not thinking of taking up with her. I'm going to marry Elsie.'

Bella Jeannie eyed him speculatively. 'I havena once heard you saying you love her.'

'I do love her,' he said, hastily. Maybe he would come to love her when the baby was born. He would have to live with her for the rest of his life, whatever, whether he loved her or not.

'Your father doesna like her any more than me.'

He knew this wasn't true. Bowfer had said more to Elsie in the three hours she had been in the house than he usually said in a month. If he didn't know his father had no time for women, he would think the old devil was attracted to her. 'Look, Mam, I don't give a damn what anybody thinks. I'm old enough to make up my own mind.'

Offended, Bella Jeannie drew in her mouth.

The three women sat round the fire in the afternoon, Lizann and Hannah staring vacantly at the leaping flames, and Lou, guessing that they were recalling happier times, saying nothing to interrupt their thoughts but giving an occasional deep sigh, because her heart was aching for them. She was about to suggest another cup of tea when she heard footsteps outside. 'Somebody's coming.'

There was no reaction from the other two, but when the door opened, they whirled round and gaped in amazement. First in, George went to his wife, whose haggard face had turned a greenish white. 'It's all right, Lizann,' he assured her. 'I'm not a ghost.'

Mick made for his mother and put his arm round her. 'Father's still sorting things out with the rest of the crew, but he said we should come and let you know we were all safe.'

Lou, the only one still thinking rationally, waited for a few minutes before asking, 'What happened?'

George was fully occupied in trying to stem Lizann's tears of anticlimax as much as relief, so it was Mick who answered, holding Hannah's hand as he told how the gales had tossed the *Hannah* about like a toy boat for hours on end before dashing her against the rocks with a force that splintered her hull, and everyone aboard was flung into the raging sea. 'I managed to grab hold of a spar that was floating by,' he went on, 'though I thought I'd be sucked under with her when she keeled over. But she went down real canny.'

Before his last words were out, Willie Alec came in, his lined face as grey as his son's and son-in-law's. Hannah stood up with a strangled sob and almost collapsed into his arms, and as he stroked her back, he said, 'It was lucky the *Girl Alice* was close astern o' us, and her skipper saw what happened. He picked every man jack o' us up, and his crew even managed to fit us out wi' dry clothes.'

Grinning, Mick looked down at the trousers he was wearing, which only reached the calves of his legs. 'This pair's half-mast on me. A couple of inches shorter and they'd be like the breeks I wore to school.'

George turned to him, his face serious. 'They did the best they could, Mick, and it was real good of them.'

Willie Alec disentangled himself from his wife to thump down on the nearest seat, then passed a weary, trembling hand across his brow. 'If it hadna been for them, we'd've been goners.'

Nobody said anything to that, each thanking God for the rescue but unable to dispel the thought of the tragedy there could have been. At last, Willie Alec groaned, 'For all that, she went to the sea bed and all our gear wi' her.'

Always more practical than her sister, Lou tried to make him look on the bright side. 'You'd had her insured, though?'

He shook his head in shame. 'I couldna afford to insure her at first, and I aye meant to take out a policy . . . but I kept putting it off.'

'Ach, well,' Mick consoled, 'you're no worse off than you were before you bought her, and you'll get a berth with somebody else.'

'You dinna understand,' his father moaned, clamping his head between his hands in his anguish. 'She's still to be paid, and I'm responsible for my crew's gear, and all.'

Mick protested at this. 'It wasn't your fault she went down, Father.'

'No, but I want to recompense every man so he can buy new . . .'

'You'll not need to worry about me and George. We'll buy our own.'

160

'Aye,' his brother-in-law nodded, 'we'll manage that.'

Lizann could hardly believe that George had agreed. It would take most of their savings to replace the boots, the ganzies, the sets of heavy underwear, the oilskins, and he could never replace the antique sextant which he had told her had belonged to Katie's great-grandfather. Besides, he wouldn't get another skipper's job, and it would take them ages on a deckie's wages till they made up their savings again. They would never furnish a house at this rate, and they had to get away from the Yardie, for her mother was always casting up about George's other wife. There was going to be big trouble one of these days.

'That still leaves Billy Peat and Robbie Fernie,' Willie Alec sighed. 'Married men wi' young bairns ... and wee Jimmicky, the cook. His mother's a widow-woman.'

Lou broke into the heavy silence which followed. 'That's only three you'll need to recom ... pay to get new gear, four counting yourself. And the shipyard'll surely wait till you're on your feet again before they expect you to ...'

'I'm not going to renege on my debts!' Willie Alec said angrily. 'I'm going to pay what I'm due every month, supposing me and Hannah have to go hungry.'

'There's no need to lose your rag at me,' Lou said, huffily, getting to her feet. 'I'd best away. I can see I'm not wanted here.'

'Ach, Lou, I'm sorry,' Willie Alec muttered. 'I'm that upset I dinna ken what I'm saying. I'd best go to my bed for a while.'

Not one to harbour grudges, Lou's face broke into a wide smile. 'Aye, things'll look better when you've had a sleep, but get something in your belly first.'

After a meal hardly any of them touched, Willie Alec went through to his bed, and after protesting for some time that they didn't need to, Mick and George were persuaded to have a rest, too.

After washing up, Lou said, 'You're nae needing me now, so I'll get off hame. You'll be glad o' some peace for a while to get over things, but it's a blessing they were all saved.'

When Lizann went upstairs a few hours later to say that supper was ready, she was glad to find her husband sound asleep, but Mick answered her call with alacrity.

With Willie Alec and George still sleeping off the effects of their ordeal, only three sat down at the table, but knowing that Jenny Cowie would be anxious about him, Mick finished quickly and went to let her know he was home safely. Hannah, who had scarcely said a word since the men came in, now murmured, 'I wouldna like to go through that again.'

'No,' Lizann agreed, 'but it's all over now, thank God.'

'Amen to that.'

At half past eight Lizann went upstairs again. 'Ah, you're wakened at last?' she said, when George lifted his head. 'How d'you feel now?'

'A lot better, but I wouldn't like to go through that again.'

'That's what my mother said and all,' Lizann smiled. 'Would you like something to eat? I can easy heat up your supper.'

'I just want to hold you. When we were in the water, I kept thinking about you, and . . . oh, God, come here, my darling.'

'I'll have to tell my mother . . .'

'Forget your mother. She'll know you've come to bed with me.'

She needed no further persuasion and, remembering her wish when she thought George was lost to her that she hadn't been so afraid of them being heard, she did her best to please him.

In the morning, Willie Alec looked round the breakfast

table. 'I meant what I said last night. I'm going to pay back every penny of my debts.'

'You should have a word with the yard,' Mick advised. 'They might come to some special arrangement with you.'

'I want no special arrangements made for me,' his father growled. 'I took in hand to pay off a certain amount every month for three year, and that's what I'm going to do. I'm giving no man the chance to say Willie Alec Jappy broke his word. I want nothing hanging over my head when I go to my grave.'

'That gives you plenty time,' Mick grinned.

His father was in no mood for pleasantries. 'Just you let this be a lesson to you, and all, Mick. Buy nothing you canna pay for in full.'

Mick's grin became somewhat rueful. 'That means I'll never be able to buy anything that costs more than a shilling or two. I'm aye skint.'

'You'll have to cut your coat according to your cloth,' Willie Alec said, firmly. 'You spend ower much on that lassie you go out wi'.'

Mick glanced wryly at Lizann, who guessed that he had been saving in the hope of marrying Jenny, and that he, too, would be left with very little after buying his new gear, but she said nothing. Mick and George would consider this as a setback to their future plans – as had she the day before – but all she felt now was thankful that they had a future.

Chapter Eleven

Three weeks later, Peter Tait married Elsie Slater in the Baptist church in Cluny Place. Her father had arranged for the reception to be held in the St Andrew's Hotel, to which forty guests had been invited, and it was almost midnight before the happy couple could go up to the room Chae had also booked for them for the night.

Peter was shy about undressing, but Elsie tossed off her long white wedding gown and underclothes then gyrated slowly in front of him. This made him forget his inhibitions, and he too cast his clothing on the floor.

'Wow!' Elsie exclaimed, when they settled back on the bed afterwards. 'That was the best yet, Peter.'

His prowess had also surprised him – it had likely been not having to worry about being seen – but he laughed off her compliment. 'That was nothing, I'm not finished yet.' The way she was fondling him had fired him again, and he proceeded to show her his boast had been no idle one.

It was only after their second wild coupling that he remembered. 'I hope this doesn't hurt the baby.'

Her big blue eyes regarded him innocently. 'What baby?' His puzzled expression made her giggle. 'There's no baby, I just said that so you'd marry me.'

She had planned her moment carefully, sure that he would forgive her anything tonight, but his expression alarmed her. Had she gone too far? Running her tongue round her already moist lips, she wheedled, 'Peter, lovey, you're nae angry at me, are you?'

'Of course I'm angry!' he barked, trying unsuccessfully

to keep his eyes away from her. 'No man likes being made a fool of.'

'I wasna trying to make a fool o' you,' she pouted. 'I wanted you to wed me, what's wrong wi' that?'

This time he did manage to turn his head away. If she hadn't spun him the story, he'd have told Lizann when he went to commiserate with her that he still loved her, and even with George turning up safe and sound again, she might have realized she would have a more tranquil life with a draughtsman than a seaman who could be lost at any time. Instead, he'd had to say he was marrying Elsie . . . and because of her bloody stupid lie, he had lost all hope of ever getting Lizann.

'God Almighty!' he burst out, viciously. 'I wish I'd known. Do you think I'd have married you if . . .'

'Do you think you could have gotten another girl to satisfy you like me?' Elsie's voice was velvet-soft, cloying, insinuating her words deep into his brain and setting it off on a different track. She was a man's woman, she knew how to get him going, she knew how to keep him going, and by God, when she wanted to, she could drive him so mad with lust that all he could think of was taking her. Anyway, he had burned his bridges behind him. They were husband and wife now, for better or worse, for richer or poorer, in sickness and health.

Feeling her stroking his shoulder, coaxing him, he looked back at her and was lost. His pulses quickened at the sight of her lissom, naked body spreadeagled by his side, her sweet red lips crying out to be kissed, but he had to teach her who was boss. 'I'll make damned sure I'll put you up the spout tonight,' he muttered, grabbing one of her breasts and squeezing.

Her hand dived down. 'Get on wi' it, then!' she grinned.

With her uncommunicative husband by her side – nothing new, for he was always like that – Bella Jeannie reached home much happier than when she set out for the wedding. 'You ken,' she said, when they were inside, 'I was near sure Elsie was in the family way, so I watched her like a hawk the whole time . . .'

Bowfer Tait held his breath, for he'd really enjoyed himself dancing with all the young things, especially his new daughter-in-law, then he relaxed when his wife went on, '. . . but her belly's as flat as a pancake. It'll likely nae be long till she is, for I could see Peter was worked up, but there'll be nae shame to the bairn when it's born.'

'Aye . . . no, that's right.' Bowfer nodded vigorously. He'd been worked up himself just looking at all the lassies, their slim supple bodies so different from Bella Jeannie's whaleboned stiffness, and when he'd held them in his arms he'd felt a long-forgotten raging heat in his nether regions. And if Elsie's belly was flat, it was the only thing about her that was. 'We'll just go up to bed, eh?' he muttered, hopefully.

'Aye, we'd be as well.'

After climbing the stairs, Bowfer had to sit down on a chair – this damned cough would be the death of him, he thought, as he fought for breath. By the time he recovered, Bella Jeannie had taken off her tent-like frock and petticoat, and though he bent down to remove his shoes and socks, he watched her out of the corner of his eye. When he was younger, he had liked a woman with a bit of flesh on her, but a man's tastes change. He'd have preferred somebody with a decent figure right now, but Bella Jeannie would have to do.

When she took off her brassiere, he was mesmerized to see her high bosom dropping a couple of inches, but it occurred to him that he should start to undress himself in case she noticed him looking at her. First pulling off the tie he had slackened when he came out of the hall, he took off his shirt and started opening his trouser buttons. He couldn't believe the size of the huge belly that flopped out when his wife unhooked her corsets; he was usually asleep before she came to bed. Her sagging breasts reached to her belly-button now, or where her belly-button should be – it must be somewhere under all those layers of fat, though he wouldn't have seen it anyway with her always keeping on her woollen vest, day and night, winter and summer.

Sighing with relief, she threw the pink instrument of torture on the chair at her side of the bed, and scratched where her skin was irritated from long hours of confinement. As her fingers gouged into the spongy rolls around her waist and hips, Bowfer felt his heat subsiding. She wasn't just fat, she was bloody disgusting!

Blissfully unaware of her husband's repugnance, Bella Jeannie hitched up her thick bloomers, put on her winceyette nightdress and got into bed, the springs protesting loudly at her weight. Starting another fit of coughing, Bowfer held his chest until it stopped, then kicked off his trousers and, in his linder and drawers, lay down on the narrow strip which was all that was available to him. He hadn't touched Bella Jeannie as a husband for many a long year, and he'd thought he was past it, but he wasn't. The young things had got him going, though he'd lost the urge again after seeing his wife as near naked as anybody would ever see her.

Bowfer closed his eyes and turned his thoughts to Elsie. Dancing with her had been a revelation, for the lassies in his day had been nothing like as forward. She'd pressed her tits into his chest, and she must have known it was turning him on, for she'd smiled and rubbed against him till he was that fired up he was feared he would disgrace himself in front of the other guests. He'd had to pretend his chest was bothering him so he could go and sit down, but she knew fine what his trouble was. By God, he wouldn't be lying here just thinking about it if it was her lying beside him. Peter was a lucky young bugger!

* * *

At his side, Bella Jeannie was also thinking. As a mother, she wished her son had chosen a better wife, a lassie she would be proud to be seen with in the street, but it was done and she'd have to make the best of it. She wouldn't let Elsie dictate to her in her own house, that was one thing sure, though it was her own fault they'd be biding here. Peter had been all for buying a house, but she hadn't wanted Elsie to have him all to herself. 'What's the sense in spending out money when there's plenty room here?' she had said.

'We wouldn't have any privacy here,' he had argued.

'You'll get all the privacy you need in your bed.'

He had flushed at that, and though she had been nearly sure he'd been at it with Elsie before the wedding, she had learned different today. He was as innocent as a bairn ... but not his wife. It wouldn't be that one's first time with a man! Not even a hundred-and-first!

Bella Jeannie recalled the shock she'd had on her own wedding night. She had no brothers, no idea of how different a man's body was from a woman's, and when she saw the huge thing that sprang out of her groom's trousers she had nearly fainted. She gave a tiny smirk in the darkness. She'd soon found out what it was for, and once she got used to it, she'd quite liked it. Of course, she'd been nice and slim in those days, but even after Peter was born and she'd put on weight, his father had still needed his nightly ration. But she'd grown fatter and fatter, and sometimes couldn't be bothered with him, and now she couldn't remember the last time he'd done it, even the last time he'd tried. At her age, she needed her sleep – and so did he!

The trouble was, he barked like a Great Dane off and on all night, and though she knew he couldn't help it, she often felt like telling him to shut up. There he was again, hawking and hawking, and gasping as if his last minute had come. Giving him a thump in the ribs with her elbow to show her displeasure, she heaved herself round with her back to him, and turned her mind to the earlier part of the evening. His bad cough hadn't stopped him from dancing with every lassie in the hall, and coming back after his dance with Elsie all flushed. And he'd sat for ages with his hands over the bulge she'd seen when he was walking to his seat, stupid old devil. He'd hardly taken his eyes off the little bitch for the rest of the evening, and little wonder, for she'd flaunted herself in front of all the men. Peter would have to watch her. If she stuck her tits in Bowfer's face every day, what would it drive him to?

With something of a struggle, for it wasn't easy to shift her sixteen stones, Bella Jeannie turned round again. 'Are you sleeping?'

Bowfer's erotic dreams were rudely shattered. 'Eh? What's that?'

'I asked if you was sleeping.'

'I was, but nae now.'

'I was thinking . . .' Bella Jeannie began, slowly, for she hadn't quite worked out what to say, '. . . about Elsie.'

'Oh, aye?' he said, cautious now.

His wife jumped right in; he had to be told. 'I could see she got you going, and I'm warning you now, Bowfer Tait, keep your hands off her.'

'Me?' he exclaimed, incredulously. 'For God's sake, woman, I've never laid a finger on her.'

'And you never will! Have you got that?'

'Aye, I've got it, but I dinna ken what you take me for. A man doesna interfere wi' his son's wife. Now, if you're finished, would you let me get some sleep?'

She closed her eyes, clicking her tongue as he began another bout of coughing which went on and on, as though he couldn't get to the bottom of it. She was about to ask how she expected her to sleep when he gave a peculiar grunt, and she wondered if the exertion of dancing had been too much for him. After all, he was past sixty and he was like a washed-out clout when he came home from his work, though it never stopped him from going out for a few pints once he'd had his supper. She waited for him to make a move of some kind ... and waited ... and waited.

A rough shove still producing no response, a cold alarm gripped her, and, unable to see anything in the dark, she hoisted herself out of bed to light the gas mantle. Hoping she could do something to help she went back to her husband, but one look was enough. His eyes – the eyes that had twinkled roguishly for Elsie and the other young girls – stared back at her with no spark of life. Stretching over to close them, she said, 'Silly old bugger, see what you've done to yourself wi' your nonsense.' There was a catch in her voice, and her legs giving way, she sat down on the chair to think what to do.

If Peter had been here ... but Peter wouldn't be till tomorrow sometime. Wondering what time it was, she looked at the alarm clock on the chest of drawers. Quarter to two. She couldn't knock on anybody's door at this time of night, but she couldn't sit here and do nothing. Nevertheless, she made no move until she recovered a little, then she stood up to put on her clothes, her trembling hands fumbling with each fastening. Fully dressed, she went down to the kitchen to make herself a cup of tea, and when her frozen heart thawed out, she decided to go and fetch Peter. She needed him, and he had to be told about his father.

Still satisfying his bride's insatiable demands, Peter halted at a sharp knock on their door. 'What the ... ?' he muttered, deciding to ignore it, but it came again, more insistent this time. 'Mr Tait! Mr Tait!'

Stark naked, he rose to find out who was there, and

when he put his head round the door, he was astonished to see the hotel manager, muffled up in a fleecy dressing-gown. 'Yes?' he asked.

The man looked embarrassed. 'I'm sorry to disturb you, Mr Tait, but a policeman's asking for you.'

'A policeman? What's it about?'

'He wouldn't tell me. You'll have to come down.'

Closing the door, Peter switched on the light, at which Elsie eyed him suspiciously. 'A bobby? What've you been up to?'

'You should know,' he grinned, then shook his head. 'There must be a mistake. It can't be me he wants, but I'd better go down and see.'

'Be quick, then, or I'll go off the boil.'

Wondering, in amusement, if she ever went off the boil, he pulled on his underpants, trousers and shirt, then went down to the hotel lobby. 'Not guilty,' he joked, holding both hands up in mock surrender. 'You've got the wrong man, officer.'

The policeman did not smile. 'Your mother wants you home.'

'What?' Peter gasped. 'This is my wedding night.'

'Aye, she told me. But I'm afraid it's bad news. Your father died.'

Peter clutched at the reception desk. 'But he was dancing here earlier on . . .' He looked pathetically at the uniformed man.

'It happens like that sometimes – no warning. I'll walk back with you, but you'll need a coat or something. It's devilish cold outside.'

'I don't have a coat here, but I'll get my jacket. I'll have to tell . . . my wife, anyway, and she'll likely want to come with me.'

Elsie was not at all pleased to leave the warm bed in the middle of the night. 'It'll make no odds to your father if we wait till a decent time,' she pouted.

'My mother sent for me. You'd better hurry, the bobby's waiting.'

'Trust your family to spoil our first night.'

But she rose and took out the bag containing her ordinary clothes. 'Put my wedding gown in there,' she muttered as she dressed, quickly because she was cold, not because somebody was waiting, 'and watch and nae crush it.'

The policeman tipped his hat when they went downstairs, and held the outside door open for them. 'Your mother was on her way here when I met her,' he said, as they hurried along the road, 'and when she told me about your father, I said I'd come and let you know, but I went for the doctor first, in case . . . well, in case she'd made a mistake.'

Dr Mathieson was still in the house when Peter and Elsie went in, having stayed with Bella Jeannie who was suffering from delayed shock. She was sitting in the kitchen and looked so pitiful that Peter crossed the room to put an arm round her shoulder.

The doctor lifted his bag. 'You'll not need me now you've got your son,' he said and, putting on his hat, he went out.

'She needs something to steady her nerves,' Peter whispered to Elsie. 'There's a bottle of whisky in the foot of the dresser, give her a good shot of it.'

The spirits brought some colour back into Bella Jeannie's cheeks, and he said gently, 'Do you feel like telling us what happened?'

'Oh, m'loon,' she said, mournfully, 'I dinna really ken what happened. We went straight to our bed when we come in, and your father's chest was bothering him for ages, and he coughed and coughed – you ken how he is – and then he made a funny kind of noise. He didna move after that, and I got up and lighted the gas, and . . .' The horror too fresh, she broke off and put her hand to her eyes.

'Don't upset yourself any more,' Peter soothed.

'I didna ken what to do, and I couldna stand being here myself wi' him so ... I'm sorry, Peter.'

'No, no, it's all right. You needed me, I understand.'

'But it was your wedding night ...' She looked across him at Elsie. 'I hope you're nae annoyed at me?'

Elsie shrugged. 'Well, I wasna expecting it to be so short, but ... ach, you couldna help it.'

'The doctor said it was the strain o' the coughing on top of all the excitement of the dancing.'

Another five minutes passed before Peter said, 'What happens now?'

His mother sighed. 'You'll have to see the undertakers, but they'll nae be open on Sunday, so you'll have to go first thing on Monday.'

'I'll do that. Now, it's still only after three, and we all need some sleep ...' He stopped, his cheeks colouring.

She didn't notice his confusion. 'Take Elsie up to your room, the bed was all ready for you, any road, and I'll just sit here.'

Elsie jumped to her feet, but Peter said, 'No, Mam, I can't let you do that. You go to bed with Elsie and I'll sit here.'

To Elsie's relief, Bella Jeannie shook her head. 'No, no. I'll be fine here. Away you go.'

When the house was quiet and she was sure that the newlyweds were asleep, Bella Jeannie crept upstairs to take another look at her dead husband. 'I was maybe wrong in what I thought about you, Bowfer,' she whispered, stroking his brow, 'but you're away from temptation now, and I'm pleased you enjoyed the last hours you had in this world.'

As she stepped back, she saw that his face had a peacefulness about it that hadn't been there when he died ... more than peace, really, almost a smile ... or was that just her imagination?

Chapter Twelve

That same night, Lizann was lying in bed worrying about her father. He had been a changed man since the *Hannah* went down, three weeks before, though he had been lucky to get a berth on the *Endeavour*. She didn't know if he was the same at sea, but he was moody and withdrawn at home . . . when he wasn't raging her mother for being extravagant.

'You ken fine we canna afford to eat meat like this,' he had ranted a fortnight ago, when she served him a plate of boiled beef and carrots.

'It was the cheapest Lizann could get,' Hannah wailed, 'and I got a big pot o' soup out o' it.'

'A bone would have done for soup,' he growled.

'It was near closing time when I went to the butcher,' Lizann had put in, 'and he was selling off what he'd left at less than half price.'

He was even worse now, she reflected. He hardly opened his mouth to any of them, his hair had turned white almost overnight and his face was greyer than ever. He had lost so much weight his clothes were hanging on him, and if he carried on like this he would make himself ill.

George and Mick were both on the *Dawn Rose*, and after buying new gear, they had given what was left of their savings to Willie Alec to help him recompense the other crew members of the ill-fated *Hannah*. Lizann didn't know how Jenny Cowie felt about it – she must have known why Mick had been saving – but she herself felt that there must be a jinx on her and George, that something would always happen to prevent them getting a house.

Lizann's mind returned to her father. The *Endeavour* had been late in landing, and when he came home he complained of pains in his chest and shoulders. 'It's the weather,' he had moaned, as Hannah rubbed in some strong embrocation, working from his chin to his waist. 'Driving rain, running down under the collar o' my oilskins. It's nae much wonder I've got rheumatics.'

Lizann suspected that it was more than rheumatics – he had been at sea since he was thirteen and should be accustomed to soakings – but she had kept her fears to herself. It would have been better, however, if she had voiced them to her mother; it might have prepared Hannah for what was to come.

On Sunday, Willie Alec hunched morosely in front of the fire all day. He had no appetite and took only a few cups of tea, but when Hannah said, after she and Lizann had eaten supper, that he should miss a trip to give his rheumatics a chance to get better, he growled, 'You ken I canna afford to miss any trips.'

Willie Alec went to bed early. When he appeared on Monday morning Lizann was alarmed at the blueness in the grey of his face and at how deep his eyes were sunk in his cheeks. He sat down at the table, waving away the plate Hannah set in front of him. 'I couldna eat anything. The top o' my stomach feels like there's a lump o' lead in it.'

'It'll be indigestion,' she said, already on her way to get the baking soda out of the press. 'Something you've ate on the boat hadna agreed wi' you.' She hadn't even opened the poke of soda when he said, 'Och, I'm going to be sick.' His hand to his mouth, he scraped back his chair and hurried outside.

'That's the first time he's ever been sick,' Hannah

observed in some concern, 'in all the time I've ken't him. I hope it's nothing serious.'

Lizann tried to allay her anxiety. 'He'll be all right when he's got rid of whatever's upset his stomach.'

'Aye, I suppose so.' Reassured, Hannah finished her porridge. Willie Alec had been a rock for her to lean on all their married life and she couldn't imagine him letting her down by being ill.

But Lizann did not feel easy, and when some ten minutes had elapsed, she said, 'He's a long time. Maybe I should go and see if he's . . .'

'I'll go. He'll not want you to see him spewing.'

Hannah had only been gone for a second when a prolonged eerie scream made Lizann rush outside. She drew in a sharp breath when she saw her mother kneeling on the ground, still screaming, with her hand under Willie Alec's head. He was lying absolutely motionless, and when Lizann put her finger on his pulse, there wasn't even a hint of a beat. As she had suspected, the pains he had complained of hadn't been rheumatism; they must have come from his heart.

She stood paralysed for a moment, then knowing that she would have to do something, she tried to pull her mother to her feet, but Hannah clung on to her husband, refusing to believe that he was gone from her.

To Lizann's relief, Jake Berry from next door came out to see who was making such a din. He took in the situation at a glance. Hoisting Hannah up, he ordered Lizann to take her inside. 'I'll go and see if young Joe Rennie's at hame,' he went on. 'He'll help me to carry your father into the house, and then I'll send him for the doctor. You'll need him to gi'e you the death certificate.'

'Thanks, Jake,' she murmured as she led her mother away.

Hannah sat down meekly, her eyes dull, her hands twitching, but when the two men took in her husband she started to scream again, reaching such a pitch that Lizann felt like screaming at her to stop. Willie Alec now in his own bed, Joe went to tell the doctor, but Jake, knowing that Lizann was being driven crazy by the noise her mother was making, went across to Hannah and, without a word, gave her a resounding slap on the side of her face.

'I'm sorry,' he said to Lizann, 'but it's the only way to stop her.'

'Aye,' she nodded. She couldn't have done it, but it had certainly been effective.

'Will you be all right now?' Jake asked. 'Or will I send Babsie in?'

'No, we'll be fine.' She didn't want outsiders around her. She wished that George and Mick were at home, but the *Dawn Rose* had sailed early this morning and wouldn't be back till Friday or Saturday. Then, like a welcome surge of heat in a chilled room, she remembered the only other person her mother would want to see, and turned to Jake again. 'Would you go for my Auntie Lou?'

'Aye, that's a good idea, lass. Rannas Place, isn't it?'

When he left, Hannah whispered, 'I aye thought I'd lose your father to the sea.'

'You should be glad he was at home,' Lizann said, gently, 'not with other folk.'

'He wasna wi' onybody,' Hannah gulped. 'He was out at the door wi' nae a soul near him. I should have been there for him.'

'You weren't to know.'

Her mother sat thoughtfully for a while then burst out, 'It's all that George Buchan's fault.'

Deeply wounded, Lizann said, 'How do you make that out?'

'If Willie Alec hadna wanted to make him a skipper, he wouldna have bought that boat and landed in debt. It was worrying about paying the shipyard that killed him.'

'That's not fair, Mother. Father said he'd always wanted a boat of his own. You can't blame George for that.'

'Willie Alec wouldna have bought it if it hadna been for him,' Hannah repeated stubbornly.

Lizann stopped arguing. Her mother was still in shock; she'd never say wicked things like that once she came to herself.

When Lou Flett came bustling in with Jockie – retired for four months now – at her heels, she said, 'I couldna believe Jake Berry. "Nae Willie Alec?" I says, and he says, "Aye, Willie Alec. It must have been a heart attack." So I shouted to Jockie, he was outside speaking.'

After closing the curtains, she went to her sister. 'I'd like a wee word wi' Lizann in private, Hannah, but Jockie'll bide wi' you till we come through again.' She beckoned to her niece to follow her into the tiny lobby. 'Where's your father lying?' she whispered.

'In his bed. There was nowhere else to put him.'

'Aye, that's what I thought. You'll be taking your mother to sleep wi' you the night, then?'

'I think I'd better. There's Mick's bed, but I don't like the idea of her being on her own. She's in a terrible state.'

'I could see that, though I dinna think it's sunk right in yet.'

'It has sunk in. She . . . blames George for it.' Lizann swallowed, then relayed what Hannah had said.

'Mercy on us!' Lou exclaimed. 'But Willie Alec's been saving for years to get his own boat, though he didna tell Hannah. George was just an excuse. So dinna take it to heart, lass, for she hadna meant it.'

They returned to the kitchen, where Jockie was standing uneasily at the fireside, his hands over his paunch, unable to think what to say to the bereaved woman. 'Sit down, for ony sake,' Lou ordered. 'You're just making the place look untidy.' She turned to her sister now, her voice softening. 'Jockie'll see to things for you, Hannah, but he canna go till the doctor's been.'

As if he had been waiting outside for his cue, Dr Mathieson walked in. A small, rather stout man, he had attended Hannah at her difficult confinements, but he had never been called in for other members of the family. Living locally he knew them all, and any time he had spoken to Willie Alec in the street he had thought him forthright and sensible. After telling Hannah how much the whole community would feel the loss of such a fine man, he drew Lizann aside and asked her to describe the manner of her father's death.

The preliminaries over, Lou took charge and ushered him through to see the body. 'It seems a straightforward coronary,' he announced, in a few minutes. 'All the signs were there, according to Lizann – the pain in the area of his chest, the blueness of the skin, the final sickness – and I doubt that I would have been able to avert it even if I had been called in yesterday. It's a sad business.'

'It is that,' Lou agreed, 'though I suppose you're used to it.'

'Unfortunately I meet with sudden death quite often, but I have never got used to it.' He sighed deeply, then, remembering his duty, he opened his bag and took out a pad of blank forms. Scribbling something down, he handed it to Lou. 'Whoever registers his death will need this.'

His departure left Jockie free to carry out the errands his wife had volunteered for him, to the registrar and the undertaker, and when he went out, Lou at last had the chance to tell her sister what had been decided for her. 'You'd best sleep wi' Lizann till after the frunial.'

Hannah regarded her in some surprise. 'I'll sleep in my own bed.'

'You canna sleep wi' a corpse, Hannah. Go wi' Lizann and you'll be a comfort to each other.'

'I'm nae going wi' her!' Hannah declared loudly, saying the last word with some venom. 'If she hadna taken that man here, my Willie Alec would still be alive.'

'Ach, Hannah, you dinna ken what you're saying.'

'I ken fine what I'm saying, and I'll sleep in the street before I'll sleep wi' her.'

Glancing at Lizann, whose mouth was trembling in her chalk-white face, Lou raised her shoulders helplessly. 'Would you go to Mick's bed?'

'Aye, Mick wouldna wish me ony ill.'

Lizann could stand it no longer. 'I never wished you ill, Mother, and neither did George. It wasn't his fault, it wasn't!' Her throat tight with the injustice of the accusations, her eyes hot with unshed tears, she had to stop. If she carried on she would go into a fit of hysteria, as her mother had done earlier.

Looking at her sympathetically, Lou murmured, 'Go and change Mick's bed for her, lass. I'll sleep there wi' her the night, Jockie'll nae mind, and she'll maybe have come to herself by the morn.'

It was two hours before Jockie returned. 'The undertaker canna come till the morrow,' he said sadly. 'They've other three bodies to see to, two up the town and one in Buckpool.'

'I wonder who died in Buckpool?' Lou said reflectively. 'You'll maybe ken them, Lizann.'

Lizann shook her head. She didn't care who else had died, whether she knew them or not. Her own sorrow was more than enough to cope with.

At half past four, Jockie eyed his wife hopefully. 'Ony chance o' some supper? I've had nothing to eat since breakfast time.'

'Either have we,' she said indignantly – none of them having wanted a dinner, she hadn't made anything – 'but I suppose we'll need something in our bellies to see us through all this.'

Hannah and Lizann scarcely touched the cheese pudding she made, Lou herself took only half of what she put on her plate, but Jockie scraped his clean. 'I was needing that,' he observed, giving a loud belch. His wife glared at him, but rose to pour the tea without making any comment on his lack of manners.

Even Lou felt the strain of sitting by the fire in the early evening with hardly a word being said, and it was only a quarter to eight when Jockie rose to his feet. 'It's time we went hame, Lou. You can come back the morrow if you want.'

'I'm sleeping wi' Hannah the night,' she told him.

Her sister, who had been looking vacantly into the fire for the past hour, looked up now. 'I want to be by myself.'

'I thought we agreed . . .' Lou began.

'No, you agreed,' Hannah corrected her. 'I'm going to Mick's bed, and I'm not having anybody wi' me.'

Lou bridled but stood up. 'I'll get my coat and we'll be off then.'

When Lizann saw them out, her aunt said, 'Try and get her to sleep wi' you, for I wouldna put it past her to sneak in beside your father.'

'I'll try,' Lizann sighed, 'but you heard what she said about me.'

'Aye, well, but try just the same. And if she'll nae go to your bed, you'd best lock her in Mick's room.'

'Oh, I couldn't! She'd kick up a terrible fuss.'

'It's for her own good. God kens what it would do to her if she went into the same bed as the body. It could put her out o' her mind.'

Jockie giving her sleeve a tug, she said, 'Aye, I'm coming, but mind what I said, Lizann, and try to get some sleep yourself, for you look like death warmed . . .' Her gaffe made her clap her hand over her mouth, and turning away she hurried to catch up with her husband.

Lizann went inside reluctantly. Her mother was almost

out of her mind already, and crossing her could be dangerous. But surely, if she got her own way, whatever she decided on, she would settle down. 'Do you want a cup of tea before we go to bed, Mother?' she asked.

Hannah kept her face averted. 'I want nothing from you.'

Fighting back an urge to shake her, Lizann said, 'And you're going to Mick's bed?'

'Aye, my son's bed.'

'All right, then, I'll help you up the stair.'

'Keep your hands off me!' Hannah shouted. 'I ken what you're up to. When you get me to the top, you'll shove me down so I'll break my neck.'

Shocked at this attack, Lizann watched her mother levering herself off her chair and making her unsteady way into the lobby, then, afraid that she would fall, she went upstairs behind her, but not too close in case she was accused of something else. When Hannah reached Mick's room, she scurried in and slammed the door in Lizann's face, leaving her shaking daughter sure that Lou had been right. In her present state of mind, her mother might easily sneak down to her own bed during the night. It would be safest to lock her in, whatever the consequences ... but the key was still on the inside!

Wishing that she had thought of removing it earlier, Lizann stood for a moment on the landing considering what to do. Should she chance going in for it? Her mother might go for her, though. It would be best to wait till she was asleep and wouldn't hear. Locking the door of her own room as a precaution, Lizann lay on top of her bed, prepared to jump at the slightest squeak.

Her mind went back to the morning, to her father ... to the beloved man she would never see alive again, and the tears she had been forced to keep under control for her mother's sake refused to be held back any longer. Even in her anguish, her thoughts ranged over the other events of the day, and the silence around her seemed to press in upon her, to magnify the horror of what her mother had said about her, about George.

Giving way to her grief did help, so that gradually the heaviness of the silence eased and she relaxed. Then, hearing a creak as if someone had stood on a loose floorboard, she shot off the bed to stop her mother going downstairs. But when she unlocked her own door, Mick's was still tightly shut and there was no sound from inside when she put her ear to the keyhole. It must have been the joists of the old house groaning, she thought, as they do in all old houses.

Deciding that it should be safe now to get Mick's key, she edged his door open, slid her hand round the corner and eased it out. She froze as the figure on the bed moved, but Hannah was only shifting position, and the breathy sighs she had been making in her sleep began again when she was settled. Letting her own breath out, Lizann inserted the key in the outside of the lock and turned it cautiously.

She had done it! She had actually locked her mother in, something she would never have dreamt she could do, would never have dreamt of doing . . . at a normal time, but this was anything but a normal time.

Awake early, Lizann unlocked Mick's door and put the key in her pocket in case she needed it again. She had the fire burning well and the toast ready by the time Hannah came down. 'I'm not eating anything you made!' she said viciously, and before Lizann could stop her she threw her toast into the slop pail followed by the contents of the teapot. While she waited for the kettle to boil again, she stuck a slice of bread on the prongs of the toasting fork and sat down at the fire. Everything to her liking at last, she walked over to the table, giving her daughter a wide berth as she passed.

Lizann heaved a desperate sigh. She felt bad enough

already without being treated like this, but if she said anything her mother might turn more against her.

They were still at the table, Hannah with her back to the door, when Lou came in. She raised her eyebrows at Lizann, then, satisfied by her niece's head-shake that nothing untoward had happened since she left, she came forward and addressed her sister. 'I hope you'd a good night's sleep, Hannah. How d'you feel now?'

Waiting until she had swallowed her last mouthful, Hannah said primly, as if to a complete stranger, 'I'm fine, thank you.' She collected her dirty dishes into a pile and stood up. 'I'm going to Willie Alec now.'

'You'd better go wi' her, Lizann,' Lou whispered.

But Hannah had heard. 'I don't want her!'

Her sister took her arm. 'Will you let me come wi' you, then?'

Lizann cleared the table, washed up the dishes and was sweeping the floor when Lou came back, looking completely defeated. 'I canna get her to leave him. She's demented.'

'I know that.'

The undertaker's men came at eleven, and after giving them a cup of tea when their task was over, Lou went outside with them. She was some time in coming back, her face agog with what she had just learned from Babsie Berry, who had called her over to tell her. 'D'you mind Jockie saying somebody in Buckpool had died, and all? Well, you'll never guess who it was. Bowfer Tait!'

'Peter's father?' Lizann exclaimed.

'Aye, he died awful sudden and all, in his bed ... on Peter's wedding night, poor laddie. The bobby had to get him and his bride out o' their hotel to tell him.'

Still holding a deep affection for Peter, Lizann wondered sadly how he was feeling. Her wedding night had been ruined by George being so drunk, but what had happened to Peter was much worse.

Noticing that her niece's eyes had misted, Lou said, 'You still think a lot o' him?'

'We'll always be good friends,' Lizann murmured. 'I'm awful sorry for him, and what must his poor wife have felt when . . . ?'

'That's something else Babsie tell't me,' Lou interrupted. 'A woman that was at their wedding tell't her it was a downright disgrace the road the bride carried on . . .'

'I don't want to hear,' Lizann said loudly. 'Some people say anything to cause trouble. Peter wouldn't have married her if she wasn't a decent girl, and I hope they'll be very happy together – once he gets over his father's death.'

She wished that she and Peter could comfort each other, like he had comforted her when she thought she'd lost George . . . but he didn't need her – he had a wife. It was strange, though, both their fathers dying suddenly like that, and hardly any time between them.

Jake Berry having spread word of Willie Alec's death, several people came during the afternoon to offer condolences and, as was the custom, to be taken to view the remains. They were taken aback, however, when Lou led them into the parlour, to find the widow seated by the coffin, clasping the ice-cold hands crossed over the shroud.

One old woman shook her head sadly when Lizann showed her and her friend out. 'Poor Hannah, she doesna believe Willie Alec's away. She asked him if he was warm enough.'

Her companion tutted her distaste for this. 'I've never seen onybody taking it like that before, but of course she just lived for him. It wouldna surprise me if it's her next.' Remembering that she was shaking hands with the widow's daughter, she added, in some embarrassment and only putting her foot in it further, 'I'm sorry, Lizann, I didna mean that, but she's nothing to live for now he's away, has she?'

185

Wanting to shout that she had a son and daughter to live for, Lizann merely said, 'It was an awful shock, but I'm sure she'll get over it.'

'Oh, aye, so she will, so she will.'

When she went inside, Lizann repeated what had been said, and her aunt looked at her apologetically. 'Maybe that woman wasna so wrong, at that. Your mother never had a lad before she met Willie Alec, everybody ken't that, and she fell for him hook, line and sinker. She's depended on him ever since, she's never had to stand on her own two feet, and when she does accept his death – though I'm some feared she'll never accept it – but even if she does, I've the feeling she'll go down the hill quick.'

'No, Auntie Lou,' Lizann muttered, tearfully. 'I won't let her give up and neither'll Mick.'

'Well, lass, you can try, but you can see how she is the now.' This reminded Lou that she still had to accomplish something. 'I'm going back to try to get her away from that coffin. She's been sitting there for hours and it's nae good for her.'

But once again Hannah refused to be shifted. 'If I leave him, he'll wonder where I am,' she wailed.

Lou put her hand under her sister's elbow. 'Come on, Hannah, m'dear.'

'Let go, I'm biding here.'

'You're upsetting Lizann. Think on her.'

'She's got a man to look out for her, and it's him that's to blame for . . .' Putting a hand to her mouth, Hannah stopped.

Gathering that, in her confusion, she couldn't remember what she had against her son-in-law, Lou said, gently, 'George wasna to blame for Willie Alec's death.'

Hannah looked up at her piteously. 'Death? My Willie Alec's dead?'

'Aye, Hannah, he died yesterday morning and it was nothing to do wi' George. It was a heart attack and I'm truly sorry for you, m'dear, but come ben the house now, like a good lass.'

Releasing the hands she was holding, Hannah stood up to obey her elder sister, as she had obeyed her since they were children. Lou put a finger to her lips when they went into the kitchen, and settled her charge in her usual armchair. 'I'll make another cuppie. That'll cheer you up.'

The tea cheered none of them and they sat silently, Lizann miserably aware that her mother was cringing away from her. Then she felt her aunt nudging her. 'We'd best see if her black frock's clean,' Lou whispered. She pushed Lizann ahead of her and closed the bedroom door behind them. 'I was thinking, if she wants to sleep in her own bed the night seeing it's clear now, dinna let her. It's next door to the parlour, and . . .'

'She'll not listen to anything I say,' Lizann muttered. 'She can't even bear me near her.'

'She's mixed up in her mind, and you'll need to go easy wi' her till she comes out o' it.'

'Will she ever come out of it?'

'Oh, lass, I canna tell you that. She aye took troubles a lot worse than me, she was never able to face up to them. But we'd better get out her black frock, she'll need it for the frunial.'

After supper, Lou offered to sleep with Hannah to make sure she stayed in bed, whichever room she went to, but Lizann said, 'Uncle Jockie'll be expecting you home, and I can lock her into Mick's room again. We'll be all right.'

'Well, if you're sure.' Lou stood up and put on her coat, but out at the door she gave her niece one last piece of advice. 'If she starts ony nonsense at bedtime, get Jake in. He'll carry her up the stair on his back if he has to.'

Lizann went inside with a glimmer of a smile on her face.

Almost an hour later, when she was gathering courage

to get her mother up to Mick's bed, Mick and George came in. It was so unexpected, and so welcome, that she jumped up. 'Oh, George,' she moaned, flinging herself at him, 'I'm glad you're home.'

He had to wait until her tears stopped before he could tell her why they were back early. 'A trawl skipper contacted us with a loud-hailer yesterday. Your Uncle Jockie had got somebody to radio him to ask him to pass on the message.'

'That must have been when he went to the undertaker,' she gulped. 'He never said, but it was awful good of him.'

'Anyway, Heck turned the boat and headed for home. God, Lizann, I'm sorry I wasn't here for you at the time.'

Hannah had also risen and was now encircled in Mick's arms, her eyes less vacant, but still dry as he murmured words of love and sympathy, and it was George who took over the tea-making. Hannah sat down when he handed her a cup and Mick went to Lizann. 'She looks kind of queer,' he whispered. 'Is she all right?'

'No, she's not.' Lizann told him what had happened, and ended, 'Auntie Lou thinks she shouldn't go to her own bed in case she goes through to Father in the middle of the night, but now you're back . . .'

'Let her go to my bed and I'll sleep in hers till she . . .'

They were all startled when Hannah suddenly flung the cup from her, the contents splashing over hearthrug and linoleum. 'I'm not drinking this. Not when he made it.' She pointed her finger at George.

While Lizann dried up the mess Mick made another pot of tea, and when Hannah emptied her cup he said, 'Right, Mother. Up to beddie-byes.'

Lizann couldn't believe her eyes when Hannah let him take her arm and went with him as docile as a lamb. Remembering the key in her pocket, she ran after them, and Mick nodded his understanding.

In another ten minutes, the house was in darkness –

Mick having sent Lizann and George to bed and going to the parlour himself to look at his father before he went to the adjacent bedroom.

Curled in her husband's arms, Lizann said, 'It's been awful, George, and my mother . . . I know she got a shock, but she's been so nasty . . .'

'I could see you were near the end of your tether, my darling, but try to get some sleep now.'

Knowing that Mick would attend to their mother if she kicked up any noise, Lizann closed her eyes and was asleep almost at once.

The funeral was an ordeal for all the family, although Hannah appeared quite normal to the other mourners. When the minister said prayers over the coffin, only the women were present, and the tears shed by the widow and her daughter were just what was expected. Many of the older men had been to Bowfer's funeral the day before, and looked tired and drawn as they stood in the street – this being the ritual – until they could walk behind the hearse to the kirkyard. Several skippers had returned to port early so that they and their crews could attend, for Willie Alec Jappy was well known and well respected, and most of them went back to the Yardie for the funeral tea, crowding in until there was barely room in the kitchen to take a breath.

When the grieving family was left alone at last, Hannah said rather tremulously, 'Well, he got a good send-off.'

Putting up a prayer of thanks that her mother was no longer confused, Lizann nodded. 'And they all had a good word for him. Now, is anybody ready for another cup of tea?'

Hannah frowned and looked at Mick. 'Tell her she's not to make tea for me, for I'll not drink it.'

'Ach, Mother, surely you don't think she's going to poison you?'

'I wouldna put it past her. She's ill-wished me for a while.'

'She blames me and George for Father dying,' Lizann muttered sadly.

About to round angrily on his mother, Mick thought better of it. 'I'll make the tea, then.'

Hannah was allowed to go to her own bed that night, and when she was out of the way, Mick said, 'I'm going to pay off the shipyard.'

Lizann was shocked. 'You can't afford to do that.'

'It's what Father would have wanted. He didn't want anybody saying a Jappy reneged on his debts, and surely Jones'll let me take over the monthly instalments.'

George seemed uncomfortable. 'I'd offer to help, Mick, but . . .'

'No, no! It's up to me. You've Lizann to think on.'

When George lay down beside his wife that night, he said, 'I hope you didn't think I was selfish saying I couldn't help Mick, but we'll have to get a house. We can't stay here if your mother's going to carry on like that.'

Lizann shook her head. 'I can't leave her on her own.'

'Mick'll be here at the weekends, and Lou would likely look in on her every day. We have to move, my darling, or we'll end up fighting with each other.'

She still looked doubtful. 'It maybe won't be long till she comes all right again.'

Hannah was not 'all right' even by the time Mick and George went back to sea over a week later, and when Lou heard what George had suggested, she said, 'Aye, it might be best if you got a house, Lizann. You're nae safe here wi' her, and it looks like she'll never get ony better.'

Over the next month, it seemed that Lou had predicted correctly. There was no sign of Hannah improving; in fact, there was every sign that she was deteriorating. No matter what Lizann did for her, she still acted as if she couldn't bear her daughter near her, and she was hardly civil to her son-in-law when he was at home. Lizann had clung to the hope that time would heal the rift, but George was growing so irritable with her – because of things her mother said – that when he came in on Friday 17 December and told her he'd heard a two-roomed house in Freuchny Road was vacant, she said he might as well go and ask about it.

He had already found out who was dealing with the property and went there straight away, hoping that the office was still open and praying that the house hadn't been let to someone else. The factor told him that it had just been vacated the day before. 'It's very small,' he went on, giving George the key, 'and I think you should have a look at it before committing yourself. Some folk leave an awful mess behind them, and I haven't had time to inspect it yet.'

'I don't care what state it's in,' George smiled. 'I'll take it.'

As he signed the Missive of Let he wondered if he had been a bit rash, but even if the place was filthy he was prepared to work at it until it was fit to live in. At least it was well away from the Yardie, and with Hannah's legs getting more tottery every day, she wouldn't be likely to visit. When he went to Freuchny Road, he was pleased to find both rooms immaculate. They were really tiny, the kitchen at the front opening into the bedroom at the back, but they would have to do till he could afford something bigger. Before going back to tell Lizann the good news, he ordered some second-hand furniture from the auction rooms in Blairdaff Street, to be delivered the following morning – only what was absolutely essential, and even that would have to be paid up so much a week.

Lizann had been having second thoughts about leaving her mother, but she had no option but to agree when George presented her with the fait accompli, and said she would start packing their belongings in the morning while he was taking in the furniture. Hannah had listened to everything and said nothing, but Mick went to get some boxes from the grocer. While he was out he slipped along to tell Jenny he would be busy all Saturday helping Lizann and George to flit. He came back with three tea chests and said he would get the loan of a hand-cart to take them to Freuchny Road when they were packed.

Lizann was inclined to be weepy next day. She hadn't had time to think properly, and she would be in a house up the town by nightfall, a house she hadn't even seen yet and didn't know anything about except that it just had two little rooms. She felt no guilt now at leaving the Yardie, however, for her mother had made it clear that she didn't want her here. When she packed the last of the wedding presents, she took a look around her room to make sure that nothing belonging to her had been overlooked. All that was left, apart from the furniture, was the picture on the wall and that wasn't hers either. She would have to give it back, much as it went against the grain.

She took it down and studied it. There was something in it that got to her, an atmosphere of . . . the only way she could describe it was . . . love. Whatever Hannah had felt about the artist, it was quite obvious how he had felt about her – as though there was a bond of some kind between him and this girl who was gazing forlornly out to sea. The creel slung over the shoulders made the figure seem more waif-like, emphasized a sadness that might not have been there in real life, although Hannah had hated selling fish from it. It would be sacrilege if the picture was hidden away again.

Lizann carried it down to the kitchen, where her mother, as usual, was huddled over the fire. 'Will I put this back in the lobby press, or will I leave it in the bedroom?'

Hannah turned round slowly, her eyes darkening when she saw what her daughter was holding. 'You're taking all the rest of your things,' she said harshly, 'so you'd be as well taking that and all.'

'But it's yours. Father had it done for you.'

'I didna encourage Robbie! I didna!'

This totally unexpected statement took Lizann's breath away. So there had been something between artist and model, but she would have to tread warily. 'Robbie? Was it him that drew . . . ?'

Hannah glanced desperately around her. 'Willie Alec didna notice at first, then he said onybody could see from this that Robbie loved me.'

And that was true enough, Lizann reflected; she had seen it herself. It seemed that her father had accused his wife of encouraging Robbie, so that was why the picture had been hidden away, but everybody had always said that Hannah never had eyes for any man except Willie Alec. Surely she wouldn't have . . .

Another detail came back to Lizann's mind. 'When I found the picture, you told me you were married to Father when you were posing for it?'

Hannah's hands fidgeted madly, and her eyes scanned the room as if for some source of delivery from this inquisition. 'Willie Alec told him he wanted me all to himself when he was home at the weekends.'

'So you were alone with Robbie on the other nights?' Lizann prompted.

'David wasna his! I never let him . . . I never!'

Astonished by the vehemence of her mother's outburst as much as by what she inferred, Lizann waited for further enlightenment, and sure enough, it came after a moment. 'Willie Alec thought . . . that's why I hid the picture away.'

Hannah's hands were now clutching wildly at her chest as if the memory of what had happened was too much for her to bear, and although Lizann was aching to know the whole story, she realized that, for the sake of her mother's sanity, she would be best to leave the matter alone. 'If you don't want it, can I have it?'

'Aye, take it away wi' you, for I want nothing to remind me of you.'

Deeply hurt, Lizann went back upstairs, but she couldn't stop wondering about the circumstances surrounding the making of the picture. Who was Robbie? Who was David? What had happened to them? Her mother had said David wasn't Robbie's, which would suggest that she'd had a baby that Willie Alec thought wasn't his. But where had that child gone?

Laying the picture on top of one of the crates, her heart lightened. It did belong to her now, really and truly, and because of the mystery behind its creation – she was sure love had flourished on both sides – she would treasure it as though it had been drawn by the best artist in the world. It would be a token of good luck, of enduring love, in her own home, and she would never, ever part with it . . . not for any reason!

Chapter Thirteen

❧

Standing hands on hips in the middle of their bedroom, Elsie said loudly, in what she imagined were the refined tones a draughtsman's wife should use, 'I'm fed up of your mother going on at me. If she'd just let me be I'd get things done, but she's aye at my back criticizing.'

Peter shook his head. 'I've tried telling her we'd be best to get a place of our own, but she makes me feel I'd be deserting her. I suppose I could look for a house without telling her – once we'd got it, she couldn't do anything about it.'

'She'll be laughing on the other side of her face in a wee while, any road.'

He looked at her apprehensively. 'How's that?'

'Her darling son's going to be a Daddy, that's how!'

'You mean you're . . . expecting?'

'Aye, and I'm certain sure, for I'm near three month.'

His face not registering the joy she had hoped for, Peter muttered, 'I suppose it was our first night?' Since his father's death he hadn't been quite so abandoned in his love-making.

'Our first night as man and wife,' she smirked, 'though we only got to enjoy the half of it. But we'll need more room when the bairn . . . the baby comes, so Bella Jeannie'll have to put that in her pipe and smoke it!'

'Don't say anything to her, she'll take it better coming from me. But I'll wait till I've found a house.'

After a night of passion in which Peter wondered if his wife had told him another untruth and was doing her best to make it come true, Elsie said, 'I think I'll have a long lie the day. Your mother never trusts me to make your breakfast.'

Bella Jeannie looked surprised when Peter went into the kitchen alone. 'Is she nae coming down the day?'

Rather put out because his mother never gave his wife her name, Peter said, pointedly, 'Elsie's staying in bed for a while. She's tired.'

The corners of his mother's mouth went down. 'Who does she think she is, Lady Muck?'

It was after ten before Elsie rose, and when she went into the kitchen Bella Jeannie looked her up and down with a sarcastic sneer. 'I'd better nae say good morning, for it's near afternoon. What was you up to last night? You look right washed out, and so did my Peter.'

'Your Peter?' Elsie screeched, this possessiveness being what annoyed her most. 'He's my Peter now, you old fleabag!'

She lifted her hand menacingly and, thinking her daughter-in-law was about to strike her, Bella Jeannie stepped back. 'You impudent besom! Wait till I tell my Peter you was going to hit me.'

'Shut your fat face!' Elsie shouted, no longer bothering to put on an act. 'I wasna going to hit you, though you bloody well asked for it.'

'You're man mad, that's what you are!' Bella Jeannie declared loudly, the old grudge resurfacing as she laid down the heavy ornament she had been dusting. 'Walking about wi' your bum wiggling to get men to look at you, and ony man would have done you, so why did you pick on my Peter?'

Almost frothing at the mouth, Elsie shouted, 'Peter couldna keep his hands off me before we was wed – it was only me having in a Dutch cap that stopped him bairning me.'

Apoplectic with rage, Bella Jeannie roared, 'You'd needed a Dutch cap for all the other men you'd been wi'!'

Realizing that she was up against a much tougher opponent than she had bargained for, Elsie made herself scarce, but as she walked towards the town she realized that she had quite enjoyed crossing swords with her mother-in-law. It might be fun to needle her for a while yet before she flung her pregnancy in the old bitch's face. That would floor her!

Lizann looked round her tiny kitchen with satisfaction, smiling as she recalled George's compliment when he left the morning before. 'You've worked a miracle on this place,' he had said, and it was true. Even with second-hand moquette armchairs that weren't a pair, and a table that didn't match the sideboard or the four chairs that were supposed to be part of the 'dining suite', she had made it presentable. The well-worn mats weren't so cosy as the clootie rugs her father used to make, but they were better than the bare linoleum the previous tenants had left. It would have been nice to have a few cushions and more china ornaments – the two on the sideboard had been wedding presents – but she hoped to pick up some things cheap when the shops had their sales.

Trying to imagine what would look best on the mantel-piece, her eyes were caught by the picture which held pride of place on the fireplace wall. Everyone who came to see her admired it, but she had not told one single person who the fisher girl was, for she could still remem-ber the rejection she had felt at the time she was told to take it. Until then she'd believed that there would come a day when her mother would forget all her imagined grievances, but that last sneering remark had shown that nothing would ever change. She had left the Yardie that Saturday afternoon with Mick pushing the hand-cart, her head held high, but, knowing she would never be wel-comed back, her legs had felt like tubes of rubber with lead weights at the ends. Luckily there had been so much to do when they reached Freuchny Road that she had soon snapped out of her depression.

When George went back to sea on the Monday morning she had arranged her things on the shelves of the kitchen cupboard to her satisfaction, and Lou had called in the evening to tell her that Hannah was speaking about putting Willie Alec's clothes to the Seamen's Mission.

'I see you've got her picture,' she observed then. 'I'd forgot about it.'

Hopefully, Lizann asked, 'D'you know who drew it?'

'He was a great chum o' your father's . . . eh, what was his name again?'

'Robbie something,' Lizann ventured.

'That's it! Robbie Chapman!'

'And who was David?'

'David? I canna think on a . . .' Lou broke off suddenly. 'How did you find out about that?'

'Mother said David wasn't Robbie's, and I guessed . . .'

'There was nothing in it, Lizann, I'm sure o' that. David come between Mick and you, but he didna live, poor thing, and your father took it in his head that the bairn was Robbie's. He tell't him never to come back, and as far as I ken, he left Buckie and never did come back. I thought Willie Alec made Hannah throw out the picture, but she musta kept it.'

Lou stopped to consider this, then said, 'I canna get ower her telling you, though. It shows she's far from right. You'd be best to keep away for a while, and you're not to worry about her, for I'll go every day and give her a hand with her housework, and I'll tell you when I think she's ready to see you.'

Apparently that time hadn't come yet, Lizann reflected, for a visit had never been mentioned again.

Although Elsie and Bella Jeannie kept up a battle of words which neither ever won, they were extra polite to each other in front of Peter. He was lulled into assuming that they had accepted each other and were prepared to live in harmony, whereas they were happy to be living in disharmony, girding up their loins for another head-on attack. If he had been more observant he might have picked up the signs of a storm brewing, but, being a peaceful man, he was slow in recognizing aggression in others.

He encouraged his wife, who still showed no outward indication of being pregnant, to take things easy. 'There's no need for you to get up,' he always told her when he left for work. 'My mother's quite happy to make my breakfast.'

Elsie wallowed in his consideration for her. It was good to be treated like an invalid, though she had never felt better in her life. But time was getting short. If it wasn't for the firm corsets she had bought to keep her bulge under control, her delicate state (that was a laugh) would be common knowledge. She wouldn't manage to keep it hidden much longer, though, and today would be as good as any to ram it down her mother-in-law's throat – once she'd had a decent rest.

It was wearing on for half past eleven when she emerged from her bedroom in a clinging satin wrap that showed more than she realized, and Bella Jeannie, having just made her bed, appeared on the landing at the same time. She gave her son's wife her usual disapproving stare, then said triumphantly, 'So I was right!'

Elsie moved a lock of bleached hair nonchalantly out of her eye. 'You think you're right about everything, but what is it this time?'

'I ken't fine you was wi' a bairn!'

'So? I've the right, haven't I?'

Bella Jeannie fixed her with a glower that would have shrivelled up a lesser mortal. 'Oh aye, you've the right, but there was nae need for you to hide it if it's my Peter's.'

'Your Peter? Your Peter?' Elsie screeched, annoyed that she had lost the upper hand. 'He's been my Peter for the past six month!'

'I still say it's nae his. My Peter wouldna land his wife wi' a bairn so quick . . .' she broke off to assess the evidence. 'By God! You're six month gone, ony road, by the look o' you! It is a wedding-night bairn!'

Elsie seized this opening to take her revenge. 'Aye, just think on it, Bella Jeannie! Peter was putting it inside me when your man was drawing his last breath, and every time you think about Bowfer you'll picture that. And it was about the sixth time he was on me, for your precious son's nae ony different from other men . . .'

'Well, you should ken!' Bella Jeannie was so incensed – as much at herself for being unable to think of anything better to say at what Elsie had just said – that she turned away and started down the stairs.

'You dinna like being bested,' Elsie sneered, close behind her as she clumped down step by step. 'But I'll tell you this, you great fat lump, it's me that's cock o' the walk here. If I asked my Peter to put you out, he wouldna think twice about it.'

Almost missing her footing on the second last tread, Bella Jeannie had to hold on to the banister to reach the lobby. She wanted to argue, to say it would be the other way round, but her heart was thumping in her mouth and she couldn't utter a word.

Pressing home her advantage, Elsie taunted, 'He doesna care a docken for you now he's got me, but you needna worry. I'll nae be asking him to put you out, though once we shift into our ain hoose, he'll never come back here to see you.'

In an effort to calm herself when they went into the kitchen, Bella Jeannie flopped awkwardly down on one of the armchairs but, misjudging her distance from it, she landed on the edge of the seat. Her sixteen stone weight made the back legs shoot up in the air and she was pitched forward, unfortunately striking her head on the corner of the table with full force before she hit the floor.

Elsie had been grinning at her enemy's humiliation, but when she saw the blood spurting from the woman's temple she rushed to help her up; it proved impossible to lift her. She stood for some minutes wondering what to do, while the dark red pool on the floor grew larger and larger. At last, forgetting her deshabille, she ran screaming out of the house and narrowly missed bumping into a tall youth going past with his father. 'Help me! Help me!' she begged.

'What's up, lass?' the man asked, taking her arm.

Recognizing him, she cried, 'Tom, Bella Jeannie's had an accident!'

They helped her back inside, and when Tom Fyfe saw the old woman, he exclaimed, 'God Almighty! She's been bleeding like a stuck pig!' He knelt down and felt for a pulse, then looked up at Elsie. 'She's gone.'

'Oh, God!' she moaned. 'That's what I was feared for.'

Having often heard the two women arguing when he'd passed the house, he asked, a little sharply, 'How did it happen?'

'She missed the seat and ... fell on the corner of the table. What'll I do, Tom?'

Her explanation held the ring of truth, and fitted in with the gouge he could see on the old woman's head. 'The first thing would be to get the doctor,' he said gently. 'And somebody'll have to tell Peter. Look lass, I was going up the town any road, so ...'

'Don't leave me here myself,' she wailed.

'No, no, I'll leave Lenny wi' you. I've some other things to do, so Peter'll likely be here before I get back.'

When Tom went out Elsie started to shake again and,

not knowing what else to do, fifteen-year-old Lenny put his arms round her and held her close. 'It's all right,' he murmured, patting her shoulder.

Young as he was, her uncorseted body excited him, and he soon let her go, his smooth face red with embarrassment, but she was still too shocked to notice.

It was much later, all the formalities having been carried out and the funeral arranged, and lying in bed with a husband too upset to give her the loving she needed, before Elsie recalled the scene and realized that Lenny had been aroused by holding her. Her dulled spirits lifted. With Bella Jeannie gone, she would be lonely when Peter was out at work, and she was sure Lenny Fyfe wouldn't refuse if she asked him in to keep her company now and again. He was a good-looking laddie, with dark hair and skin to match, and Peter was asking for it, for he had never once told her he loved her and only made love when she set herself out to fire him with her body – sometimes not even then. Besides, it would be great fun to show the virgin Lenny the facts of life.

Another six months had passed, and Lizann was sitting at her fireside waiting for her aunt's nightly visit. After that one rally, when Hannah had disposed of Willie Alec's clothes, Lou said she had gone back into her shell and wouldn't speak about him or her daughter. All her reports since then had been the same, and Lizann was convinced that she would never see her mother again.

Glancing at the clock, she started in surprise. Lou usually came about ten to seven, and it was after eight already. What had happened that she was so late? Lizann got to her feet meaning to go and find out, but her aunt walked in at that moment, her eyes snapping with excitement.

'I've ran near all the road,' she puffed, 'for I'm dying to tell you.'

Lizann sat down, her heart palpitating at the thought of hearing good news for a change. 'Has Mother . . . ?' she began, hopefully.

'I was coming away,' Lou interrupted, 'and she come to the door wi' me and Peter Tait was going past and he says, proud as a peacock, "Would you ladies like to come and see my son? He was six weeks old on Monday." I didna think she'd go, she hasna been outside the door since your Da died, but she says, "Let me put on my coat," and then he took her arm for she was a bittie wobbly, and oh, Lizann, what a bonnie bairn it is. Peter, after him, though they're calling him Pattie to save a mix-up.'

'I'm pleased for him. It'll make up for losing his mother, but it's a shame Bella Jeannie didn't live to see her grandson.'

Lou gave her a peculiar look, but went on, 'If Bella Jeannie was alive she'd die o' shock if she saw her house the day. She never bothered much about herself, but she aye kept her house clean and tidy.'

'It must be difficult when there's a baby,' Lizann pointed out.

'It wasna just untidy, it was . . . filthy! And that madam sitting wi' a fag at the corner o' her mouth, and her hair bleached, and that much lipstick on she looked like she'd cut her face. Oh, Lizann, you've nae idea! And you could see right through her goonie!'

Thankful that her aunt couldn't see the filmy night-dresses she wore, Lizann said, 'She hadn't been expecting visitors so late.'

'It was only suppertime, so it had been for Peter, and him turning turkey red at the sight o' her. I'm sure he could hardly wait for us to leave so he could put another bairn inside her.'

'Ach, you're imagining things, Auntie Lou.'

'Your mother said the same when we came out. But

she was fair taken wi' the infant, and I thought . . . if you and George was to . . .'

'You think a grandchild would stop her hating us?'

'There's only one road to find out,' Lou grinned, 'and it wouldna be ony hardship to you, would it?'

Colouring, Lizann said, 'I don't think George wants a baby yet.'

'Keep at him, Lizann. Doll yourself up like that Elsie, that'll put him in the mood. I wish I'd persevered wi' my Jockie, but he wasna that way inclined, worse luck. He liked his sleep ower much, still does, the lazy devil.' Lou gave a deep sigh. 'Hannah didna ken how lucky she was wi' Willie Alec, for he wasna like that. I shouldna be telling you this, but I used to fancy him myself, and me wed on Jockie by the time him and Hannah was courting. Well, well, I'd best be off.'

Her aunt left Lizann something to think about. Would a grandchild make her mother change her attitude? Surely it was worth trying?

Smoothing her skin-tight jumper over her breasts, Elsie looked at her reflection in the wardrobe mirror. Her figure was nearly back to what it used to be, and here she was, away again. She'd hated her body when she was carrying Pattie, though Peter had loved running his hands over her belly and waiting for the infant to move. That had always got her going, though nothing she did had made him touch her anywhere else, which is why Lenny Fyfe had been such a godsend. He was serving his time as a baker now, working from two in the morning till ten, and she'd caught him on his way home the first time. He'd been shy and embarrassed that day, but he'd learnt real quick. He'd been so hot for her, he'd come in every forenoon for a week and she'd had to tell him folk would start speaking if they saw him. So he'd made it Tuesdays and Thursdays till she grew too big, and he'd stopped till after

Pattie was born. And now, with a second damned bairn on the road, she'd only have about four or five more months with him.

If Peter would just kittle himself up a bit, take her every night like he used to, she wouldn't need anybody else, but he still hadn't got over his mother's death. She hadn't told him about the fight she'd had with the old bitch, though. She'd told him the same as she told Tom Fyfe and she hadn't needed to pretend to be shocked; she'd never been so shaken in all her life.

The wailing of her son brought Elsie's musings to an abrupt stop, and she turned round impatiently to pick him up and give him his bottle.

As always, Peter took a look at his son as soon as he went in from work. 'He's the bonniest baby I've ever seen,' he beamed.

Elsie rushed across to kiss him. 'Hannah Jappy must think that, and all, for she was in again the day to see him.'

Peter had a feeling that there was more to Hannah's interest than met the eye. If Lizann hadn't married George Buchan, Pattie might have been Hannah's grandson, and that could be how she thought of him. Once again, the old aching for his lost love pulled at him, and he tried to keep his voice steady as he said, 'Poor Hannah, she must be lonely.'

Ladling soup into a big plate, Elsie said, 'If she's needing a bairn to look after, she can have this next one for all I care.'

'Next one? You're not expecting again, are you? Already?'

'It's your fault!'

'It takes two.' He was angry at himself as much as at her. He should be able to withstand the temptation of her curves. He did, occasionally, but there were times when they drove him frantic with desire.

205

'If you're too proud to buy French letters,' she was sneering, 'I'll have to get something, for I've no intentions of calving every year.'

Shocked at her choice of word, Peter gave a nervous smile. 'We needn't worry now till after you've had this one.'

'Hannah was saying you and her Lizann was engaged at one time.'

'Not for long. I broke it off.'

'That's not what Hannah said.'

'She's blethering,' Peter burst out, feeling guilty at the lie. 'She's been turned in the head since Willie Alec died.'

'I'd like to know why she put Lizann out.'

'It was nothing to do with me!' At least that was the truth, Peter told himself, though he had often wondered about it himself. Mick had just shrugged when he asked, as if he didn't know either.

Elsie couldn't let the subject drop. 'Did her and you ever . . . ?'

'I never touched Lizann, if that's what you're getting at.' That, too, was the truth. 'You're not jealous of her?'

Elsie gave a scornful laugh. 'Jealous? What needs I be jealous, when you come straight home from the yard every night and never go out again?'

Mick having once casually referred to Lizann being at Freuchny Road, Peter had often thought of going to see her on his way home – George Buchan was only there at the weekends – but he was thankful now that he hadn't given in to his longing to know how she was. Elsie would have torn him limb from limb if she'd found out.

Sitting on George's knee at the fireside, Lizann murmured, 'Lou thinks we should have a baby.'

'Does she now? And what business is it of hers?' But he was smiling.

'She thinks a grandchild would make my mother come round to us.'

'We're happy enough the way we are, aren't we?'

'I'm happy when you're at home,' she assured him. 'It's just, when I'm on my own, I often wish I could go to see her.'

His face sobered. 'Maybe you should, it's . . . how long now? Ten months? I'll go with you the morrow, if you want.'

'I'd rather go myself the first time. I'll wait till you're away.'

'Suit yourself, but I'll tell you this, Lizann, when I want to make a baby it'll be for us, not your mother. I want to enjoy you for a while longer without an infant coming between us.'

She wished he hadn't added the last bit, but had to admit that it was good having him all to herself. She turned round and kissed him. 'I love you, George.'

'And I love you. If I ever lost you, I wouldn't want to live.'

'Life's got to go on, whatever happens,' she whispered, thinking of her mother, 'but if I lost you . . . the night the Hannah went down . . .'

'Forget about that, my darling. Lightning never strikes twice in the same place, and my turn's past.' He was about to pick her up and carry her through to bed when someone knocked on the door. 'Damn!' he growled, as she stood up. 'Who on earth could that be?'

'It's either Mick or Auntie Lou,' she said, making sure that her skirt was straight before she answered the summons.

It was her brother and his girlfriend. 'We haven't come at a bad time, have we?' he grinned.

Conscious of her mussed hair and hot cheeks, Lizann glanced at Jenny, who always looked as if she'd stepped out of a bandbox. Her beautiful chestnut tresses were swept up on top of her head, with not one single strand out of place ... but her grey eyes were apologetic. 'No,' Lizann said hastily. 'We were just sitting speaking ...'

'Canoodling, more like,' Mick teased.

George grinned. 'Sit down, we've all our lives to canoodle.'

'Is anything wrong with Mother?' Lizann asked, anxiously.

'No, she's still the same,' Mick told her. 'Some days you'd think she was back to normal, then the next day she's looking out of the window for Father coming along the road.'

'Do you know if she's eating properly?'

'When I'm there she does, and she says Lou makes her suppers when I'm away, though she likely doesn't cook anything for her dinners. But Jenny often takes her in something.'

'Oh,' Lizann exclaimed delightedly, 'that's good of you, Jenny.'

The girl looked flustered. 'I went to see her one day on my road home from the town, and she was so embarrassed at not having biscuits to give me with the cup of tea, I started baking scones and things for her.'

'That's why we're here,' Mick explained. 'Jenny would like the recipe for your sponge cake. She didn't like to ask you herself.'

'You shouldn't be shy with me, Jenny,' Lizann scolded, gently. 'You know me well enough by this time, surely? I'll let you write it out.'

The two women went to the table with paper and pencil, and George sat down next to Mick. 'Are you two thinking of getting wed?' he teased. 'Is that why Jenny's after recipes?'

Mick pulled a face. 'I wish we could, but I've nothing to offer her. It's taking me all my time to make the payments to the yard and give Mother enough to keep her going. And there's Jenny's folk. They're poor things, the pair of them, and I couldn't take her away. They need what she takes in from her sewing.'

'Could you not marry her and move in there?'

'They haven't room, and what about my own mother? No, George, I've puzzled and puzzled, but it's hopeless.'

'How long before you clear the debt to the yard?'

'Near two year yet, but even when it's paid up, I could hardly keep a wife and two houses going.'

'Aye,' George sighed, 'you've got a problem. I wish I could help you, but I'm still paying up our furniture.'

'I wouldn't take anything from you, any road.'

When the recipe had been written out Lizann looked round, and seeing her husband and brother deep in conversation, she murmured, 'I've been thinking on going to see my mother when George goes away. Will she want to see me, do you think?'

Jenny considered for a moment. 'It might be easier if I came with you. She wouldn't kick up a fuss in front of me.'

'That's a good idea! George wanted to come, but he'd be like a red rag to a bull to her. When could you manage?'

'What about Sunday afternoon? Mick's promised to paint old Jack Hay's shed – he was on the *Silver Star* with your father and him at one time, and he's retired now and bent with arthritis – and I heard George saying he'd give him a hand.'

'That's fine, and we won't tell them.'

Having arranged to meet Jenny at two o'clock, Lizann tapped gently on the door of her old home on Sunday afternoon, but when her mother opened it, her face went stony. 'Oh, it's you.'

Jenny stepped forward. 'And me, Hannah,' she said, brightly.

Obviously in a quandary as to whether to welcome them or shut the door in their faces, it took some seconds for Hannah to mutter, 'Come in.'

'How are you, Mother?' Lizann had decided not to ask for forgiveness, because she had done nothing that needed to be forgiven.

'I'm fine ... and you're looking well.'

Lizann was relieved that her mother was actually speaking directly to her. 'I am well. George and me are very happy.'

'You should see their house, Hannah,' Jenny put in. 'It's really nice inside.'

'We haven't much,' Lizann smiled, 'but you're welcome to visit us.'

Hannah's eyes hooded. 'I never go outside my own door nowadays.'

'Auntie Lou said you sometimes went to see Peter Tait's baby.'

'Lou has nae business carrying tales.'

'She was pleased you'd been going out, and she always comes to let me know how you're doing.'

'I don't know how I'd have managed if it hadna been for her ... and for Jenny here. She's been like a daughter to me.'

This was too much for Lizann. 'You could still have your own daughter if you hadn't ...' She broke off. It would do more harm than good to drag it all up again.

Hannah's brow wrinkled in perplexity, and Jenny said quickly, 'Will I make some tea for you, Hannah? So you and Lizann can speak?'

As Jenny moved to get the teapot, Lizann said softly, 'I want us to be friends, Mother. I'd like to come and see you now and then.'

'Nobody's stopping you.' Hannah's fingers were meshing and unmeshing as if she had no control over them. 'I never put you out.'

As good as, Lizann thought, but the situation was too delicate to say it aloud. 'Can I come once a week, then?'

'If you want.'

'I do want. Oh, Mother, I've missed you.' Tears hovered on Lizann's eyelashes and she held out her hands in appeal.

Unable to stand by and see the woman hurt her daughter again, Jenny gave her a gentle prod from behind. 'Go on, Hannah. You need her as much as she needs you.'

'I don't need her,' Hannah said, stubbornly, but her eyes were moist.

'You do,' Jenny cried. 'I know you do, if you'd just admit it.'

Spotting a tear starting to run down her mother's cheek, Lizann jumped up and ran round the table. 'I'm sorry,' she gulped, enfolding the frail body in her arms. 'It's not true what you thought of me, but I'm sorry, just the same. I would never have done anything to hurt you, you should know that.'

Still sitting ramrod straight, Hannah sniffed, 'Willie Alec's gone.'

'I know, and I'm sorry about that, too, but it wasn't my fault, nor George's. Please, Mother, say you don't blame us any longer.'

Her back suddenly caving in, Hannah burst into tears. 'Was that what I was blaming you for? I couldna mind, I just ken't it was something bad.'

Lizann, also sobbing now, squeezed her shoulders affectionately. 'We didn't do anything bad, but I suppose you were so upset you had to blame somebody.'

'I'll have to tell Willie Alec I was wrong about you.'

Gasping at this, Lizann looked up at Jenny, who shook her head. 'You can see she's still not right,' she whispered. 'Now, go and sit down and I'll pour the tea.'

She produced half of the sponge cake she had made that morning from Lizann's recipe, and Hannah accepted the slice she was given. Lizann, however, was too distressed by her mother's lapse to eat anything.

When they were leaving, Hannah said, 'You'll come back, Lizann?'

'Yes, Mother, I'll come back.'

'And bring your man wi' you . . .' She looked at Jenny now. 'And you'll come back, and all?'

'As often as I can.'

Knowing that she was standing watching them, neither of them dared to speak until they were out of her sight. 'I'd better come home with you,' Jenny said then. 'I can see you're awful upset.'

Lizann nodded tearfully, unable to trust herself to say anything.

She had recovered slightly by the time they reached Freuchny Road, and with George and Mick still out they discussed the visit. 'It could've been a lot worse,' Jenny consoled. 'She wasn't as bad as I've seen her.'

Lizann sighed deeply. 'I thought she'd got over it. Was it seeing me that made her get muddled again?'

'No, she's up and down and sometimes I don't know how to take her. But she asked you back, don't forget.'

'Will she remember, though? She might turn on me the next time I go.'

'I think she's seen sense about that, but the brain's a funny thing.'

This did not make Lizann feel any more confident about going again, though she knew what Jenny meant. 'Why don't you come and see me more often?' she asked. 'You don't need to wait for Mick to take you, I'd be glad to see you any time.' It would be good to have a friend to talk to when George wasn't there, she thought.

'I didn't like to come without being invited.'

Lizann managed to smile. 'You've a standing invitation now. Any time you're up to the shops, come in for a cup of tea. And thanks for coming with me today. It would have been a lot worse if you hadn't been there.' She paused, then said, 'I'm not going to tell George I went, not till I see how things go the next time.'

'I won't say anything to Mick either, then.'

While she was doing her housework on Monday, Lizann's thoughts turned to her visit to the Yardie. It had been going so well at first, awkward but not really difficult, and with the reconciliation, she had thought her mother had regained her senses . . . till she began speaking as if her dead husband was still alive. That showed she wasn't clear in her mind yet, nothing like it. Maybe she never would be, but her daughter would do everything she could to help . . . if she was allowed to.

Chapter Fourteen

❦

The cold snap at the beginning of 1938 had had a devastating effect on more than one family in Buckpool. Several old people succumbed to it, including Jenny Cowie's parents who died within a week of each other. Fortunately, Mick had been at home on both occasions and was a great comfort to her, but after the second funeral, which had cleaned out her father's meagre savings, he told her he still couldn't afford to marry her. 'We'll have to wait till after I finish paying the shipyard,' he said, regretfully.

'But we'd be living here, and I could keep on with my sewing . . .'

'I'm not having my wife working, and there's my mother to think on.'

'She's got Lizann and your auntie.'

'Lou's getting on, she's five years older than Mother.'

Jenny gave a deep sigh. 'I don't think you want to marry me at all.'

He gripped her shoulders. 'Don't say that, Jenny. I've wanted to marry you since we started going steady, that's how long I've been saving, but it's been one damned thing after another. First I'd to buy new gear when the *Hannah* went down, and then having to pay the yard . . .'

'You didn't need to take that on,' Jenny muttered. 'The insurance folk would surely have settled what was still owing . . .'

'Father didn't have her insured, worse luck, and I'd to ask Jones to reduce the instalments, so it's going to take a while to clear.'

'I could sell my house,' Jenny offered. 'If I gave you what I get for it, that should be enough to pay off . . .'

'I can't let you do that!' Mick declared. 'I took in hand to settle it myself and I'll settle it! Any road, where would you bide if you sold this house?'

'If you'd marry me, I'd come to the Yardie as your wife, and I'd look after your mother.'

Mick was tempted, but like his father he was fiercely proud of his integrity. 'I don't want folk thinking I'd to depend on you for money.'

'You're as thrawn as an old mule,' she burst out. 'I should look for somebody else and stop wasting my time with you.'

'Oh, Jen,' he pleaded, 'don't do that. You know I love you, and if you loved me you'd wait.'

'Aye,' she sighed, 'that's just it. I do love you, Mick Jappy, and I don't want anybody else. I'll wait, for as long as you want.'

Lizann went to see her mother every forenoon now, even at the weekends, though George didn't come with her every time he was home; sometimes he went to see his own mother, but not very often. The first time they'd gone to the Yardie together had been worrying; Hannah had eyed him with suspicion as if she wondered why she didn't feel easy with him. Lizann had been afraid that she might cast up his divorce, or throw out the old accusation that Willie Alec's death had been his fault, but she had held out her hand after a moment and said, 'So you're Lizann's man? I'm real pleased to meet you.'

George had looked hurt because she hadn't remembered him, and Lizann had frowned to let him know not to say anything, so he shook hands and the confrontation she feared was averted. She herself had learned to take every day as it came, cleaning the house and cooking little treats for her mother to encourage her to eat more, and only occasionally did Hannah speak as if Willie Alec might walk in. Lizann would always humour her. 'There's enough dinner for him,' or 'I'll make him something when he comes.' That satisfied Hannah and, her thoughts having no continuity, she reverted to speaking about Mick or praising Jenny, who looked in most days, or pondering over some gossip Lou had given her.

Only once had a delicate subject been touched upon. 'Peter Tait's got two right bonnie bairnies,' Hannah had said, looking speculatively at her daughter. 'There's nae sign o' you starting a family?'

Lizann hadn't been sure at the time and had shaken her head, but she had good news today: between Christmas and Hogmanay, or maybe into 1939, her mother would get the grandchild she longed for.

Hannah looked up from her armchair when she went in. 'The kettle's boiling.'

Her senses sharpened by the anticipation of what she was going to say, Lizann noticed with dismay that her mother's eyes were dull and sunken, her cheeks hollow, her brow rutted with deep furrows. And she was so thin that anyone who didn't know better would think she'd been starved.

Feeling a rush of pity for her, Lizann took a few minutes to make the tea and get everything ready, then pushed the breadboard across the table. 'Have a bit of the teabread I took in. You could do with being fattened up a bit.'

She was pleased when her mother took a slice and spread it thickly with butter. 'You and Lou's a pair,' Hannah snorted. 'She's aye saying I'm wasting away to a shadow.'

'So you are.' Lizann waited until her mother's plate was empty before she ventured, 'Mother, d'you remember asking when I was to be starting a family? Well, I'm due at the end of the year, so you'll be a granny.'

Hannah's proud smile was followed by intense bewilderment. 'But me and Willie Alec's got two grandsons already . . .'

Her spirits plummeting, Lizann said cautiously, 'No, you haven't any grandchildren, Mother. You must be thinking about Peter's two boys.'

'But Peter's your man, isn't he?'

'No, I'm married to George, and this'll be our first baby, though I haven't told him yet.'

'George? George Buchan? Him that . . .' Hannah halted, screwing up her face in her effort to remember. 'He did something bad to your father.'

'George has never done anything bad to anybody!' Lizann couldn't stop her voice from rising. 'He's good and kind and . . .'

'He'd another wife before you, though.'

Having often wished that her mother would regain her memory properly, Lizann wished now that she hadn't remembered so much. But she would soon forget again, and it was wisest to ignore her last remark. 'Do you want me to change your bed this morning?'

Hannah's face cleared. 'Aye, there's a good drying wind.'

No further reference was made to either George or Peter, and when Lou turned up in the late afternoon Lizann said, 'I'll leave you to take in the washing, Auntie Lou. I'll do the ironing the morrow.'

Her aunt went to the door with her. 'You look a bittie upset. What's she been saying to you?'

Lizann didn't want to speak about it. 'Just the usual.'

'About Willie Alec? I some think she'll never be right about that. Are you expecting George back the night?'

'He's due home, though I never know exactly when.'

'Take a day off the morrow, it's time you'd a rest. I'll come and see to your mother after I've had my breakfast.'

'Thanks, Auntie Lou, it'll be good to have a whole day

at home with George. Not that he ever says anything about me coming here, but . . .'

'He's a good man. Nae like some that like to be waited on hand and foot . . . my Jockie, for one.' Lou went inside laughing.

When George came in that evening, Lizann didn't mention her mother's flash of remembrance. She had something better to tell him.

She waited until supper was finished and they were both seated at the fire, but he forestalled her. 'You look kind of peaky. What's wrong?'

'Not a thing,' she assured him, wondering how he would take her news. 'Except . . .'

'I knew there was something. Is it your mother?'

'Well . . .' Lizann hesitated, then, not considering it a peculiar way of telling him, she murmured, 'She's going to be a grandmother.'

He looked puzzled. 'She's going to be a . . . ?' When her meaning struck him, he gasped, 'We're having a baby?'

His awestruck face didn't tell her what he thought. 'At the end of the year. Are you angry?' she asked, timidly.

'Angry?' With an exuberant whoop he jumped up, lifted her from her chair and whirled her round. 'Anything but! I'm pleased . . . more than pleased. I'm delirious!' Setting her down, he kissed her until she had to struggle for air.

'I wasn't sure if you wanted a baby.'

'I wasn't sure if we could afford to feed an extra mouth.'

She gave a shy smile. 'I'll be feeding it myself for the first eight or nine months.'

He patted her stomach gently. 'I can't get over it! I'm responsible for the little being that's in there.' He kissed her again. 'Oh, Lizann, it's wonderful, and I don't care if it's a boy or a girl.'

'Just as well,' she smiled. 'We'll have to take what comes.'

He sat down again and pulled her on to his knee. 'You'd better take things easy, though, for I don't want anything to go wrong. Stop going to your mother every day, one house is enough for you to keep clean.'

'But I can't leave her to do everything. She's not fit.'

'Lou'll help her.'

'Lou has enough to do. Anyway, I'll not have to take it easy till nearer the time.'

'Promise me you'll stop when it gets too much for you.'

'I promise. I'll stop when I get too big to bend.'

'And no lifting anything heavy.'

'No lifting anything heavy.' She laughed at his over-protection.

Leaning back, he gave a sigh of contentment. 'A little Buchan!'

'A wee George?'

'Or another Lizann?' he grinned.

'What if it's twins?'

'Like you said, we'll have to take what comes. God, I love you.'

Her heart full, she pulled his head down and kissed him. 'This is only the start of our family.'

'One'll do for a while, till we see how we manage.'

'We'll manage however many we have.'

Saturday being a lovely May day, they took a walk in the afternoon, and as they strolled arm in arm along the open road – the green grass of the verges brightened by the pink of campions, the yellow of buttercups, the blue of forget-me-nots, the white of the Stars of Bethlehem and a host of other wild flowers – George looked across at the herd of cows grazing at one end of a huge field and laughed. 'They're daft, aren't they? All that space and they crowd into one wee corner.' He slipped his arm round his wife's waist, hugging her closely and kissing her before letting her go again. 'This is heaven. It's so peaceful, and just the two of us . . .'

'And the cows,' she giggled. Two had already poked their heads over the paling beside them, and the rest were ambling up, too, curious to know what was going on.

As she pulled some grass and held it out to the nearest animal, George gave a sigh of pleasure. 'When the baby comes, we'll be taking it out in the pram and letting it see all this . . . I can hardly wait.'

'You'll have to,' Lizann smiled, 'for seven months, and I'll grow fat and horrible before that, and waddle about like a . . .'

'As long as I can get my arms round you . . .' he teased.

'Maybe I'll get so big they won't go round me.'

'I won't care, I'll still love you. I'm just sorry it's you that's got to put up with all the pain and discomfort.'

'You can't have the baby for me,' she chuckled.

On Sunday, despite her protests that he didn't need to bother, George insisted on accompanying her to the Yardie in the afternoon. 'How are you this fine day?' he asked Hannah breezily when they went in.

'Not too bad,' she replied, smiling sweetly at him.

'Will I chop some kindling for you?'

'Aye, if you wouldna mind.'

Hannah turned to her daughter when he went out. 'He's a good man. Does he ken you're expecting?'

Surprised that she had remembered, Lizann nodded. 'Aye, I told him on Friday night, and he's delighted.'

'So he should be, you've waited long enough.'

Lizann looked round the kitchen. 'Where's the ironing?'

'Lou did it yesterday.' As she watched Lizann swilling the teapot and putting in three heaped caddy-spoonfuls of tea, she said, 'Would you get me some wool the morrow, so I can knit some things for the bairnie? I'm tired doing nothing. I'm getting so I can hardly move about at all.'

'You're not strong enough to be moving about much.' Lizann had noticed how spindly and weak her mother's legs were. 'Righto, I'll buy wool on my road here in the morning. Now, I'd better go out and see if George wants a flycup.'

When she asked him, he said, 'No thanks, I'll just carry on with this. Your mother's failing, isn't she?'

'She couldn't manage without somebody helping her.'

'I can see that, but mind what I said. No tiring yourself.'

After washing up the two dirty cups and saucers, and knowing that her mother wouldn't let her do any housework on the Sabbath, Lizann opened the cupboard. 'What's for supper? I'd better start cooking it.'

'Lou made a pot o' soup yesterday wi' a big bit o' rolled mutton. We can have it sliced cold.'

'I'll pare some tatties, then,' Lizann smiled, filling the basin with cold water.

Hannah said nothing for some time, then she observed, 'I'm surprised Willie Alec's nae hame yet, but he's likely went somewhere wi' Mick.'

'Aye, likely.'

Another five minutes elapsed before Hannah spoke again. 'Ach, you must think I'm off my head, Lizann. I ken fine your father died, but I canna stop thinking he's still alive.'

Not knowing what to say, Lizann murmured, 'It's only natural, Mother.'

'I get awful muddled sometimes, and my mind goes back to the days he was here. We was that happy, Lizann, and we never had a fight. Little arguments, but nae a real fight.'

'I know that, but you'd be better to forget the old days if thinking about them makes you muddled.'

'That's what Lou says, and all, but her and you dinna ken what it's like to lose your man.'

Her eyes were so strange that a shiver passed over Lizann's heart. It was almost as though her mother could foresee some terrible tragedy in store for either her or her aunt, and crossing her fingers she prayed it would involve her uncle, not her husband. She was instantly shocked at her own selfishness, for Lou must love Jockie, though surely not as much as she loved George.

Supper was ready by the time Mick came in, and when Lizann told him that George had made enough kindling to last for weeks, he winked to his mother. 'So he's taking over my jobs now?' Hannah's expression made him add, with a laugh to show he wasn't displeased, 'About time, too.' Then he turned to his sister. 'I'll manage to attend to our supper if you two want to get off home.'

'Good man,' George beamed, rising to his feet and clapping him on the shoulder. 'Before we go, I'll give you a surprise. You're going to be an uncle. What d'you say to that?'

'Uncle Mick? By God, that's something, right enough. How do you feel about being a grandma, Mother?'

'It's old news to me, Mick, for I was tell't first. I just wish your father was still alive. He'd have been fair proud.'

His eyebrows shooting up, Mick said nothing until he went to the door with Lizann and her husband. 'Was I hearing things? Was Mother really admitting Father's dead?'

Lizann nodded. 'I think she's accepted it now . . . if she doesn't slide back again.'

On the way home, George said, 'And she didn't blame me for anything, thank goodness. I feel like a free man.'

'She said you were a good man.'

'Praise be! We should have made this baby months ago.'

'I told you that.' She couldn't resist saying it.

The hot August was making Hannah more irritable than usual, yet she persisted in hugging the fire, which had to be kept burning to boil the kettle for the many cups of tea she needed, as well as for cooking. The heat also made Lizann feel her pregnancy more of a burden than it should be, and when her mother complained one day, 'The sweat's just hailing aff me,' she snapped, 'If you'd shift to the couch, you wouldn't sweat so much. It's daft sitting half up the lum.'

Hannah turned on her angrily. 'Ho! So I'm daft now, am I? I dinna need to put up with cheek from you, so just you go hame and . . .'

'I'm sorry, Mother, but you would feel cooler on the couch. Come on, and I'll help you over to it.'

'Leave me be! You needna think you can boss me about now you've got a man to make a fuss of you. You never carried on like this when you were engaged to Peter!'

Lizann swallowed the retort she felt like making. George was too busy listening to the wireless or reading in the papers about what Hitler and his troops were doing to pay much attention to her these days, and Jenny said Mick was the same. Goodness knows why they were so interested in the man everybody said was mad.

Mick and his girlfriend visited Freuchny Road every Sunday evening now, the two young women being left to sit and chat while the men went into a huddle, their faces grave, their voices low, and it wasn't until Neville Chamberlain returned from the Munich conference at the end of September waving a piece of paper and declaring 'Peace in our time!' that George told his wife about the rumours of war which had been circulating for some time. 'It's all right now, though,' he grinned. 'Our Prime Minister got Hitler and Mussolini and the French – Daladier, I think his name is – to sign a pact, so there'll be no war.

Germany's been given a bit of Czechoslovakia as a ... well, to keep him sweet.'

Lizann was put completely at ease by this, not realizing – as so many other people did not realize – that this bribe to Hitler was to have the effect of encouraging further German aggression.

A very cold spell had started at the end of October, and as Lizann made her way home one dark night at the beginning of November she had to watch her step, the roads were so slippery. Just one wrong move, she thought, as she strained her eyes to see where to put her feet, and she could land flat on her back. It wouldn't be her first fall on ice, but it would be a disaster with her confinement so near. Reaching Freuchny Road in safety, she let herself into her house with fingers scarcely able to grasp the doorkey, then, about to take off her coat and muffler, she decided to keep them on. It would be a waste lighting the fire when it was after seven already, and she could do with an early night.

While she waited for the kettle to boil for a cup of tea to heat her, she made up her mind to tell her mother tomorrow that she'd have to stop coming for a while. George had been right when he left last time – she shouldn't be trailing there every day. She'd felt quite queer ever since she got up this morning, and if anything happened to the baby he would never forgive her. Besides, she was quite worried that she hadn't felt it moving for a while, though when she'd mentioned it to Babsie Berry, the old woman had said, 'It often happens late on. I'm sure the bairnies have a wee rest afore they've to make their way out into the world.'

The tea poured, she sat with her hands round the cup until the feeling came back to her fingers, then draining it quickly, she went through to the bedroom, the only other room there was. It too was bitterly cold, so she wasted no time in getting into bed, wishing that she could afford to buy a winceyette nightgown, but with rent to pay, food to buy and all the other things she needed, there was nothing left at the end of each week. She couldn't get warm whatever she did, for the linen sheets – a wedding present from George's mother – were as cold as charity.

She had been in bed for over an hour, unable to sleep because of the chill seeping right into her bones, when a thunderous knocking made her sit up in alarm. At the next assault she jumped out of bed and pulled on her coat to go and see who was at her door; when she beheld Mick, his face white and his eyes starting out of his head, she was sure she knew why he had come.

He barged right in, and she closed the door to keep out the wintry blast. 'Is it Mother?' she asked anxiously.

Giving a loud groan, he gathered her in his arms. 'No, Lizann, it's worse than that. Oh God, I wish I didn't have to tell you.'

'Tell me what? Oh, Mick, what's happened?'

'It's George! We were on our way back to port, and . . . the sea was that rough it was coming right over the bows, and he was walking from the wheelhouse . . .'

The pause made her cry out, 'Tell me, Mick, tell me!'

'I can hardly bear to say it. You see, another wave came up and took him over the side.'

'Is he hurt? Is he badly injured?'

Dissolving into tears, Mick burst out, 'We couldn't see any sign of him! We couldn't save him! Oh, Lizann, we did everything we could. We circled round and round for hours, but he never surfaced. I'm sorry, I'm sorry!'

His arms tightened round her, and although she hadn't yet taken it in properly, she had the feeling that if he hadn't been holding her up her legs would have buckled under her. Great sobs were shaking his body, and she automatically stroked his head for a few moments before she was struck by the awful realization of why he was crying. With the cramping of her stomach in grief, she screamed, 'Not George! Not my George!'

'I'm sorry!' Mick repeated. 'I wish to God it had been me!'

Their tears bonding their cheeks together, they stood for some minutes holding each other as if afraid to let go, then, to her further horror, Lizann recognized the down-bearing pains of childbirth. 'Oh, Mick,' she gasped, 'I think the baby's coming!'

He released her so abruptly that she reeled back and he had to grab her arms to save her from falling. 'Oh Christ!' he groaned. 'The shock must have brought it on.'

She tried to keep calm, but her eyes were pleading and her voice shook as she said, 'You'll have to help me, Mick, there's no time to get the midwife.'

He looked at her helplessly. 'You'll have to tell me what to do.'

She stared back at him, equally helplessly. 'I don't know myself.'

In an effort to reassure her he said the first thing that occurred to him. 'You'll have to take off that coat, and I'd better boil the kettle. We'll need a lot of hot water.' He didn't know why, but he had heard it somewhere and it sounded efficient.

Already shivering with dread at what she would have to go through, she murmured, 'I'll have to go back to bed, I suppose, so you'd better light the fire through there.'

As he went into the bedroom, another fierce pain made her moan, but thankfully it didn't last long. Unbuttoning her coat, she looked down at her swollen belly, the skin stretched taut across it, and suddenly felt embarrassed that her brother would see it through her old nightie. But what did it matter? He was going to see a lot worse than that before he was done. She sat down to wait until he had the small fire going in the other room, fighting against the lump of sorrow for her husband that was obstructing her throat. She had to keep up – she couldn't lose the baby . . . as well as George.

'That's it burning,' Mick announced, when he came in again. 'Will you manage to walk through?'

Putting a hand under her elbow, he helped her out of the chair and kept hold of her while she waddled towards the connecting door. His face turned scarlet when her coat flapped back, and, trying to make a joke of it, she said, 'I'd look like a woman in a brothel if it wasn't for this lump.' He didn't laugh, and she wished that she hadn't said it. 'Oh, I forgot!' she exclaimed. 'You'd better put the rubber sheet on the bed first. It's in the press.'

As he turned away, she gasped and doubled up in a pain so excruciating that she thought she would die, a pain that wouldn't stop, a pain that told her the baby was not going to wait a minute longer.

Her screams made Mick rush back to her. 'Are you all right, Lizann?'

'I . . . can't go any farther . . . put my coat down on the floor.'

Horror-stricken as he realized what she meant to happen, he removed the garment and spread it on the linoleum and, still screaming, she put out her hand for him to help her down on it. 'I could carry you to your bed,' he muttered, but she shook her head and pulled her nightdress up around her waist. This lack of modesty proved to him beyond doubt that the birth was taking place there and then, and not knowing what else to do, he hunkered down in front of her.

Her previous screams had alarmed him, but the sounds issuing from her now made his hair stand on end – long unearthly howls between the loud animal grunts she gave each time she bore down. Beads of perspiration were pouring down her face, and he whipped out his handkerchief to wipe them away, glad that he could do this at least for her.

Her tortured eyes showed her gratitude before they closed to make one more push, her body heaving as she roared out in agony, and her bare feet were suddenly drenched with the breaking of her waters. Sure that she could do no more by herself, she issued some instructions, the words coming out in guttural, staccato jerks. 'When you . . . see the head . . . ease it out.'

In a daze, Mick slid his hands between her legs and put his fingers round the slimy roundness he could feel. Before he could do anything, however, Lizann made one final, superhuman effort and the baby plopped out in a rush of blood and mucus, the cord twisted around its neck.

Mick leaned over it in an attempt to prevent her from seeing it, but she pushed him away and looked down on the purple face of her dead son.

Chapter Fifteen

Waiting for his sister to come round again, Mick's thoughts returned to the trauma, and marvel, of a human birth. He would never have believed the agony a woman had to go through if he had not taken part in the event itself and what followed. He'd had to force himself to do what was needed and it would stay in his memory for ever. His first instinct, when Lizann fell back unconscious, had been to lift her and carry her through to her bed, but he was faced with a problem – the lifeless infant was still attached to her. Not daring to cut the cord in case he did some damage to her, he had tugged gently but insistently to try and free it. To his surprise, something else came out, and only then did he recall having read somewhere that there was an afterbirth. He had searched for some towels to staunch the blood, and with three stuffed between her thighs took her to the bedroom, his mind set on seeing that she came through her ordeal.

Twenty minutes later she had opened her eyes and looked at him for a few seconds before drifting away again. Afraid that she was giving up he had watched her anxiously over the past hour, but thank God, her breathing remained steady.

When she began to move again he leaned forward and stroked her brow. She was fully conscious this time and stared up at him piteously. 'Oh, Mick, tell me it's not true . . . about George.'

He would have given his own life to be able to reassure her, but he had to say, 'Lizann, I'm sorry, but it's true, right enough.'

For the next two hours he sat on the edge of the bed, holding her as she moaned and wept, tears in his own eyes and a hollowness in his heart that was almost beyond endurance. 'If only the baby could have lived,' she hiccupped, at last. 'It was part of George, and now I've nothing left – nobody!'

Completely out of his depth, Mick murmured, 'You've got me, Lizann . . . and Mother. She'll always need you.'

'It's not the same.' She buried her face on his shoulder, and though they'd always been close he was stunned by the depth of his love and compassion for her at that moment.

When she asked him to tell her again how George had been lost, he went over it with her, reluctantly, but more lucidly than he had done the night before. When he finished tears were brimming in her dark, sunken eyes. 'D'you think he suffered at all?'

'Don't think about it, Lizann. If you go on like this, you'll never get better.'

'I don't want to live, any road. What have I got to live for?'

'Oh, don't say that, little sister.'

The old endearment was intended to comfort her, but succeeded only in making tears flood out again; he watched her hopelessly. What could anybody say that would console her for losing the husband she'd had to fight so hard to get, the husband she'd had for so short a time?

When she recovered she said, 'I'm sorry.'

'I understand,' he whispered, taking her hand and stroking it. 'I know how I'd feel if anything happened to Jenny.'

'Mick,' she gulped, 'will you make me some tea, please?'

'Surely.' He was glad to be asked to do something, for it was feeling so useless that got him down.

When he went into the kitchen he almost tripped over something and took a moment to remember what had been left lying there. Making his way carefully to the gas ring at the fireside, he struck a match and lit the mantle in the lamp at the side of the mantelpiece. When he turned round, a grisly sight met his eyes, even worse than it had been the night before – or maybe it just appeared that way because he was no longer in shock. Looking at the dead infant lying amongst the debris of the birth on the blood-soaked coat, he couldn't help shuddering, and he was about to bundle it all up when it occurred to him that Lizann's doctor should see it first . . . and take a look at her, too.

When he took through her tea he said, 'Will you be all right if I go and tell the doctor to come?'

He swept aside her protests that she didn't need a doctor, and being told that she was still with Dr Mathieson, he went out. At quarter past seven on a November morning it was still dark, and the sleety rain made him pull up the collar of his jacket and hold his head down. Turning out of Freuchny Road he nearly bumped into someone coming along Commercial Road. 'Peter!' he exclaimed, the familiar face going a little way to lighten the black despair that had descended on him.

'What's up, Mick? You look a bit rattled.'

'If you knew what I've been through . . .' He broke off, for he couldn't bring himself to describe it. 'I'm going to get the doctor for Lizann.'

Peter's eyes darkened with concern. 'Has something gone wrong? Is her baby coming early?'

'I haven't time to speak. Can you walk along a bit with me?'

'I was on my way to work, but . . . ach well.' Peter turned about. 'Now, what's up?'

'What's not up would be more like it,' Mick sighed. 'You'll not have heard, of course.' He gave an account of what had happened to George and went on, 'The skipper said it would be best if I broke the news to Lizann, and it's a good thing it was me that went, for when I told her, she lost the baby.'

'When you were there?'

'I'd to do the needful, and I haven't got over it yet. She's in an awful state, but the doctor'll have to see the ... and I'll ask him to check on her.'

Peter was on the point of saying that he would fetch the doctor when a better idea occurred to him. 'Would it be any help if I went to her, so she's not on her own?'

'It would be a godsend, but what about your work?'

'I was early, and anyway, they'll manage without me for a while.'

'Thanks, Peter, I'll not forget this.'

Changing direction again, Peter hurried to Freuchny Road and knocked at the door before going in. Averting his eyes from the gruesome mess in the kitchen, he called, 'It's Peter, Lizann. Can I come in?'

He was in her bedroom before she could answer, and although she pulled the blankets up around her bare shoulders in embarrassment, he was sure she was pleased to see him. 'I met Mick,' he explained, 'and I said I'd keep you company till he comes back. I'm sorry, Lizann, really I am ... about George ... and the baby.'

Forgetting her deshabille now, she held out her arms. 'Oh, Peter!'

Kneeling by the bed, he held her tightly, her grief his only concern, because he had never wished George Buchan any ill.

'You don't know how much I loved him,' she sobbed.

'I think I do.'

'You're so good to me,' she gulped and lifted her head to kiss his cheek. 'I don't deserve it after what I did to you.'

'I'll always be your friend. You know that, don't you?'

'Thanks, Peter.'

When Mick came back he hesitated in the doorway, frowning at the sight of his newly widowed sister in the arms of the man who had once been her fiancé. Neither of them looked guilty, though, and as Lizann lay back and covered herself she said, 'I needed somebody, Mick.'

Her brother's face cleared. 'The doctor said he'll come as soon as he can, and we'd better not keep Peter any longer. He's half an hour late for his work already.'

Standing up, Peter said, 'Aye, I'll have to go, but is it all right if I come back to see you?'

'You don't need to worry about me. I'll be fine.'

At the street door, Peter looked apologetically at Mick. 'Whatever you thought when you came in, you were wrong. She wanted me to hold her, and that's all there was to it.'

Recalling how she had needed him to hold her earlier, Mick said, 'Aye, I can believe that. I did tell you she was in an awful state.'

'I still love her, Mick,' Peter admitted, softly.

'I was some feared for that.'

'But if I come back, it'll just be as a friend. I promise you that.'

'She'll need all the friends she can get now, but you've your wife and bairns to think on.'

'Aye, how could I forget?' Peter turned and walked away.

Returning to his sister, Mick said, 'I went to tell Jenny, as well as the doctor, and she'll be coming to see you.'

'Did you tell Mother and all?'

'No, I thought I'd better wait.'

When Jenny arrived she ordered Mick to go home. 'I've nobody to worry about now,' she went on, 'so I can stay with Lizann till she's on her feet. Hannah'll need you.'

Dr Mathieson came in shortly after this, and she stayed in the kitchen to let him examine his patient. 'She's very weak,' he reported in a few minutes. 'She's had two bad shocks, and it will take her whole system a long time to recover. Are you to be staying here with her?' At Jenny's nod, he continued, 'Good. If she is left alone, she could fall into a deep depression, which in turn ... well, just keep a careful eye on her. Now, go through to her until I attend to things here.'

After making a thorough inspection of the still-born infant and the other remnants, he called Jenny through again. 'The birth will have to be registered even if ...' He paused, his mouth screwing up. 'The father has been lost, of course, but I can explain all the circumstances to the registrar. What name shall I give the child? William, after her father?'

'That's fine.'

Dr Mathieson having taken everything away in the blood-saturated coat, Jenny cleaned the kitchen floor and organized the supper, keeping up a loud one-sided conversation to let Lizann know she hadn't forgotten her. When she went through to the bedroom and saw her charge lying with her face to the wall, clearly not wanting to speak, she sat down in the chair, ready to give solace when it was needed.

Mick had been in the house for some time before he plucked up courage to tell his mother anything. With his mind occupied by the sad mission he had to carry out, he had come off the boat the night before without even waiting for a fry of fish, so he had bought some mince on his way from Freuchny Road. Hannah talked to him quite sensibly while he made it ready, and ate a good plateful, but now, with the table cleared and the kitchen tidied, he could procrastinate no longer.

'You're awful quiet, Mick,' Hannah said suddenly.

'What's bothering you? Is something wrong wi' Lizann? She didna come the day.'

'Will you promise not to get upset if I tell you?'

Her eyes narrowed with apprehension. 'I'll try not to.'

'Oh, God!' he groaned. 'I can't whitewash it for you. You see, George Buchan was washed overboard yesterday.'

'Lizann's man? Oh, poor soul, she'll be awful . . .'

'I'd to go and tell her, and she . . . lost the baby.'

'Oh, my dear Lord! Oh, if only I could go to her.'

'I was with her all night, and Jenny's there now.'

'It's me should be wi' her, but I'm hardly fit to walk nowadays.'

'She knows you can't go, and Jenny'll look after her.'

After several minutes of silence, Hannah said, 'I blamed George for your father dying, you ken. I said it was his fault for making him buy that boat, when naebody could've made Willie Alec do anything he didna want to do.'

Mick was taken aback by what she was admitting, but he hoped that, as seemed likely, this second shock had cleared his mother's brain of the confusion she'd been labouring under. 'Don't blame yourself, Mother,' he soothed. 'You haven't been . . . yourself for a long time, and Lizann'll be pleased you're better.'

'When you go back to see her, tell her how sorry I am, about George and the poor wee bairnie . . . and for the things I said to her and her man. Oh, and tell her nae to worry about me. Lou'll see to me.'

Marvelling at the change in her, Mick just nodded.

When Peter arrived home, Elsie said, 'Did you know Lizann Jappy's man's been drowned?'

He decided to be completely honest. 'I met Mick on my way to work, and he told me . . . and she lost her baby, as well. He was going for the doctor so I said I'd go and sit with her till he came back.'

Elsie's top lip curled. 'Oh, aye? Playing Santy Claus, was you?'

'I did what any friend would've done.'

'You must have been a lot more than friends when you was engaged.'

Scowling, he retorted, 'I loved her, but I was never her lover!'

'Pull the other one,' she sneered. 'This one's got bells on.'

'Look, Elsie, I didn't need to tell you I'd been to see her, but I didn't want to keep it secret from you.'

'In case you was found out? And I suppose you'd been cuddling her and whispering sweet nothings in her ear?'

'I did try to comfort her. Poor Lizann, she was nearly out of her mind and I . . .'

'Poor Lizann my backside!' Elsie snapped, forgetting all her pseudo-refinement. 'Nae content wi' one man, she kept you dangling on the end o' a string, and all. You needna think I didna ken.'

'You're a callous bitch!' he shouted. 'She only wanted George Buchan, and now she's lost him, and their baby! Have you no pity for her?'

'For the woman my man's been lusting after for years? I'm nae blind, Peter Tait. You look like a love-sick young laddie when anybody speaks about her. I wouldna be surprised if you wed me to make her jealous!'

This was too much for him. 'I went out with you to make her jealous, but I married you because you said you were expecting my child.'

'Oh, aye, I forgot. But you wasna long in putting a real bairn inside me, was you? And starting Tommy just weeks after Pattie was born.'

Wanting to hurt her now, he yelled, 'What did you

expect, the way you sat about with everything you had on show?'

She smirked now. 'That was the way to get you going, wasn't it? One look at my paps and your tongue was hanging out.'

'That's disgusting!'

'It's true, though. I could twist you round my little finger any time I want, nae like your prim fancy woman.'

Peter's face flamed with guilty shame. Elsie could set him ablaze with an animal lust, no matter what he thought of her as a woman. She was an addiction, while what he had always felt for Lizann was reverent love.

'That made you think,' she crowed now. 'I'm right, amn't I?'

'Aye, you're right,' he sighed. 'You're like a drug I can't give up.'

In the evening Jenny sat down again by the bedside and, thinking that Lizann looked slightly brighter, she said, 'I believe you'd Peter Tait seeing you this morning?'

'Peter's another good friend.'

'More than a friend at one time? You got engaged to him.'

'That was . . . before George came back to me.'

Lizann's lips had started to quiver, so Jenny changed the subject. 'I meant to ask you before, where do you keep your spare blankets?'

Lizann looked surprised. 'What d'you want blankets for?'

'I'm going to make a bed on the two easy chairs in the kitchen.'

'There's no need for that, you can sleep with me.'

'Are you sure?'

'Quite sure.'

When Jenny finally went to bed, she was so tired that she fell asleep almost at once, and Lizann lay wide awake beside her, thinking about George and the plans they had made for the baby. Then she recalled her premonition on the day her mother had looked so queer. She had been sure that something awful was going to happen, but she hadn't foreseen this double tragedy, husband and child both gone. Not wanting to disturb Jenny by giving way to her grief again, she bit on her bottom lip, but the tears still edged out and rolled down her cheeks.

She would never see George again. There would be no more love-making, no more babies. It was goodbye to the family she had planned to start, goodbye to all her dreams.

She was too distraught to realize that without a husband, there would be no money coming into the house, either. That worry was still to come.

Chapter Sixteen

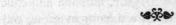

Heck Lindsay appeared the following day, and although
Lizann was not really up to receiving visitors, Jenny
showed him into the bedroom in case he had something
important to say. A short, stout, florid man, George's
skipper stood at the foot of the bed twirling his flat cap
in his hands.

'I'm devilish sorry, Missus Buchan, it was a terrible
thing to happen, and the other lassie said you lost the
baby, and all. I ken it doesna help, like, but for what it's
worth, you've my deepest sympathy, for he was a fine
man. I wouldna intrude on you, but ... well, George
would have been due ...' He paused before ending
uncomfortably, 'The thing is, I didna even cover my
expenses this trip seeing we'd to turn back so early ...'

Having told the widow a deliberate lie – they had come
back because the catch was so poor – his lined, weatherbeaten face took on a redder tinge. Then, clearing his
throat as well as his embarrassment, he went on, 'I
thought you'd be needing some cash, so here's something,
for ... compensation, like.' He laid an envelope down
on the bed. 'What would you like done wi' his seabag?'

Unable to speak, Lizann shook her head helplessly, and
it was Jenny who said decisively, 'Give it to Mick. She'll
maybe want to keep some of George's things.'

'Aye, of course. Well, I'll be on my way, Missus
Buchan, and I hope you'll soon be up and about again.'

When her brother brought the seabag to her, Lizann
told him to keep it and everything in it. 'You may as well
get the good of his seaboots and oilskins and ...'

'There's only a shirt and ganzy, and his spare set of underclothes,' Mick mumbled. 'He was wearing the rest when he . . .' His face scarlet, he broke off.

Frowning at him, Jenny said, 'Take it away, you've upset her.'

Lizann withdrew into her own dark world now, and for the next two days she hardly spoke to Jenny, pretending to be asleep when she heard her brother or her aunt coming in.

'Poor soul,' Lou sighed to Jenny, 'but maybe sleep's the best thing for her.'

'I'm worried about her,' Jenny confided. 'She hasn't eaten anything, yesterday or today.'

'Dinna force her. She'll eat when she feels like it.'

It didn't seem right to Jenny to let anyone keep refusing food. She said nothing when her patient left her breakfast untouched, but she couldn't hold her tongue at dinnertime. 'You'll never get your strength back if you carry on like this,' she scolded gently, when Lizann shook her head. 'Come on, try some of this lentil soup, it'll do you good.'

Lizann picked up the spoon listlessly, but after a few mouthfuls, she set it down again, her lips pursed. Wondering if she should coax her appetite with invalid foods, Jenny made scrambled eggs for supper, and was about to take through the tray when someone knocked at the door.

It was Peter Tait. 'I'm not coming in,' he said. 'I just wanted to know how Lizann is now.'

'She's not eating,' Jenny told him, sadly, then inspiration hit her. 'Would you take this through to her? She might eat it for you.'

Love for Lizann almost choked him when he saw that she looked even worse than on the morning she'd been sobbing in his arms, but he managed to joke. 'It's the waiter, Lizann, and the chef'll sack me if you don't eat every mouthful.'

A ghost of a smile touched her lips. 'Oh, Peter.' It was

all she said, but he was sure he could detect a fondness in her voice.

He stood over her until the plate was empty then moved the tray to the chest of drawers and sat down on the bed. Taking her hand, he said, 'I don't like to see you so down, my dear. You're not the Lizann we knew, so will you please try to come back to us? Please, for me?' The pressure of her fingers encouraged him. 'I know you're suffering, and you likely think you'll never get over this, but George wouldn't want you to give up. You're young, you're a lovely girl . . .'

Her eyes clouded, and he said quickly, 'I'm speaking as your friend, Lizann, but I'd better go. My wife'll be wondering why I'm late. You'll remember what I said, now?'

She nodded weakly and when he stood up, she murmured, 'Thanks, Peter, it was good of you to come.'

Jenny was delighted to see the empty plate when he took back the tray. 'You've fairly done the trick, Peter. You should be here all the time.'

Wishing that were possible, he smiled and took his leave, but on his way home he wondered if Jenny knew how he felt about Lizann . . . but she wouldn't have made that last remark if she did. He had wanted to tell Lizann herself that he still loved her, and it was only her unease when he said she was a lovely girl that had stopped him. It was also why he had mentioned his wife.

As he had expected, Elsie was angry when he went in. 'Where the hell have you been?' she demanded. 'Your supper's been ready for the past hour.'

'I'm just half an hour late,' he said, calmly. 'I went to see Lizann.'

'Again? You know I don't like you going there.'

'I'm glad I went, for she hadn't been eating. Jenny asked me to take through her supper.'

'I suppose she ate it for you.'

'She did, and not before time – she's just skin and bone.'

'You'd surely had your arms round her again to know that?'

Peter looked at her with distaste. Her face was plumper than when he first knew her, and after two children her waist had thickened. Not that either of that would have mattered if he loved her, but he didn't. He never had! 'No, Elsie,' he said, 'I didn't have my arms round her, much as I wanted to.' Her gasp gave him a small degree of pleasure.

Furious inside, Elsie tried to laugh it off. 'So you can keep your hands off her, but I bet you can't keep your hands off me.' She came forward now, her breasts swelling almost out of the low-cut nightdress she always wore for him, and with her dark-ringed nipples so close to him, he groaned hopelessly. 'No, you bitch! I can't.' He pulled her into his arms and thrust himself against her as she laughed in his face.

When Jenny had finished tidying up she went into the bedroom. 'How do you feel now?' she asked, solicitously.

'Like a washed-out clout,' Lizann sighed.

'Did Peter tire you?'

'A wee bit.'

'It'll take you a while to get over things.'

'I'll never get over them.'

'Aye will you, it just takes time.'

'I've plenty of that, then,' Lizann muttered despondently.

Next day she felt the desperate need to talk. 'If only I'd had George longer, it wouldn't be so bad. I thought we'd grow old together and have sons and daughters to look after us, and now . . . I can understand why my mother turned funny after Father . . .'

'You're made of different stuff from Hannah,' Jenny declared. 'She depended on Willie Alec for everything,

242

but you've always had a mind of your own. You had to fight to marry George, and then you were tied down seeing to her.'

'George and me were never free to enjoy our marriage,' Lizann agreed. 'I used to wish she was dead, sometimes, so we could do what we liked. You'll be thinking I'm terrible, saying that, but I couldn't help it. I pictured us going for walks with our children, a wee George and another Lizann, watching them growing up . . .' Her voice broke.

'Don't upset yourself, Lizann. It's better not to think on what might have been and concentrate on what's going to be.' Jenny stopped and gave a little smile. 'Ach, I sound like one of yon old wives.'

'No, you're a true friend, Jenny,' Lizann said, earnestly. 'And it's true, I can't turn the clock back.'

Noticing the increasing pallor in her cheeks, Jenny stood up. 'I've made you speak too much.'

The following morning Lizann said she felt like getting up, and so, relieved that she was improving, Jenny let her sit in the kitchen for half an hour, but the recovery did not last. She was moody all the next day, and wouldn't move when Jenny told her she should try being up for a little longer.

Determined not to let her relapse, Jenny sat down by her bed after supper. 'Lizann,' she began firmly, 'I think the time's come for a bit of straight talking. The longer you lie in that bed, the worse you'll get, till you'll be like your mother, with legs that weak you'll not be able to walk at all.' Noticing that Lizann's eyes had filled with tears of self-pity, she hardened her heart and continued, 'I'm telling you for your own good, so you'll dress yourself tomorrow and come through for your breakfast, and if you feel tired you can have a rest in the afternoon. You're not an invalid now.'

The 'straight talking' worked; in another week Lizann

was staying up all day and, although she was rather shaky on her legs and exhausted by bedtime, she had her mind set on being left on her own. 'I'll manage to look after myself,' she told Jenny, 'so you'd better go back to your own house. It must be inches thick with dust by this time.'

Not very happy about it, Jenny went home to Main Street, but asked Lou Flett to call in on Lizann every night on the pretext of reporting on Hannah, as she had done while mother and daughter were estranged.

On her first day alone, Lizann was still in bed when she heard someone knocking on the outside door and walking straight in. Supposing it was Jenny come to check on her, she wished she'd remembered to turn the key in the lock the night before, and turned round to defend herself for not being up at half past nine. But it wasn't her ex-nurse/housekeeper.

'Mrs Buchan!' she gasped, her already white face blanching even more, her hand flying to her mouth in guilt, for she hadn't given George's mother a single thought.

'Aye,' the woman said grimly. 'It's a good thing I've got friends, or I wouldna have ken't my son was lost.'

'Oh, I'm sorry, but I . . .'

'I'd have thought it was the first thing you'd have done, but . . . ach, I ken't the minute I set eyes on you, you was bad luck. Well, are you to be lying there a' day, or will I have to make myself a cup o' tea?'

So distressed that she hardly knew what she was doing, Lizann threw back the bedcovers and swung her feet to the floor, and it was only when she saw the expression on her mother-in-law's face that she remembered how transparent her well-worn nightdress was. Along with that awful thought came the realization that she didn't have a coat to cover it. 'Oh, Mrs Buchan,' she wailed, unable to call her anything else, 'I don't know what you must think, but I . . .'

'I'll tell you what I think,' Ina Buchan sneered. 'If I'd ever wore a goon like that, my man woulda thought I was a whore. He wouldna have had nothing to do wi' me, but the young men nowadays are different, and I can see how you trapped George into leaving his wife.'

Too weak to deny the accusation, Lizann lifted her skirt off the chair and stepped into it, wondering if her legs would take her through to the kitchen, and if she'd have the strength to light the fire if they did. Ina handed her her blouse. 'Here, cover your breists, and all!' she ordered, then her obvious repugnance was replaced by perplexity as her brain registered what her eyes had seen. 'The last time George came to see me, he said you was expectin'. Did you get rid o' it, or what?'

An unexpected and totally uncharacteristic wave of anger swept through Lizann. How dare this woman speak to her like that? 'I lost the baby when I heard about George,' she said quietly, with all the dignity she could muster.

This did knock Ina Buchan out of her stride. 'Oh . . . oh . . . well,' she stammered, 'I'm sorry about that.'

'And I'm sorry you've lost your son,' Lizann went on. 'I should have asked my brother to tell you, but I was in such a state . . .' She paused to regain control of herself. 'I did love George, you know, with all my heart, and I don't think I'll ever get over losing him.'

'I lost my man to the sea, and all,' Ina said, ruminatively, 'but I never thought I'd lose George the same road.' Her hand shot out to steady Lizann, who had taken a shaky step forward. 'Look, I'd better leave you. You're ower upset, and . . . so am I. You likely think I'm nae grieving like I should, but I grat for near two whole days after I heard, though I kept thinking it couldna be George that had gone overboard, for you'd surely have had the decency to . . .' Her voice hardened again. 'Then I made up my mind to come and tell you what I thought of you.

You never come wi' George the few times he visited me . . . oh, I ken he said you'd to look after your mother, but surely you coulda . . . ?'

Recognizing that nothing she said would change her mother-in-law's opinion of her, Lizann chose to ignore this last complaint. 'I think you'd be as well leaving, Mrs Buchan,' she said firmly. 'Thank you for coming, but there's no point in us seeing each other again, for we've nothing in common now.'

Clearly not accustomed to being brushed off by anyone, Ina glowered at her. 'Some women get decent daughter-in-laws,' she muttered, 'but I havena been so lucky, though my son had two wives. Katie uptailed and left Cullen, and you . . .' Clicking her tongue in offended exasperation, she swept across the kitchen and stalked out.

It took several seconds for the reaction to set in. When it did, Lizann collapsed back on her bed, hot tears scalding her cheeks, her throat closing in sorrow and self-pity, and it was over half an hour before she resolved to tell nobody that George's mother had been there and to forget the horrible things the woman had said.

'I canna believe it,' Lou remarked to her niece, some evenings later. 'It's like there was never nothing wrong wi' your ma, and her mind's a lot clearer than mine, for I'd forget where my head was if it wasna fixed on.' Lizann giving a wan smile, Lou went on, 'You're still looking peaky, are you sure you're eating enough?'

'Yes, Mary Droppie next door gets butcher meat for me, and anything else I need.' The old woman's nickname had been bestowed on her years before for her habit of saying, 'I think we'll get a droppie rain,' which sometimes changed to, 'I'm sure we're in for a droppie snow,' or, as Lizann had lately found out, 'Will I get a droppie mince for you?'

Lou smiled. 'I'll nae need to worry about you, then.'

With a cheery wave she walked away, and Lizann closed the door and went inside. If Lou only knew how things really were, she thought. She was having to watch every penny she spent. The 'compensation' Heck Lindsay had handed over was nearly all gone already, and what would she do when there was nothing left . . . and nothing coming in? Maybe it was just as well the baby hadn't lived, for how could she have bought clothes for it? Or a pram?

Her throat tightened with remorse as she was struck by something else. She'd blamed George's death for making her lose the baby, but it must have been dead before. That was why she had felt no movements. George had pleaded with her to stop doing so much and she hadn't listened to him. She had gone on cleaning the two houses, climbing up on chairs to scrub high shelves, going down on her knees to polish floors . . . it was all her fault! But she hadn't wanted to harm the child – she had felt so well she hadn't thought that what she was doing could be bad for it. If she hadn't been so headstrong, she would have a son to compensate for her husband. She would have managed somehow. She would have worked her fingers to the bone for him.

She shook her head. She wasn't fit to look after herself, let alone a baby. She was still weaker, physically and mentally, than she cared to admit, though she'd made Jenny go home. And Mary Droppie kept telling her she wasn't eating enough to keep a mouse going, but she couldn't afford to buy any more. If she was stronger she could take a job, but the only job she'd ever had was gutting fish in Yarmouth, which was how she'd met George. Maybe some folk would say she should be thankful to have been his wife for almost three years, but it wasn't nearly long enough. Could this be God's way of punishing them for what they had done there? Putting her hands to her face and making no attempt to control herself, she wept bitter tears for all the years they should have had together.

Peter had made up his mind not to see Lizann again, but on his way home from work one night he thought there was no reason why he shouldn't go to ask how she was. They were still friends, and friends were expected to be concerned for one another's well-being.

Having hoped she would be well on the way to recovery, he was saddened to see how haggard her face was when she opened the door. Her once shiny black curls were hanging lank, and the eyes that had sparkled brightly seemed to have no life left in them. He longed to take her in his arms and beg her to let him look after her.

'It's you, Peter,' she said in a flat voice. 'You'd better come in.'

It wasn't a warm welcome, and he wished now that he hadn't given in to his whim. 'Jenny's not with you, then?' he asked.

'I made her go home.'

'You shouldn't have. You need company.'

'I don't want company.'

'You'll get over it, Lizann,' he told her, gently. 'It takes time.'

'That's what everybody says.'

An awkward silence fell, both staring into the barely-glowing embers in the fire, then Lizann murmured, 'How's your wife? And your boys?'

'They're fine. Pattie's a little devil, into everything, but Tommy's quieter. It's funny how brothers can be so different.'

'Aye, I suppose so.'

Noticing tears glistening before she turned her head away, he guessed that she was thinking of her own son, the son she had lost on the same day as she lost her husband, and his heart went out to her. Not knowing what else to say, he murmured, 'You shouldn't be on your own yet.'

Her lips lifted in a thin smile. 'I'm better on my own.'

'But you might . . . do something stupid.'

The smile faded. 'I've thought about it. What have I got to live for?'

'Everything! You're still young, you'll get your looks back and . . . I have to say it, no matter what you think, you'll find another man.'

'I could never love anybody else, and you needn't worry, Peter. I'm not going to do away with myself. If I'd only myself to worry about, I might have done it, but another bad shock might turn my mother's brain again, and I couldn't do that to her.'

'Thank God! You had me worried.'

'I think you should go now, but don't tell Mick what I said.'

He got to his feet at once. 'I won't tell anybody, but remember, if there's ever anything I can do for you, Lizann, you've only to let me know, whatever it is.'

Rising, too, she shook her head. 'There's nothing anybody can do for me, Peter, for I've lost the only man I've ever loved.'

'I know that,' he said, wryly.

When he went home, Elsie looked at him suspiciously. 'You're late!'

'I went to Freuchny Road to see Lizann, and before you start shouting, let me tell you something. If you'd seen her the night, you'd have been as sorry for her as I was. She's as far down as anybody could be, and I'll not stop seeing her, whatever you say.'

'Did she turn her dark eyes on you and bewitch you again?'

'She was like a skeleton, with her eyes sunk right into her head.'

'Would you go running if she asked you?'

'If she asked me for help, I'd go running,' he said, truthfully, 'but she won't. As for what you're meaning, my place is here with my family.'

'Aye well,' his wife smirked, 'and don't you forget it.' She snuggled up to him in her usual seductive manner, but for once – maybe because he was so anxious about Lizann – it had no effect on him. 'Get off, Elsie!' he exclaimed, shoving her away. 'Can you not leave me in peace?'

The initial surprise in her eyes became anger. 'I might have ken't!' she shouted. 'You've laid your fancy woman the night! You've aye hoped you'd get her, that's why you've kept going there, and now you've had her, you dinna want me!'

Something in Peter snapped. 'Have you no sense, woman?' he bellowed. 'She's not in a fit state for anything, and I've never had her, tonight or any other night. But I love her so much I'd lay down my life for her if I thought it would help, and I can't even tell her, for she still loves George Buchan!'

Taken completely aback by his outburst, Elsie stared at him with her mouth gaping, then, snapping it shut, she flounced away. He sat down, head in hands, appalled at what he had said in his fury. She would do her best to get back at him, and he'd be wise to stay away from Lizann ... for a while, at any rate, until Elsie cooled down.

As usual, Mick went to see his sister when he came off the boat and was dismayed at the change in her. She had looked a bit better the last time he'd been, and now she was as bad as ever. 'Are you sure you're eating properly?' he demanded.

Nearly at her wits' end as to how to keep going, Lizann burst out, 'I haven't any money left.' Not having meant to let him know, she clapped her hand over her mouth, but the damage was done.

'I thought the skipper gave you compensation,' Mick gasped.

'Just five pounds, and it's all gone.'

'Five pounds? Was that all? The hungry bugger! To hear him, folk would think he'd lashed out a hundred.'

'Don't say anything to him, Mick,' she pleaded. 'I shouldn't have told you. It's not your worry.'

'It is my worry, though I likely wouldn't get any more out of him if I did tell him what I thought of him.'

'I'll get by. I'll think of something.'

'Like what?' he said, harshly. 'You'll not be able to work for a long time yet, and I can't let my little sister starve.' Hesitating, Mick did a quick mental calculation. 'I'll give you something every week to let you get some decent food.'

'I can't let you do that!'

'You can and you will! I'll only manage ten bob, will that do? Just till you get your health back.'

Although Mick was not taking her other expenses into account – rent, coal, gas, cleaning materials – Lizann said gratefully, 'It's plenty, but I wish you wouldn't.'

He stuck his hand into his trouser pocket then handed her a crumpled ten shilling note, which she accepted reluctantly. 'I'm sorry I can't offer you a cup of tea, Mick. My caddy's empty.'

'I'll get when I go home. Do you want me to go and buy some things for you first, or can you walk to the shops yourself?'

'I haven't been out at all yet, but I'll give Mary Droppie next door a list when she comes in the morning.'

'What about your supper the night?'

'Jenny took in a pie this afternoon. She's been awful good to me.'

He smiled broadly. 'Aye, she's a good-hearted lass, my Jen.'

Cheap nourishing food having restored a little of Lizann's strength, she had started going to the shops, letting Mary Droppie accompany her the first time in case the walk was too much for her. Then she insisted on going alone, because she didn't want her neighbour or anyone else to see what she meant to do. At first she sold only one of the teasets which had been wedding gifts and had never been used, but what she got for it didn't last long, and she gradually disposed of all four, and six tablecloths which had also been presents. They had all been stored in boxes under the bed, so neither Jenny nor Mick knew they were gone.

Although Lizann's health had improved, the same could not be said for her spirits. Every night before she went to sleep, she shed tears for her husband, for the child she had borne but never suckled, and in her dreams she pictured herself with George, swinging their little boy by the hands as they walked. She knew that Jenny was judging her by the brave face she put on and thought she had got over her losses, but it was nearly two months, and she herself didn't think she would ever get over them. To add to her worry as to what would happen when she had nothing left to sell, Mrs Buchan's venomous utterings came back to haunt her. She might have remained in this precarious state indefinitely if two things hadn't happened to make things even worse.

Elsie Tait's mind had been on only one thing for weeks, and this Monday was no different. She'd known for ages that Peter didn't love her, and she had seen by his eyes, when he said he loved Lizann, that it was a love that was tearing him apart. She'd felt like killing him at the time, but she didn't want to lose him . . . she knew when she was well off. He kept her in comfort, he didn't begrudge her the clothes she bought and he was a good father. She had always known how to arouse him, but since their last quarrel she could hardly get him to touch her at all. Although she consoled herself with Lenny Fyfe, she couldn't bear the thought of Peter making love to Lizann. He swore he hadn't, but he couldn't pull the wool over her eyes and she was determined to put a stop to it.

Having planned what to do, she left her two sons with the woman next door and set off to put it into action, gloating that the little bitch in Freuchny Road didn't know what was coming to her.

'I'm Peter Tait's wife,' she announced, when Lizann opened the door.

The girl looked surprised. 'Is something wrong? Is he ill?'

Her patent concern inflamed Elsie even more. 'If you let me in, I'll tell you,' she snapped. Pushing her way inside, she plonked herself on a chair. 'You should ken what's wrong.'

'Me? I'm sorry . . . ?' Lizann murmured, utterly bewildered.

'Dinna play the innocent wi' me! I ken what you've been up to – trying to take my man away from me.'

'I don't understand.'

'You couldna wait to get rid o' Jenny Cowie so you could get Peter to yourself when he came to see you.'

'That's not why . . .'

'I ken what's been going on, and let me put you wise to something. You maybe think he loves you when you and him are at it, but he doesna.'

Lizann shook her head in disbelief. 'You're making a big mistake, Mrs Tait. There's never been anything like that between Peter and me.'

'I dinna believe you.'

'Oh, this is ridiculous! Please leave.'

Elsie was enjoying herself now. 'You canna stand hearing the truth, is that it? You was engaged to him once, so dinna tell me . . .'

'Nothing happened, I swear.'

'You was just a young lassie, and you canna tell me you never wanted a man inside you?'

Remembering her wish to find out what came after the kissing, which had led to her making love with George in Yarmouth, deep colour flooded Lizann's pallid face, and Elsie pounced in triumph. 'So it's true!'

'No!' Lizann screamed. 'You don't understand!'

'I understand right enough, and listen to me, my fine lady! You leave my Peter alone! Next time he comes here, tell him nae to come back! Tell him you've found somebody else! Tell him onything you like, but send him hame to me! If you dinna, I swear I'll spread it the length and breadth o' Buckie that you've been taking up wi' my man for years!' Breathless from the increasing volume of her tirade, Elsie laid her hand on her chest for a moment before she carried on. 'You'll be the speak o' the town, and you'll be wishing you'd never set eyes on him . . . wishing you'd never been born!'

Getting up, she went to the door, but before going out, she said, 'And dinna tell him I've been here, or it'll be all the worse for you!'

Lizann was still shaking next morning. Unable to get the vindictive face out of her mind, she had lain awake all night, wishing – as Elsie had said she would – that she had never been born. How could that woman have said all those things? Peter was a friend, a very dear friend she would be forced to turn from her door because of his wife's insane jealousy . . . but maybe it would please Mrs Tait more if she left Buckie altogether?

She was still agonizing over it when Jenny arrived, eager to tell her about a wedding party she'd seen going into church on Saturday. Trying to show some interest, Lizann saw that Jenny's eyes were moist when she described the bride's gown and, without taking time to think, she said, 'Why have you and Mick never got married?'

'We can't afford to, as long as he keeps giving all his wages away,' Jenny said, rather sharply.

Too upset already to remember that most of what Mick gave away went to the shipyard, Lizann took this to be a hit at the ten shillings he gave her. She had never given a thought to how Jenny would feel about it and, mortified with shame, she could say nothing.

'Ach, don't mind me,' Jenny smiled in a moment. 'I was just jealous at seeing the bride so happy.'

She proceeded to describe the outfits of some of the women guests, but Lizann hardly heard her, and when Jenny left she sat down to think. She was a burden to Mick, a burden he would willingly carry for ever though he shouldn't have to. If it wasn't for her, he could marry his Jenny and live happily ever after. Her mind dwelt now on all the things her older brother had done for her over the years. He had always defended her from bigger boys when she was little; he had gone to see George when she was confined to the house, had given him the advice which had been the means of her father letting her marry the man she loved; he had come to tell her himself that George was drowned, when he could have left it to the skipper; he had looked after her as well as any midwife could have done when she lost the baby. All that, as well as giving her money he could ill afford.

It was her turn to do something for him now, but what? If she told him what Jenny had said, he would be angry at his girlfriend, not her, and he would still insist on giving her the ten shillings. Then it occurred to her that, if she left Buckie as she had thought of doing, she would be killing two birds with one stone. She wouldn't tell anybody where she was, and both Peter and Mick would be free of her . . . but where could she go? It would have to be within walking distance, for she'd have to keep what little she had in her purse in case she didn't find work straight away. Most of the fishing villages round about had their own women to gut what their boats took in.

She pressed her hands to her temples. It was too difficult to think, for she hadn't recovered from Mrs Tait's terrible accusations. And she still hadn't got over George . . . and the baby . . . Maybe she would be best to go to bed and leave the thinking till her brain was clearer. Rising out of her chair, she studied the picture hanging above the fire and wondered if this girl had ever been faced with as many troubles as she'd had. She drew in her breath. She had always loved the picture for its atmosphere of peace and love, and she had nearly forgotten that the girl was her mother, who must have felt something for Robbie Chapman because she had kept the sketch he had so lovingly made.

Lizann's heart jolted. Her mother had once sold fish from a creel, and if her mother could do it . . . ? People still needed fish, people who lived too far from shops or the sea. She likely wouldn't make a good living, but as long as she could exist on it, she wouldn't mind.

Her mind made up, she started to plan how to go about it. She had sold so much already that there wasn't much more than the old furniture left in the house, just her using dishes and some ornaments, and the bedding. She wouldn't get much for any of them, but every penny would help. She would go to the auction room in Blairdaff Street tomorrow and ask if they'd clear the house for her, and with what she got she would pay her rent arrears and hand in the key. Lou had said, when she was leaving on Sunday, that she wouldn't be back for about a week because she was going to be cleaning, Jenny had said yesterday that she'd a big load of sewing to do and wouldn't see her for a few days, and Mick wasn't due home till Friday or Saturday. She could be well away before any of them discovered that she had gone.

In spite of the shock Jenny had given her, and the knowledge that she would soon have to fend for herself with no friends or relatives to turn to, Lizann slept soundly that night and rose in the morning anxious to put her plan into action.

She hung back for a moment before she went into the auction room, but the man asked no awkward questions. When she realized that he believed the house to be cleared belonged to someone who had died, she did not correct him. It was better than having to admit the truth. While he was laboriously writing down the address, she had a quick glance around her, gasping incredulously when her eyes fell on an old creel propped up in a corner. Taking it as a good omen, she asked, 'Is that creel for sale?'

The man's eyes lit up. 'It'd make a fine display in a room wi' a bunch o' heather in it, or ...'

'How much do you want for it?'

Averse to being rushed into making decisions on the spot, he said, 'We can agree on that when we've settled this business.' He tapped on the pad in front of him. 'When do you want me to take away the stuff?'

'As soon as you can, please.'

'This is Wednesday ... would tomorrow morning first thing suit you?'

'That's fine.' It was better than just fine, she thought, for old Mary Droppie slept at her daughter's every Wednesday and wasn't home till the next night, so she wouldn't be there to see what was going on.

'There's just one thing, though,' the man cautioned. 'I never carry any cash with me, so you'll have to come here to be paid, and I'll take the price of the creel off that.'

Lizann went out, satisfied with what she had accomplished so far.

At eleven o'clock the following morning she wasn't quite so happy. The entire contents of her house – including the picture she had sworn she would never part with, and she had done so with tears running down her cheeks – had yielded only £4 2s 6d, and with the cost of the creel deducted, all she got was £3 15s. She had nearly told the man he hadn't given her enough for her belongings and seven and six was too dear for an old creel, but she hadn't felt up to arguing with him.

Thirty minutes later she was trudging along the coast road with the creel slung over her shoulder. Inside was the bundle of clothes which was all she had to her name apart from the three pound notes in her pocket – the fifteen shillings had gone to the factor for rent – and when it hit her that she had left home and friends for ever, her step faltered. For a moment she wished bleakly that she hadn't been so rash and was on the point of turning back when she remembered that she was doing this for Peter, and for Mick and Jenny.

Heaving a deep, shivering sigh, she carried on.

Chapter Seventeen

Because Lizann was his main concern these days, Mick made straight for Freuchny Road when he came ashore at half past six on Saturday night, a day later than usual. He knew he would feel better if he made sure she was all right before he went home.

When he saw that there were no curtains at her window, he assumed that she had taken them down to wash and hadn't been able to get them dry – it had been drizzling steadily all day. Finding the door locked, and getting no answer to his knock, he dug into his wallet for the key he'd had cut in case of an emergency – not that this was an emergency, but she might have fallen asleep and he didn't want to stand outside longer than necessary.

Swinging the door open, he stood stock-still in astonishment. Instead of the shabbily cosy room he had expected to walk into – Lizann had made quite a presentable home from all the second-hand bits and pieces; she had hand-stitched covers for the cushions she picked up at sales; she had crocheted lace doyleys to stop her ornaments scratching the old sideboard; she had cleeked a rug for her hearth – he gazed round a room bare of any form of comfort . . . totally bare. Too bewildered to feel any sort of emotion, he walked across the wooden floorboards and glanced into the bedroom, but it too was completely empty.

When he heard someone coming in, he turned, hoping it was Lizann, but it was Mary Droppie, puffing from the unaccustomed effort of hurrying. 'I was hoping you'd come the night, Mick, for I didna ken what to do.'

'What's happened?' he asked in bewilderment, the nape of his neck prickling now with fear for his sister. 'Where's Lizann?'

'God knows! I didna ken she was awa' till I saw Jeannie Tosh – next door on the other side – coming doon the street aboot four o'clock the day, and she said a lorry flitted her oot on Thursday morning. I wasna here, you see, so I'd nae idea . . .'

'Have you asked if any of the other neighbours know anything?'

'Of course I asked. D'you think I didna care aboot her?'

It was obvious to Mick that the old woman was offended that Lizann had not confided in her – he knew she had felt a responsibility for the young widow. 'I'm sorry, Mary, I know you did a lot for her.'

She looked embarrassed at this. 'Aye, well, I did what I could. Ony road, Jeannie Tosh was the only body that saw a thing, and she thought Lizann was going back to her ma's.'

Not having given one thought to his mother, Mick exclaimed, 'Oh, my God! Maybe Lizann's had to go . . . I'd better get home double quick.'

He shepherded the old woman out and locked the door behind him before he set off, taking long strides at first then breaking into a run when the drizzle developed into a heavy downpour. By the time he reached the Yardie it was bouncing off the street and he burst into the house like a wild thing, startling Hannah, who was sitting by the fire reading.

'What a fleg you gave me!' she frowned, hand on her palpitating heart.

He had to hold on to the back of a chair to get his breath back and to get over his disappointment that Lizann wasn't there, though he knew he should be glad that his mother was the same as she usually was. Needing to share his worry with a person of some sense, he said, 'I was running to get out of the rain, it's bucketing down, but I'm wet through any road, so I might as well go and let Jenny know I'm home.' He dashed out before his mother could say anything.

In his panic, he banged open Jenny's door, too, when he reached it, making her jump up in alarm. 'What's wrong, Mick? Is it Hannah?'

'It's Lizann. She's . . . gone away.'

'Gone away? What d'you mean?'

Irritated, he said, 'Gone away! Cleared out her house and vanished.'

'Cleared out her house?' Jenny's expression grew contrite. 'Oh, Mick, I knew I shouldn't have left her so long on her own, but I'd a whole pile of sewing to finish . . .'

'When did you see her last?'

'Tuesday morning, and she never said anything about leaving . . .'

'She didn't say anything to anybody, not even Mary Droppie, but she was seen going away in a lorry and she could be far enough by this time. God Almighty! What the hell could have made her go away so suddenly?'

There was a moment's silence, then Jenny let out a horrified gasp. 'Oh, Mick! I've just minded!'

'Minded what? Tell me, for God's sake!'

'I was telling her about a wedding I saw, and she asked me why we'd never got married . . .' She stopped and looked at him in dismay.

'Go on,' he urged.

'I said we couldn't afford it as long as you gave all your wages away. I meant what you gave the yard, but maybe she thought I was complaining about the ten bob you give her.'

Shoving her away from him, Mick shouted, 'She's touchy about that. You should have known that's what she would think.'

Jenny burst into tears. 'I never thought . . .'

'You never thought,' he repeated, harshly. 'God Almighty, you should have thought! You know the state she's been in! She never wanted money from me, and if she thought you weren't pleased about it . . . oh God!'

'Mick . . . I'm sorry.' Sobbing loudly, Jenny threw her arms round his neck in entreaty. 'Please, Mick, say you don't blame me.'

About to say that there was nobody else to blame, his anger vanished, and with a low moan he clasped her tightly to him, rubbing her back to calm her. 'I know you wouldn't hurt her deliberately, Jen, but I wish you hadn't said that.'

They stood thus for some time, then sat down to discuss what could be done, but no matter how hard they tried, they could think of nothing. Presently, Jenny gave a start. 'Would she have gone to Cullen?'

'To George's mother?' Mick looked a little happier. 'I'll bet that's where she is! It's too late the night, I'll get the first bus tomorrow.'

Ina Buchan looked at her caller in astonishment. 'What made you think she'd come to me? She never bothered wi' me afore George was lost . . .'

Thankful that he didn't have to tell her about her son, Mick murmured, 'She'd to look after my mother . . .'

'. . . and keep her man from seeing his?' Ina sneered. 'She's a thankless besom, for she near aboot threw me oot when I went to see her.'

'You went to see her? When?'

'Once I got ower it myself . . . but she . . . there's nae love lost atween me and her, and I'm the last body she'd've asked if she was needing help.'

She'd be the last person he'd ask for help, too, Mick thought. 'I'm right worried about her, Mrs Buchan, she's emptied her house, and I've no idea where she is. She's been in an awful state . . .'

The woman nodded stiffly. 'Losing her man and her bairn at the same time . . . that would be enough to put ony woman aff her head.'

Thinking it best to leave her under the impression that Lizann's mind was totally deranged – which maybe wasn't so far off the mark – Mick said, 'I'll have to go, my mother's not fit to be on her own for long, but if Lizann does come here, you'll let us know?'

'I will, but she'll likely be hame in a wee while.'

'I hope so.'

Going home in the bus, Mick felt that all hope of finding his sister had gone, and when Jenny opened her door to him she could see by his look of defeat that he'd had no luck. Trying to cheer him, she said brightly, 'I just thought when you were away . . . would she be at Lou's?'

A shaft of hope came into his drawn face. 'My mind's like a sieve. How could I have forgotten Lou? We'll go when we've had our dinner.'

In his own house, he had to parry his mother's questions as to where he'd been, saying that he'd had some business to attend to and refusing to tell her what. Then, when he said he was going out with Jenny, Hannah snapped, 'You're hardly ever in when you're ashore nowadays. You'd be as well taking your bed along there.'

Lizann was not with Lou, who was more concerned about her than Ina Buchan had been. 'She'll be like a bairn if she's among strangers. Is there nobody else you can try?'

Mick heaved a shuddery sigh. 'I can't think of anybody.'

'Oh, well,' Lou said staunchly, 'we never died a winter yet, and one o' us'll surely manage to come up wi' something ower a cup o' tea.'

The cups of tea had no miraculous effect, nothing

coming to any of them until Lou suddenly hit one hand with her other fist, and looked at them smugly. 'Why did I nae think on it afore? She musta got that lorry in Buckie, so somebody here musta driven her and kens where she's went, and me and Jenny'll just have to ask till we find him.'

It came to Jenny that Lizann could have got the lorry from wherever she had gone, but she didn't like to say anything to dim the sparkle which had appeared in Mick's eyes. 'We were a day late in coming in,' he smiled, 'so I'm not sailing till Tuesday. I'll ask round the fish houses after I pay the shipyard in the morning.'

They made a list of every place they could think of that might have a lorry and settled on which of them would go where next day, then Lou asked, 'Have you tell't Hannah, Mick?'

Looking shamefaced, he shook his head. 'To tell the truth, I couldn't face it, but it's up to me and I will do it, when I'm ready. Now, we'd better go, Jenny, or Jockie'll be home and his supper not ready.'

On the walk back, he said, 'Mother was saying I should take my bed to your house seeing I'm there so much.' Seeing a flush spreading across Jenny's face, he murmured, 'In just two month, I pay the last instalment on the *Hannah* and then I'll be able to provide for you. We'll get wed, and you can sell your house and move into the Yardie.'

'Oh, Mick, I can hardly believe we'll be man and wife at last.'

'We've waited long enough,' he said gruffly.

When they reached her house, he asked, 'Can I come in?' Noticing that she looked doubtful as to his intentions, he added, 'I'm not trying to jump the gun, but I haven't kissed you for three whole hours.'

Giggling, she unlocked her door and took him inside.

* * *

Neither Jenny nor Mick, on their separate missions, had any luck on Monday, and what Lou told them when they reported at Rannas Place in the evening made them even more depressed. 'I could've grat when the factor said Lizann had gi'en up the hoose,' she said, sadly. 'I'd been hoping they'd moved her oot so's they could repair her roof or something like that, that's why I went and asked first thing, but she's handed in the key, so there's nae chance she'll be back.'

'I'd better give you the key I got made, then,' Mick murmured, 'and you can hand it in.'

Lou's mind was still on the most important matter. 'Now, you'll be back at sea the morrow, Mick, and there's nae need for you to waste your sewing time, Jenny, so I'll carry on myself. There canna be much places left to ask, just the littler shops.' She would take no argument and so it was left at that.

Mick couldn't sleep for worrying that night, but he was finishing his breakfast when he remembered that Peter had sometimes visited Lizann. Would she have confided in her old sweetheart? For his own peace of mind, he would have to go and ask before he joined his ship.

His question only succeeded in worrying Peter and clearly annoying Elsie, so he hurried home to pick up his seabag and get to the harbour. He felt so helpless; he couldn't even report Lizann as missing to the police, not when she took all her belongings with her.

It was Tuesday afternoon when Lou came to the auction room in Blairdaff Street, and she wondered if it was worth asking in such a run-down place. Telling herself that needs must when the devil drives, she hitched up her skirts and went in, her nose wrinkling at the musty smell. The man who came forward struck her as a shifty character, so she came straight to the point. 'Do you have a lorry?'

He smiled ingratiatingly. 'Was you wanting to buy some furniture?'

Horrified that he thought she was the kind of person who would buy furniture out of a place like this, Lou drew herself up to her full five feet, half an inch. 'I'm not buying, I just asked if you'd a lorry.'

His fawning manner vanished along with his smile. 'No!'

'Thank you.' She made a sweeping exit, little knowing that if she had been less abrupt, or if she had phrased her question differently, she would have been given a fuller answer. David Roth had not told a lie, for he hired a lorry on the rare occasions he had a heavy load to shift, but even if he had told Lou this, he couldn't have told her what she really wanted to know. He had taken Lizann and her belongings back to his shop, and he had no idea what she had done after he paid her.

When Jenny arrived that evening, Lou had to admit defeat. 'She must have got the lorry from wherever she was going.' She made a brave show of cheerfulness now. 'She must have found another house, seeing she took her furniture, though I canna understand why she went away at all.' This had bothered Lou ever since she heard about it.

'It's my fault,' Jenny admitted, and explained a little tearfully.

Lou looked staggered, but patted the girl's hand. 'It's likely nothing to do wi' you, lass. She ken't Mick was paying the yard, and it looks like she doesna want nae-body to ken where she is. We'd best get on wi' our ain lives and let her get on wi' hers.'

When Peter left for work on Wednesday, Elsie told her two sons to get ready to go out.

'Oh, we're not going to the Yardie again, are we?'

She looked at Pattie's screwed-up face and couldn't

help sympathizing with him. Because of the interest Hannah had taken in the boys when they were smaller, Peter had asked his wife to take them in to see her now and then, since she wasn't fit to go out herself. Elsie hadn't minded at first – Hannah always gave them a sixpence each, which had pleased them – but they were getting too big to be cooped up inside with a woman who kept kissing them like they were still babies. 'I promised Hannah I'd look in the day,' she told Pattie, 'but you and Tommy can bide here and play if you want. I'll ask Rosie McIntosh to keep an eye on you.'

As she dressed herself, her thoughts returned to what had been uppermost in her mind since Mick's visit the previous morning. She'd only given Lizann a warning, she'd never dreamt the stupid bitch would run away, but it was probably a good thing. If Lizann had stayed on in Buckie, Peter would likely have wanted a divorce so he could marry her; that would have been a financial disaster for his wife, for she would never get another man to hand over most of his wages.

Half an hour later, Elsie knocked on Hannah's door and walked in. 'I'm going up the town,' she announced, breezily, 'so if there's anything you need, I'll get it for you.'

'Is the boys nae wi' you?' Hannah asked, her expression matching the whining accusation in her voice. 'My wee grandsons?'

This really got Elsie's dander up. If Hannah thought she was the boys' grandmother, she must think Lizann was their mother. Well, Elsie Tait wasn't going to stand for that! No, by God! The old bitch was asking to be told a thing or two. Drawing up a chair, Elsie said, with feigned concern, 'You'll be real worried about Lizann?'

'I am that. Mick says she still hasna got over George and the bairnie. I wish I could go and see her but I canna get outside my door nowadays.'

'You wouldna be able to see her supposing you could,' Elsie said, in a deceptively gentle manner. 'You see, she was taking up wi' my Peter and I went to tell her to let him alone, and Mick says she's ran away and naebody kens where she is.'

'Taking up wi' your Peter?' Hannah gasped, absorbing only one of these facts. 'But he's her Peter.'

This was Bella Jeannie all over again, as far as Elsie was concerned, but she had to be more careful this time. 'It's me that's Peter's wife,' she corrected, 'but Lizann was encouraging him to her house. Nae that he needed much encouraging, for I'm sure he's been at her oftener than he's been at me since her man was drowned.'

'No, no.' Hannah shook her head convulsively.

'I warned her I'd tell the whole o' Buckie if she didna let him be, but I never thought she'd run away.'

'My Lizann's run away?' It got through to Hannah at last, and her face crumpled, her bewildered eyes took on a wildness that made Elsie wish she hadn't tried to cause trouble. 'I thought Mick would've tell't you,' she muttered as she jumped up, guilt making her add, 'It's a secret, so you'd better nae tell onybody, and for ony sake, dinna let Mick ken I tell't you. Mind now, Hannah. It's a secret!'

As she had taken to doing every forenoon, Jenny went to see if Hannah had something for her dinner and, opening the door, she was astonished to hear her saying, 'Mind and turn my mattress afore you put on clean sheets, Lizann.'

Thinking in delight that Lizann had come home, Jenny passed Hannah with a smiling nod, but there was no one in the bedroom. Back in the kitchen, she noticed that Hannah's eyes had a unnatural darkness to them. 'Who were you speaking to just now?'

'You, of course,' Hannah frowned. 'And mind and

polish the stair, and all, for you havena done them this week yet.'

'Lou's going to do them this afternoon,' Jenny said, gently.

'No, no, Lizann! You're nae to leave them for Lou.'

Her legs threatening to give way, Jenny grasped the edge of the table. Hannah was mistaking her for Lizann! She'd been all right yesterday, so what had brought this on? 'Has anybody else been in to see you the day?'

Hannah smiled. 'Just Jenny.'

Unable to be sure if there really had been someone or if the old woman was just imagining it, Jenny asked, 'What was she saying?'

Hannah appeared to think about this, but her eyes were darting hither and thither slyly. 'I canna mind. She was just in a minute.'

Jenny decided that it had been imagination. Her mind was gone again, poor thing, and she shouldn't be left on her own.

Lou arrived when dinner was over. 'I made rice broth for her,' Jenny whispered, 'and I'd to spoon it to her, for she's lost the use of her arms now, as well as her legs. And she's all muddled, for she thinks I'm Lizann. I don't know what's happened, but it's a good thing Mick didn't tell her anything before he sailed.'

Lou sighed deeply. 'We'd better nae say onything, either, for she might go bizerk all together . . . and I'd best sleep wi' her the night.'

'What's you two whispering about?' Hannah demanded, sharply.

Lou gave her a forced smile. 'Jenny was saying she made rice . . .'

Hannah's brows shot down. 'Jenny? Is she back? I thought it was just Lizann that was here.'

The other two exchanged agonized glances, then Jenny

said, 'I'm going home now, Hannah, but I'll see you the morrow.'

Hannah looked at her sister in perplexed suspicion when the door shut. 'But she went away before Lizann came in. I'm near sure it was her that tell't me . . .' She broke off, gripping her lips tightly.

'Tell't you what?' Lou prodded, though she could hardly think that Jenny had anything to do with Hannah's sudden deterioration.

'Never you mind!' Hannah snapped.

Not wishing to upset her further, and believing in any case that she was havering, Lou stopped probing. If she and Jenny had got together and tried to get to the bottom of it they might have stumbled across the truth, because Peter Tait's wife was the only other young woman who ever visited Hannah. As it was, Elsie's unpremeditated villainy remained undetected.

PART TWO

1939–1942

❧

Chapter Eighteen

'There's something at the back o' my mind about you, Lizann,' Hannah observed one afternoon in March, frowning with the effort of trying to remember, 'if I could only think what it is.'

Jenny had stopped correcting her about the name. It was easier to let her mother-in-law believe what she wanted to believe. She wished Mick had told Hannah the truth at the time, for there might come a day when her brain cleared and she would realize that it wasn't Lizann who washed her, dressed her, spoonfed her, potted her, put her to bed, and what would happen then? But Mick hadn't been capable of coping with the state his mother would have got herself into if she knew about Lizann. Oh, he had done his best to hide how he felt, Jenny couldn't deny that, but it wouldn't have taken much to knock him off balance altogether. That was why she had forced him – it had been easy since his resistance was at its lowest ebb – into marrying her as quickly as he could.

'You need a wife to help you over your troubles,' she had declared, 'and I've enough money to tide us over till you've squared the yard.'

They had been married immediately the banns had been cried, and the debt to the shipyard had been cleared, yet Mick still seemed to be living on a knife-edge, though he was everything she could have wanted as a lover.

She watched for him the following day and went out to speak to him before he came in. 'I think your mother's beginning to know something's wrong. She said yesterday she'd something at the back of her mind about Lizann. Maybe you should tell her.'

Mick blew out a long breath from puckered lips. 'But she still thinks you're Lizann, doesn't she? No, I think I'll leave it a while yet.'

Next morning, as Jenny was dressing her, Hannah said, 'Your father'll be hame the day, Lizann. You'll have to make a big pot o' soup for him.'

As usual, Jenny just smiled at this, though she longed to shake the confused woman and tell her Willie Alec had been dead for years. 'I'll get a bit of boiling beef after we've had our breakfast.'

'She's back to thinking your father's still alive,' she whispered to Mick while they walked to the butcher's shop together.

'Lou'll maybe be able to bring her out o' it,' Mick said, hopefully.

'Lou wasn't feeling well yesterday, so maybe she'll not be coming.'

When someone knocked on the door in the middle of the forenoon, Jenny wondered why Lou was early and why she hadn't walked in as she normally did, so she was alarmed to see Sarah Smith, Lou's next door neighbour.

'Your auntie sent me,' Mrs Smith explained. 'She was in terrible pain wi' her stomach the whole night, and Jockie had to go for the doctor at seven this morning, and the ambulance took her to the hospital.'

'Oh, my goodness!' Jenny gasped. 'D'you know what it is?'

'It sounded to me like a ulcer, or something like that.'

'I'll tell Mick, she's his auntie. Thanks for letting us know.'

When Mick was told, he said, 'It must be serious before she was put in the hospital, I'd better go and see her, for she's aye been good to us.'

He was gone for so long that Jenny prepared herself

for bad news, but she was still shocked at his drawn face when he returned. He shook his head sadly. 'She died before I got there. They said it was cancer, and she should have seen the doctor ages ago.'

'Cancer?' Jenny exclaimed, her eyes as round as saucers. 'Oh, my God! Yesterday was the only time I ever heard her complaining.'

They had both forgotten Hannah, who had been listening to every word but had got it wrong. 'Lizann's got cancer?' she cried, hands jumping about on her lap. 'But she's still a young lassie.'

Jenny burst into tears, and Mick knelt down beside his mother. 'No, it's not Lizann. It's Lou.'

'Lou hasna got cancer,' Hannah declared firmly. 'She's never had a thing wrong wi' her. It was me took everything when we was young.'

'Lou died in the hospital,' Mick said, slowly and gently, as if to a child, but his mother looked at him with blank eyes.

Standing up, he turned to his wife, who held out her arms and he went into them with a strangled moan. 'Oh, Jen, I don't think she'll ever get over this, it's too much for her. It's too much for me.' His noisy sobs went on for some time, and Jenny, tears coursing down her own cheeks, held him tightly.

She saw a silent Hannah to bed earlier than usual that night, then went back to the kitchen. 'Why were you away so long?' she asked Mick, who was sitting staring into the fire.

'I'd to see this doctor and that doctor, and wait for them to sign a death certificate. Then I'd to go and look for Jockie. God knows how Lou put up with him since he stopped working, for he was in and out bars all day. He must have started after Lou went away in the ambulance, for he was blazing drunk by the time I found him. I said he'd better wait till he was sober before he arranged the funeral, and he started to cry and say he was sorry for how he'd treated her, and I'd to stay with him till he calmed down. Oh, Jenny, it's been awful.'

'I could see you were worn out when you came back. I'm feeling a bit tired myself, so we'd be as well going up to bed now.'

He transferred his pity to his wife. 'Oh, I shouldn't be carrying on like this when you ... you must always be dead tired looking after my mother the way you do.'

'I do get tired,' she admitted, not noticing his unintentional pun, 'but just ordinary tired. I'm fine in the mornings.'

He fell asleep minutes afterwards with his arms around her, and Jenny smiled ruefully as she listened to his steady breathing. She had hoped for some loving, but he'd be feeling Lou's death even more than she did. As for Hannah ... well, she'd probably forgotten all about it already and would be sound asleep by now.

Hannah was not sound asleep. Her unhinged mind was grappling with things she could not understand. Her sister couldn't be dead. Lou had always been healthy ... like Lizann. Lizann? But it wasn't Lizann that had put her to bed, it was the girl that had looked after her ever since ... ? Since Willie Alec died? No, that had been Lizann right enough, to begin with ... and she'd still come every day after she left the Yardie.

Hannah drew a deep breath, striving to remember why Lizann had stopped coming, for she had stopped, that was sure. Ah! She'd been expecting and then ... something terrible had happened. Her man ... had been drowned and ... she'd lost the bairnie. But why had she never come back?

Her head spinning, Hannah did her best to delve through the mists that fogged her brain. There was something else! Something somebody had said. Not the girl who looked after her now – that was . . . Jenny Cowie! – it was another girl, not a nice girl. Peter Tait. Why had she thought about him? He'd been engaged to Lizann, but . . . he'd married . . . a blond hussy with a painted face . . . ? What was her name? Elsie! Aye, that was it, and it was her that had come and said . . . ? What was it she'd said? About Lizann?

Hannah felt herself shying away from it, but having enough sense to know she would lose the thread of her thoughts altogether if she let go of them, she persevered until it came back to her. Elsie said Lizann had run away. But why had she run away, and where was she?

Losing her concentration suddenly, Hannah's thoughts took a jump back in time. She didn't want Lizann here. It was her fault Willie Alec was dead. Her and that man she took to the house, that . . . George Buchan from Cullen. She didn't want them here! She managed fine with Lou coming in every day, and Mick's girl bringing in things she'd baked. Now she was a nice lassie, a thoughtful lassie, and Mick couldn't do better if he took her for a wife.

Satisfied that she'd sorted everything out, Hannah fell asleep.

When Peter Tait saw Lou's death in the newspaper he decided to attend the funeral, but when he told Elsie her eyes narrowed. 'How do you know this Louise Flett, any road? It says she was seventy-three.'

Thankful that his wife hadn't connected her with Mick's Auntie Lou, he answered cautiously. 'I've known her for years. She's a nice old body.'

'I've never heard you speaking about her, and you're not going. They might dock it off your wages, and we can't afford it.'

'I am going . . . whatever you say!'

He sighed as she flounced away with her mouth

screwed up. She got more on his nerves every day, and if he hadn't his two sons to consider he would walk out on her. He suspected that she took other men in when he was at work, though the only person he had ever caught in his house – one day he had come home early with a streaming cold – was young Lenny Fyfe, and he was just a kid.

Having asked off work for an hour, he took his black tie in his pocket the following morning. He didn't expect to know many of the people at the funeral, but when he turned up at Rannas Place the only person he recognized was Mick Jappy. His eyes going round the men assembled in the street and remembering Mick once saying his uncle took a good bucket, he guessed that the wee man with the red nose must be Lou's husband. He looked as if he'd had a good few drams already . . . to steady his nerves.

When the service in the kirkyard was over, Mick came across to speak to him. 'It's good of you to come, Peter.'

'Och, well,' Peter said, slightly embarrassed because he wasn't there for the reason Mick thought, 'you've always been my best pal. How's your mother taking this? I hope it hasn't set her back again.'

Taken by surprise, Mick burst out, 'She went out of her mind again not long after Lizann went away. You'd think she knew, but none of us ever told her.'

An icy hand clutched at Peter's stomach. 'So you've never heard from Lizann, then?'

Mick shook his head sadly. 'Not a word.'

'Does Hannah not wonder where she is?'

'She's that muddled she thinks Jenny's Lizann, and I can't see myself ever telling her. God knows what it would do to her.'

Peter touched his shoulder sympathetically. 'Aye, it's maybe better to keep it from her. It's a good thing you've got Jenny.'

Noticing the other mourners moving away, Mick said, 'Are you coming back to Lou's house?'

'I'm sorry, I've to go back to work.'

'Right. Well, I'd better see to Jockie. He looks like he'll keel over any minute, and God knows what he'll be like by the end of the day.'

'You'll let me know if you ever hear from Lizann?'

'Aye, I'll do that.'

As Peter walked back to the yard, he wondered again where Lizann had gone, and why she had left. It must have been sudden, when she hadn't told a soul she was leaving. Not even the clamour of metal hammering against metal, reverberating non-stop through the window, could get Lizann out of his mind for the rest of the day, and when he went home he was still puzzling over her disappearance.

'Did you see anybody you knew at the funeral?' Elsie asked.

He hadn't meant to tell her, but it came out. 'Just Mick Jappy.'

'Mick? Did he know the old woman, and all?'

'She was his auntie.'

'Lou? I didn't realize ... oh, I see now why you were so anxious to go. Has he heard anything from Lizann?'

'I don't think he ever will ... not now. I wish I knew why she went off like that.'

Elsie longed to tell him it had been her doing, but, knowing what his reaction would be, she said instead, 'Mick thought it was something Jenny said, didn't he?'

'That's what he said, but I can't believe it. Jenny's a nice girl, a kind girl. She wouldn't hurt anybody. I wish I'd gone back to see Lizann again, and I would have, if you hadn't kicked up such a stink about it. She mightn't have gone away if she'd talked things over with me.'

'She might have made you go with her,' Elsie sneered.

Past caring what she thought, he said, 'If she'd asked me, I'd have gone to the ends of the earth with her!'

Stung, she lashed back, 'That wouldna have bothered me, for there's mair than one man waiting to get into my bed.'

'You can take whoever you like into your bed as far as I'm concerned,' Peter said quietly. 'I'll not be sharing it with you again.'

'Oho,' she taunted, 'and where'll you sleep?'

'With the boys . . . when I'm here.'

She looked wary now. 'When you're here? What d'you mean by that?'

'I'm going to sign on a boat to get away from you.'

'The hard work would kill you!'

'I'd be better dead than sleeping with you!'

Realizing that she had pushed him too far, Elsie sidled up to him. 'It wasn't true about the other men. I just said it to get back at you. Come up the stair and I'll show you.'

He shoved her away. 'I wouldn't touch you if you were the only woman on this earth.'

'You didna aye think that.'

'More fool me. I should have known what you were from the minute I set eyes on you.'

'Oh, aye? What am I, then?'

'A common tart. My mother was right, I should never have married you.'

'Your mother was a goddam't nosy bitch!' Elsie shouted.

'She was a damn sight better a woman than you'll ever be!'

Wanting to wound him, she was on the point of telling him what had really happened on the morning of her last row with Bella Jeannie when it occurred to her that he would blame her for his mother's death and might lash out at her in his anger. Instead, she started to undo the buttons of her blouse, hoping to tempt him into forgetting why they were at each other's throats.

'Stop that!' he roared. 'You're wasting your time!' He spun round and stalked out, slamming the outside door behind him. He was disgusted that baring her breasts was her answer to everything; they didn't excite him any more. God, he wished he hadn't tried to do the right thing by her in keeping away from Lizann.

He walked for hours, welcoming the night when darkness engulfed him. His heart was aching for the woman he loved, yet he had begun to smart from the vile insult his wife had thrown at him. It was degrading to think that while he'd been working to provide her and their sons with a decent standard of living, she'd been entertaining other men, for he hadn't believed her when she said she'd lied about it. She must have laughed at him on the rare occasions he'd needed her over the past few months, likely compared him with her other lovers.

Peter was miles away from home when he eventually sat down on a bank at the side of the road to take stock of his situation. He had said, on the spur of the moment, that he would sign on a boat to get away from her and he damned well would. At least he would be free of her for five days at a time; he could surely manage to put up with her for the two days he would be ashore.

Shafts of daylight were peppering the black sky before he reached his house again, in time to wash and shave and change into a clean shirt before going to work, but when he went in he was annoyed to see Elsie sitting by the fire with a blanket wrapped round her. Thinking she was asleep, he tried to creep past but her eyes jerked open.

'So you've come back at last?' she said sarcastically. 'Where have you been till . . .' She shot a quick glance at the clock, '. . . till twenty past six in the morning? You must have been wi' bloody good company.'

'The best!' he snarled. 'I was by myself . . . walking and thinking.'

'And have you changed your mind about going to sea?'

'No.' He made for the door into the lobby but she jumped to her feet, the blanket falling to reveal that she was wearing nothing underneath.

Pressing against him, she looked up at him seductively. 'We could have a quarter of an hour . . .'

His arms went round her automatically, her large breasts firing him in spite of himself, and feeling his arousal, a slow smirk spread over her face. This was what brought Peter to his senses, and he gave her such a desperate shove that she reeled back with her mouth gaping. 'You bitch!' he said harshly. 'You bloody, whoring bitch!'

Rubbing her chestbone, she cried, 'If you leave me, Peter Tait, I'll sue you for desertion! I'll take every penny off you!'

At the foot of the stairs now, he said, 'Who said I was leaving you? I'm going to sea like half the other men in Buckie – you can't sue me for that. I'll have to work my notice at the yard, so I'll sleep with the boys till I go and every time I'm back. So keep away from me.'

When he came downstairs she had the blanket round her once more, and his dark expression as he strode past her kept her from making any kind of remark, derogatory or otherwise. He had let her know what he thought of her, Peter congratulated himself, and she wouldn't bother him again. He would live in the same house, eat the meals she cooked, wear the clothes she washed and ironed, but he would never sleep with her again, and he wouldn't care who she slept with when he wasn't there . . . or even when he was there.

Feeling better, he strode out jauntily, and he had almost reached the shipyard before Lizann crossed his mind. His step faltered for a moment, then, telling himself that she was part of his past and that she clearly wanted a new life which didn't include him, he went inside, determined to go and see Mick Jappy that night about getting a berth.

Astonished that Peter Tait was standing up so well to the rigours aboard the *Dawn Rose*, even in fierce March gales, Mick gave him a poke in the ribs as he passed. 'You'll soon be an old hand at this game, eh?'

Peter grinned. 'It's great what a couple of weeks will do.'

Mick continued on his way. He'd been having a confab with the skipper about a slight leak from the boiler, but they'd agreed it wasn't anything to worry about . . . yet. Back in the engine room, he wondered what had made Peter throw up the steady job he had. He hadn't mentioned it on the day of Lou's funeral, yet he'd set his mind on it by the next day and it was sheer good luck there was a job going on the *Dawn Rose*. He hadn't even had to work the month's notice he was supposed to give the shipyard as a salaried draughtsman – surely the manager knew the kind of wife he had and took pity on him.

Elsie was the speak of Main Street with her dyed hair and face caked with make-up, and he'd heard from more than one source that she was taking up with Tom Fyfe's laddie. It was a mystery why Peter had ever married her; she wasn't his type, and it hadn't been a shotgun wedding. It had been fully nine months till Pattie was born . . . but it was likely her curves that kept Peter with her, for their second had been born less than a year later.

Mick leaned forward to check the bucket he had put under the boiler, and finding only one drop of water in it, he sat back and relaxed. Poor Peter. His wedding hadn't been long after Lizann's, so it looked like he'd married Elsie on the rebound, and there was something in his eyes even yet when he spoke about Lizann that showed . . . a longing. Elsie was bound to have noticed it, as well. Maybe that was why she carried on the way she did. Another thought struck Mick. Had it been something to do with Peter that made Lizann go away? On the day after she lost George he had admitted he still loved her, but surely he wouldn't have been so unfeeling as to say that to her? No, it must have been what Jenny said that did it, Mick concluded sadly, though Lizann should have realized he was still paying the yard. And she must have remembered that by now, so why hadn't she come home? He would surely have heard if anything had happened to her, so wherever she was, she must be happy. That was the only way to look at it.

His heart always aching to find his missing sister, he turned his mind to what his skipper had told him a few minutes before.

'Heck says the government's offering twenty pounds to any seafaring man who's willing to join the Royal Navy,' Mick observed, as he and Peter walked homewards along the street. 'They're sure there's going to be war, after all.'

Peter was dreading having to spend the next few days with Elsie and was paying no heed to what Mick was saying. 'Oh, aye?' he muttered.

'I've been thinking – they'll conscript us any road, if there is a war, so I've made up my mind to take them up on it.'

Peter looked at him now. 'Take who up on what?'

'Have you got cloth ears, man? I'm volunteering for the Navy.'

'You surely wouldn't leave Jenny and you not long wed?'

'I don't want to, but I feel I've got to. They say Germany's got a big fleet of ships waiting to invade us, and we'll have to stop it.' Mick eyed Peter expectantly. 'Are you on?'

'You're not asking me to join up with you? I couldn't leave Elsie with our two.'

'It would get you away from her,' Mick said craftily.

'Aye, so it would!' Peter was pensive for a moment. 'By God!' he burst out then. 'I can just see her face if I did!'

'The money'll help Jenny and me to get on our feet quicker, but I'm not looking forward to telling her. I just hope she'll understand.'

'Jenny's a gem, she'll understand. But I've my boys to consider, so I'd better have a proper think about it first.'

Mick lifted his shoulders briefly. 'Aye, maybe you should. I've had a few days to turn it over in my mind since the skipper told me. I'm going to go tomorrow to see about it – if you want to come, fine.'

The two men parted at the Yardie, and Peter, whose feet normally dragged along the last few hundred yards, suddenly stepped out briskly, for he had made up his mind already. He was grinning as he went into his own house. When Elsie looked up, he was surprised to see that she had tarted herself up for him; she hadn't made the effort for a long time. 'Pattie and Tommy in bed already?' he asked. 'I thought I'd see them for a wee while.'

'And I thought it was time we ... had an evening without them.'

There was a smirk on her painted face that told him she was trying to tempt him into making love to her, so he decided to take the wind out of her sails. 'I've something to tell you. I'm putting my name down for the Navy tomorrow with Mick.'

The smirk disappeared. 'You're what?'

'Joining the Navy with Mick,' he grinned. 'So I'll be away from you, thank God.'

'You bugger!' she cried, springing to her feet and searching for a way to take the smile off his face, but not having expected anything like this, her devious mind failed her for once.

*　　*　　*

Jenny was weeping softly in her husband's arms. 'Oh, Mick, why are you doing it? You know I don't care about money.'

'Twenty pounds is a fair bit, though. Think of the things you'll be able to buy for yourself, things I haven't been able to get for you.'

'I don't care, I love you and I don't want you to go.'

Mick sighed. 'I have to. Call it patriotism or whatever you like, even a stupid sense of my own importance, but my heart tells me I must answer the call. Anyway, there's going to be a war, that's certain, and it'd just be a matter of time before I'd be forced to go.'

'If you waited, I could have you for a few more weeks, maybe months.'

'I don't want to leave you, don't think that, it's going to be an awful wrench, but . . .' He ended with a shrug.

Recognizing that nothing she said would make him change his mind, Jenny murmured, 'I'll miss you when you're away.'

'I'm away for days at a time now,' he pointed out, smiling.

'That's different. I know you'll be home at the weekends.'

She raised her head, and he saw that her grey eyes were filled with pain at the thought of what he intended to do, but he still had to do it. He was a Jappy, and Jappys had to do their duty no matter how hard it was. His father would have been ashamed of him if he'd let his wife talk him out of it. Yet he would feel their parting as deeply as Jenny did, he told himself, and a lump rose in his throat as he bent his head to kiss away her sadness. The first kiss began a whole series of kisses and caresses that ended with two sated bodies lying back sighing.

Ever resilient, Elsie had bounced back quickly, but did her best to appear subdued in front of Peter when he was home at the weekends. He and Mick had both kept working while they were waiting, but she was glad when he got word to report to Chatham. Nevertheless, she did feel a pang of regret when he left to catch the train.

Looking on the bright side, of course, she told herself, his going meant she was free for Lenny Fyfe for longer than five days at a time. He had shaped up pretty well and did everything he could to please her; she would prefer a more dominant lover, but he would do meantime.

She and Jenny having something in common now, they took to discussing the letters they received – Elsie having to invent the endearments she pretended to read out, because she was green with envy at the things Mick wrote to his wife.

When the two men came home after their initial training, Peter was so full of what they had been doing that he described it in full to Elsie, keeping back for as long as he could the one item of news he knew would annoy her. 'We're not in the Navy proper, just the R.N.V.R., that's the Royal Naval Volunteer Reserve, for the duration of the war, if it comes. Mick's been made a petty officer, but I'm just a rating.'

'Why's that?' she asked, frowning.

'Because he's been at sea a lot longer than me.'

'That shouldn't make any difference,' she pouted.

'He's a qualified engineer, but I'm going to be a clerk, I'm not sure yet what grading I'll get.'

Peter was flattered by his sons' pride that he was in uniform, and he had to chuckle to himself at the renewed interest Elsie was showing in him, but he stuck to his own rule and did not sleep with his wife – he knew his own failing. Occasionally, however, when they were sitting having a last cup of tea together in the kitchen, he couldn't keep his eyes from straying to her bosom; she had perfected the art of exposing as much as she could without risking being accused of baring it. And what wasn't actually exposed could be seen through her filmy nightie, so he emptied his cup quickly and left her. Unfortunately, much as he despised her, he returned to his ship with a picture etched on his brain of the two delectable mounds and their dark-ringed nipples which had driven him mad for years.

On his first day home, Mick watched his young wife lovingly as she bustled about, drinking in her shapely legs, her slim figure, her narrow waist. His eyes lingered slightly on her breasts – surely they were fuller than they used to be? – and then moved up her slender neck till they reached the mouth he was longing to kiss but couldn't, for Jenny was shy when his mother was in the kitchen with them. Her cheeks were paler and her lovely chestnut hair wasn't as shiny as he remembered – was all the hard work turning her old before her time? He shouldn't have let her tie herself to marriage and looking after his mother.

When Hannah was settled for the night, he murmured, 'We could go to our bed as well, couldn't we? It's been a long time, Jen darling.'

Snuggling down under the blankets, he said, 'You're looking a wee bit under the weather. Are you sure you're not doing too much?'

She looked at him shyly. 'Can't you guess what it is?'

His brow wrinkled in thought for a moment, then he let out a whoop of joy. 'You're expecting?'

'Sshh!' she breathed. 'You'll waken your mother. I wasn't going to tell you till I was sure, but ... well, I'm nearly sure.'

His eyes grew serious, and his voice was a little thick, as he said, 'Jenny Jappy, did I ever tell you how much I love you?'

Chapter Nineteen

❦

Lizann had never been used to grandeur or ostentation, but this was the bottom of the barrel, she decided, taking stock of her surroundings; yet it was all she needed, and at least the blankets on the rickety bed were clean. It would have been nice to have a more comfortable chair to sit on – her bottom grew numb after five minutes on the unpadded seat of the wooden one, which had one leg shorter than the rest – but there wasn't room for an armchair. The grate was so small it wouldn't send out enough heat in the dead of winter, so it was just as well there was only a wee skylight in the sloping roof. The trouble was, it didn't let in much air even when it was open, and she had been stifling all night. The little primus stove was a blessing though; it would have been unbearable if she'd had to light the fire to boil the kettle.

Sighing in resignation, she went downstairs and out on to the winding road which descended steeply to the village proper and the sea. Even at six o'clock, the July morning gave promise of another scorching day, and she hoped it wouldn't be so oppressive as it had been yesterday – not that she should complain; it would be a lot worse in winter. She could take off her cardigan if she was too hot, but she had no extra clothes to wear if she was cold. The only coat she'd possessed had been . . .

Manoeuvring her way carefully round the end of a house sitting on a sharp bend, she turned her mind hastily to other garments she'd once had. She had only worn the pink taffeta dress about half a dozen times, and the blue crêpe-de-chine once, on her wedding day. They had hung in her cupboard in the Yardie, protected from moths by balls of camphor, until she transferred them to the closet at Freuchny Road. Later, they'd been packed in a box and sold along with her other belongings. They'd have been cooler for her now, but too fancy to wear to sell fish.

Turning right at the foot of the brae, she walked along the seafront, passing the ancient hotel and the picturesque cottages snuggling under the overhanging cliffs. She'd only seen a couple of people on her way down, but the small harbour at the far end was abustle with men in long seaboots and ganzies, sorting out their catches and haggling with shopkeepers from inland villages and towns, who could charge what they liked but were reluctant to pay the asking price themselves.

As she stood watching, an elderly man approached her. 'I've a lot o' undersize haddocks the day, Liz,' he said softly, giving her a gaptoothed smile, 'and some herring and ling.'

His crafty wink told her that they weren't really less than the length stipulated by the authorities, who never came here to check anyway. 'Thanks, Murdo,' she grinned. He had been the first to give her the chance to buy cheaply, and she would always be grateful to him.

'I kept them separate,' he whispered, 'and you can have them for the same price as last time.'

Having already heard the other men charging more that day, she smiled, 'That's good of you.'

'How's things going wi' you, Liz?' he asked, presently, dumping a heavy box at her feet and watching her gut its shimmering contents with an expertise that told of experience.

'Fine. I've built up a good round, though I wouldn't have known where to start if you hadn't told me about the fishwife that died.'

'Aye, old Betsy. She'd been on the go for as long as I

can mind, and poor old soul, she should have retired years ago. But you've thrived on it, Liz. You look a lot better than the first time I saw you.'

Her smile was somewhat self-conscious. 'I told you, I'd been ill.'

He turned away to attend to another buyer, and she recalled the story she had spun him to explain why she had come to be selling fish from a creel. 'My man was lost when his boat went down,' she had said, afraid to tell the truth in case he'd heard of the man who went overboard from a Buckie drifter last November. To further distance herself from that tragedy, she had given her name as Liz Benzies and said she came from Lossiemouth. 'I didn't want to ask my mother for money, for she never wanted me to marry him, and when I got over the shock, all I wanted was to get away.'

Murdo had looked at her in pity. 'I'm sure your man's folk wouldna have let you starve, if you'd asked them.'

It had never crossed her mind to go to George's mother, not even when she went through Cullen, not after what the woman had said. In any case, she had been wishing she still had Peter as a friend ... but his wife had scuppered that.

Murdo had seen her distress, and after telling her he would sell her the fish she wanted at a fair price each time he took his boat in, he had added, 'I'll let the rest o' them ken it's old Betsy's round you've taken on, though it's nae a job for a bonnie young thing like you.'

She had found out how right he was, she thought ruefully. The weight of a full creel had been almost too much for her at first, but she had trudged over the countryside doggedly. To begin with, the wives of the farmers and fee'd men hadn't been keen on buying from a stranger, but when she told them old Betsy had died, they realized that if they didn't buy from her they wouldn't get fish at all, and they looked for her every week now. She had worked out Betsy's routes, a different one for each day of the week, and even if she didn't make much profit and had to live very frugally, she was surviving.

As it often did, her mind went back to the day she had left Buckie, weak and sore at heart, and she wondered how she had ever managed to get as far as Pennan. She had walked only a few miles when she'd had to stop and sit down at the side of the road to rest, and, remembering that the money she had left from the sale of her furniture had to last till she earned some more, she had put her arms on the creel and wept bitterly. When she recovered, she had felt as if the tears had cleansed her of her anger at God for depriving her of her husband, her hurt at George's mother's lack of understanding, her resentment at what Elsie and Jenny had said. Determined to overcome what Fate had sent her, she'd carried on past Portknockie, then seeing a baker in Cullen, she had bought a mince pie to eat while she went along. She hadn't been capable of logical thought, but she knew that Cullen was too near Buckie for her to stop there, and she had continued on her way, through Portsoy and Banff to Macduff, where exhaustion had forced her to take a bed for the night in a cheap hotel by the harbour.

Revived, she had gone on again in the morning, past Gardenstown and Crovie, until she came to the next steep road down to the sea, the road to Pennan. She didn't know why she had decided to settle here – maybe because the first little cottages she saw appealed to her, perched as they were on the side of the cliff – but she was glad that she had. She wouldn't have met Murdo otherwise, though the climb up from the village was an awful strain on her every day.

She rented her room, no food provided, from the wife of one of Murdo's friends. She told her landlady nothing of her circumstances, and kept herself to herself as much as she could. There was the occasional night when she thought of all the lonely nights stretching ahead of her, and she had to fight back the fear of growing too old to carry on, telling herself not to be morbid. She would weather the storm, she would find a haven she could call her own some day, when she could afford to buy a small house. The thing was, she couldn't save a ha'penny from what she made, and there wasn't much left of what she had started out with – she'd had to dip into it several times to pay the rent of her room.

Letting out a long, dejected breath, she lifted the old box Murdo had given her to hold the guts and tipped them into the sea, at which the gulls stopped their circling and screeched as they dived in after them. She packed her creel now, shovelling some of Murdo's salt over each layer as a preservative, and slung it over her shoulder.

'You're off again then, Liz?' Murdo smiled.

'Aye, once again.' Having paid for her purchases, she started up the steep slope, looking longingly as she passed at the neat cottages standing in tiers on the hillside, but not stopping at any of them. She had no customers in Pennan, for the fishermen took fries of fish home to their own wives and to the widows of friends who had been lost. She had to go well into the hinterland beyond the turnpike.

It took her nearly an hour to reach her first port of call, the farm of Easter Duncairn. She was always fascinated by the peculiar kink in the chimney here; it had a devil-may-care-look about it, a rakishness that she kind of liked, yet the farmhouse itself was solidly constructed and gave the impression that it would still be standing when the trump of doom sounded. There was a well-kept garden in front, with a gravel path running between the symmetrical rectangles of flower-bordered lawns and leading to the green front door. In her ignorance, it was this door she had gone to on her first day, but she had been told by a scraggy old woman in no uncertain terms to go round the back. At the time she had thought this unpleasant person was the farmer's wife, and having somehow expected a stout jolly person, she'd been quite disappointed; but she had learned from the cottar wives that Meggie was just a housekeeper. Whatever she was, she was an absolute pain to deal with.

As she usually did, Meggie spent ages making up her mind what to buy and then complaining that the fishwife was charging too much. Lizann wasn't to be browbeaten, however, and they were still trying to come to an agreement when a man came round the corner, and the housekeeper's manner changed like quicksilver. 'I'm buying some fish for your supper, Mr Fordyce,' she simpered ingratiatingly.

'It sounded as if you were arguing about the price,' he frowned, 'and I'm sure this young lady wouldn't cheat you.' He smiled at Lizann.

'No, sir,' she said, smiling back shyly.

'Give her what she asked, Meggie,' he ordered, and waited until the coins were put in Lizann's palm before he walked off.

'He's nae idea what things cost,' Meggie complained. 'His father wasna like that, though – I'd to account for every ha'penny to him. Of course, Dan's just been back since old Duncan died, and he never wanted to be a farmer, ony road.'

'What did he do before?' Lizann enquired idly.

Pleased to brag about her employer, Meggie said, proudly, 'He went to the university in Aberdeen, and he got a job wi' a soil research place somewhere round there. He was well up, near running it, when his father died, but Easter Duncairn had been in the family for generations and wi' being the only son, he felt obliged to carry it on.'

'You've got to admire him for that, then,' Lizann murmured.

'Oh, aye,' Meggie conceded, 'he believes in doing his duty, and he's a good man to work for, but he's aye experimenting – different chemicals for different crops – and the men dinna like it.'

'Some folk don't like changes,' Lizann agreed, 'but if his ideas work, they'll come round.' Anxious to get on, she heaved up the creel. 'I'll see you again next week.'

She went on now to the farm's cottar houses, glad that the wives of the hired men didn't haggle over the prices, but because she knew they had to watch what they spent, she sometimes took a copper off for them. At the second of the small group of houses she gratefully accepted a cup of tea from a white-haired woman who looked too old to be a fee'd man's wife and she took to be a mother. Whatever she was, she was very kind and pressed the girl to taste one of her newly made pancakes.

Leaving the fifth and last house, Lizann carried on along the road to the next farm, Mains of Duncairn. Here it was the farmer's wife who came to the door, another woman who dithered about what she wanted but didn't argue about the price. At one of the cottar houses there a young wife came out with an infant attached to her breast, at which a stab of pain pierced Lizann's heart. It brought back the memory of her own baby, the baby that had never drawn breath, and she had trouble in keeping the smile on her face.

'This little bugger's teething,' her customer said, delving into her purse to pay for a piece of ling. 'Skirling from morn to night, and the only road I can stop him's to keep him at my pap.'

A little revolted by the last word, Lizann wondered how she would have coped with teething problems, and decided that she would have tried some other way to soothe her child . . . if he had lived. Dropping the coins she received into the old handbag she used as a moneybag, she said, 'Thanks, and I hope his teeth've come through by the next time I see you.'

The woman gave a screech of laughter. 'God, I hope so, or I'll ha'e nae paps left.'

By the time Lizann had gone round Wester Duncairn, the next farmtoun, as she had heard the little communities called, the sun was high in the sky, and it was so hot that she looked for a shaded place to sit down for a little while. Finding a large oak tree, its branches spread wide, she laid down the creel – not so heavy now – where the sun wouldn't get at it and took a paper bag out of her pocket. Inside were two slices of bread sandwiched together with a thin spreading of margarine. She wished that she had something to drink, but even if she could have afforded a bottle of lemonade, it would have been too much extra weight for her to carry, and she could get water from a burn farther on.

Her repast over, she lay back on the grass and closed her eyes. It was very pleasant here, no sound except the buzzing of the bees as they made their way from buttercup to buttercup and the occasional clicking of a grasshopper. If only she could stay for ever ... if only George was beside her, she would be in heaven. It was still too painful to think of him, so she turned her mind to something else. She was glad she had made it possible for Mick to marry Jenny, for her mother would have a daughter-in-law to look after her – Auntie Lou was too old to keep going to the Yardie every day for much longer. Jenny wouldn't mind taking on the job; she was a good-hearted girl.

Lizann gave a small sigh. At the time she'd been easily upset, touchy about the least little thing, and after what that horrible Elsie had said she had taken Jenny's little outburst too much to heart. She had since realized that Jenny had likely said what she did without thinking, but the resentment must have been there. If Lizann had stayed in Buckie, Mick would have kept giving her money and it could have caused rows between him and Jenny.

It suddenly occurred to Lizann that Mick had also been paying off the debt to the shipyard. Had that been what Jenny meant? Had she, in her foolish, nervy pride, jumped to the wrong conclusion? There could only have been a few instalments left to pay – it would likely be settled by now – and what he had given her was just a fleabite. She took a moment or two to consider this. She, like Jenny, had acted on impulse, and it was too late to go back. She'd done the only thing possible by leaving, though there had been times, when she was feeling really low, that she regretted it.

But if she didn't keep away, Peter's wife would spread her lies about and he could lose his job. It put new heart into Lizann to think she was repaying his kindness to her at the time of her bereavement, even though he would never know, and if her new life was far from ideal, things were bound to improve. She was still in her twenties, after all.

Feeling more optimistic now, she went over her day so far. Her sales had been good, and she shouldn't have any more trouble with Meggie at Easter Duncairn. She'd always dreaded going there, the old woman had been so difficult, but surely she would be more reasonable now. The farmer had seemed a nice man. She judged him to be around fifty, average height, fairly broad and not very good-looking. Not that he was ugly . . . his eyes were a kindly grey and his brown hair had a cute wave at the front. At first glance she had thought he was very serious, grim even, and then he'd given her that attractive smile and she knew that he had a lighter side to him. She had, however, got the impression that nothing would change his mind once it was made up and hoped that his new ideas would soon meet with his men's approval. But she couldn't sit here all day thinking about a man she would never see again, didn't particularly want to see again. The air was cooling, and she still had fish to sell.

Dan Fordyce sat down in the parlour for his usual after-dinner smoke. Meggie was rattling around in the kitchen, so she wouldn't bother him for a while. Lighting his pipe, he leaned back in the old leather chair to think. He hadn't been able to get that young lassie out of his mind since he saw her. Her faded blouse, darned in several places, had been sticking to her back, and her skirt had been crumpled. Her black curly hair had been a bit untidy, the tendrils round her face damp with sweat, but it was her eyes that haunted him. A dark, dark brown with jet black centres, and fringed with the thickest, longest lashes he had ever seen, they had held a deep sorrow which a girl her age should not have known. She had come through some terrible trouble, something she had not got over yet, and she had looked so vulnerable that he'd wanted to usher her inside to take care of her.

Never in all his adult years having given any girl a second glance, he could not understand why she'd had such an effect on him. If he had been younger ... but he would be forty-three next month, and she must only be ... about seventeen? To her he would be an old man ... and so he was. Old and stuck in a rut. Granted, the rut was not of his making, but he was deeply entrenched in it now.

In the kitchen, Meggie Thow was also thinking. She had seen Mr Fordyce's eyes lingering on the young fishwife, though the lassie herself hadn't noticed, which was a blessing, for it might have put ideas in her head. Dan would be a catch for any woman, and he could have his pick of dozens of farmers' daughters, so his housekeeper wasn't going to stand by and let him make a fool of himself over a creature young enough to be *his* daughter.

That was often the way with men in their forties – a flutter of some young thing's eyelashes and they fell like a stone.

Thumping a shining copper pan on to a shelf, it dawned on Meggie that it wouldn't matter who Dan took for a wife, she would still be out of a job. She had been employed here as housemaid to his mother before he was even born, and had been taken on as housekeeper when Mrs Fordyce passed away, eighteen years ago. She would soon be sixty, but she would defy anybody to better her at cooking and baking, though a new mistress would want somebody a lot younger. It would be the finish of her, for nobody would want to employ a woman of her age.

Well, Meggie thought, grimly, she could do nothing if he took a fancy to some suitable maiden lady, but he wouldn't set eyes on that fishwife again if she could help it. She could hardly tell the creature to stop coming, the master liked a bit of fish, but she would buy whatever was at the top of the creel, pay what was asked and send her on her way. He would soon forget her, for he wasn't a ladies' man, thank goodness.

Never having given much thought to how the changing seasons affected those who worked on the land, Lizann was amazed to find that the workers from one place helped the neighbouring farms to bring in the harvest in August. In addition to the big brosy men whose muscles rippled under leathered skin as they bound the sheaves and stooked them to wait for the cart to take them to the mill, or to be built into huge ricks for drying out, several young maids were running about keeping them supplied with things to eat and drink. Even grumpy Meggie could be seen carrying out steaming kettles of tea.

The men, always out for a laugh, young and old, shouted to Lizann as she went past – 'Hey, lass, come and gi'es a kiss' or 'My God, where have you been a' my life?' – and sometimes she was surprised by a young buck who had crept up behind her to pinch her bottom. The first time it happened she hadn't known what to do, but she had soon realized it was just part of their fun and could now laugh along with them.

She sometimes wished she could be part of this happy throng, and considered asking one of the farmers if he wanted another girl to help, but the fear of being turned down in public held her back. When things seemed to be wearing to an end, one of the men, a young strapling a few years younger than herself, caught her round the waist. 'Would you like to come to the meal and ale the morn's night wi' me?'

She was tempted to accept until it crossed her mind that he was likely teasing, so she shoved him away with a laugh and went on her way.

Just after eleven on the third day of September, her landlady called upstairs to her. 'That's Chamberlain saying on the wireless we're at war wi' Germany.'

Although Lizann waited for an invitation to go down and discuss this upsetting news over a cup of tea, nothing came, and she sat down sadly to think about it herself. She had no idea what happened in a war – she had never known any men who had fought in the last one; surely all the fighting would be in Europe? But she had heard the men down at the harbour saying Hitler would like to conquer Britain, and she wished now that she'd listened to Mick and George when they were speaking about it. But surely the Germans wouldn't reach Scotland? And even if they did, they wouldn't attack the fishing boats from the Moray Firth, so Mick wouldn't be in any danger. And Peter was a draughtsman, so he'd be all right as well. And they wouldn't be called up, not when they had such important jobs.

*   *   *

Jenny Jappy had also been listening to Neville Chamberlain's speech, and her face was ashen by the time it ended. She had never believed Mick's gloomy predictions, but it seemed he'd been right, and now he'd be at Hitler's mercy. She glanced at Hannah, to see if she had taken in what the Prime Minister had said, but her head was buried in the *Sunday Post* Jake Berry had taken in. She was so upset by the news herself, however, that she rose in a moment to brew some tea to revive her. There had been so many men killed in the last war. The local names were on the memorial in Cluny Square, and when this war was over there would be a lot more ... but please God, not Mick Jappy's. Not Mick Jappy's!

After dinner, Jenny wished she had someone to talk to, and so, telling Hannah she was going to see Elsie for a wee while, she hurried along to Main Street. Being six months pregnant, she was quite breathless when she reached the Taits' house, and Elsie, in the middle of washing up her dishes, was glad of an excuse to stop. 'What's up, Jenny?' she asked, giving her hands a perfunctory wipe on a grubby towel.

Hardly able to credit that she hadn't heard, Jenny said, 'Were you not listening to Chamberlain this morning? Britain's at war with Germany.'

'Oh well, everybody said it was coming.'

'Are you not worried for Peter?'

'Worried. What about?'

'Oh, Elsie. Him and Mick are in the Navy, they'll be sent to wherever they're needed ... to fight the Jerries.'

A frown crossed the other woman's face, natural as nature intended for once. 'D'you think they might ... be killed?'

'It's possible.'

'Oh, Jenny, and I was really nasty to Peter when he was home.'

Elsie looked so distraught that Jenny regretted alarming her. 'They'll likely be safe enough.'

'Oh, I hope so. You see, I was angry at him for joining the Navy and leaving me wi' two boys.' She stopped and eyed Jenny's rounded stomach. 'And you'll be left wi' an infant. When's it due again?'

'Round about Christmas, and Mick thought he should be home in time for the birth. I just hope he doesn't have to act midwife for me like he did for Lizann.'

'Oh aye, Peter tell't me about that.' Recalling how Peter had come by the information, Elsie's heart hardened against him. If he hadn't been taken in by that pasty-faced widow, he would still have been a proper husband to her, and she wouldn't have needed Lenny.

Sensing a change in her friend, Jenny said she'd have to get back to Hannah. 'Thank goodness she hasn't the wit to know about the war.'

Having had several soakings over the past two weeks, Lizann was growing worried about the winter. It was only October, but already the ground was white with frost in the early mornings, though it soon cleared. The soles of her shoes were so thin now that every tiny stone she stood on felt like a boulder, and worse still, they didn't keep out the wet. She had resorted to packing them with wads of any old newspapers she found, because she couldn't afford to buy a new pair, nor a coat, nor a thicker cardigan. Her hands were raw and hacked, and her legs were a blotchy red with the chilblains caused by brine running out of her creel.

It was clear but cold when she set off up the hill one morning, and she was surprised when a woman from one of the cottages called out: 'I hope you dinna mind, but I see you going past every day, and ... I was going to throw out this old coat o' my man's, but I thought maybe you'd be glad o' it.' Looking anxiously apologetic, she held out a shapeless black garment with a green tinge to it that spoke of having been stored in a damp cupboard for many a long year.

It would have gone against the grain at one time for Lizann to accept such a monstrosity, but she had no pride left. 'It's very good of you,' she smiled. 'Thanks very much.'

The woman watched her putting it on. 'It's a bit big, but it'll keep you warm,' she observed before going inside.

The coat would have gone round Lizann twice, and its hem practically touched the ground, but it would keep her warm, she decided, and shield her poor legs from the brine.

Working along with the 'tattie howkers' – mostly children who got a week off school to help gather the potatoes – Dan Fordyce spotted a peculiar figure coming along the road. He was very short, and his long black coat was flapping round him though he was doing his best to hold the front edges together. Thinking he was a tramp, Dan kept his eyes on him, and it was only when the stranger turned into the farm track and he saw the creel that he realized it was the young fishwife.

Bending his back to his task again, he was glad that someone had given her a coat. He had seen her from a distance a few times since the onset of the cold weather, and had felt so sorry for her that he'd considered giving her one of his, or asking Meggie if she had something she could spare, but she might have thought he was interested in the girl. He was interested, but only in her welfare. He wondered if the lass knew how incongruous she looked but supposed she had no mirror – and what did it matter anyway, if it kept out the cold?

When he saw her leaving the farmhouse just minutes later, he knew that his housekeeper had not even given her a cup of tea. He wished that he had the courage to go and speak to the poor thing – a kind word might lift that attitude of dejection – but if he did it would be all round the district that he was chasing after her. Besides, what could he say? She would think it strange if he said he was glad someone had given her a coat. It was none of his business, and she would likely tell him so.

When he went in for his lunch, he expected Meggie to remark on what a sight the girl had been, but she didn't mention it, and neither did he.

Chapter Twenty

❧

Lizann was forced to take a break at the end of December, because none of the boats went out. With nowhere else to go, she huddled over the driftwood smouldering in the tiny grate in her room, rising only to get a bite to eat occasionally. She was worried that her stand-by money, as she called it, was so low, only shillings left after buying the loaf and the bottle of milk, but luckily one of the cottars' wives had given her three eggs and a lump of home-made cheese last time she was there.

On Hogmanay she let her little peep of fire go out, and went to bed long before the New Year came in. This last month had been really hard, she mused, shivering between sheets that felt, and probably were, damp; without the old coat, she doubted if she could have survived the howling winds and driving rain. There had even been days when the coat was still so wet in the morning that she'd had to leave it behind. No wonder she had a never-ending cold.

Thankfully, there hadn't been much snow yet, though it would come with a vengeance in January or February, and she wasn't looking forward to battling against blizzards. Curling into a tight ball in an effort to get warm, she prayed that 1940 would be a better year for her than the one just ending.

'Lizann, come and pick up my paper!'

Jenny couldn't help frowning at the whining voice. It was bad enough to be called by the wrong name without being interrupted when she was bathing her month-old baby. 'My hands are wet. I'll pick it up when I'm finished here.'

'Hurry up, then!' Hannah had no patience now, and expected attention immediately she demanded it.

To take her mother-in-law's mind off the newspaper, Jenny said, 'I still can't get over Peter Tait giving up his fine job last year and going to sea. And then joining the R.N.V.R. with Mick. If he'd stayed at the shipyard, he'd have been exempt.'

'Peter's a good laddie,' Hannah observed. 'You should stick to him, Lizann, for there's some men . . .' She tailed off, looking more confused than ever.

'Lizann broke off with Peter, d'you not mind?'

'Oh aye, he wed that . . .' Hannah's eyes swivelled away, darkening with the thought that there was something there she didn't want to remember. Even this left her troubled mind in the next instant. 'You got another man, though, didn't you, Lizann?'

'Lizann married George Buchan, but he was drowned. Mick and me called this wee lad after him.' She poked her tiny son, who gurgled with glee.

'George Buchan?' Hannah muttered, reflectively. 'Aye, I mind something about him. Did he nae come from Cullen?'

Jenny was delighted at this. 'That's right,' she encouraged.

'But there was something bad about him.'

'He wasn't bad. Lizann was truly happy with him.'

'Are you nae Lizann?'

'I'm Jenny, Mick's wife.'

Her eyes clearing a little, Hannah said, 'Jenny Cowie, I mind now.'

Although she had been Jenny Jappy – a comic name really – for almost a year, she bit back a correction. It was a step in the right direction that Hannah remembered her maiden name. Jenny had dried her wriggling infant and was putting on a clean napkin before the older woman spoke again. 'Mick and Jenny, Lizann and Peter,' she said, in a sing-song chant. 'Mick and Jenny, Lizann and Peter.'

Jenny sighed. 'Lizann and George. Say it, Hannah. Lizann and George.'

Hannah shook her head stubbornly. 'Lizann and Peter!'

Jenny gave up and concentrated on manoeuvring her squirming baby into his vest and nightgown, then pinned up the foot to form a bag so that his feet wouldn't be cold. Taking him over to the fireside, she laid him on his grandmother's lap. 'Here, take Georgie till I empty his bath.'

Hannah's crooked hands went round the little bundle, her expression softening as she crooned, 'Who's his Mammy's little dearie, then?'

Jenny lifted the enamel bath from the floor, and took it outside to pour down the drain, then she dried it thoroughly before hanging it up on a nail at the back porch, smiling as she heard Hannah making baby sounds and chuckling to herself.

'He minds me right on Mick when he was a bairn,' she said, when Jenny took him from her.

'So he should,' Jenny laughed. 'He's Mick's son.'

'Aye, so he is.' But Hannah didn't look convinced of this.

When Jenny came down from settling the baby into his crib, she said, 'Are you ready for your bed and all?'

'It's early yet, isn't it?'

'We'll wait a while if you like, but I'd like to get all Georgie's things washed, and I've a pile of ironing to do.'

'Oh, if it's like that, you'd better put me to my bed right now!'

Hannah sounded offended, but Jenny didn't argue, it wasn't worth it. 'Right, I'll give you a lift up.' She hoisted her mother-in-law out of her seat, and then, supporting her round the waist and taking nearly all her weight, helped her through to her room. 'Shoes off first,' she said brightly, making Hannah sit on the bed, 'then stockings.'

Hannah submitted to the nightly routine as if she were no older than her grandson, and Jenny removed layers of clothes before struggling to get her into her winceyette nightgown and woollen cardigan – she always felt cold. 'That's you ready, then,' she said, swinging Hannah's pathetically thin legs up on to the bed.

She wasn't grateful. Glaring malevolently at Jenny as the bedclothes were tucked round her, she spat out, 'You canna wait to get rid o' me, can you? I'm just in your road.'

'That's stupid! I just want you settled before I start washing.'

Hannah's expression changed, her voice took on its usual complaining tone. 'There'll maybe come a day when you've to depend on somebody else to do everything for you.'

Jenny patted her hand. 'Aye, I suppose there will. Now, I'll leave the light on for you to read a while, and I'll come back and put it out.'

She went outside to the standpipe to fill a pail with cold water to soak the dirty nappies overnight, then she filled the kettle and two pots to have hot water to wash the rest of the baby clothes. That done, she laid past the Johnson's powder and the zinc and castor oil ointment, then started to sweep up the crumbs Hannah had dropped from her mouth at suppertime. Looking after her was more tiring than attending to wee Georgie, Jenny thought; not that she minded doing it, but there were times, like tonight, when she was so tired it would have been heaven just to sit down and relax for a while.

Not for the first time, Jenny wished that Mick hadn't volunteered. He'd been a great help to her when he was on leave over Christmas and New Year, when she'd been so big and heavy the smallest jobs had been an awful effort for her, but she could still do with him at home. Babsie Berry had done her best for two days after wee Georgie was born at the beginning of January, but the cleaning, cooking, washing, running up and down the stairs with trays, topped by attending to Hannah, had been too much for her. She hadn't wanted to give up but hadn't argued much when she was ordered home. And so, Jenny thought, with a slight shake of her head, her lying-in time had been cut drastically short. Still, she was young, she could cope, and when Hannah got on her nerves, as she so often did, she just had to remind herself how much the old woman loved wee Georgie. Besides, it would soon be two months since Mick had gone back to his ship, so it shouldn't be long till he was home again.

Having cheered herself, Jenny laid the ironing blanket over the table and picked up the iron she'd been heating at the fire. She still had yesterday's washing to attend to.

The snow was getting deeper and deeper every day, and Lizann's shoes and the old coat were almost falling apart with being wet so much. She had overcome the first problem, to a certain extent, by cutting up some old canvas she found and making bags to tie round her shoes, but she couldn't do anything about the coat. She had no money to pay rent, let alone buy clothes. When she gave up her room she had told her landlady she'd found somewhere else, but she was actually having to take shelter anywhere she could. She had slept in what had once been a sail-maker's shed for a week until the roof was blown off. She had crouched under a bridge once, but she'd been so cold and stiff in the morning she could hardly walk. Then she had found a ruined house with broken windows, but she hadn't had a wink of sleep for the wind howling in and the flurries of snow it brought with it.

Her homelessness was not her only hardship. She hadn't had a proper meal for weeks, only the odd cup of tea and a scone from a customer. She was exhausted, therefore, and weak with hunger, when she trailed down to the harbour one early morning in February. Her plight worsened when she saw that Murdo's boat had not been out, and only two of the others had braved the storm. Their prices would be so high she'd not be able to buy much, which meant less takings and even less could be bought tomorrow. She was caught in a vicious spiral, and where would it end?

With her creel only half-full, she struggled up the hill and ploughed slowly along what she hoped was the road, though the snow was so deep she couldn't really tell. Her heart was pounding from the exertion of lifting one leaden foot after the other when the old picture flashed into her mind. It had been her good luck token, and if she hadn't had to sell it, things might have gone better for her. It did not enter her poor benumbed brain that her bad luck had begun before that, with her husband's death, because she had become convinced that George's drowning was God's punishment for their sin in Yarmouth.

But she needed her full concentration to keep going, and carried on until she was almost sure that she had lost her way and would have to turn back. Then, taking a brief rest, she glanced around and nearly cried out with relief at the welcome sight of a familiarly-angled smoking chimney away to her right. Everything was all right! It was the farmhouse of Easter Duncairn, her first call.

Keeping her head down against the biting wind which held the first flakes of what promised to be a bad storm, she trudged on, but the sky was darkening ominously, the snow doubled in intensity, and she stood for a moment debating whether or not to go on. If she didn't, she would have to throw away her fish – she had no means of cooking any for her own use – and she couldn't buy any tomorrow. She had to carry on.

Her strength was giving out; she could see nothing through the raging blizzard, and the going was so difficult that she had to halt every few steps to get her breath back. She did not realize that she had wandered off the road, and she would have missed her first set of customers if the snow hadn't eased briefly and given her another chance to see the smoking chimney, now to her left and slightly farther away. She turned towards it thankfully, and found herself, some twenty minutes later, at the front of the farmhouse. Searching for the back door, she tottered round the side of the building.

Her fingers had no feeling, and she held her creel out when the door was opened in answer to the tap she made with her foot. Meggie seemed surprised to see her, but went back inside for a plate to hold the fish she would be buying. 'You'll be charging the earth for them the day,' she remarked, sourly, when she returned, 'but I suppose I'll just have to pay up or do without.'

The tantalizing smell of baking made Lizann long for something to eat, but the housekeeper didn't offer her anything and took quite a time to choose what she wanted. 'Well,' she demanded when she lifted out two large haddocks, 'how much d'you want for them?'

Lizann gasped out her price through chattering teeth, and the woman dropped the coins into her moneybag, muttering, 'If I was you, I'd go hame afore the storm gets ony worse.'

Lizann shook her head and staggered off. At the time of the harvest, when all the workers had been involved in getting the grain in as long as the weather was dry, she had been hailed by several of them as she went past, had been allowed to share in what the wives took out for them to eat, had felt at one with the rough, laughing, red-faced men whose muscles rippled under their browned skins. They had made her welcome, it had been a friendly place . . . but now there wasn't a soul to be seen, not even an animal she could cosy up to for warmth.

Already chilled to the bone, she had started to feel really queer. Her head was spinning and there were pains in her chest – but some invisible force impelled her forward. Every now and then her feet were swallowed up in a snowdrift and she wasn't conscious of making the effort to pull them out. She inched on stubbornly despite having lost all sense of direction, until a high-pitched buzzing started in her ears. She shook her head vigorously to dispel it, but that only made her feel dizzier, so she stopped and put her hands to her head in despair. For several seconds she stood swaying on her feet, then her senses left her altogether. Her body made no sound as it hit the cushion-soft whiteness of the ground, the falling creel spewing its contents around her head in a wide arc.

And the snow kept falling relentlessly.

Martha Laing looked up in surprise when her brother came out of his room wearing his heavy oilskin coat, his white hair tousled but a look of determination on his lined face. 'You're not going out in that blizzard, Adam?' she burst out.

'The beasts need fed whatever the weather,' he replied, sitting down to pull on a pair of well-worn rubber boots.

'But Mr Fordyce wouldn't expect you to . . .'

'It's what I'm paid for,' Adam said, stubbornly. 'I'm not fit for much else nowadays, and he's been good enough to keep me on.'

Martha said no more. Adam was an obstinate old man, had been obstinate even when he was a young man, and there was no point in arguing with him. She rose to put some more coal on the fire so it would be burning better for him coming back. It was good of Mr Fordyce to let him keep his job. She had been afraid, when old Duncan died, that his son would make a clean sweep and she and Adam would have to get out of the tied house, so it had been a great weight off her mind when he said he was keeping on all the farm hands. Of course, he likely had no idea that Adam was wearing on for seventy, but it was a godsend just the same, for where could they have gone if they'd had to leave?

Adam had been at Easter Duncairn since he was about thirty, not long after he'd got married. Most farm servants moved on every six months, but Peg had liked this place so much she'd made Adam stay put. When she died, coming up to fourteen years since, it had been like he'd lost his purpose in life, so that was why Martha, fifty-eight at the time and still a spinster, had offered to come and keep house for her young brother. They got on well and never an angry word had passed between them, though they had their little differences.

She shouldn't have let him go out just now, not with his bad chest. If he got soaked he could land with pneumonia, and Mr Fordyce wouldn't put up with a man who wasn't pulling his weight. Martha gave her head an impatient shake. Och, she was just a worrying old woman! Adam had on his boots and his oilskin coat, what harm could come to him? He would be back in no time, and she'd best heat some fresh underwear for him.

After hanging a clean linder and drawers over the string under the mantelpiece, Martha sat down again to weigh up what they would lose if Adam was sacked. The cottage was a bit bigger than most cottar houses, with a kitchen and two rooms downstairs – one meant as a parlour, but when she moved in, Adam had said she could have it as her bedroom: his daughter Margaret likely hadn't wanted to share her attic room. All the rooms were a fair size, and old Duncan Fordyce had got water piped in about six years ago, so they could have a sink with a cold water tap in the kitchen. And a lavatory had been built on at the back, with its door put in under the stairs. What a boon that had been, Martha mused. She used to hate trailing away up to the far end of the backyard to the dry lavvy in the dark winter nights. She had put off going, and gone through agony till her bladder had been at bursting point.

Her eyes took an admiring glance round the kitchen, and she couldn't help thinking how much better it looked now than when she'd first seen it. Adam and his young wife hadn't long been married at the time, and they'd only had a few bits of furniture, but it hadn't taken Peg long to make it into a proper home. As she used to say, 'It's the love that's in it that makes a home.' She'd been a right one, had Peg, a hard worker who hadn't been afraid to scrimp in order to save for the things she wanted. She'd had her heart set on a moquette suite she had seen on one of her rare visits to Banff, and though it had taken her years, she had eventually managed to buy one which was very similar. The armchairs were a bit worn after so long, but they were still comfortable . . . once you knew where the loose spring was. If you didn't, you soon found out!

The couch, being less sat upon, still looked brand new . . . almost. Only an area on the right-hand side, slightly lighter than the rest and with a tinge of pink to it, showed where Peg had scoured off the ochre Adam had spilt on it when he first painted the kitchen walls. That was in the days when wallpaper was too costly for cottar folk, and only available in shops in the towns, anyway. So it had been a case of ochre – a sickly yellow or an equally sickly dark pink – or whitewash. Being houseproud, Peg had opted for whitewash after the fiasco, and it had certainly made the room look brighter, even if the least little mark showed. Give her her due, though, she had never once complained about the extra work it gave her.

Martha suddenly recalled her mind to the present.

Adam was taking an awful long time, over an hour, but he'd likely be finding it difficult to cross the fields in this weather. And he'd likely stay a while with the beasts once he'd fed them, for he liked to speak to them, to gentle them as if they were bairns. And he did look on them as bairns, she supposed – his bairns.

Another hour passed before Adam appeared, by which time his sister was imagining that he had fallen into a snowdrift and couldn't get out, but her relief was tempered with dismay when she saw that he was holding his chest. 'Are you all right?' she asked.

'Give me a minute to come to myself,' he puffed.

She filled the teapot while she was waiting, but forgot about it when he said, 'I'll need you to come outside and help me.'

Puzzled, but asking no questions, she put her shawl round her head and flung her coat round her shoulders before following him out. 'Leave the door open a wee bit,' he ordered.

She wasn't prepared for what she saw in the slim shaft of light that sneaked out from the kitchen lamp, and clutched at her breast in horror. 'Heaven help us! Is it a man or a woman?'

Not bothering to explain how he knew, Adam muttered, 'It's a woman and I'd say she's at death's door, so we'd best get her inside.'

The woman wasn't heavy, but it still took them some time to lift her rigid body off the barrow and through the doorway. They laid her on the sofa, and while Martha went to get something to cover her, Adam looked down on the prostrate figure with critical eyes. 'She looks like a gypsy to me.'

Coming in, Martha said thoughtfully, 'I'm not sure I want a gypsy in the house, she could put a curse on us.' But she tucked the blanket all round the woman's legs. 'Her coat's frozen solid,' she murmured, then, recognizing the black garment, she peered at the bloodless face. 'It's the lassie that comes round with the fish! Oh, the poor soul!'

She lifted the blanket and held up one of Lizann's legs. 'Look, she's had to tie bits of canvas round her shoes.' Without undoing the strings, she pulled canvas and shoes off together, then, going down on her knees, she gently massaged the almost black toes poking through the holes in the stockings. 'I hope she hasn't got frostbite. You'll have to fill a pig for her, Adam.'

She was rubbing the hacked hands when her brother came over with the earthenware hot water bottle, and she put it between the layers of the doubled blanket. 'It would be agony for her if her feet touched it.'

For the next fifteen minutes, Martha did her best to coax her patient back to life while Adam stood helplessly beside her. At last, the young woman gave a low moan and moved her head. 'She's coming round,' Martha said jubilantly.

'Thank God!'

At the sound of their voices, Lizann opened her eyes and looked from one hopeful face to the other in strained wonderment. Martha took her hand. 'Just rest there a while.'

Her mission accomplished, she rose to fill the kettle again, and when she was setting it on the fire, she motioned to her brother to join her. 'It was a close thing,' she whispered. 'If you hadn't . . .'

'Aye,' he nodded. 'God knows how long she could have lain there.'

'How did you find her?'

'I was coming back from the byre, and I tripped over something . . . I thought it was a stone off the dyke . . . and I bent down to shift it . . . in case somebody else fell and hurt themselves . . . but it wouldn't move.'

He stopped for breath, but Martha urged him on. 'The

snow melted with the heat of my hands ... and I saw it was a head ... so I raked about till I got an arm and there was still ... a pulse. So I went for the old barrow, though I'd an awful job getting her on ... and I took her here ... it was nearer than the farmhouse.' He leaned back on his chair, exhausted by saying so much.

Martha gave a humourless laugh. 'Meggie Thow wouldn't have thanked you if you'd taken her there.' The kettle on the boil, she poured out the tea she had infused before and made fresh.

Going over to Lizann, she slid one arm under the girl's head and held the cup to her lips. When it was empty, she said, 'I'm going upstairs to make a bed ready for you.'

Always uncomfortable alone with females other than his sister, Adam sat down by the fire, but in a few minutes Lizann croaked, 'Was it you ... that took me here?'

Embarrassed, he bobbed his head a few times, but when she attempted, unsuccessfully, to put her feet on the floor, he burst out, 'Bide there till Martha comes back.'

'Your wife?'

'My sister.'

When Martha appeared again she said, 'Are you feeling better, lass?'

'She's not fit to walk,' Adam observed.

'The bed's made up, but I'll ...' She looked at Lizann apologetically. 'I'm sorry, lass, I'll have to wash you first. We thought you were a gypsy, your face is that ingrained with dirt.'

'I'd nowhere ... to wash myself.'

Martha felt even more pity for her. 'I'll soon have you clean. Get the bath through, Adam, and make it ready for her.'

'Oh, no!' Lizann protested, weakly, glancing at the man.

'He'll bide in his room till we're finished,' Martha said, firmly.

The bath filled, Adam helped to move Lizann to the fireside before he left the kitchen, then Martha stripped her and took her weight till she sat down in the warm water. 'I'll leave you to soak,' she said, and went through to Adam. 'Her underthings are just in rags, so go into my chest of drawers and get one of my vests for her, and a nightgown . . . and a pair of knickers, I'll come for them when she's ready.'

Returning to Lizann, she set about getting her clean, which turned out to be quite a difficult task because, embarrassed at being seen naked, she persisted in trying to hide her intimate parts. 'Modesty's all right in its place,' Martha muttered, 'but we'll never be done at this rate.'

Defeated, Lizann remained still and stared at the fire while the old woman scrubbed every inch of her body until she was satisfied that it could be made no cleaner. The drying and dressing would have overcome a woman with less determination than Martha, but at last she got Lizann decently covered and called to Adam. 'You'll have to give me a hand to get her up to Margaret's room.'

Brother and sister made a cat's cradle with their hands for Lizann to sit on, but when they reached the stairs, they saw that there wasn't room to take her up that way. 'I could carry her,' Adam offered.

Martha was about to say he wasn't fit for that, but having seen how sharply the girl's ribs and shoulder blades protruded from her emaciated body, she changed her mind. 'Well, there's nothing of her, so I suppose . . . just watch and not strain yourself.'

Holding her under the knees and round her back, he lifted her in one seemingly effortless movement. 'She's light as a feather,' he smiled, as he started up the steps.

When he laid his burden on the bed, he looked at Martha for guidance on what to do next. 'Go down and fill the pig again,' she told him.

'Who's Margaret?' Lizann asked, when he went out.

'Adam's daughter. He was forty when she was born, so that would make her nearly twenty-eight now. She was working in an office in Edinburgh and married the boss, but they emigrated to Australia five years ago.'

When Adam took up the hot water bottle, Martha wrapped it inside an old pillowcase and pushed it under the bedclothes. 'I'll leave you to rest now,' she told Lizann. 'You'll not be fit for anything for a long time yet.'

'But . . .'

'You're welcome to bide here for as long as you need.'

'But I can't pay . . .'

'I'm not wanting anything from you. Good gracious me, if you knew how often I've wanted another woman to speak to, instead of sitting every night with that brother of mine. He's that dour, it takes him all his time to string a couple of sentences together sometimes.' She went out, leaving Lizann with a faint smile on her face.

'I'd right like to know why that poor thing was in such a state,' the old woman said when she went downstairs. 'She looks like she hasn't had a square meal for ages, and you'd think somebody would've noticed she wasn't fit to be trailing about like she did. She'll not sell any more fish for a good while.'

'She's real bonnie when she's clean,' Adam remarked, self-consciously. 'Curly black hair and brown eyes . . . and fair skin. She's nothing like a gypsy now.'

'She'd have been better looked after if she *had* been a gypsy.'

Adam stroked his nose. 'You'll have to give her something to eat.'

'Empty bellies shrink, so I'll just make a bowl of saps when she's had time to come to herself. That'll be a wee bit of nourishment.'

When she took up the saps – two slices of bread soaked in hot milk and sprinkled with sugar – Martha had to spoon it into the girl's mouth, and was pleased that she supped most of it. 'Are you thawing out yet?'

'My feet's tingling now,' Lizann said, shyly.

'That's a start. Would you like the pig filled again?'

'No . . . thank you.'

Martha shook her head sadly when she went downstairs. 'She's not used to folk doing anything for her, the poor soul, and what'll she do when she's on her feet again? She wouldn't make much from selling fish, and I think she's been living rough. That's why she hadn't been able to keep herself clean.'

They sat pensively for some time, then Martha picked up the poker and stirred the coals in the fire. 'Adam, you wouldn't think of letting her bide here?'

He looked at her in astonishment. 'For good?'

'Aye. Once she's better, she could help me in the house, and maybe in the summer she would help you in the garden. We're not so able nowadays to do things, and we're aye getting older.'

'We can't pay her anything.'

Martha had already thought of that. 'It seems to me she's hardly had any money to herself for a long time. I think she'd jump at the chance to work for her keep.'

Adam chewed this over for a few minutes, then said, 'She'll need new clothes. You said yourself she was in rags.'

'There's still some of the things Margaret took here before she went to Australia, and they're about the same size.'

Adam had no answer to this. 'We'll see, then.'

Knowing her brother as she did, Martha was satisfied that the battle was as good as won. It all depended on the girl herself agreeing to it.

Chapter Twenty-one

❦

Going into the byre the following morning, Dan Fordyce found that his cows had been given their usual ration of hay, cattle-cake and mashed turnips, and he was very thankful to have a man like Adam Laing in his employ. The old man never neglected his work whatever the weather, and it was to be hoped that he hadn't suffered any ill effects. Continuing on his way, Dan discovered that the overnight gales had blown most of the snow against the dykes and the ground had a thick covering of solid ice. There would be no outside work done today again, he mused glumly, but he was soon to make a more disquieting discovery.

Carrying on his round of inspection, he decided to go and ask about Adam when he was finished, but twenty minutes later, as he made his way carefully over the ice, his eye was caught by something in the field to his left. On investigating, he saw that it was a creel, almost submerged under a frozen drift. 'God Almighty!' he exclaimed, remembering the fish he'd had for supper last night, though it hadn't dawned on him that his housekeeper had bought them from the young fishwife. Even in the blizzard, that poor girl had called as usual, but why had she cast her creel off here? She couldn't have had much to sell in this weather, so possibly she had sold all she had and gone home without the basket. It would have been an encumbrance to her with conditions underfoot so bad.

His mind eased, he aimed a few idle kicks at the base of the drift and had another nasty shock when he saw

several fish embedded in the chunk of ice that sheared off
... and even more in the space it left behind. The creel
hadn't been empty! The girl wouldn't have abandoned
what was her livelihood! Had she felt ill? Had she collapsed somewhere farther on? His eyes circled the vast
expanse of whiteness but saw nothing apart from several
round, iced eruptions which he knew were really the large
boulders which bedevilled his ploughmen, a legacy from
Pictish times that nothing would shift. Desperate to find
out what had happened to the girl, he went back to his
house to ask if Meggie knew anything.

'She was a good bit later than she usually is,' she told
him, vaguely.

'When was she here?' he demanded, his stomach tight
with dread.

'Oh now, it would have been ... maybe twelve, maybe
a bittie after. I didna think to look at the clock.'

Her sarcasm angered him. 'Why didn't you take her
inside, woman? The storm had started by then.'

'She was anxious to get on. She did look kind o' funny
though, now I come to think on it.'

'And you still let her go? Good God, Meggie, why
didn't you take her inside? Wherever she gets her fish,
she ...'

'I think it's Pennan.'

'That's a long way to come in weather like this.'

'She didna need to come,' Meggie said, defensively,
'and if she'd had ony sense, she wouldna.'

'She probably couldn't afford to lose a day's takings.
I can't think how she managed to get as far as this, and
it looks as if she didn't get any farther. Her creel's lying
out there.'

Trying to make up for what he evidently considered
her short-comings, Meggie muttered, 'Maybe one o' the
cottars' wives took her in.'

He was off before she finished, going as quickly as he

could over the treacherous ice. Judging by where her creel was, she had not been going to his cottar houses, but she could have been disorientated . . . she might have realized her mistake and found her way there eventually. It was worth a try. About to knock at the first door he came to, he spotted the old barrow he'd always meant to burn standing on the next path and wondered why Adam had been using it. A possible solution coming to him, he vaulted the dividing fence and rapped on the Laings' door.

It was Martha who opened it. 'Oh, it's you, Mr Fordyce. Come in.'

'I won't come in, thank you. I came to ask if you saw the fishwife yesterday. You see, I found her creel, and I . . .'

'Adam found her,' Martha smiled. 'He took her here in that barrow.'

'Thank God for that!' he cried, not caring what she thought of his concern for the girl. 'I was afraid she was lying dead somewhere.'

'She was near death when we took her in, but she's young and she'll get over it, though it'll take her a while to get her strength back. I'm sure she hadn't had anything to eat for weeks, she's like a skeleton, but I'll feed her up.'

'She couldn't be in better hands.' Remembering that he had meant to call here anyway, Dan said, 'I saw Adam had fed the cattle yesterday. He shouldn't have gone out in weather like that. Is he all right?'

'It's a good job he did go, or he wouldn't have found the lassie, but don't worry, he didn't come to any ill. A wee sniff, that's all.'

'Tell him to take a few days off. I'll get the other men to attend to any of his jobs that need doing, and I'll see to the animals myself.'

'I'll tell him, Mr Fordyce, but I can't guarantee he'll

listen. He's not a one for sitting about on his backside doing nothing.'

Dan's eyes twinkled as he touched the peak of his lugged bonnet and turned away. He wished that he could have seen the girl for himself. He couldn't come and ask about her again, because he didn't want to give Martha or Meggie any cause for gossip. But ... why shouldn't he use the creel as an excuse? Returning the girl's property would be regarded as an act of kindness, but he would have to wait until he could get it out of its ice prison.

Looking around the room, Lizann gave a sigh of contentment. It was just as sparsely furnished as her last room – only a tallboy and a padded chair in addition to the bed – but so much nicer. There was a cross-stitch runner on top of the drawers, the padding on the chair picked out one of the colours on the pristine cover on the quilt. The linoleum was highly polished, with a mat at each side of the bed. Although an attic, it had a proper window which made everything look really bright. There was a tiled fireplace, not that much bigger than the one she'd had at Pennan, but sending out far more heat. It had been burning when she woke, but she didn't know which of her benefactors had come up to light it.

Martha had taken up her breakfast at eight, a soft-boiled egg mashed with a little butter, and had come back with a cup of tea at ten. It would be heaven to live in this old cottage with nothing to worry about, but she couldn't. As soon as she was fit she would have to leave; she couldn't take advantage of the Laings' kindness.

At twelve, when Martha came bustling in, she said, 'You'll be ready for your dinner?' Setting the tray down on Lizann's knees, she went on, 'Mr Fordyce was asking about you.'

'How did he know I was here?'

'He found your creel, and he thought you were lying

dead somewhere. He was real worried about you.'

'I don't remember much about it.' Lizann sighed. 'I think I was at the farmhouse . . .'

'That must have been the last place you were before you collapsed.'

Lizann nodded, 'If it hadn't been for your brother . . .'

'I wasn't pleased at him for going to feed the beasts, but I didn't stop him, thank goodness. Now, I strained that soup for you, so sup it before it's cold.'

The soup was followed some minutes later by a small plate of thin custard, but it was like a feast to Lizann. Still feeling very weak, she dozed off but was roused again at three. As she was to discover, Martha was as regular as clockwork in everything she did, every snack and meal dead on the hour. 'Here's a flycup for you,' the old woman smiled, 'and I thought I'd take mine up here, and all, for it's time we'd a wee chat . . . if you feel up to it?'

It was the moment Lizann had been dreading. Not one question had been asked yet, and the Laings were bound to be curious about her background. 'Yes, I'm up to it,' she murmured.

Martha took a sip from her cup before she began. 'What are you going to do when you're back on your feet?'

Lizann's throat constricted. 'I'll do what I was doing before, and I'll leave as soon as . . .'

'Have you got money to buy your fish?'

'I think I'd some in my bag, not much, but I don't know where it is.'

'It's likely lying under the ice and somebody'll find it when the thaw comes.' Martha eyed her speculatively. 'Do you want to go back to that life? You weren't really making a living, were you?'

'I was . . . managing,' Lizann muttered, looking away.

'You weren't managing very well. If you were any thinner, I'd be able to see right through you.'

Lizann gave an uncomfortable smile. 'I'll be all right when the better weather comes in.'

'That'll be a while yet. Now, I'm going to ask you something, so just listen till I've finished. Me and Adam was speaking last night, and we thought it would be a good idea if you bade here to help us. We'll not be able to pay you anything, but you'd have your bed and all the food you need.' Noticing Lizann biting her lip, Martha said, a little sadly, 'Never mind, lass. If you can't face biding with us two old folk, just tell me. I'll not think any the less of you.'

In tears now, Lizann gulped, 'It's not that, Martha. You've been so kind to me already, and now . . .'

Stretching out, the old woman laid her hand over the girl's. 'M'dear, we weren't trying to do you a favour, we need you. I'm seventy-two, and Adam'll be sixty-eight in June, and we're finding things getting a bit much for us. You'll have to work hard, mind, the garden as well as . . .' She broke off, shaking her head. 'No, it's too much to ask.'

'No, no! I'd love to do it!'

'I'd better tell you . . . if Mr Fordyce makes Adam retire, we'll have to get out of the house. It goes with the job.'

Lizann wiped her eyes. 'I'll come with you, wherever you've to go.'

Martha leaned back, her own eyes suspiciously moist. 'Now we've got that settled, you'd best tell me your name.'

Her future taken care of, Lizann gave her real name this time – Liz Benzies was dead and buried under the snow – and told Martha a little of her history.

'Oh, you poor thing!' the old woman exclaimed, when she learned of the double tragedy. 'I don't know how you came through that.'

'I hardly know myself,' Lizann gulped. 'I was in a

terrible state, and then somebody ... two folk ... said things ... and I just had to get away.'

'Have you never thought on going home?'

'What would have been the point?'

'You'd have saved being near starved to death for want of food.'

'I didn't want to upset my mother again. It's best I stay away, and I'll be with you and Adam now and I'll never go hungry again.'

'Not if I can help it,' Martha beamed.

'I'll let Lizann get dressed to come down for a wee while the day,' Martha told her brother one morning in the middle of March. 'She's been up an hour every day this week, and I think her legs are strong enough now to try the stair.'

'Aye,' Adam smiled, 'she looks better every day.'

'There's a bit more flesh on her now, and her face has filled out and all. Besides, she's desperate to try herself. Once I've tidied up down here, I'll look through Margaret's things with her and she can choose what she wants. They're out of fashion, but they'll be better than what she used to have on.'

Recalling the ancient black shapeless coat and the threadbare skirt the girl had been wearing when he took her into the kitchen, Adam nodded his agreement to that.

Lizann was astonished when Martha turned out the contents of what had once been Margaret Laing's wardrobe, a cupboard at the side of the fireplace. Even after five years, the skirts, jumpers and blouses seemed as good as new. 'It doesn't look as if Adam's daughter ever wore them,' she exclaimed.

'She was aye awful extravagant. Her man had plenty of money, and he'd promised to buy her new clothes when they got to Australia, so she left all this with us, the best of quality and all. There's four sets of underwear, and goodness knows how many pairs of stockings; thick lisle for the winter, chiffon lisle for the summer, and silk for the parties they went to. And look at all that shoes! She never saved a ha'penny.'

Gathering that Martha had not thought much of her niece, Lizann said, 'They're too good. I can't take . . .'

'They're lying here going to waste.'

Lizann let a silk stocking slide across her fingers, no longer red and rough. 'It's like getting years and years of presents all at one time.'

Martha couldn't hold back a sniff. 'Get dressed,' she said, a little sharply to cover her emotion, 'and I'll help you down the stair.'

Lizann chose a London tan skirt and mustard twin-set, both of which suited her colouring, chiffon lisle stockings and a pair of brown shoes, all of which fitted her perfectly. 'I feel like a duchess,' she told Martha when she was ready.

Having walked several times across her room on previous days, she had thought she would need no help, but she found that her legs were not as strong as she thought and had to grip Martha's arm on her way down to the kitchen. Sitting by the fire, she gave a gasp of surprise at what was propped up near the window. 'How did my creel get here?'

'Mr Fordyce handed it in weeks ago.' Martha hadn't mentioned it at the time because she was afraid that the girl, in her weakened state, might think the farmer had his eye on her. He was quite concerned for her, but he would feel responsible since she'd been found on his land. There was nothing else in it!

Dan did not recognize the girl working in the Laings' garden at first, and wondered if the daughter Adam had once told him about had come back from Australia. Sensing that someone was watching her, she raised her head, and his heart jolted. The young fishwife! She looked so different from how he remembered, willowy but not skinny, and her black curls sat round her sweet face most becomingly. Adam had said her name was Lizann, a beautiful name for a beautiful girl! He pulled himself together. 'It's a lovely morning,' he called.

She smiled shyly. 'Yes, it is.'

'I'm glad to see you up and about. Are you feeling better now?'

'Yes, thank you.'

He could prolong the moment no longer and, giving her a nod, he walked on, wondering why she was still with the Laings when she looked the very picture of health. Not that he wanted her to leave; he would rather she stayed here for ever so that he could see her occasionally.

When he came to where Adam was furring soil round the potato shaws, he stopped to speak to him. 'I see you've still got Lizann with you?'

Adam's smiling face changed. 'She's going to stop with us, if you've no objections, Mr Fordyce?'

'None. She'll be better with you than trailing round the countryside selling fish. That was no job for a young girl.'

'She's not so young as she looks,' Adam volunteered. 'Her birthday was three weeks ago, and she said she was twenty-eight.'

Dan's spirits lifted. He'd thought she was much younger, and sixteen years wasn't insurmountable. But he looked much older than forty-three and she wouldn't consider him as a prospective husband, even if he ever plucked up the courage to tell her how he felt.

When Martha carried out a cup of tea, she said, 'Was that Mr Fordyce I heard speaking to you?'

She watched Lizann closely for any sign of confusion, but her smile was perfectly open. 'Yes, he was just passing. Oh, should I have thanked him for handing in my creel?'

'I thanked him at the time. You've made a real good job of staking the peas, but watch and not do too much.'

Lizann's laugh was loud and clear. 'I'm as fit as a fiddle now.'

'Aye, well, I'm not wanting you to have a relapse. Oh, it's that warm I think I'll take out a chair and sit a while.'

Enjoying the sunshine, Lizann straightened up to admire what she had done. Never having done any gardening before, she'd had to depend on Adam to show her what to do, but everything was in good shape now, though she had a steady job keeping down the weeds. It was hot for May, but she would much rather be wielding a trowel, or even a spade, than lugging a heavy creel around. Her present life was paradise compared with that, and Martha and Adam were as good as mother and father to her.

Her thoughts wavered for a moment, but she pulled them resolutely away from the past. She had found contentment and happiness with the Laings, and she wouldn't let anything spoil it, not even old memories.

When one of his collies had pups, Dan Fordyce couldn't help wishing he could give one to Lizann, but it would be difficult to give her a gift without causing talk. The puppy was six weeks old before he thought of giving him to Adam. Neither he nor Martha were fit to do much walking – the old man shouldn't really be doing any work, but he hadn't had the heart to tell him so. The day would come, of course, when he would be forced to lay him off, but sufficient unto the day . . .

'What would I do with a pup?' Adam asked in surprise, when the offer was made. Then, rubbing his nose, he muttered, 'I suppose Lizann would like him. He's a real taking wee thing.'

Lizann was delighted, and called the black and white handful Cheeky. 'He's got such a cheeky face,' she explained to Martha, who wasn't at all pleased about having an untrained puppy in the house.

'As long as you keep him under control,' she warned. 'If I find any puddles or such on the floor, or if he chews up anything, out he goes.'

And so Lizann had another chore to attend to twice a day, sometimes three times, when she took Cheeky out to make sure his bladder or his bowels didn't evacuate indoors. Not that she regarded it as a chore; she loved the small bundle as much as he loved her, and he frisked round her as she weeded and hoed, or jumped away when she ran the old mower over the tiny patch of bleaching green at the back. She varied the direction of their walks, but her favourite, and Cheeky's, was to follow the burn that ran along the far end of one of the fields, until she judged that they'd gone far enough and turned back.

Dan Fordyce often watched them, the puppy racing ahead and taking a stick back for Lizann to throw, and he longed to join her, to be part of her life like the dog. Sadly, she wasn't aware of how he felt. Any time she met him, accidentally as she thought, she just gave a shy smile and hurried on, but the smile remained with him for the rest of the day. She was like a ray of sunshine brightening his dull existence, and he found himself waiting expectantly for her to appear and weave her magic round him. When she didn't come, he felt bereft.

Lizann paid no attention to what was going on in the world. She did hear Adam speaking about thousands of soldiers being evacuated from Dunkirk, but it meant nothing to her. Her days revolved round Cheeky. Sometimes she saw the farmer when they were out, but he never gave any indication that he had seen them. She wondered if he was angry at her for going along the burn, which ran quite near his house, but he never looked angry and the puppy wasn't destroying anything. Maybe she should pass the time of day with him some time, but he made her feel shy. He was Adam's boss, after all, and it had been good of him to allow her to live with the Laings. Some farmers wouldn't have.

'I saw Mr Fordyce again,' she told Martha when she went home one day. 'I don't think he knows I see him, but he . . . watches me, sometimes.'

Having often stood at the window watching girl and dog cavorting like two bairns, Martha wasn't in the least surprised by this. 'There's no harm in Dan,' she told Lizann. 'You're a sight for sore eyes, you're that taken up with the pup.'

'I was wondering if I should speak to him, but I don't like.'

Martha nodded wisely. 'It's best you don't. Bosses don't mix with the workers.'

It did not occur to either of them that Lizann did not work for Dan Fordyce, and it would have made no difference if they had. As far as they were concerned, he was gentry, and the gentry were a class apart.

When Adam came in for his supper, he thumped down in his chair. 'God dammit, but I'm tired the day,' he sighed.

'Watch your language,' his sister snapped, worrying that he would lose his job if his health failed.

Lizann went across to him. 'I'll take off your boots for you.'

Looking at the crown of her head as she knelt on the floor in front of him, he said, 'This is the first time in my life anybody's ever taken my boots off for me.'

'And she'll not be making a habit of it,' Martha declared. 'What would Mr Fordyce say if he thought you weren't fit to take them off yourself?'

'Oh, don't rage him,' Lizann begged. 'He didn't ask me to do it.'

Letting Cheeky off his lead, Lizann sat down to watch him bounding away through the trees at the side of the burn. He would soon come back to her and push his cold nose into her hand, urging her to get up and play with him. Sure enough, he padded up again in a few minutes, somewhat bigger than when Adam brought him home first but still not fully-grown, and danced around her with his dark eyes pleading with her to get up and have some fun. He had a short, fat stick in his mouth, and when she tried to take it from him he hung on to it, his head going this way and that in his delight that she was playing his favourite game. She knew the rules and waited a short time before letting it go, at which he laid it beside her, his tail wagging as he waited for her to pick it up and throw it for him.

'You're a torment,' she laughed. 'I'm too lazy to play with you.'

He cocked his head to the side, looking hopefully from the stick to her and back again, then a sound made him prick up his ears. 'Somebody's coming,' she told him, wondering who it was, because nobody ever came here in the evenings. Cheeky rushed off to investigate, and she heard a male voice saying, 'You've come to meet me, have you, boy?'

Lizann stiffened. It sounded like the farmer, and she was always a bit scared of him, though he'd only ever spoken to her twice.

Coming into sight, Dan smiled. 'What's his name?'

'I called him Cheeky, Mr Fordyce,' she murmured timidly, thinking now that it sounded childish.

'That's a good name for him. He's as cheeky as they come. Do you mind if I sit down?'

'Oh no, I don't mind.' It was his land, after all, and he could sit where he liked.

Hitching up the legs of his trousers he sat down at her side, still fondling the dog's ears in a way that had Cheeky almost bursting with contentment. 'You're Lizann?' he observed. 'Adam said you were living with them now.'

'Martha and him have been awful good to me,' she said earnestly.

'You're looking better than the first time I saw you.'

He was regarding her moss green skirt and jumper with approval, and remembering how untidy and ragged she had been before, she felt ashamed that he had seen her. 'Martha gave me Adam's daughter's things to wear,' she explained.

'Green suits you,' he smiled.

She was flustered by the compliment, and they remained silent for a few moments, Cheeky paying more attention to the man than to her, and he to the dog. She didn't know if he expected her to say anything or not, but felt obliged to. 'Thank you, Mr Fordyce.'

He looked at her again, his eyes holding hers until she dropped them in confusion. 'My name's Dan,' he said, softly. 'Mr Fordyce makes me sound like an old man.'

She glanced at him cautiously, and finding that he was tickling the dog's belly, she had a good look at him. Her first impression of him had been that he was about fifty, but he didn't look as old as that now. His ruddy face wasn't lined, and she'd noticed that his eyes were grey and had a twinkle in them as if he found something funny, but he hadn't been laughing at her. His thick hair was wavy, much the same light brown as George's had been, but neater, and he wasn't in his usual old tweeds. Was it the flannels and sports jacket that made him look younger?

When his head turned towards her again she looked away guiltily and he let out a deep, rumbling laugh. 'Now you've had a good look at me, how old do you think I am?'

'Oh, I'm sorry, Mr Fordyce, I didn't mean to . . .'

'I told you to call me Dan, and I'll be forty-four on my birthday. I suppose that is old to you?'

'Oh no, Mr . . . um, Dan,' she gasped breathlessly. 'That's not old.'

'I'm keeping you from your walk.' He stood up and dusted down his trousers. 'It's been nice talking to you, Lizann, and you too, Cheeky.'

Patting the collie's head, he strode back the way he had come, leaving Lizann wondering why he'd been there if he wasn't going anywhere. Maybe he'd come out for a walk because he was tired of sitting in the house . . . but it was none of her business. Lifting the stick Cheeky had forgotten, she flung it forward and laughed as he raced after it.

'Did you have a nice walk?' Martha asked, when she went home.

'Mr Fordyce was out for a walk, too, and he sat down with me for a while. He's really nice.'

'Aye, he is that.'

'He told me to call him Dan.' As soon as she said it, she wished that she hadn't.

'Don't start getting ideas about him,' Martha frowned. 'He's not the marrying kind.'

Lizann laughed at this. 'I just said he was nice, and you think I'm after him. I loved George, Martha, and when I lost him . . . well, I don't want to get married ever again.'

When Lizann went up to bed, Martha said, 'Did you hear that, Adam?'

'Hear what?' her brother said, cautiously.

'Mr Fordyce told her to call him Dan. What do you make of that?'

After giving it some thought, Adam snorted. 'I'd say

he was needing a bit of company, and she's the only body round here with any gumption in her. He's got more sense than let a lassie her age turn his head.'

Chapter Twenty-two

❧❧❧

Jenny decided to wait until she had given her mother-in-law her dinner before telling her the news. She had got so frail over the past few months that the least little thing put her off eating. Carrying over a bowl of potato soup, she sat down to spoon it to the elderly woman, with a cloth ready to wipe any dribbles that ran down her chin.

'When's Mick due hame?' Hannah asked, when the bowl was empty.

'He just went away this morning, and he's not expecting to be back for about six months this time.' Jenny's heart was sore, for this would be the longest time they had ever been apart. 'Now, would you like some rice pudding?'

'If you havena put raisins in it.'

'There's no raisins in it. I know you don't like them.'

'A wee drop, then.'

Standing up to serve the rice, Jenny had a look in the pram to make sure her six-month-old son was coping with the bottle she'd had to put him on when her own milk dried up. Poor wee soul, his grandmother took up most of her attention ... but he seemed to be thriving.

'I'll wait a while for my cup o' tea,' Hannah remarked, when Jenny gave her the last spoonful of rice. 'I'm full up the now.'

Having gulped her own pudding down during the feeding, Jenny laid the empty plate on the table. 'Hannah, I've something to tell you.'

'Something good, I hope.'

Jenny had to smile. 'I'm having another baby . . . about Christmas again.'

She couldn't help recalling what Mick had said when she told him – in bed on the first night of his last leave. 'George was supposed to be at Christmas, and all. Is it you or me that functions better in March?'

She had laughed. 'They say a young man's fancy turns to thoughts of love in the spring.'

'Just thoughts of love, not filling your wife's belly again. Oh, I'm sorry, Jen, in more ways than one. First, I shouldn't speak men's talk to you, and second, I didn't mean us to have another baby yet. You've enough to do without that.'

'Mick, I want you to be as glad about this baby as I am.'

'But I've been selfish . . . just thinking of my own enjoyment.'

She had put her fingers over his mouth. 'Do you think I don't enjoy it? Mick, my darling, I wouldn't mind if you put a dozen babies in my belly . . . as long as they weren't all there at once.'

They had both laughed . . . until an animal lust took hold of them, the three months of enforced separation making it all the fiercer yet all the sweeter. Remembering all the other times they'd made love before he went back to his ship, a hunger swept through Jenny, a hunger that wouldn't be assuaged until the child she was carrying had left her womb.

'Another baby?' Hannah barked suddenly. She obviously didn't think it was good news. 'And how d'you think you're going to look after it when you've me and wee Georgie depending on you and all?'

'I'll manage. The thing is, Mick says he'll apply for Christmas leave, but there's no guarantee he'll get it, and Babsie's not fit to help now, but Elsie's offered to come and keep house. She says Rosie Mac'll not mind looking after Pattie and Tommy.'

'Elsie?' There was a deep scowl on Hannah's face now. 'Her that comes in on Thursdays?'

Jenny smiled. 'That's right. You'll be fine with her.'

'No, I dinna like her. There's something . . .' Hannah halted, fingers plucking at the rug over her knees.

Wondering why she'd taken such a dislike to Elsie – it had been going on for a long time now, like she'd a grudge against her – Jenny said curtly, 'It'll just be till I'm on my feet again.'

Hannah's mind was already off what she was trying to remember about Elsie. 'Folk would think I was stupid, Lizann, the way you speak to me. Your father would soon tell you.'

Jenny gave a deep sigh. 'Nobody thinks you're stupid.'

'When'll Mick be hame?'

'Not for months.' Jenny didn't bother reminding her she'd asked that less than half an hour ago. She often asked the same thing a dozen times a day and took offence if it was pointed out to her. And she was always getting worse. Goodness knows what she'd be like by the time the baby arrived.

Since Dan first spoke to Lizann and Cheeky by the burn, she had made a point of never varying their route, and he put in his appearance on most nights. She had lost her initial awkwardness with him, and could talk to him freely, as he seemed to do to her. He had told her about his time at university, about Ella, his sister in Aberdeen who had let him lodge with her while he was studying, and he had drawn her out to tell him something of her earlier life. To begin with, she had limited herself to her childhood in the Yardie, but little by little she told him about how she had met George, why they'd had to wait so long until they could be married, and when Dan asked the other night why they were no longer together, how she had lost him.

Dan had placed his large, rough hand over hers then, and murmured, 'I knew by your eyes the first time I saw you that you'd had some tragedy in your life, but I didn't dream ... Oh, Lizann, I'm truly sorry.'

Recalling this one hot morning in September, she wondered what they would speak about tonight if she saw him. Should she tell him about losing the baby as well? She didn't want his pity, but if he believed that was why she'd run away from Buckie and started selling fish, it would save her having to give any other explanation. The thing was, it would make her sound as if she had no backbone, when it wasn't really what had made her flee like a coward. It had been the culmination of a whole lot of things: George being drowned, the baby, lack of money, what Elsie had accused her of doing and the threat, topped by Jenny's remark, which she had likely misunderstood – she'd been in such a state.

Her reverie was interrupted by Martha saying, 'Here's Adam and the soup not dished up.'

Flinging his cap on to the couch when he came in, her brother took his seat at the table without a word, and she eyed him anxiously. 'Your face is just running with sweat. You shouldn't be working in this heat.'

'The day I stop working'll be the day they put me in my box,' he said dolefully.

'It's not just the heat that's bothering you, though.' Martha knew her brother inside out.

'I was minding ... it's a year ago the day since war was declared.'

'But it's not affecting us.'

'It will. I can mind the stories the men told when they came back from the last war, the ones that came back, and some of them never got over the terrible things they'd seen.'

340

She could say nothing to that, and he went on, 'It's going to be a lot worse this time, for Hitler's been preparing for war for years, the time we were hiding our heads in the sand like ostriches.'

For a few moments he seemed to be thinking, then he said, 'I wasn't conscripted the last time, for I was a married man and coming up for forty-three, but Mr Fordyce, old Duncan, he'd to attend I don't know how many tribunals to try to keep the young men from having to go. It didn't make any odds though, for they were still taken.'

'So he had to get other workers?' Lizann asked, finding this history lesson fascinating.

'There was nobody to get – they were all away fighting. There was just him and me and a fourteen-year-old laddie to keep the whole place going and it was damned hard work, I can tell you. Old Duncan had to ask some of the wives to help with the harvests and they worked as well as any of us, my Peg for one.'

Remembering his wife he lapsed into silence, and was so morose when he came home for his supper that Lizann was glad to go out after the meal was over. When she saw Dan, however, he too could talk only about the war. 'I'd love to do my bit, but I have to keep running the farm.'

'I'm glad you won't have to fight ... you might be killed.'

'Would you care?' he asked softly.

'Of course I'd care!' Hoping she hadn't given him any wrong ideas, she hurried on, 'I'd care if any of the men I know got killed.'

'I hope they don't take too many of my men. My father used to tell me about the trouble he had last time.'

'Adam was speaking about that at dinnertime, the most I've heard him say for ages. But this war'll not last so long, surely?'

'I sincerely hope not. The Germans are trying to prevent

Britain from importing the foodstuffs we need, so pressure's on us farmers to produce as much as we can.'

Over the next few days, Martha continued to be worried that Adam was overtaxing his strength. He was utterly exhausted when he came at night, sometimes too tired to eat, but when she told him he should be taking things easy at his age, he said sharply, 'And let Mr Fordyce say I'm not fit for my job?'

'I can see him dropping down dead somewhere,' she confided to Lizann the following forenoon, 'but will he take a telling? Not him. And it'll be worse once they start gathering in the tatties.'

Lizann tried to comfort her. 'He'll ease up if he feels it's getting too much for him.'

'If anything happens to him . . . we'd be put out of this house.'

'Nothing's going to happen to him. Sit down and stop looking on the black side. I'll make some tea, that'll make you feel better.'

Ten minutes later Martha said she would dust the kitchen, seeing the floor had been swept, and Lizann went through to do the other two rooms downstairs. She, too, was worried about Adam, though she'd tried to set Martha's mind at rest. If anything did happen to him – heaven forbid – his sister would be inconsolable, for there was a close bond between them. But surely the farmer wouldn't put them out. He was too kind for that . . . yet he'd need the house for the man he engaged to replace Adam. Maybe he'd give them time to look for somewhere else, but how could they afford to live anywhere else with no breadwinner?

This was too distressing to think about, and she assured herself that she was worrying for nothing. Adam would live for years yet even if he was nearly seventy. Both beds made, she rolled up the rugs and put them under her arm. Going into the kitchen, she said, 'I'm going to shake the mats,' then saw that Martha was dozing, the duster in her hand.

The mats well shaken, she went back inside, and was pleased that the old woman hadn't moved. Poor old soul, she thought, fondly, she likely hasn't been sleeping at nights for worrying. After finishing the second room, she went up quietly to clean her own.

She had everything ready when Adam came in at twelve o'clock, his face wet with perspiration, his breathing erratic as he pulled out a chair to sit at the table. Glancing at Martha, he said, 'You'd better waken her, Lizann, or she'll not sleep the night.'

'I don't think she'd much sleep last night.' But Lizann went over and touched the old lady's shoulder gently. 'Dinnertime, Martha.' Getting no response, she tried again. 'Come on, Martha. Your dinner'll get cold.'

It was Adam who realized first. Struggling to his feet, he burst out, his voice hoarse with emotion, 'She's not sleeping!'

Lizann looked round at him and caught his alarm. 'Martha! Martha!' she shouted, and shook her roughly. 'Oh, Adam, she won't waken up.'

'No,' he whispered, mournfully, 'she'll never waken up again.'

Refusing to believe it, Lizann felt for a pulse, but there was nothing and she turned to Adam. He put his arms round her awkwardly, and they stood for some time, her tears starting his, for they had both loved Martha deeply in their own ways.

At last Lizann said softly, 'You should sit down, Adam, you're as white as a sheet.'

'So are you.' Nevertheless, he did sit down, his hands shaking so much that he hid them under the tablecloth.

Lizann stared at him with wide, sorrowful eyes. 'We'll

have to get a doctor to . . .' she whispered. 'Has Mr Fordyce got a telephone?'

Too overcome to speak now, Adam gave a slight nod but, as she went out, his head dropped down and she could hear his deep sobs even from the foot of the garden. She ran all the way to the farmhouse, but when she asked the housekeeper to phone the doctor, the woman jumped to the wrong conclusion. 'He didna look well last time I saw him. He shouldna be working so hard.'

'No, no!' Lizann gasped. 'It's not Adam! It's Martha!'

'Martha? What's wrong wi' her?'

'I think she's . . . dead.'

'Dead? Oh, dearie me! Dearie me! That's terrible!'

Meggie was so affected by this unexpected tragedy that Lizann had to remind her why she was there. 'Please phone . . . right now. I don't want to leave Adam on his own too long.'

Meggie's hands fluttered nervously. 'Oh, lassie, I'm nae use wi' that contraption. I'll have to get Mr Fordyce.'

She disappeared inside and Dan came running out in just a moment, his mouth still full. 'Meggie says Martha's . . . ?'

'Please, Mr Fordyce, will you phone and ask the doctor to come?'

He gripped her elbow. 'Come inside. You look as if you need a seat.'

The telephone was on a small table in the hallway, and he made her sit on the chair beside it. He asked the operator for the number, and while he waited to be put through, he said, 'Adam didn't say she was ill.'

'She wasn't ill. I thought she was sleeping and . . .'

A reedy, metallic voice brought her to a halt, and the farmer turned his head away. 'Dr Munro? It's Dan Fordyce, Easter Duncairn. Could you call at my cottar houses as soon as possible? The name's Martha Laing.' Laying down the receiver, he looked at Lizann again. 'He'll come as soon as he can. Now, you were telling me, she was asleep . . . ?'

'I thought she was sleeping, but I couldn't get her to waken for her dinner . . . and when I felt her wrist, there wasn't a pulse.'

Trembling with delayed shock, Lizann was not aware how near she came at that moment to being taken in another man's arms, nor how hard Dan had to fight against the urge to crush her against his chest. All she knew was that he was looking at her with a strange expression. 'I'm sorry I've bothered you in the middle of your dinner,' she whispered.

'Don't be silly.' The sharpness covered his concern. 'I had better take you back.'

Calling to Meggie not to keep his meal hot, he pulled Lizann's arm through his and propelled her outside. 'I'm really sorry about Martha, Lizann,' he said, when they were on the rough track. 'I know you thought a lot of her. And how is Adam taking it? He hasn't been looking too good himself these past few weeks.'

'No, he hasn't, and he was sobbing fit to break his heart when I left him. He'll miss her something awful . . . and so'll I.' Lizann blinked in an effort to stop a tear, but it still spilled over and she knew, by the extra pressure he put on her arm, that the farmer had seen it.

Knowing that both Lizann and Adam were too shocked, Dan promised to arrange everything. He also told Adam to take a whole week off, which he considered, if not enough time to let him get over his loss, should help him to build up his strength a little.

When at long last they were left on their own, the doctor having helped Dan to carry Martha's body through to her bedroom, the old man and the young woman sat down at the fireside, thankful that the stir was past for the time being. After staring for a short time at the bowl of flowers Lizann had set in a corner the

345

previous day, Adam looked across at her, tears brimming in his eyes. 'What am I going to do without her?'

'We'll both miss her, but we'll have to carry on.'

'For as long as I'm able to carry on,' he muttered, morosely.

'Oh, Adam, you're good for a lot of years yet.'

He fixed his faded eyes on the flowers again. 'What's going to happen to you when I . . . ?'

'Oh, Adam, don't think about it.'

After a long pause, he mumbled, 'Any road, Dan Fordyce sees fine I'm on my road out, and . . .'

'He's a good man, he won't sack you. Look, it's daft sitting here, we should go to bed.'

Rising, she helped him to his feet, and he grasped her hand. 'You'll never leave me, will you, Lizann?'

'Never! Get some sleep, for we've the funeral to get through yet.'

She saw him through to his room, and in her own bed she prayed that the funeral wouldn't be too much for him. Her thoughts turned in spite of herself to her mother. She wasn't as old as Martha, but she had been in a far worse state of health. Was Lou attending to her properly? But it would be Jenny who was looking after her now, for she and Mick must be married by this time.

Tears coursed down Lizann's cheeks as she remembered all the dear ones she had left behind, the dear ones she had tried so hard to banish from her memory, and when her mind touched on Peter Tait, she had to clap her hand over her mouth to stop her from sobbing aloud. She still loved him, but it was only the pure, simple love for a very close friend, a friend who had been a deep source of comfort to her more than once. If he had been here today . . . but his wife had put an end to all that; they could never be friends now, even if they ever met again.

She had been happier with Martha and Adam than

346

she'd thought possible after losing George, and now it looked as if it wouldn't be long till she was homeless and friendless again.

Work at Easter Duncairn went on as usual, the harvesting of the potato crop in October, the ploughing in November, but Dan Fordyce made sure that Adam was given only light jobs. Since Martha's death, he had been quiet to the point of taciturnity, speaking when spoken to only if an answer was expected, and even then in as few words as he could.

As the winter drew in, Lizann grew more anxious about his health, but she knew that it was no use saying anything. All she could do was to make sure he was well wrapped up when he went out and have warm clothes ready for him when he came in. In the evenings they normally sat in silence, listening only to the news bulletins on the wireless, for Adam did not think it was fitting to be laughing at comedy shows or enjoying the big bands when they were still in mourning.

'Martha used to like Henry Hall,' Lizann said, tentatively, one night. 'She wouldn't mind us listening to him.' But Adam shook his head, and she didn't suggest it again.

Chapter Twenty-three

❦

When she made her Thursday visits to the Yardie, Elsie was always afraid that Hannah might unthinkingly reveal the 'secret', but as time passed – with the elderly woman glowering at her for a minute and then ignoring her – she came to the conclusion that it had joined all the other things buried beyond recall in what passed now for Hannah's brain.

With 1940 wearing to a close, Jenny was well through her eighth month and still in the best of health. Elsie couldn't understand why some women seemed to bloom when they were carrying, while she'd blown up like a balloon both times. Still, as Lenny Fyfe had told her after Tommy was born, she'd got her figure back real quick. Lenny had the knack of making her feel good, though she still sometimes hungered for a man that would dominate her like she had always secretly yearned to be dominated.

On 20 December, Elsie asked her neighbour to keep an eye on her sons till she went to the Yardie. 'They're just a pest wi' Jenny so near her time,' she explained. 'She's nae due for a few days yet, but she wasna looking great yesterday, and I'm feared it'll come early.'

Rosie McIntosh smiled. 'I'll ken what's up if you're nae back, and dinna worry about your bairns. I'll keep them like we arranged.'

'Thanks.' Elsie hurried off gratefully.

'Yoo-hoo!' she called, as she opened the Jappys' door and walked in. 'It's just me.'

To her surprise, Hannah said, 'Thank God you've come! I think she's started.'

Jenny was curled over the sink, her face ashen when she turned round. 'You'd best get Tibbie, Elsie.'

Elsie nodded, then, looking at the wee mite in his high chair, his eyes round with terror, his thumb in his mouth as a comforter, she said, 'And I'll put wee Georgie in to Babsie Berry's, out of the road.'

Jenny wished that her mother-in-law could also be sent out of the way, but another pain tore at her, and she gave a quick nod before hugging the sink again.

When Elsie returned, she was accompanied by the middle-aged woman who acted as the local midwife. Tibbie Taylor took one look at Jenny, then said, 'I'll help you ben to your bed.'

'It's Hannah that sleeps ben there,' Elsie pointed out. 'Jenny's bed's up the stair.'

Another pain beginning, Jenny gasped, 'I don't ... think I'll manage ... to get up ...'

'I'm nae having a bairn born in my bed!' Hannah burst out.

'Nobody's asking you!' Elsie snarled.

Her eyes wild, Hannah cried, 'You ... you ... it was you! It was you!' Her words deteriorated into a series of unintelligible grunts, but no one was paying any attention to her.

Past caring where she would go as long as the infant came out, Jenny said, 'I'll have to ... have it here. You can put ... the rubber sheet on ... the mat ...'

Tibbie scowled. 'And have me breaking my back bending? I suppose ... if you was on the couch ...?'

She took a large waterproof apron out of her bag and tied it round her as she waited for the sofa to be made ready, and then Elsie helped Jenny to put on an old nightgown of Hannah's she had found in the press when she was looking for the rubber sheet.

349

The confinement under way at last, Hannah – her mind momentarily taken off her previous agitation – directed operations from her ringside seat like a queen from a throne, and after ignoring her for some time Tibbie turned on her angrily. 'Be at peace, for ony sake, Hannah, or I'll get Elsie to carry you through to your bed.'

Hannah was having none of this. 'Lizann's my lassie, and I've to make sure nothing goes wrong!'

'Lizann?' Tibbie shouted. 'Naebody's seen your Lizann for months. It's Jenny that's having the bairn! Mick's wife!'

Tibbie having brought Lizann's disappearance back to her mind, and how she had previously been told about it, Hannah tottered to her feet, her outraged face as red as the tartan rug which slid off her knees. Elsie jumped to support her but wasn't quick enough to stop her landing in a heap on the floor. Unable to lift her, she looked at the midwife in desperation. 'What'll we do with her?'

Rattled by all the commotion, Tibbie snapped, 'Leave her there. She'll maybe keep her mouth shut now.'

Hannah certainly stopped interfering, but kept saying, 'It was her! It was her! I mind now!' Her finger pointed at Elsie for a moment, then her memory left her again, and dropping her hand, she kept up a steady flow of low moans, which, although more disturbing to Jenny and Tibbie, wiped the look of apprehension off Elsie's face.

After a while, piqued that no one would help her, Hannah whined, 'I could get my death lying here and naebody cares.'

'Never heed her,' Tibbie whispered, and Elsie turned to Jenny as she let out another agonized scream.

At least two of the occupants of the room would never forget the next few hours. Jenny was too intent on forcing the infant out of her womb to hear Hannah's sporadic accusations, and Hannah herself was no longer aware of what was going on, but at one point Elsie put her hands over her ears and groaned, 'It's like a bloody circus in here,' and Tibbie muttered, 'I've never heard nothing like it.'

At last the sweating midwife gave a triumphant cry. 'Ha! The head's crowning,' and concentrated on guiding the infant out. 'It's a girl,' she announced in a few minutes. She got the slimy, blood-streaked baby crying and then handed her to Elsie. 'I'll wash her when I've finished wi' Jenny.'

As Elsie wrapped the infant in a towel, Hannah looked up at her slyly. 'Lizann . . .' she began, and an evil smirk crossed her face as she ended, '. . . and Peter!'

'Shut up!' Elsie screamed. 'It's a bloody asylum you should be in, you mad old bitch!'

The afterbirth having come off, Jenny lay back weakly and Tibbie took the baby. 'Get some water ready,' she told Elsie, 'and stop carrying on. You're as bad as the auld wife.'

Elsie went over to the fire and lifted the kettle to fill the basin. 'You wouldna like her saying your man was taking up wi' somebody else.'

Tibbie looked surprised. 'She never said nothing like that to you.'

'It's what she meant.'

'Stop it,' Jenny pleaded. 'Her mind's back to when Lizann was engaged to Peter. That's all it is.'

'Lizann and Peter,' Hannah repeated, grinning vacantly.

Moving towards the sink, Tibbie said, 'That's enough, Hannah. Just lie there and be quiet, and once I've got the bairnie clean, Elsie and me'll lift you back on to your seat. You're ravelled wi' falling, but you'll be fine when we get you up off the floor.'

The soft voice soothed Hannah, but she glared at Elsie again as soon as she was returned to her chair. The venom gradually left her eyes, and she lay back and closed them.

When Jenny was changed and settled in her own bed with the baby at her breast, Tibbie went home and Elsie sat down to recover, her thoughts on what Hannah had said ... too dangerous for comfort, though she hadn't come out with anything specific. The old besom was sleeping now, but when she woke up she might remember a lot more. It would have been a blessing if she'd had a seizure in her rage ... but maybe that could be arranged yet. All it needed was to goad her into losing her temper, and with any luck it might be the finish of her.

An hour later, as she was taking some dishes out of the dresser, Elsie eyed the old woman coldly. 'I'm putting you to your bed after your supper.'

Hannah's brows came down. 'That's ower early for me to go to my bed.'

Tossing her bleached head, Elsie said, 'I'll go to your bed, then, and you can bide in that chair all night.'

The familiar searching look came into Hannah's eyes. 'You'd do it and all. You're a bad woman, I ken that!'

Elsie pretended she didn't hear this. 'When you're settled, I'll nip home for some things, seeing I'll be biding here the night. Rosie Mac said she'd keep Pattie and Tommy for me.'

'Pattie and Tommy?'

'My two loons.' Elsie filled three plates with stew.

'But Pattie and Tommy's my grandsons.'

Not wanting the quarrel just yet, Elsie kept her attention on spooning out the potatoes. After taking a tray up to Jenny, she came back to feed Hannah, who took one taste of the meat and screwed up her nose. 'That's nae fit for pigs! I couldna eat that!'

'Please yourself!' Elsie whipped away the plate and sat at the table to eat hers.

Hannah sat in a brooding silence – shaking her head at the semolina she was offered later – until the table was cleared and the kitchen was tidied again. 'I'm nae going to my bed!' she declared then.

'Aye are you!' Elsie heaved her up and half carried her to her room. 'You can maybe get round Jenny, but nae me!' Dumping her on the bed, she undressed the frail body roughly and yanked the nightgown over her head.

'I said you was bad,' Hannah quavered, 'and now I can mind why!'

'Shut your mouth or I'll shut it for you!'

But Hannah's eyes were no longer wild or vague. 'It was you that made Lizann run away, wasn't it? You said she'd been taking up wi' Peter, and you tell't her to keep away from him. But I ken she wasna fit to take up wi' onybody, she wasna that kind ony road, so that was a load of lies you made up.'

Elsie rammed the skinny arm into the old cardigan. 'Supposing it was, what can you do about it? You'll never get Lizann back ... and neither'll Peter.'

Hannah looked up at her balefully. 'I'll tell Mick what you did.'

'He'll nae believe you, everybody kens you're aff your head!' Yet, even as she lifted the other arm and twisted it roughly into the second sleeve, Elsie was doubting this. Mick must know that Hannah had short rational spells and, naturally, he would believe what his mother said rather than take an outsider's word ... especially an outsider with an axe to grind. Knowing Mick, the first person he would tell would be Peter, and then ... she'd be right in the shit! Peter would throw her out, without her bairns, and she couldn't go back to her parents. Her father would half-kill her for what she'd done. She'd likely end up on the streets, and though there were some men she wouldn't mind pleasuring, men who would treat her with respect, she had heard there were perverts who couldn't get satisfaction unless they were causing pain.

Her entire future at stake, she tried desperately to think

of a way to avoid being found out, and as she looked down at the old woman who posed such a threat to her, a strange sense of excitement arose in her. The old bitch was so frail she couldn't live much longer, but being her, she might hang on just long enough to spill the beans before she popped off – the beans that would destroy Mrs Peter Tait. Yes, Elsie decided, Hannah had signed her own death warrant and there was no point in being squeamish.

Bending down, she lifted the grey head for a moment and gently removed one of the pillows. 'That'll help you to get a nice long sleep,' she murmured, then, waiting until the faded eyes closed, she pressed it down over the nose and mouth, not relaxing until the feeble struggles stopped – in only a matter of seconds.

She stood up now, her breathing rapid and ragged, but it wasn't long before a cold smile stole across her face. Going upstairs, she went into Jenny's room. 'That's her sleeping like a baby. Rosie's keeping my two, but I'll have to go hame for my nightie and things. I'll nae be long.'

Walking to Main Street, she had misgivings about what she had done. Bella Jeannie's death hadn't exactly been her fault, but Hannah's was ... definitely. Would the doctor know she'd been smothered though her face wasn't blue? She hadn't put up a fight, for she'd been on the verge of dying anyway ... hadn't she? She was better away! It would be a big relief to Jenny and all.

Having thus dismissed her fears, Elsie went to her neighbour's house to check on her sons before collecting what she needed from her own, and was back at the Yardie in less than twenty minutes. Undressing in front of the fire, she felt an irresistible urge to make sure everything was as it should be, and slipped through to the other room. Giving a shivery sigh of relief that nothing had changed, she jeered, 'Aye, Hannah Jappy, you'll nae be telling Mick or naebody else what I did to your Lizann.'

354

Chapter Twenty-four

❧

When Mick arrived home the following night – having moved hell and high water to be there in time for the birth of his child, and not knowing that he'd missed it by twenty-four hours – he was surprised to find Elsie Tait by the fire, tired and distressed. His first thought was for his wife. 'Is anything wrong with Jenny?'

Elsie had passed a traumatic day, pacifying her patient and telling lies to the doctor, who, she had thought at first, seemed suspicious at Hannah dying so suddenly, so her voice was genuinely low and unsteady. 'She'd a baby girl yesterday, and they're both fine, but . . . your mother . . . died some time last night.'

'Oh, God!' His shocked face worked spasmodically, and he was obviously torn between which of the two women he loved to be more concerned about.

'Go up and see Jenny,' Elsie murmured, 'and I'll tell you about Hannah when you come back.'

Still in a fragile state, Jenny burst into tears as soon as she saw him, and holding her shaking body he said, 'Don't upset yourself, my pet. Mother hasn't been herself for ages, and she's had her life. We're just starting ours. Now, let me see my daughter.'

Drawing aside the covers, he looked down at the tiny bundle in the cradle. 'Oh, she's a wee darling, Jen. What'll we call her?'

Hastily drying her eyes, Jenny said softly, 'I think we'll have to call her Lizann. That'll be a George and a Lizann together again, and she said herself that's what she'd wanted to do.'

Her husband's face showed his pleasure at her thoughtfulness. 'Jenny, it's no wonder I love you.' His expression sobered. 'I just wish to God I knew where she is, for she'd be pleased about this. Now, I suppose I'd better go and speak to Elsie.'

He had never liked Peter's wife, but he was inclined to feel sorry for her now. 'You must have got an awful shock this morning,' he said, when he went downstairs.

'I haven't got over it yet, though I should have expected it for your mother was in a terrible state yesterday. You see, Jenny couldn't manage to get up the stairs when Tibbie came, and Hannah wouldn't hear of them using her bed, so she saw everything.'

'What d'you mean, she saw everything?'

'Jenny had the baby on the couch, and Hannah was screaming things, and she fell on the floor, and I couldn't get her up . . .'

'God Almighty!' Mick could visualize the scene, with his mother trying to get attention, her peace disrupted, and no one having time to bother with her. Taking out his handkerchief, he wiped his clammy brow. 'I'm sorry you got the brunt of it, Elsie. I bet you'll never forget the day my wee Lizann was born.'

He was quite correct in this, and not only because of the circumstances of the birth. Her peculiar expression, however, was anger at learning his daughter's name, not, as he thought, agreement with what he had said. 'Will I make you a cup of tea?' he asked sympathetically.

At her nod he put the kettle on to boil, then went into his mother's room. She looked so peaceful that he found it hard to believe she was dead, but he was glad that she had passed away in her sleep. She hadn't had much of a life since his father died, and it was a good thing she hadn't known about Lizann. That was one heartache she had been spared. Heaving a gusty sigh, he went back to the kitchen.

It was only when Elsie rose to wash the dirty cups that he remembered something. 'Who's looking after Pattie and Tommy?'

'Rosie Mac.'

'Well, Peter got his leave changed at the last minute as well, so you'd better get home to him. I'm here to look after things, though I wish I'd been here ... Oh, before you go, has anything been done about the funeral yet?'

'No. Jake Berry said he would ask your uncle ... Jockie?, but I thought you'd want to do it yourself. I'll be glad to get to my bed, Mick, for I'm fit to drop, but I'll be back in the morning to see how Jenny is.'

He stood up and, to his own surprise as well as hers, kissed her on the cheek. 'Thanks for all you've done, Elsie.'

When she went out, he closed the front of the fire and went upstairs, where Jenny said, 'I've been thinking, Mick. I didn't really take in what was happening yesterday, but I can mind Hannah going on at Elsie, accusing her of something, but she couldn't get it out. What could it have been?'

'Nothing, likely. You know how muddled she was, and Elsie said all the commotion made her a lot worse.'

'She got awful upset,' Jenny said, thoughtfully. 'She was pointing at Elsie and shouting, "It was you!", and when Tibbie told her to be quiet, she said, "Lizann's my lassie."'

'She was always thinking you were Lizann,' Mick said gently.

'But Tibbie told her nobody had seen Lizann for months.'

'Oh, no!' Mick groaned. 'And I thought she went to her Maker without knowing that.'

'That was when she fell trying to stand up, and Elsie couldn't lift her, and Tibbie said to leave her lying. Then after the baby was born she started saying "Lizann and Peter", and Elsie screamed at her that she should be in an asylum.' Jenny looked at her husband pathetically. 'She shouldn't have said things like that to a poor old woman.'

'She'd've been all on edge.'

'It's funny, though. Tibbie said she was as bad as Hannah, the noise she was making, and Elsie said, "How would you like it if she said your man was taking up with somebody else?" It was like she thought something had been going on between Lizann and Peter.'

Mick's face screwed up. 'I know she was jealous when Peter went to see Lizann after George was lost . . .' He stopped, recalling how he had found his sister in Peter's arms that morning, then shook his head vehemently. 'No, no! There was nothing going on, I'm sure of that.'

Nonetheless, he couldn't help wondering as he got into bed if Elsie had been right. Had Lizann been carrying on with Peter? Had she run away because she felt guilty about him being unfaithful to his wife? It was a more reasonable explanation than Jenny's remark, and he knew Peter had always loved Lizann, but still . . . No, he couldn't believe it.

He was almost asleep when he thought of a different angle. Had Elsie in her jealousy gone to Lizann and accused her of having an affair with Peter? It couldn't have been true, but his sister wasn't strong enough at the time to cope with anything like that . . . she would have wanted to get away from it. That was why she'd left Buckie! It must be! She'd had nobody to confide in, with Mother stuck in the house, and Jenny and Lou both too busy to visit her. The agony she must have gone through!

His peace totally ruined, he decided to confront Elsie in the morning . . . then he remembered how much she had done for Jenny. He was grateful to her for that, and with no proof of what he thought it would be best to say nothing. Anyway, he was probably wrong.

* * *

358

When Peter arrived home he was astonished that nobody was in the house, and sat down at the fireside to wait for his family's return. Noticing that the fire hadn't been lit, he presumed that Elsie had taken the boys to visit their grandparents. She hadn't been expecting him home for at least another month, of course.

After ten minutes, he felt quite chilly, and contemplated lighting the fire in the parlour so that it would be warm when he went through to the couch. Then, realizing that it was just after seven o'clock and it could be two or three hours before Elsie came back, a better idea came to him. Why shouldn't he have a lie down upstairs? He would shift out when Elsie was getting the boys to bed.

Just taking off his blouse and trousers, he stretched out on the big double bed, absolute heaven after the hard bunk he was used to ... when he had the chance to go to it. Still feeling cold, he shifted himself until he was under the blankets, and then he heard a key in the outside door. Propping himself up on one elbow ready to call to his sons when they came upstairs, he frowned when only Elsie appeared. 'Where the hell have you been?' he asked angrily. 'And where's the boys?'

'They're with Rosie,' she sighed, opening the waistband of her skirt with trembling fingers, for she was too tired to quarrel with him. 'I've been at the Yardie. Jenny had her baby yesterday, and Hannah's dead, and I just got away because Mick's home, so don't start going on at me.'

His mouth had dropped open, but she looked so worn out that he felt a warmth for her in his pity. 'I'm sorry.' Watching her undressing, he said, 'How did Hannah die?'

'The stir must have been too much for her. She got in an awful state, and I'd a job getting her to her bed. But she was sound asleep when I left her, so I near passed out when I found her dead this morning.'

'She died in her sleep? Oh well, it's the best way to go.'

'I suppose so.' Elsie unfastened her brassiere and took it off, but not with the usual flourish and lifting of her breasts, which, if she had but known, had disgusted rather than titillated her husband since the night of Lou Flett's funeral.

But it was this lack of awareness of her body that titillated him now, and as she slipped on her skimpy nightgown and lay down beside him, he became fully aroused. His arms went round her, and she turned to him with a sob in her throat. 'It's been awful.'

'It must have been,' he muttered thickly, gripping her buttocks. He could feel her nipples hardening against him, and soon she was moving her pelvis in the old familiar way. 'Oh, Peter,' she murmured happily, 'I never thought you'd do this again.'

Neither had he, and he despised himself for it.

In the morning, when her hand crept round to try to rouse him again, he pushed it away and growled, 'No, Elsie. Last night was a mistake. I shouldn't have touched you ... I didn't want to ...'

Her momentary scowl changed as she leaned over the bed until her breasts were dangling in front of his face. 'Take a hold of them, Peter, and then tell me you don't want me.'

The masses of soft flesh did not have the effect she wanted. Turning his head away, he snarled, 'Get up and cover yourself!'

Jumping back, she cried, 'Mick likely thinks his mother didna ken Lizann had ran away, but I tell't her at the time – the day after he came here asking if you'd seen her. That was what Hannah was trying to mind when Tibbie was there yesterday, and she kept pointing at me and saying, "It was you! It was you!", but she couldna tell onybody what I'd done.'

Satisfied by his thunderstruck expression, she sneered, 'That took the feet from you, but it was time Hannah ken't her precious daughter didna care a damn about her. She aye went on about how good Lizann was, but it was Jenny that looked after her.'

'You're a din-raising bitch!' Peter yelled. 'I told you Mick didn't want Hannah to know, and that was a helluva thing to do to her.'

'She's made Jenny's life a misery.'

'Jenny never complained.'

'Jenny's a fool!'

'Jenny's a damned fine girl! An angel!'

Elsie looked at him suspiciously. 'Have you got your eye on her now?'

'Don't be bloody stupid! Lizann wouldn't have gone away if something hadn't made her ... or somebody! I'm positive it wasn't what Jenny said. Poor Lizann, she ...'

For one brief moment, Elsie had almost confessed that she was the somebody who had made Lizann leave so suddenly, but Peter's concern for the girl made her interrupt him. 'Poor Lizann my backside! She ken't fine what she was doing! Making on she was broken-hearted at losing George Buchan and getting you to comfort her. Comfort her? If that was comfort, you gi'ed me a right dose o' it last night! You put another bairn in my belly, I'm sure o' that.'

This consequence of his ardour had escaped him, and he slumped back heavily on the bed, while his wife stood, hands on hips, gloating at his distress. Then she said, hopefully, 'You'll not say anything to Mick about me telling Hannah Lizann was away?'

He looked up at her, wondering why he had never tumbled to her sheer maliciousness before. In spite of what she had done, all she was worried about was saving her own skin. 'I'll not tell him, but for his sake, not yours

– he'll be feeling bad enough about her dying. For God's sake, get out of my sight!'

When she flounced out, clothes in her hand, he lay back against the pillows. What kind of man was he to let her off so lightly? He should march her to the Yardie, tell Mick and let him do what he liked to her. She was poison ... but she was the mother of his two sons, and, God help him, maybe a third. Yet if Lizann ever did turn up again, he'd gladly leave them all to be with her.

Mick and Peter were restrained with each other when they walked together to the station at the end of their leave, Mick afraid to mention Elsie in case he let slip what he thought she had done, and Peter because he thought he knew what she had done. He did have the feeling that she had kept something back, but he hadn't even the slightest suspicion that her misdeeds had culminated in committing the ultimate crime ... murder!

By the time they were going aboard ship again, they had relaxed into their old friendship, and in just over a month, Peter said sheepishly, 'Elsie's expecting again.'

Without thinking, Mick said, 'I thought you said you weren't getting on with each other. Are you sure it's yours?'

Peter hung his head. 'It's mine, right enough.'

'There's no need to be ashamed of knocking your wife up,' Mick said, a little stiffly. 'It's nothing to do with me.'

Peter hesitated, then, because Elsie's confession had been preying on his mind and he wanted to get it off his chest, however angry Mick would be, he said, 'I've something to tell you, but not here. I'd better wait till we dock somewhere.'

The landing did not come for another three weeks, however, by which time he regretted saying anything; so when they were seated in a bar in Portsmouth and Mick asked what he'd been going to tell him, he laughed it off.

'Och, it was nothing. Elsie and me had a right set-to after I'd ... you don't want to hear about it. Like I told you before, you're lucky having a wife like Jenny.'

When Elsie told him that she was expecting again, Lenny Fyfe muttered plaintively, 'I thought you said you never let your man touch you now.'

'It was only once,' she reassured him. 'The night after Jenny Jappy had her baby and old Hannah died. When he started pawing at me, I was ower tired to fight him, and to tell the truth, it made me feel better.' His sulky face warned her to be careful. 'He'll not get near me again, though, I'm making him sleep on the parlour couch. Ach, Lenny, you're nae jealous, are you? I've told you dozens of times you're best.'

He had perked up at that, and since then, after every time they made love, he boasted, 'Peter didna thrill you like that, did he?'

Peter had thrilled her, Elsie reflected later, but just when he felt like it, and Lenny wasn't too bad. He swore he never went out with girls his own age, and she believed him when he said he loved her. She was quite fond of him, though she wished he wasn't so gentle. He treated her like a piece of bone china, when she wanted to be roughed up, to be mastered. He wasn't twenty yet, of course, and he was a lot better than he'd been at first, so maybe he'd get more forceful as he grew older. But she'd only a few months to enjoy him before they'd have to stop ... till after this baby was born.

The doubt she had tried to stifle for weeks raised its ugly head once more. Was it Lenny's child she was carrying? Peter was blond, and her bleached hair was naturally fairish, so how would she explain if the infant she produced had dark hair and sallow skin like Lenny? What a tongue-wagging that would cause in Buckpool!

Elsie's resentment that her husband had only made love

to her once since he joined up was being replaced by anger that he hadn't taken any precautions at the time. They got issued with French letters in the forces, so she'd heard, and they didn't need to use them when they were away, for they got stuff in their tea to stop them getting horny. He must have had a stock of them, and he'd been in her bed waiting for her, so he must have meant to give her a bairn. The bugger!

Because their corvette had been scheduled for a refit in the middle of March, the roster for leave had been on display in plenty of time for the men to let their wives or mothers know when to expect them. Peter was pleased to see that Mick would be travelling home with him again. It was a mighty long journey when you made it on your own.

On the train, their conversation was kept mainly to discussing the reports on how London had stood up to the blitz, which was still going on to a certain extent, and to the various other towns and cities which had had more than their share of attention from German bombers. After a few hours, however, they fell silent and dozed off. They'd had hardly any sleep for the past two weeks because of enemy activity around them, and it was good to be able to lie back and relax.

When they changed trains at Aberdeen there was an air raid warning in force, but a porter told them that the Jerries had been and gone. They had quite a wait for their connection, which was a slow train, stopping at almost every station on the way, but at last they were swinging their heavy kitbags on their shoulders and walking towards their homes.

Coming to the Yardie, Mick said, 'Would you like to see my daughter, Peter? She's a real smasher!'

In no hurry to go home, Peter went in with him to find Jenny feeding the infant by the fire. Her face colouring, she pulled her cardigan over her exposed breast, but he couldn't help thinking what a lovely picture of motherhood she made. 'I'm sorry to butt in,' he told her, 'but Mick wanted me to see the baby.'

'It's all right,' she murmured. 'She'll be finished in a minute.'

'Peter says Elsie's expecting again,' Mick observed.

A little miffed that her friend hadn't told her this, Jenny still smiled. 'Oh, that's good. Congratulations, Peter.'

Having noticed the odd glance she gave Mick before she spoke, Peter guessed that she suspected how things were between him and his wife. 'It was a mistake,' he admitted. 'We haven't slept as man and wife for ages, and we'll not be doing it again.'

Thoroughly embarrassed by his bluntness, Jenny murmured, 'I don't know what to say, Peter.'

'There's nothing you can say. Some marriages work out, mine didn't.'

'Can you not try to make a go of it ... for the boys?'

'They're the only reason I didn't walk out on her. I know now I should never have married her.'

'Why did you?' Jenny turned scarlet at asking so personal a question. 'I'm sorry, Peter, it's none of my business. I've always got on with her, and I couldn't have done without her when wee Lizann was born.'

His heart cramping at the beloved name, he said, 'I suppose she's got her good points. She's been a good mother, but she's ...' Breaking off, he looked at Jenny uncomfortably. 'I can't burden you with my troubles, you've had enough of your own, with Hannah dying and ...'

'Hannah couldn't get it out of her head that you and Lizann were still engaged. Even the night she died, she was shouting, "Lizann and Peter, Lizann and Peter."' Jenny, too, broke off, dismayed by how close she had come to revealing the accusation directed at his wife.

'That was part of the row we had,' Peter said wryly. 'Elsie was always jealous of Lizann. I'd better go, though, and let you folk get to bed.'

Striding along Main Street, Peter wished that he had the guts to leave Elsie altogether. The only thing was, he would miss his sons . . . and there was another baby on the way, damn it. Still, if she was already pregnant it would be all right to sleep with her, in the biblical sense, for he couldn't do any more harm and he needed some release.

The boys were sleeping when he went up to them, looking like angels though he knew they could be devils when they liked. Not that they were badly behaved, he thought with a smile, just boys being boys. His smile faded when he went into the other bedroom and saw Elsie's sour face.

'You're awful late,' she snapped. 'Where've you been?'

'We were late getting to Buckie, and Mick wanted me to see his baby.'

She lifted her head and frowned at him. 'Did they tell you they called her after your fancy piece? But you'll soon have a new bairn of your own to look at, and you can't blame me for it this time.'

It occurred to him that he might not be to blame for it, either. For all he knew it could be some other man's, for Elsie wasn't the kind to sit at home like a nun when he was away. His inside twisting in disgust, he knew he couldn't face lying down beside her, tonight or any other night. 'I'll get a couple of blankets out of the press. I'm going to sleep on the couch in the parlour from now on.'

'Suits me! You're a waste of time, any road.' She snuggled down and pulled the bedcovers up round her head as he went out.

Downstairs, a wave of anger beset him. She was making

out it was his fault their marriage was a failure, when he'd done all he could in the early stages to make it work. If only he had met a decent girl after Lizann broke their engagement, things would have been different.

Chapter Twenty-five

❦

There had been some snow in January, but February brought much heavier storms, and when Adam came home one night, tired and blue with the cold, Lizann wondered how much longer he could stand up to it. Handing him the fresh clothes she had been heating for him, she said, 'Change into them at the fireside. I'll turn my back.'

She began to dish up the supper, but in a few minutes he said, 'My fingers are that stiff, I can't fasten my spaver.'

When she turned round and saw how pathetic he looked, she went across to him. 'I'm sorry,' he shivered, 'I shouldn't expect you to . . .'

'It's all right,' she smiled, 'I don't mind.'

They were both embarrassed as she did up his trouser buttons, but when he was decent, he said, with a catch in his voice, 'I was just minding, Lizann, it's a year the now since I took you into this house.'

'So it is,' she exclaimed in surprise, 'though it feels like I've been here a lot longer than that.'

'You must be fed up biding with an old man like me.'

'I'll never be fed up.'

'You're like a daughter to me, Lizann,' he muttered, a trifle self-consciously, 'better than my own, for she's even stopped writing.'

'Oh, Adam.' Lizann's throat was choked. 'I love you like a father, and I'll always be here for you.'

'What if I've to stop working and we're put out?'

'We'll find somewhere else and I can take a job to keep

us. Now stop being so sentimental and let me see a smile on your face for a change.'

The outer edge of his lips curved up fractionally. 'Aye, you're right. I'm just a stupid old fool worrying about things. Martha would have told me off for it.'

'She wouldn't have wanted you to grieve for her so long, either.'

Despite Adam's brave attempts now at keeping cheerful, Lizann could see that his health was steadily deteriorating, but she went along with his pretence that nothing was wrong. They listened to Henry Hall again, to Geraldo and Roy Fox, and laughed at Arthur Askey and Stinker Murdoch in *Band Waggon*. They enjoyed most of the other comedians, too, although Adam wasn't too keen on Max Miller's risqué jokes. Gradually, Lizann put her fears for him to the back of her mind.

Feeling quite down one afternoon in June 1941, Jenny wished she had someone to talk to, and so, putting wee Lizann in her pram and making Georgie hold the handle, she walked along to Main Street.

Elsie was still washing up her dishes, but left them in the sink while she spoke to her visitor. 'This heat gets me down,' she sighed, putting her hands under the swell of her belly, 'and I was going to put my two horrors out to play for a while, so's I can get some peace.'

Jenny looked contrite. 'Oh, I'm sorry. I'll come back another time.'

'No, no, it's just them I want rid of. Georgie can go with them, if you like. Pattie'll take care of him.'

Jenny hesitated. She had never entrusted her eighteen-month-old son to anyone else and Pattie wasn't four yet, but it would give Elsie and her a chance to talk. 'All right,' she murmured. 'Be sure and keep hold of him all the time, mind.'

'I'll mind,' the boy assured her, 'but I'm going to get

my black sugar ellie first.' He raced upstairs and came back with a bottle of water blackened by the chunk of rock-hard liquorice he'd been shaking in it since the afternoon before, which process had also formed a creamy froth on top.

'I'm going to play bools,' Tommy announced, taking his bag of marbles out of his pocket, 'and I'll let Georgie play if he wants.' At only three, he was almost as tall as his brother.

'Me and my chums'll likely be playing Hoist the Flag,' Pattie said, adding condescendingly. 'Him, and all, if he wants.'

'Out you go,' Elsie laughed. 'I'm not caring what you do as long's you keep away from the old harbour.'

The boys scampered off, and making sure that baby Lizann was asleep in her pram, Jenny looked at Elsie. 'Have you been listening to the wireless lately? Or reading the paper?'

'I'm nae interested in the war, if that's what you're asking. I've enough to keep me going wi' two loons and this lump.'

Gasping, Jenny said, 'But things aren't going well for Britain. Does it not worry you that your Peter could be killed ... and my Mick?'

'They'll not be in the fighting. It's likely all on land.'

'There's been a lot of ships lost already.'

'I didn't think ...' Elsie's mouth tightened.

Sorry for putting her worry into her friend's mind, Jenny forced a smile. 'Ach, they'll likely be all right. As my father used to say, "The devil looks after his own." Mick did say in his last letter it looked like the balloon was going up, but I thought he was joking, and surely they'll get home before they're sent away anywhere.'

Their conversation took its usual turn now, with Jenny telling Elsie that Georgie was poking his fingers into everything nowadays, and Elsie recounting the trouble her two caused. Almost an hour had passed when an avalanche of small bodies burst in again, demanding something to eat.

Jenny gave a horrified gasp. 'Look at the state of you!' she scolded her son.

Elsie roared with laughter. 'They're like three blackies. What've you been up to, Pattie?'

He stuck out his bottom lip. 'Why is it always me you pick on?'

'It's you that always needs picking on.'

'It wasn't my fault this time. It was Johnsy Elrick that lighted the fire, and we was just jumping over it.'

'You could have got burnt!' Jenny exclaimed, imagining Georgie falling in the fire and being rushed to hospital.

'It wasn't blazing,' Pattie defended himself. 'The sticks was damp, so it was just a lot of smoke.'

'It's a good scrub you'll need,' Jenny told her son angrily. She had almost forgotten her daughter, who gave an indignant howl now at being disturbed by all the noise. 'We're going home now, pet. Georgie's been a bad boy.'

Elsie laughed again. 'Your troubles are just beginning. I'm used to it. Sometimes my two's clarted in a lot worse than smoke.'

When she was outside, Jenny grabbed Georgie by the hand and hauled him along the pavement. 'It's not only you I'll have to scrub. Everything you've got on as well, so there'll be no rest for me after suppertime.'

Once she got him home and saw the tear balanced on the edge of his bottom eyelid, however, she relented. Leaving the baby in the pram, she took him in her arms for a cuddle, not realizing until after she let him go that she had got soot on her clothes, too. 'Och,' she sighed. 'I'm as bad as you now.'

* * *

Pattie and Tommy had gone out to play again, so it was only when they came in for supper that Elsie filled the galvanized bath and left them to scrub each other, shutting her ears to the noise they made as she laid the table. When she went back to them they weren't much cleaner, because the water had so much soot in it. Making them stand, she sluiced them down with cold water from the kettle, laughing herself when they started to giggle. She filled a basin for them to wash their feet, and shook her head ruefully at the black scum left sticking to the sides of the tub when she emptied it.

By the time she had cleaned it thoroughly, Pattie and Tommy had dried themselves, but, because the supper would spoil if it wasn't dished up, she made them sit down as they were. Looking at the bare sturdy bodies, reddened by all the scrubbing and rubbing, she thought that Peter would have enjoyed the whole carry-on, and so, after putting the boys to bed, she sat down to write to him. She never had much to say, but tonight she filled four whole pages describing the afternoon's incident. She paused when she came to an end, because she usually just signed her name, but this time, she wrote, tongue in cheek, 'Your loving wife, Elsie.' He could make what he liked of that, she thought.

As her pregnancy wore into its seventh month, Elsie's fear that Lenny Fyfe was the father began to border on certainty, but she knew she could do nothing about it. She should have tried to get rid of it much earlier on; it was too late now. She couldn't even confide in anybody; a single woman having an illegitimate child caused a dreadful scandal, but a married woman . . . ! It would be enough to make the walls of Jericho come tumbling down – or, nearer to home, the doors of her father's kirk to slam in her face.

The hot July was followed by an even hotter August,

and sitting one day with Jenny beside the old Buckpool harbour, in the full rays of the sun, Elsie moaned, 'You ken't what you were doing, having your bairn at the end of the year. You hadna been puggled wi' the heat like me.'

Jenny had sensed some time ago that Elsie wasn't happy about this third baby, and supposed it was resentment at Peter for putting her in this condition as much as the heat that was making her ill-natured. 'You should stay inside or sit in the shade, then. Um, are you to be having Tibbie . . . ?'

'I'd be just as well. And my mother's volunteered to come for a week.' Elsie dragged a weary hand across her brow and then down between her breasts. 'I'm sick fed up o' this, Jenny. I wish it was past.'

'Not long now,' Jenny smiled.

'Six damned weeks!'

As it happened it was only three days later that Elsie was relieved of both child and fear when her mother said, 'It's a girl – blond with bonnie fair skin like her dad's.' Then she turned to the midwife. 'I aye thought a seven-month baby had nae nails, but this ane's got perfect wee fingers.'

Tibbie, still pushing firmly on the mother's stomach, muttered, 'Ach, it was just an old wives' tale.'

Feeling the afterbirth slipping out, Elsie closed her eyes thankfully.

Peter arrived home when Norma was two months old, and as soon as he saw his lovely daughter he felt ashamed of his previous doubts. No one, not even he, could dispute that she was his. But it didn't make him feel any more charitable towards Elsie.

Not able to sleep well on the couch, he wasn't sorry when it was time to rejoin the corvette on which he and Mick both served. 'I don't know when I'll be back,' he told Elsie, when he was leaving. 'It depends on where we're sent, and it could be long enough . . . a year or more.'

Lizann had been worried for weeks by Adam's hacking cough – not helped by the hard work of the harvest – and when he came home for supper one day, the greyness in his face made her jump up in alarm. 'Adam! Are you feeling all right?'

He seemed to have some difficulty in sitting down, and she went across to help him, but suddenly he stiffened, his hand going to his chest. 'Oh lass,' he moaned, 'the pain . . . the pain . . .'

His eyes were fixed on her as if asking her to do something, but she didn't know what to do. 'Lie back,' she urged. 'Lie back and rest.'

Fighting for breath now, he shook his head, and she realized from the look in his eyes that he was frightened. 'You'll be fine in a minute,' she assured him, praying it was true, and to her relief he did lie back in a minute. 'Pains . . . for days,' he admitted. '. . . that's . . . the worst.'

'Try to relax, Adam, and I'll go and ask Dan to phone for the doctor.'

She didn't like leaving him, but being so anxious about him that her brain wasn't working, she didn't think of asking one of the neighbours to go instead. She ran out with Cheeky at her heels, and tore up the track to the farm, ignoring the stitch that started in her side. She rapped on the door, and gasped as loudly as she could, 'Mr Fordyce! Mr Fordyce!'

Meggie Thow reached the kitchen door as Dan came out of the dining-room, and he pushed her aside roughly in his haste to find out what was wrong. 'It's Adam!' Lizann panted. 'Phone the doctor!'

As he turned away she took off again, but when she burst into the cottage she could see she was too late.

Dropping to her knees, she took hold of the still warm hands. 'Oh, Adam,' she wailed, 'if I'd known ... I wouldn't have left you on your own.'

The lifeless eyes looked back at her accusingly, and she rocked back and forth like a child with shame, tears edging down her cheeks.

When Dan ran in a few moments later he took in the situation at first glance and pulled her to her feet. 'Lizann,' he crooned, enfolding her in his arms, 'don't take it so badly, my dear. You must have known it was coming.'

Her tears flooded out then, and she wept quietly on his shoulder until the doctor arrived.

Waiting until two weeks after Adam's funeral, Dan Fordyce made his way to the Laings' cottage. He could procrastinate no longer, otherwise his workers would start asking questions.

When Lizann opened the door to him her face fell, and knowing that she thought he was going to tell her to vacate the house, he smiled to allay her fears. 'May I come in? I want to discuss something with you.'

When they were seated at opposite sides of the fire, he said, 'Meggie is finding it difficult to do as much as she used to, but she has been with my family so long I haven't the heart to pay her off. I thought of retiring her on a pension, but knowing how proud and independent she is, I'm sure she wouldn't agree to it, and I don't suppose she has anywhere to go. The only solution is for me to engage someone to help her.' He paused, his eyes searching for some reaction to let him know how the wind blew, but Lizann was gaping at him as if she didn't know what he was getting at. Sighing, he carried on. 'I'm asking you if you'd like to take on the job?'

Her mouth closed and her eyes widened. 'Me? But Dan, you've been so good to me already. I can't take any more favours from you.'

375

'I'm not doing you a favour. I need your help, honestly.'

'But ... what would Meggie say?'

'It's not up to her to say anything, but she should be pleased.'

'What about Cheeky? She wouldn't want him in her kitchen.'

'Probably not, but he can go in with the other dogs. I shouldn't have sprung it on you like this, so I'll let you think it over and I'll come back tomorrow. It'll save you having to look for another job, remember, or finding somewhere else to live. I don't know how much Martha and Adam paid you ...'

'They couldn't afford to pay me anything, I worked for my keep.'

'You will have wages plus your keep if you agree.' He stood up. 'Don't feel I am forcing you, my dear. It's only a suggestion.'

Reaching the farm track, Dan let out a long sigh. It was up to Lizann now. If she accepted the job, he would see her every day, and she might come to feel something for him. If she refused, she would go away and he would never see her again. That was unthinkable.

Lizann remained sitting when Dan went out. He had surprised her so much that she still hadn't got over it, but she would have to think about it. Like he said, it would save her having to find a job, and she would have a roof over her head. That was what had been worrying her. She couldn't have faced living as she had done before the Laings practically adopted her, but working with Meggie Thow? She didn't fancy that.

Looking round the kitchen, Lizann realized that, whatever she decided, the cottage would have to be cleared out so that the new man could move in. If she asked, Dan would likely hire a lorry to take Adam's furniture and things away, but he wouldn't help her with anything else if she turned down the job he had offered. Should she take it? She would get on all right with him – Adam always said he was a good boss – and working with Meggie might not be so bad.

As she tried to picture what it would be like, it dawned on her that Dan couldn't go for walks with her and Cheeky when she was his maidservant; Meggie would have a fit if he did. She hated the thought of losing his companionship, but she would lose it anyway if she had to leave Easter Duncairn.

Lizann fell asleep that night still going over the pros and cons, but when she took Cheeky out in the morning and let her eyes sweep round the familiar scenery – the dry-stone dykes, the standing stones, the large oaks and horse chestnut trees, the tilted chimney at the farmhouse, the snow-capped mountains in the distance – she knew that she couldn't bear to leave them.

Dan turned up in the late forenoon and stood uncertainly in the middle of the kitchen floor when she took him in. 'Have you decided?'

She didn't know that his heart was racing erratically as he waited for her answer, but she did see that he was relieved when she said, 'Yes, Mr Fordyce, I'll take the job, and thank you.'

'Pack your belongings,' he smiled, 'and I'll get someone to take them up to my house in the evening. You can sleep there tonight and start work first thing in the morning.'

'But I'll have to clear this place,' Lizann gasped, amazed by the speed of his arrangements, 'and clean it ready for the new people.'

'I'll get someone to do that, and when I go home I'll tell Meggie to make a room ready for you . . .'

'I could do that myself, Mr Fordyce.'

He looked at her sadly. 'You usually call me Dan.'

'I can't now, not when I'm working for you.'

'Ah, I see what you mean. Well, why don't you call me

377

Dan when you're alone with me, and Mr Fordyce in front of Meggie?'

'I might get muddled.'

He didn't bother to answer this. 'I'll leave you to get organized and I'll see you at breakfast tomorrow.'

After packing her own clothes into an old box, she tried to leave at least the kitchen as clean as she could. She wasn't so sure now that she was doing the right thing, but she would have to stand by her decision.

Chapter Twenty-six

Although Lenny Fyfe had resumed his affair with her, Elsie's need was for a real man. With Peter going to be away for so long, she made up her mind to make the most of her evenings, but couldn't think who to ask to mind her children. Rosie Mac was too old to put up with two boisterous boys and an infant for hours at a time, and her other neighbours weren't friendly; she guessed they'd seen Lenny slinking in – or out – and knew what was going on. But Jenny Jappy seemed to be content to sit at home.

On her next visit to the Yardie, Elsie cautiously suggested that they could take it in turns to look after each other's bairns now and then. 'We deserve some nights off to enjoy ourselves.'

Jenny said she didn't feel like going out to enjoy herself. 'But I'll look after your three any time you want.'

Elsie started by parking her children on Jenny once a week and going to the seamen's bars, laughing and joking as she was plied with drinks, but taking care not to take too much. But this wasn't enough, and it soon became twice a week – much to Jenny's disapproval though she didn't like to say anything – and when she began to take a man home sometimes, she didn't tell Jenny. Most of her pick-ups were satisfied with the half-hour or so which was all she allowed before collecting her brood, but there came a time when she herself wanted more. She made her sons go out to play on the forenoons she and Lenny transported themselves on the parlour couch, but it stuck in her craw to make love with any men in her bed at nights when her bairns were asleep in the next room.

It didn't take her long to figure something out. Telling the trusting Jenny that her mother was very ill, she asked if she could leave her children overnight sometimes, so that she could go to North Pringle Street to let her father get a good night's sleep. It worked like a charm, but she didn't try it too often in case Jenny got suspicious.

As Elsie applied her rouge and mascara one evening, she congratulated herself on taking the precaution of getting a Dutch cap fitted again, so there was no risk of falling with a bairn. That would finish her carry-ons, once and for all. Lifting her lipstick now, she outlined a large cupid's bow and filled it in, grinning as she thought it wouldn't take long to be kissed off. She didn't even have to go out tonight; she had invited Paddy Flynn to the house. He was an Irish navvy who had helped with the setting up of Dallachy Aerodrome and laying the runways, and he had stayed on in Buckie, a big rough man with enough blarney to charm the birds off the trees and the kind of blue eyes that made her insides shiver. His black hair was receding at the temples, but what did that matter when he could thrill her like she'd never been thrilled before? If she could risk asking Jenny . . . he could be here every night and she could tell Lenny Fyfe to get lost.

She had just reached the foot of the stairs when the knock came, and she opened the door with a flourish. 'Ta-rah!'

'Holy Mother of God!' Paddy exclaimed, his eyes popping at the sight of her provocative nightdress. 'You'd be as well with nothing on.'

'D'you like it?' she smirked, pushing her breasts up with her hands.

His answer was to swing her off her feet, carry her upstairs and fling her on the bed. Pausing only to tear off his clothes, he flung himself on her, and the bed was rocking when someone else knocked on the outside door. 'Don't answer it,' Paddy muttered.

A second knock was ignored, and by the third, neither of them could have stopped even if they wanted to, so it also went unheeded.

'She's not there, either,' Jake Berry told Jenny when he returned to the Yardie.

Cuddling a crimson-faced, screaming child, her own face white, Jenny burst out, 'Where is she? Wee Norma's not any better, what'll I do?'

'Will I go for the doctor?'

'It's maybe nothing, and I know bairns are up and down, but it's not so bad when they're your own. Yes, you'd better get the doctor, Jake, it's better to be safe than sorry.'

Pacing the floor in an effort to pacify the unpacifiable baby, she felt angry with Elsie. She'd said she was going to see her mother, but her father had told Jake she hadn't been there, and she wasn't at home either. Surely she wasn't out gallivanting at this time of night? 'Hush, my pet,' Jenny soothed the roaring bundle. 'Hush now.'

It was only minutes until Dr Mathieson came in, though it seemed like hours to the anxious young woman, and after examining the infant, he smiled. 'It's just colic. Have you any gripe water in the house?'

'I think there's still some in the press.' She looked rather stunned. 'Colic, is that all it is? Lizann had colic, and Georgie when he was a baby, and they weren't half as bad as this. Of course, Norma's not mine, and we can't find her mother, that's why I panicked.'

'Well, there's nothing to worry about. The gripe water should settle her and she'll be asleep in no time.'

'I'm sorry I bothered you, doctor,' Jenny murmured, tendering the half-crown he usually charged.

He waved it away. 'It's what I'm there for, my dear.'

When Dr Mathieson went out, Jake said, 'I bet that's a relief. Will I hold her till you get the gripe water?'

Only half an hour later, Jenny was able to go to bed. Norma was tucked up beside Lizann, both sound asleep, and everything was peaceful again. But as she waited for sleep to claim her, she decided not to let Elsie off with the lie she had told.

It was seven o'clock the following morning, and none of the children were up when Elsie walked in, a beaming smile on her face – Paddy Flynn hadn't left her until half past six. The smile annoyed Jenny more than ever. 'I'm glad you're pleased with yourself,' she said sarcastically, 'for I was up half the night with your Norma.'

'Oh God, what happened? Is she all right?'

'She is now, but where were you? You said you were going to sit with your mother, but when I sent Jake Berry to get you, your father told him you hadn't been there at all.'

Terrified that Jake had found out everything, Elsie said, 'Did my dad say anything about my mother? How she was?'

'I don't suppose Jake asked. I sent him to your house after that, but you weren't there either. I hate being told lies, Elsie, and I'm not putting up with it. I'm not keeping your bairns to let you stay out all night with men and you needn't think it.'

Elsie had never thought so quickly in her life. 'I'm sorry, Jenny,' she began. 'I was getting ready to go to my mother when I . . . took awful pains in my stomach, I was doubled up wi' them, and then the diarrhoea started.'

'You've got over it awful quick.'

'I'd some mixture I got at the chemist a while back, and that stopped it, though it was two in the morning before I got to my bed.'

Jenny was weakening, but there was still something not explained. 'So you'd still been up when Jake was there?

Why didn't you answer the door? He said he knocked three times.'

'Oh, it was him, was it? I was in the lavvy, you see, and nobody was there by the time I got to the door. I wondered who it had been, but I never thought ... Oh, Jenny, I'm sorry you've had all the worry.'

Satisfied now, Jenny smiled. 'It wasn't your fault. I did get a scare, though, for Norma wouldn't stop screaming. That's why I made Jake go for the doctor. I'd better get the boys wakened now. It's time your Pattie was getting ready for school.'

When the Taits left, Jenny got her own two washed and dressed then started on the housework, her mind still on what had happened. She'd often had doubts about Elsie's nights with her sick mother, had even wondered if the woman really was sick, but now she had doubts about her doubts. Peter's wife might not be perfect, but she loved her bairns; she wouldn't palm them off on anybody else so she could be with a man.

She had misjudged Elsie, Jenny concluded, and she'd have to be extra nice to her in future to make up for it.

Elsie deemed it best not to push her luck with Jenny, who had hit home with her suspicions on the morning after Norma's colic. Although she had been fobbed off that time, trying it again would just be asking for trouble. But, Elsie told herself, she couldn't stop seeing Paddy Flynn. He was the best thing that had ever happened to her.

Burning her boats altogether, she told him that he could sleep with her twice a week until she saw how things went, as long as he was gone before her sons woke up. If Pattie saw him, he would think nothing of telling Rosie Mac or Jenny or whoever he happened to be speaking to that there had been a strange man in his mam's bed.

'Of course,' she reminded the Irishman, 'you'll have to

stay away when Peter's on leave, but that shouldn't be for a long time yet.'

The arrangement worked very well, Elsie discovered, because her three children slept like logs and never heard a thing, not even when she and her lover got carried away in their passion. Only one thing niggled at her – she had no qualms about deceiving Peter, but it didn't feel right to deceive Paddy by keeping Lenny as a stand-by.

The next time the young man arrived, therefore, she waited until he was leaving. 'We'd better stop this, Lenny. We've been at it for years now, and somebody might . . .'

He looked at her in disbelief. 'You're not finishing with me, Elsie?'

'It's the best way, lover-boy,' she murmured, finding it easier as he swallowed each lie. 'There's nothing in it for you. You should find yourself a nice girl and get married.'

'I don't want anybody else. I love you.'

'And I love you, but . . .' She stopped and stroked his cheek. Was she being stupid? She did think a lot of him – loved him, in a way – but Paddy was the strong man she had always been looking for, and if he found out about Lenny he'd never come back. 'It's better this way, Len. It would be awful if we carried on till you got tired of me.'

'I'll never get tired of you,' he vowed. 'Oh, Elsie, please . . . ?'

Realizing, with an inward shudder, that it was more likely to be Paddy who would tire of her, she decided to hedge her bets. 'Give it a try, eh? Just for a while? It'll do us both good, put some new life into us.'

Still not convinced, he sighed. 'Okay. But just for a wee while.'

Her fervent kiss sent him home sure that it would all work out.

*   *   *

Elsie could have screamed when she read Peter's letter. He'd said he would be away for about a year, and it wasn't much more than two months. With a heavy heart, she waited for Paddy to appear that night. 'Peter'll be home at the end of this week,' she told him, 'so I won't be able to see you till he goes back.'

The big man didn't look at all pleased, and to sweeten him she added, 'Once he's away, you could be here more than twice a week.'

'Would you let me sleep with you every night, mavourneen?'

'Aye, why not?' she said, recklessly. 'You can bide here if you want.'

'I'll hold you to that,' he grinned. 'How long will he be at home?'

'He didn't say, but I tell you what. I'll leave my front room curtains open to let you know he's gone. You'll just have to keep coming past and watching for my signal.'

Exhausted after the long journey from Portsmouth – which he wouldn't have made if it hadn't been for his children – Peter slept like a log on his first night home, but after a week of being cramped on the parlour couch he longed for the freedom to stretch his long legs, the comfort of a proper bed. On board the corvette he had to be ready to jump any minute in the short spells in his bunk, but he didn't need to make a martyr of himself at home. Why shouldn't he sleep with Elsie? She seemed to be indifferent to him now, hadn't tried any of her old tricks on him.

When he told her in the morning that he had decided to share her bed again, he made it quite clear that he would stand no nonsense from her and that she needn't expect anything of him. Late that night, however, after she had gone upstairs, he sat by the dying fire wondering if he could trust himself. He knew how the heat of her soft body would affect him, the appealing curve of her back.

He turned his mind desperately to something which had been niggling at him for some time. He'd thought about it a lot, remembering how utterly devastated Elsie had been on the night after Jenny Jappy's baby was born ... the night after Hannah had died. Died? It seemed to him that his wife wouldn't have been so badly affected by an ordinary death, sudden though it was. Not only sudden – providential, as far as Elsie was concerned. Every time she was at the Yardie she must have been scared that the old woman would come out with what she had been told and, pressed as to who had told her about Lizann's disappearance, she would name Elsie.

Jumping to his feet, he climbed the stairs. His suspicions had no real substance, but he had to prove or disprove them.

Elsie, obviously sure that his defences would fall, smiled seductively when he went into the bedroom, but he didn't respond to her. 'Tell me again what you said to Hannah about Lizann going away.'

Elsie tutted testily. 'Why are you digging that up again? It was ages ago, and she'd forgotten all about it. She thought Jenny was Lizann.'

'I still want you to remind me.'

Annoyed at him for destroying what she thought would be a night of love, and irritated that he had interrupted her affair with Paddy, his wife took no time to cast her mind back to her previous confession. 'I told her I'd made Lizann run away.'

Peter's gut twisted but he had to be certain. She hadn't admitted this before, but he had better gentle her along until he learned the truth. 'What was it you said to her?'

Too late, Elsie realized her error and tried to correct it. 'Oh, no, I mind now. I said somebody must have made Lizann run away.'

'I'm more inclined to believe your first answer,' he said, dryly.

'No, that's the gospel truth.'

His stomach muscles tightened. 'You're lying! Tell me exactly what you said to Hannah!'

Fear of what he might uncover made Elsie tell another untruth. 'That first time, I just said Lizann had ran off, but the night Jenny's baby was born and I was putting the old wife to her bed, I said ... it was me that made her leave.'

Diving over and grabbing her by the throat, Peter shook her so hard that her head wobbled and her teeth rattled. 'So it was you! What did you do, you bitch? Tell me, for God's sake!'

'Let me go!' She tried to struggle free, but Peter had her in a grip of steel, and in her anger she spat out the truth. 'I told Lizann to stop asking you to her house, or I'd ...'

'She never asked me there, you bloody fool!' Peter roared. 'I went to her ... as a friend, though I loved her as much as any man could love a woman. But come on, what else did you say to her?'

Elsie tried to excuse herself. 'I didna ken she would run away, I was just ... warning her to let you alone, or ...'

'You threatened her?'

'I said if she didna stop seeing you, I'd tell the whole o' Buckie she'd been taking up wi' you for years and years.'

'Christ almighty, woman! She'd not long lost her husband and her baby, and you said that to her? She must have been out of her mind with ... no wonder she went away.'

'I didna mean it! I just wanted to get you to myself again.'

At last he had learned why Lizann had left, but it was

small comfort to him now, and he said icily, 'You never had me in the first place!'

'How can you say that? My body used to be sore from the times . . .'

He flung her from him and straightened his back. 'Yes, Elsie, your body had me, I can't deny that, but Lizann always had my heart, and even if I never see her again I'll love her till the day I die.'

Peter became wrapped up in his own thoughts. If Elsie had told people that he was unfaithful to her – and she would have done if Lizann hadn't gone away, exaggerating out of spite – he could have lost his job, which meant everything to him then. Lizann would have realized that and, even though she was completely innocent of the accusation, she had left to save him being publicly shamed. She wouldn't care about herself, but she had cared enough for him to try to protect him.

Wishing that she had waited and told him about Elsie's threat, Peter was more glad than ever that he had joined up. He could never forgive Elsie for driving Lizann away, and if he'd still been coming home every weekend it would have meant endless fights between them.

His anger at her bubbling up again, he said, 'God, I could kill you for what you did.'

'Carry on,' she sneered, sure that he wouldn't. 'It'll nae bring your darling Lizann back.'

Having to admit to himself that this at least was true, he remembered what had prompted him to embark on his interrogation in the first place. He still hadn't learned what he wanted to know, just enough to make his mind go round and round, but not in circles. It was on a spiral course, driving him inexorably towards a crucial point, a point he felt himself shying away from. Skirting round it, he muttered, 'You told Hannah that on the night Jenny had her baby?'

Fighting against the discovery of her greatest crime,

Elsie said, as plaintively as she could, 'She was getting right up my back wi' what she was saying.'

'When you were putting her to bed?'

'And her fighting against me all the time.'

'She died that same night?'

There was something in the way he was looking at her that told Elsie she was on treacherous ground, so she blustered, 'She was sleeping when I left her.'

'Was she?' He had started out with only a sliver of suspicion, but her fidgeting hands and the fear in her eyes made him certain that he wasn't far off the mark. 'Are you trying to tell me she died from shock? Or did you do something to shut her up for good?'

Her pupils dilating, she shrank against the pillows without admitting anything . . . nor denying, and bile rose in his throat. How could he have married this poor excuse for a woman? He felt no anger, no pity, just a desperate need to get away from her. She had taken spite at him out on a grieving young widow, then on a defenceless old invalid. Furthermore, he was positive she had been the cause of Hannah's death, however she had done it, but nobody would believe him – and the one person he must never tell was Mick Jappy. If he knew what Elsie had done to his sister and his mother, he would kill her . . . and he'd be the one to swing from the end of the rope.

'What are you going to do?' Elsie quavered, as he stepped back.

'I should report you to the police,' he barked.

She flung out her arms in appeal. 'You'll not tell them? Think about Pattie and Tommy and Norma.'

'It's them I am thinking about,' he said, quietly. 'I just hope your conscience never lets you rest. You've as good as murdered Hannah, and I feel like throttling you for what you did to Lizann, but I can't deprive the children of their mother.'

Her patent relief turned his stomach. 'When I walk out

of here, I'll never come back, though it'll break my heart not to see my sons again.'

Peter had expected her to become cocksure again at being let off the hook, and he was astonished when she said gently, 'You're welcome to come and see them as often as you like. They'll want to see you.'

'Norma doesn't really know me, and it won't take Pattie and Tommy long to forget me.'

'So that's us finished, is it?' she asked, wistfully.

'That's us finished, and it's all your own doing. It was your jealousy and spite that brought us to this. I'm leaving now, Elsie, and as Hannah herself might have said, may the good Lord have mercy on you.'

He turned towards the door, wondering where he would go at this time of night, but Elsie, said, 'Wait, Peter. I know I've been a bad wife to you, and you could never think kindly of me after this, but please bide. This is your house, your home. Go and see your bairns and then tell me you can leave them for good.'

Knowing full well what the sight of his two sturdy sons and sweet wee daughter would do to him, he nevertheless tiptoed in to look at them, and the flushed angelic faces were enough to convince him that Elsie was right. He couldn't bear to leave them for ever.

When he went back to her, he said, 'I give in, but before I come back I want you to buy some kind of folding bed I can put up in the kitchen. The parlour's always freezing, and the couch is too short. And from now on you'll be my wife in name only, and we'll have to keep up a pretence of being happy in front of the kids.'

'Thank God for that. I didn't want folk to be laughing and saying my man had walked out on me.'

This proof that it was still only herself she was considering made him snap, 'They'd say a lot worse than that if they knew what you'd done.' He hadn't meant to cast it up. He had committed himself to keeping her secret, and it was best never mentioned again. 'You haven't said if you agree to my terms.'

'Oh, aye. Anything you say, Peter.'

He went down to lie on the couch, knowing he would keep thinking about the dreadful crime he was sure she had committed, the crime he should have reported to the police, but without proof . . . ?

What a bloody mess his life had turned out. With seeing so many ships blown up lately, he had become increasingly conscious of his own mortality. With no Lizann, there was nobody left to mourn if anything happened to him. He wondered if Elsie had learned a lesson tonight. Should he try to salvage something from his marriage? Not yet, though. What she'd done was too fresh in his mind. He'd be best to leave it till he was home for good. Maybe he would see things differently. All he had to do now was to get through the next two days peaceably.

Chapter Twenty-seven

❦

Peter having left on the early morning train, Elsie spent the forenoon, unusually for her, wrestling with her conscience. He likely thought she would turn over a new leaf after being found out in her lies, but surely he wouldn't expect her to be faithful when he was away for so long at a time? She loved her three bairns, but they would drive her up the wall if she had no diversions to look forward to. Maybe she should ask Jenny how she coped when Mick was away.

'Lonely already?' Jenny smiled, when she opened her door. 'Me too.'

Setting Norma down beside wee Lizann on the mat, Elsie began, 'Does Mick ... does he make love to you every night when he's home?'

Jenny flushed. They had never talked about intimate matters, but she could see her answer was important to Elsie. 'Yes, did Peter not ... ?'

'Oh, aye,' Elsie prevaricated. 'Do you not miss it when Mick's away?'

'I miss him, but I wouldn't dream of taking another man, and neither should you.'

'But if you think about Mick making love to you, do you not want ... ?'

'You've gone far enough, Elsie. I've hated thinking you're unfaithful to Peter, for next to Mick he's the nicest man I know, but I can't stop you if that's what you want. Just don't tell me about it.'

'Aye, you're right, Jenny. You see, Peter got me all fired

up when he was home, but I'll not do anything. It wouldn't be fair to him.'

'No, it wouldn't.'

Elsie kept Jenny's lecture in mind for only three days, then, unable to bear being parted from Paddy any longer, she decided to let him know the coast was clear by giving him the prearranged signal.

After settling her children in bed, she lit the fire in the parlour, then made herself ready for her lover, painting her face, splashing herself with the 4711 cologne he had given her for her birthday, and putting on a gossamer-thin nightdress. Her juices were boiling as she sat down to await his arrival and when he knocked she jumped up to let him in, flinging herself into his arms as soon as he was inside.

He grabbed her and steered her into the parlour, where the fire was burning up nicely. 'I'm desperate,' he moaned. 'I've been watching your window every night for two weeks.'

'I was trying to be a good girl, but I can't.'

'Thank God for that. The worse you are, the better I'll like it, and I can't wait a minute longer.' His mouth came down on hers now, draining away the tiny seed of guilt that she hadn't realized was there, and in a few seconds they sank naked on to the couch, so frantic with passion that Elsie forgot to close the curtains.

Lenny Fyfe had been in the Harbour Bar since the doors opened at half past five, and with quite a few whiskies and beers inside him by half past eight, his mind had turned to Elsie. She had told him to keep away, but he had to have her and he knew Peter had gone back off leave.

Going along Main Street he saw a light at her front window, and was surprised that the warden hadn't been round knocking on the door. Then it dawned on him that it was the flicker of a flame and, thinking that the house was on fire, he sprinted forward to save his paramour. When he came closer and saw that it was only the fire in the grate, he wondered who Elsie was entertaining; only honoured visitors were ever taken into parlours.

His mission aborted, Lenny decided to have a peep inside. If it was the minister he wouldn't stay long – she would be free in half an hour or so. He let out a horrified gasp when he saw that it wasn't the minister, and though his heart, and his desire, had sunk like a stone, he couldn't tear his eyes away from the nude bodies on the couch. The bitch! The bloody bitch! No wonder she had told him to stop coming to see her; she was having it off with another man!

Blind fury boiling up inside him, he edged the door open and tiptoed inside. He meant to wait until they finished the act before he made his presence known, but the ecstatic moans and animal grunts were too much for him. 'You bloody whore!' he screamed.

Elsie's astonished face, blood-red with lust, turned towards him, but the man was beyond stopping. Giving one massive thrust, he shuddered for a few moments before he slid off her on to the floor. 'What in the name of Jaysus is he doing here?' he demanded, scrambling to his feet with his hands over his genitals.

'What in the name of Jesus are *you* doing here?' Lenny countered.

'Please, Lenny,' Elsie begged, her hands jumping from her breasts to her pubis in a vain effort to cover herself. 'It's not what you think.'

'What am I supposed to think when he'd his prick inside you?'

Struggling to get on his trousers, Paddy snarled, 'What business is it of yours?'

'She's mine! That's what business it is! She's been mine for years!'

Paddy burst out laughing. 'For years? You're just a kid. You don't know what you're speaking about.'

'Ask her!' Lenny screeched. 'She'll tell you!'

His hands fumbling with his trouser buttons, Paddy turned angrily to Elsie. 'Is that true?'

Wishing Lenny in hell, she shouted, 'Get out, get out!'

'Tell him it's true!' Lenny yelled.

Slipping on his shirt, Paddy roared, 'I don't give a monkey's damn if it's true or not. I'm finished with you, you tramp!' Lifting his jacket, he made for the door.

'Don't go, Paddy!' Elsie pleaded. 'I didn't mean you!'

He looked at her contemptuously as he went out, and she jumped to her feet and punched Lenny in the chest. 'See what you've done, you stupid young bugger?'

At that moment a shrill voice outside called, 'Put out that light!'

Lenny collapsed on to the couch in a fit of uncontrollable laughter, but Elsie went to the door and gave the warden a mouthful of curses as well as a full view of her bare body. As he reeled back in amazement, she banged the door and went in to yank the curtains together. Turning to face Lenny, she spat out, 'D'you really think I wanted a half-grown idiot when I had my pick of anybody I wanted? I only fooled about with you because Peter had stopped touching me, but Paddy's a real he-man and ... now I'll never see him again.'

Her tears made Lenny get up to put his arms round her, but she shoved him away. 'Get out of my sight, for God's sake!'

He stood for a moment, then walked slowly towards the door, but as he opened it he looked at her again. 'You're an evil bitch! I'll not let you get away with what you've done to me.'

'Get lost, little boy,' she sneered. 'Run home to your mammy and see what she thinks of you for interfering with a married woman.'

Lenny pulled the door shut quietly. Her last remark had made him feel like strangling her, yet remembering how beautiful she looked standing naked in front of him, he knew he would go running back if she crooked her little finger at him. But she wouldn't have anything more to do with him now, and he would damned well carry out his threat. She deserved to suffer as much as she'd made him suffer tonight. He didn't know exactly what he would do, but he'd think of something!

Jenny couldn't believe her ears. The two women in the butcher's had been saying some awful things about Elsie. 'And it must be true,' one of them had crowed gleefully. 'Eck Stewart couldna mak' up a story like that.'

Lifting the change from the ten shilling note she had tendered, Jenny walked out of the shop seething and strode home so fast that Georgie had to run to keep up with her, while her little daughter laughed with glee at the new game. When she spotted the ARP warden at the other side of the road, she crossed over to tackle him about the rumour he had spread.

'It's not a rumour, it's gospel,' he said, puffing out his chest. 'I shouted to Elsie to put out her light, though it wasna really a light, just the flames from her fire, and help my bob, she comes to the door in her birthday suit, as bold as brass. I didna ken where to look. I've never seen a body like hers before, not without being well covered, and there she stood, swearing like a trooper. Not only that, I saw a man running out with his jacket in his hand a minute or so afore, and there was still a man in wi' her. So what had she been up to?'

Feeling sick, Jenny said, faintly, 'You must have imagined it, Eck.'

'It wasna imagination that made my cock stand up . . . oh, I beg pardon, Jenny. I shouldna be saying things like that to you. But I thought I was well past it, and that proved I wasna.'

'You shouldn't go telling folk, though. Whatever she was doing, it was her own business.'

The warden was taken aback at this, but muttered, 'I dinna think her man would look on it like that.'

Feeling a deep compassion for Peter, Jenny made up her mind to go and find out what Elsie was playing at. One lover would be bad enough, but two at the same time? Maybe when she knew it was being bandied about she would listen to her old friend . . . though it seemed she'd paid no attention to the advice she got before. Leaving her children with Babsie Berry, Jenny made for Main Street.

Elsie looked a mess when she came to the door, her face still bearing traces of make-up, black streaks where tears had made her mascara run, her bleached hair uncombed. 'I can't speak to you just now,' she said.

Ignoring this, Jenny pushed past her. 'What was going on in here last night?' she demanded. 'And don't pretend you don't know what I'm getting at, for Eck Stewart's telling everybody.'

'Eck's got a dirty mind. I'd a bath at the fire, and I'd just finished drying myself when he knocked at the door and shouted something, and I opened it without thinking.'

Gullible Jenny was prepared to believe this, yet something was still bothering her. 'Eck said he saw one man running out of your house and another man was still inside.'

Elsie threw back her head and let out a loud laugh. 'That Eck! He got a right eyeful of me, and he's made up a story to spice it up a bit.'

'Are you sure, Elsie?' Jenny wasn't really convinced, but was prepared to give her friend the benefit of the doubt.

'There was nobody here except me and the bairns. Even

if I'd wanted a man, d'you think I'm as stupid as take two in together? What do you think I am? Depraved?'

'I'm sorry, I shouldn't have believed him.'

'A fine friend you've turned out,' Elsie muttered, looking offended.

'Don't say that. I was only wanting to save Peter being hurt.'

'Peter? Are you after him now? I never dreamt . . .'

'You know fine I'm not after him, but it was awful to think you'd been unfaithful to him.'

'Well I haven't been, so go home and think twice before you accuse me of anything again.'

'Are you still friends with me, Elsie?'

'I shouldn't be, after what you said . . . but all right. Still friends.'

When Jenny wrote to Mick that night she did not mention the incident. Eck had been making as much as he could out of it, and that's what she would tell anybody who asked her about it.

She might have known Eck would clype on her, Elsie fumed, and all the old bitches in Buckpool would be watching her house every minute of the day now to see what they could see. It had been a piece of cake palming Jenny off, but some of her neighbours wouldn't be so easily hoodwinked, so she'd better give them time to forget before she took another man in.

Lenny's threat didn't worry her. It was a natural reaction. If only he hadn't walked past her house when he did, everything would have been hunky-dory, though it was her own fault for forgetting to shut the curtains – Paddy had driven that right out of her head. Of course, she shouldn't have gone to the door starkers, that was her biggest mistake. She hadn't been thinking clearly at the time. She'd only meant to shock the warden, but she'd ended up landing herself right up to the eyeballs in shit.

Always able to rise above her troubles, Elsie stood up and shrugged her shoulders. To hell with Eck Stewart! To hell with Lenny Fyfe! To hell with Paddy Flynn! And to hell with the whole lot of narrow-minded harpies that couldn't stand to see a girl having a good time.

Chapter Twenty-eight

Lenny had asked a few girls out over the past six nights, but they had all been too young and innocent to satisfy him properly. It was like a man having skimmed milk on his porridge when he was used to cream. Lying in bed, frustrated because the girl he'd been with had slapped his face for putting his hand up her skirt, a way to punish Elsie suddenly came to him. He would go back to her – she'd have cooled down by now – and make her think he was still under her spell. He would lay it on real thick, swear he loved her, and then ... as soon as there was any sign that she loved him – really loved him, not just pretending this time – he'd give her the dirty heave.

He should have known what she was up to before, just letting him see her in a forenoon. It had left her free to take another lover later on. So ... he'd be the one to go in the evenings from now on.

The following day he got a loan of a sex book one of the older bakers had bought because his wife had told him she was fed up with how he made love, and spent the afternoon reading it in his bedroom. It was a revelation to him – all those different positions when he'd thought you could only do it with the man on top. His eyes widened at the diagrams, he'd never seen anything like them, and they almost fell out altogether when he came to the photographs – actual photographs of ...

The fire in his loins reaching fever pitch, he slammed the book shut. It was a true saying that half the people didn't know what the other half was doing, but he'd have to keep his heat for Elsie.

Having told his mother that he was going out for a drink, he knocked on Elsie's door that night. She didn't look very pleased to see him, and stood with her hands on her hips. 'What d'you want?'

'I've come to say I'm sorry for ... you know ... last week.'

'So now you've said it. Cheerio!'

He managed to stick his foot out to stop her closing the door. 'Please, Elsie, will you not let me in?'

The pathetic, pleading way he was looking at her made her realize how much she had missed him ... actually missed him. It hadn't been his fault. 'All right, come in and let Elsie show you she's forgiven you.'

He needed no second bidding, and having seen how she liked the Irish navvy roughing her up, he let himself go as he worked mentally through as much of the sex-book as he'd read. After a couple of hours, when he was having a quick smoke to give his flagging desire time to kindle again, she leaned over him. 'Oh, God, Lenny, if I'd known you could do things like that, I'd never have looked at Paddy.'

Congratulating himself on being so clever, Lenny blew a smoke ring past her ear. 'You ain't seen nothing yet,' he bragged, not bothered that he had to start work at 2 AM.

It only took another two nights for him to be sure Elsie meant it when she said she loved him, for she was looking at him like she'd never done before. When he sprang his surprise on her – but not till he'd sampled a lot more of this abandoned sex – it would shake her to the dark roots of her hair.

Lenny's idyll, however, was to be rudely shattered. When he went home from the bakehouse one forenoon just three weeks later, a long buff envelope was lying on the table. Opening it, he gave a loud gasp.

'What is it,' Mrs Fyfe asked in concern, for he'd been

in a strange mood this while past and she was sure something was bothering him.

'My calling-up papers!' He'd had to register two years ago, but because he was a baker and his boss had put in an appeal, he hadn't thought he'd have to go at all.

Unable to eat his breakfast, he went up to his room to think, and after about ten minutes sat up with a delighted grin. The army had played right into his hands. He had already planned every detail of the ditching and this would make the grand finale even grander.

'You're awful quiet,' Elsie murmured that evening, lifting her blond head from the pillow to kiss him. 'Is anything wrong?'

He hadn't meant to tell her yet, but it came spilling out. 'I've been called up.'

Her face fell. 'Oh God! Already?'

He affected great despondency. 'We've just a week left.'

'Is that all?'

Neither of them said anything for a few seconds, then Elsie raked her fingers through the dark hairs on his chest. 'We'd better make the most of it, eh, Len?'

He nodded eagerly. He would give her a week she would never forget, and the crunch would come on the last night.

'Mrs Fyfe was telling me Lenny's been called up,' Jenny observed as she poured a cup of tea for her visitor.

Elsie wondered if there was any hidden meaning intended, but decided there wasn't. 'Aye, so I believe.'

'He's grown up into a right handsome man, hasn't he?' Jenny continued. She was trying to find out if there was any truth in the rumours she'd heard about him lately. 'He used to be a scraggy streak, but he's fairly filled out.'

Elsie couldn't help smiling at this. 'One bit of him, any road.'

Jenny's eyebrows shot up. 'Elsie! You haven't been . . . not with *him*?'

'I was only joking,' Elsie said hastily. 'He's never been near me.'

But Jenny wasn't to be fooled. 'I don't believe you.'

Angry at herself, Elsie went on her high horse. 'Please yourself. What business is it of yours what I do and who I do it with?'

'What about Peter?'

'Why are you aye so bloody worried about Peter? If he'd been as good as Lenny and Paddy, I wouldn't have needed them.'

Something clicked into place in Jenny's mind. 'It was true what Eck Stewart said, wasn't it? It must have been this other man that ran out of your house that night, and Lenny had still been inside. Did he catch the two of you at it?'

Stung because she'd hit on the truth, Elsie said, 'You're just jealous I'm having a good time, that's what's wrong wi' you, and I'll tell you something else. I was wi' a man every time . . .' Realizing how indiscreet she was being, she tailed off, her eyes seeking assurance that Jenny was not a jump ahead of her. She was out of luck, however.

'Every time I kept your bairns?' Jenny said, her face darkening with anger. 'When you were supposed to be sitting with your mother? Where were you the night Norma had her colic and Jake Berry couldn't find you? In some hotel with one of your fancy men?'

Elsie shook her head. 'I was in bed wi' Paddy . . . my own bed.'

'You mean, when Jake knocked, you were . . . ? Oh, no!' That seemed even worse to Jenny.

'So you see the kind o' wife your precious Peter's got!' Elsie gave a stifled sob. 'Oh God, Jenny, I'm ashamed when I think on the things I did!'

'And so you should be,' Jenny said, stiffly. 'If I'd known what was going on . . .'

Raising her streaming eyes, Elsie mumbled, 'I'm sorry, Jenny, I just couldn't help it. I love my bairns, but . . . I've aye needed a man. Peter saw through me and wouldna touch me, and that's why I went daft with any man that wanted me, but I've learned my lesson. You'll likely laugh when I tell you, but I've gone and fell in love wi' Lenny, and . . .' Stopping to gulp several times, she ended in a rush, 'He goes away next week and I'm near sure I'm expecting . . . and it's nae Peter's . . . or Paddy's.'

Jenny was too taken aback to laugh. 'It's the price of you, Elsie. I'm surprised it hasn't happened before, the way you've carried on, and don't expect me to stick up for you when folk start speaking about you.'

'Jenny, please? I've nobody else to turn to . . . my father'll kill me . . .'

'You're still just thinking about yourself,' Jenny said, scornfully. 'What about Peter? How's he going to feel when he comes home and finds you're having a baby to Lenny Fyfe?'

'Nobody'll ken it's Lenny's except you.'

'Peter'll know it isn't his, so what'll you tell him?'

Elsie's hands tore at her hair now. 'Ach, Jenny, I'm all mixed up. I didna mean to tell you about the bairn.'

'I wish you hadn't,' Jenny said, coldly. 'You've put me in a terrible spot. Peter's Mick's best pal, and I'll have to tell him.'

'Tell him what you like! I never loved him!'

Jenny jumped to her feet, her face red with rage. 'Get out, Elsie, and don't dare to set foot in my house again!'

When her erstwhile friend had trailed out Jenny collapsed into her chair again, utterly shocked by what she had been told. She believed that Elsie, for all her bravado, did love her children, and bitterly regretted ignoring Jake's knocks on the night of Norma's colic – but if even half the things she'd confessed to doing were true, she deserved what she'd got. Poor Peter!

Lenny made all his arrangements one afternoon, and was fizzling with excitement when he went to Elsie's at night.

'You're looking awful pleased with yourself,' she observed, surprised that he was so happy when they had hardly any time left to be together.

'I am pleased,' he beamed. 'What would you say to coming to Elgin with me? I've booked a room in a hotel for my last two nights.'

'Lenny!' she exclaimed, in delight. 'I'd never have thought you could be so romantic.'

'Get somebody to take your kids . . .'

Her face fell. 'That'll be a problem.'

'Will Jenny Jappy not have them? You're pally with her, aren't you.'

'Not now. We'd a bit of a set-to.'

Lenny was bitterly disappointed. Surely this wasn't the kiss of death on his marvellous scheme? 'Can you not ask somebody else?'

'Nobody's very friendly with me these days.' Her nose wrinkled for a moment as she thought deeply. 'I suppose I could ask my mother, but I'll have to find a damn good excuse for being away two nights.'

The tightness in his chest eased. 'You'll manage that. I'll come for you the morrow about five, then.'

Lenny couldn't sleep that night. His stomach was churning with fearful anticipation of how Elsie would react to what he meant to do. Would she laugh in his face and tell him she didn't care? No, she would care. She loved him, he was sure of that, so she'd probably be absolutely livid . . . beside herself with fury at being taken in. That's what he wanted . . . as long as she didn't cut up rough. He didn't want to arrive at Catterick with a couple of black eyes and a broken nose.

Elsie was all smiles when he knocked at her door at ten past five the next day. 'All set!' she boasted. 'I told Ma I'd to go to Aberdeen to sort out some squabble over my allowance book from the Navy, and I said I'd be as well having a look round the shops seeing I was there. She wasn't keen on me being away two nights, but I said it would be a wee holiday for me, away from the bairns.'

Lenny couldn't help but admire her ingenuity, though he felt his own plot was even more ingenious. 'We'd better go and catch the bus.'

In Elgin, Elsie was like a young girl, hardly ever wanting to leave their hotel room and telling Lenny how much she loved him, how much she would miss him when he went away. His passions heightened by a touch of doubt that he might come off worst, he played along with her, vowing that she was the only woman for him. As the time went past, however, his nerves were playing havoc with him, and all he could think of was to get it over. But he couldn't jump the gun; exact timing was essential.

At six o'clock on their second and last day, he suggested having a walk to blow the cobwebs off them. He had expected her to beg for more time in bed, and was prepared to say she had worn him out, but she surprised him by agreeing. 'We'll take our things with us,' he said casually. 'There's no point in having to come back, is there?'

Both having something momentous to say that was weighing heavily on their minds, they spoke very little as they strolled through Cooper Park for a good three quarters of an hour and then made their way back to the centre of town. When they came to the small tearoom on the opposite side of the street from the bus station, Lenny said, 'What about having a wee snack? It's another half hour till the bus leaves.'

He held the door open for her and made her sit with

her back to the window, then he bought sandwiches and a pot of tea, not grudging what he spent. When she gave him his cup, his hand was shaking, but he forced a loving smile. 'Will you miss me, Elsie?'

'Oh yes, Lenny,' she breathed, stretching over to lay her hand on his. 'I never loved Peter as much as I love you, and when I think you'll be going away in the morning, it's like there's a great big stone in my stomach. I don't know what I'm going to do without you.'

Feeling like saying she'd find plenty of other men, he took a bite of his corned mutton sandwich instead, though he had a problem getting it down once he had chewed it.

'Lenny,' she said, more serious than he had ever seen her, 'you won't take up with anybody down there, will you?'

He evaded the question skilfully. 'What d'you think I am?'

'So you really do love me?'

'I've never felt this way about any other girl.' That was true, Lenny thought, then he noticed that their bus was now sitting at the terminus and had a quick look at his watch. Ten minutes yet, though Elsie thought they had a lot longer than that. Pouring some milk in first – he had taken no sugar since it went on ration – his trembling hand raised the cup to his mouth, but after one sip, he laid it back in his saucer. Oh God, this waiting for the right moment was agony.

'Lenny,' Elsie began again, then stopped.

This time, it occurred to him that she looked worried . . . about him, more than likely. Women always worried about their men when they went off to war. But he wasn't her man, not even her fancy man, not any longer. His mind replayed the scene that had haunted him every night since he had witnessed it. He saw again the two naked bodies thrashing about on the couch in their lust; he heard the ecstatic moans and triumphant cries ... Oh Christ, she deserved what was coming to her!

'Will you write?' she murmured now.

'Every day.' He could have said every five minutes, it wouldn't have been any more of a fib. Looking out of the window again, he saw that the bus was already half full, and praying that his watch wasn't slow, he turned round to check with the clock on the wall behind him. Spot on! Five more minutes.

He took another sip of tea, grimaced and put the cup down again. He couldn't take any more. Speak about a lump of stone – he had a bloody great boulder in his throat! Elsie, her eyes fixed on her plate, was crumbling the edges of her sandwich as if she too couldn't swallow anything. They both looked towards the door when two young boys came in.

'You were about the same age as them when . . .' Elsie faltered and then went on, '. . . when I gave you your first lessons in love.'

Recalling the raw youth he had been, Lenny smiled a little at the last word. Love hadn't come into it. 'I ended up showing you a thing or two, though.'

'Lenny,' she started once again, 'we're good together, aren't we?'

But his eye was caught by the clock, and his stomach jolted. This was it! It was now or never! Shoving back his chair, he got to his feet.

'Is something wrong, Lenny?' Elsie inquired, anxiously.

His heart beating twenty to the dozen, he leaned across the table. 'You're what's wrong, you bloody two-faced whore! I'm finished with you, so see how *you* like being ditched!'

He strode to the door, expecting her to come after him, but a quick glance back showed her sitting with her mouth gaping, as if she couldn't believe what was happening. So much the better, he thought, it hadn't been as bad as he'd thought. Reaching the bus as it started to move, he jumped aboard and plumped down on a seat. His palms were sweating, bile was coming up in his mouth, but he'd done it!

Congratulating himself on the success of his plan, which had gone like clockwork, Lenny was amazed that he'd had the nerve to see it through. He had fooled Elsie right up to the end, and by jingo he'd got his own back on her for what she did to him.

He went over it all again. When he'd first come up with the idea, he hadn't been too sure of what would happen afterwards. He had planned to get the last bus; Elsie would have to stay in Elgin all night and she'd really have been after his blood when she got home. She might have come storming to his house and he wouldn't have put it past her to stand outside in the street and broadcast to all and sundry what she thought of him. But as it was, by courtesy of the army, he would be long gone by the time she got home.

He was quits with her, more than quits with her, and he would soon be taking his pick from the girls around Catterick.

It was fortunate for Lenny that he did not see the consequence of his revenge. It had taken Elsie's shocked brain a full minute to register what he said – she had been concentrating on trying to tell him she was expecting his child – and when she saw him sprinting towards the bus and it dawned on her that he was leaving her in the lurch, she sprang to her feet and dashed blindly out on to the street . . . straight into the path of a huge army truck.

Chapter Twenty-nine

After an initial period of resentment on Meggie's part, she had become more friendly towards Lizann, even encouraging her to go out for walks after her day's work was done. On her first such outing she had gone to collect Cheeky from the shed where all the collies were housed at night. His ears had gone up when he saw her, but he had stayed where he was, and she supposed he got enough exercise during the day. He was a farm dog now, not a pet.

She didn't bother to go near him now and usually made her way along the burn, which had always been her favourite walk. She didn't mind going by herself ... though it would have been nicer if Mr Fordyce was with her. Still, he wouldn't think it proper since he was her boss.

One Thursday night – Meggie's day for visiting the cook at Wester Duncairn – Lizann set off down the path from the back door. She passed the little wooden bridge because she liked to go along the near side of the burn and cross the water by the stepping stones about a mile farther on. As she strolled along, contentedly breathing in the smell of moss and bracken, the sound of heavy feet behind her made her look round.

'I thought this is where you'd be,' Dan said as he came alongside her. 'It was so stuffy in the house, I needed a breath of fresh air, and when I came through the kitchen, there was no one there.'

'Meggie's out seeing her friend.'

'Does she go out every Thursday?'

'Usually.'

'Um . . . I've missed our little chats, you know.'

'So've I, Mr Fordyce.'

'It's Dan, remember? Would you mind if I came with you every Thursday? Meggie wouldn't be here to get any ideas.'

'Yes, Dan, I'd like that.'

They kept walking slowly, talking about this and that, but sometimes not saying anything at all, merely enjoying each other's company. When they returned to the house Dan said goodnight and left her, but she was really pleased that they were good friends again, even though she would be with him for only an hour or so every Thursday.

'Mrs Jappy?'

The sight of the tall policeman had made Jenny's mouth dry up, but she managed to murmur, 'Yes?'

'Can I come in?'

Once inside, he took off his hat. 'I believe you're acquainted with Mrs Elsie Tait?'

'Yes?'

'She was involved in an accident in Elgin last night.'

'Oh, no! What happened?'

'I don't know. I was just told to take you to Doctor Gray's Hospital. Apparently she wants to see you.'

'Me?' Jenny could hardly credit this when they had parted on such bad terms. 'I'll have to get my neighbour to look after my bairns, but I'll not be a minute.'

In half an hour she was at the reception desk of the Elgin hospital asking for Mrs Tait. When she found the correct ward, the sister detained her before she went in. 'Mrs Tait's condition is critical, but in her brief spells of consciousness she is very agitated and keeps asking for you. I think she wants to get something off her mind, so let her tell you if she can, but whatever she says, try not to upset her.'

Judging by the woman's grave expression, Jenny guessed that Elsie was not expected to live, and she was turning away when the sister said, 'We know from letters she had that her husband is in the Navy, but is there anyone else we should notify?'

'Her mother and father live in North Pringle Street in Buckie. I don't know the number, but their name's Slater.'

'The police'll trace them from that, I'm sure. I'll tell the almoner.'

She hurried away and Jenny went into the ward, but when she saw the white, still figure on the bed she thought she was too late. As she stood uncertainly, a young nurse came over to her. 'Mrs Jappy? Let her know you're here, but don't stay longer than a few minutes.'

The girl went to attend to another patient and Jenny leaned forward. 'Elsie, can you hear me? It's Jenny Jappy.'

The eyes opened. 'Jenny?' It was very faint, the lips scarcely moving. 'My bairns . . . wi' my mother . . . be all right . . . have to tell you . . .'

The fidgeting fingers told Jenny that she was about to learn something she wouldn't want to hear, but she bent her head to listen.

'I . . . made . . . Lizann . . . run away.'

Jenny was shocked, but the tic flickering at the pain-filled eyes made her murmur, 'It's all right, Elsie.'

The voice became a fraction stronger. 'I said . . . I'd tell . . . she was . . . carrying on . . . with Peter.'

Knowing that this was not true, Jenny couldn't help gasping. She had thought she was the cause of Lizann leaving, but what Elsie had said to her was far worse.

The hoarse, low voice started again. 'I . . . told Hannah . . . at the time.'

Another piece of the jigsaw slotted into place in Jenny's mind. It had been Elsie who made Hannah change so suddenly for the worse, and that was why the old woman had shouted, 'It was her!' when the baby was being born. She had always been puzzled about that. Sick at heart, she could only say, 'It's all right, Elsie. I won't tell anybody.'

But Elsie wasn't finished yet. 'There's more.' Her hands fluttered frantically now. 'The day ... your Lizann was born ...'

Her voice tailed away, and Jenny waited anxiously, afraid that Elsie would die before confessing the rest. After about ten seconds, however, she seemed to dredge up enough strength to carry on. 'I couldn't stand ... any more ...'

Her eyes fixed on Jenny, she hesitated then whispered, 'A pillow ... over her ... face.'

Aghast, Jenny couldn't think what to say. How could she give comfort to this woman, this murderer, when she wished with all her heart that she was dead. She had known Elsie wasn't to be trusted, but she had never dreamt that she was so evil.

'Jenny?'

'Yes?'

'Sorry.' It was the merest breath, and in the next instant there was no movement, no life.

In a panic now, ashamed at what she had been thinking, Jenny looked around for the nurse, who came hurrying over. 'I think she's ...' Jenny murmured.

The girl went to the bed and felt for a pulse. Then she looked up and shook her head. 'Yes, I'm afraid she's gone.'

With the nurse eyeing her in pity for losing her friend, Jenny went out to the corridor and sat down heavily on a chair. She shouldn't have come. She should have let Elsie go to her grave with everything on her conscience ... but she hadn't known what she was going to hear. She had imagined it would be something more about being unfaithful to Peter, which would have been bad

413

enough, but this? She daren't tell Mick. It would be enough to send him clean off his head. She couldn't even tell Peter, for he'd been as upset as any of them when Lizann left, and she couldn't hurt him even more by telling him that his wife had murdered Hannah. In any case, neither of them could do a thing about it now. Nobody could.

'Did Mrs Tait die?'

The voice startled her. She hadn't noticed the policeman waiting to take her home. 'Yes.'

Gathering that she didn't want to talk about it, he said, 'I'm sorry,' but asked nothing more. Nor did he say anything on the drive back to the Yardie, but as Jenny got out of the car, he said, 'Are you sure you're all right? You look a bit shaky. Do you want me to come in with you?'

'No thanks, I'm fine.'

She let herself into the house, and put on the kettle, hoping that a cup of tea would help her to pull herself together. She couldn't drag her mind away from what she had learned, however, and eventually came to the conclusion that she would have to face up to being burdened with Elsie's secret for the rest of her life.

Life on board a corvette in the Mediterranean was even more hectic than in the Atlantic; the whole German Navy seemed to be concentrated here. The crew of the *Hercules* had had very little sleep for weeks. Several battleships had been sunk, and morale was beginning to slip. Being stuck in the engine room, Mick hadn't seen Peter for some days, so when he came on deck one night for a breath of air and saw his friend leaning over the rail, he went across to him. 'How long'll this calm last?'

'God knows,' Peter muttered, 'but it's bloody welcome. I've lost count of the times I thought we were goners.'

'Aye, it's been hairy.' Mick hesitated for a moment, his

eyes on the water below. 'Peter, it's maybe bad luck to say this, but if . . . anything happens to me, will you make sure Jenny's all right?'

'Nothing's going to happen to you, man.'

'If it does . . . do you promise?'

'Of course I promise.'

Mick had expected to be asked to look after Elsie, but after a short pause Peter said, 'Will you promise me something, and all? If Lizann turns up again, will you tell her . . . I've never stopped loving her?'

'But . . . you said you might try to make a go of it with Elsie.'

'I thought about it, but there's no way I . . .' Peter sighed. 'Lizann's worth a hundred of Elsie's kind. It was Lizann's face I kept seeing every time I thought we'd had it, and I know I'll be thinking of her when I die . . . in the war, or from old age. I'll never forget her . . .'

The shrill hooting of the alarms blocked out his last words, but as they moved to man their action posts, he shouted, 'Promise me, Mick?'

'I promise.' Reaching the hatch, Mick yelled, 'Fingers crossed we come through this,' before he swung himself round to go down to the engine room again.

Rumours were flying fast in Buckpool, each person's speculation being added to when it was passed on, and by the time Jenny heard them she wondered how much was true. One version was that Elsie had gone to Elgin to meet an airman from Lossiemouth and he'd pushed her into the street because she'd been flirting with some-body else. Another was that she'd been running away with a Seaforth Highlander who had shoved her out of his lorry when she told him she was married with three children.

Jenny wished now that she had been more sympathetic towards Elsie when she came to the Yardie that last time.

Maybe, when she told Lenny she was expecting, he'd denied it was his; with him turning his back on her as well as the woman she'd thought was her friend, would that have made her desperate enough to kill herself? Jenny couldn't believe that. Elsie was a survivor. She would have found a way out. Besides, she hadn't needed to go to Elgin to throw herself under a truck; there was a never-ending stream of trucks, lorries and buses whizzing along Main Street every day. She had led a reckless life and done some awful things, but whatever she had done didn't warrant a death like that. It would likely come out that she'd been pregnant, and with Peter having been away for so long, folk would know it wasn't his. When he came home he'd be a laughing-stock, and poor soul, he didn't deserve that on top of everything else.

Jenny was surprised when Elsie's mother came to her door in a terrible state. Mrs Slater introduced herself, then said tearfully, 'She used to say she was great chums with you, so do you know what was going on? She asked me to keep the bairns till she went to Aberdeen, but it was Elgin she was in.'

'I don't know anything.' Jenny wished she hadn't been dragged into it. 'We'd words, you see, and I never saw her again, except at the hospital for a wee while.'

'Aye, they told us she'd asked for you. Did she not say anything?'

Hating herself for having to lie, Jenny said, 'She wanted to make it up with me, that's all.'

'Did you know she was expecting?'

Feeling a guilty blush creep up her neck, Jenny could not deny this. 'That's why we'd the row.'

'Did she tell you who the father was?'

Crossing her fingers at this second falsehood, Jenny muttered, 'No.'

Mrs Slater wiped her eyes. 'I suppose I'll never know, and what does it matter now? You know, Jenny – you don't mind if I call you Jenny? – she's aye been a handful, and I thought I'd be landed looking after . . .' She stopped to wipe her eyes again. 'Thank God the three she had were legitimate, the poor wee mites, and maybe they're better with me, though I never thought I'd be looking after bairns again at my age. But me and Chae'll see they want for nothing.'

Lizann had not seen much of Dan lately, the weather had been so cold and stormy. It would have been no pleasure to wade ankle-deep in snow, no matter how much she looked forward to talking to him. Anyway, Meggie hadn't ventured out, either, and he didn't want her to know. Not that she could find any fault with what they did, Lizann thought, for it was all very innocent.

On the first dry night in March, Meggie having taken the chance to go to Wester Duncairn, Lizann decided that she may as well go out too. It wouldn't matter if Dan didn't come, it would be good just to get out in the fresh air again. She went upstairs for her coat, and when she went down he was in the hall putting on his.

'I thought you'd be going out tonight,' he grinned.

They had to keep walking smartly – it was too cold to have a seat on a fallen tree as they had done in the Indian summer of September and early October. Lizann was happy listening to Dan's deep voice telling her that he was thinking of buying a tractor, and what a help it would be during the ploughing, planting and sowing.

They went as far as their usual turning place and were coming back on the other side of the burn when he said, 'I hope you're still getting along all right with Meggie?'

'We're not exactly chums, but we get on fine.'

'I know she can be a bit difficult, but she's been . . . well, practically mistress of the house since my mother died. She still treats me like a wee laddie sometimes.'

Without stopping to think, she said, 'Have you never thought of taking a wife?'

He was so long in answering that she realized how forward she'd been and was about to apologize when he gave a soft, humourless laugh. 'Yes, I have thought about it, but I know the lady won't have me if I ask.'

'But you . . .' she stopped, because her tongue had almost run away with her again. 'I'm sorry, it's none of my business.'

'We're friends aren't we?'

'You've been a very good friend to me, Dan,' she said, earnestly. 'I'd never have got through the two funerals if it hadn't been for you, nor been able to pay the doctor and the undertakers. And you sent all Adam's things to a roup and gave me what they sold for when it wasn't mine to take.'

'It wasn't much, and I know he would have wanted you to have it. Now, tell me what you were going to say a minute ago.'

'You said your lady friend wouldn't have you if you asked, but how do you know? You should try . . . she might say yes.'

There was another pause before he said, 'I'll consider it.'

'Don't take too long, then. She could meet somebody else.'

Dan came to a halt when they crossed the wooden bridge, and neither of them noticed the dark figure dodging out of sight behind a tree. 'Here we are again.' He gave a long sigh, as if reluctant to leave her. 'I'll say goodnight here, my dear, sweet Lizann.' He bent his head and kissed her cheek before striding away in the direction of the byre.

Astonished by the kiss and the endearment, she didn't move for a few moments, then, telling herself that they had been a thank you for the advice she had given him, she walked on into the house, still unaware of the watcher who had seen and heard both.

When the kitchen door closed behind the girl, Meggie came out of her hiding place, her face darkened by an almost apoplectic rage. If she hadn't had a sore head and come back early, she'd never have found out what was going on. 'My dear, sweet Lizann,' the master had said, and it hadn't needed the kiss to prove something was brewing – had been brewing for a good while, by the look of it. And it was all that young madam's doing, for Dan Fordyce wouldn't have done that if she hadn't encouraged him. But if she thought she could trap him into making her mistress of Easter Duncairn, she had another think coming. Meggie Thow wasn't going to stand by and wait till her job was taken out of her hands. She would watch the little monkey like a hawk now, and make her life such a misery she'd be glad to pack her bag and leave.

Lizann could not understand why Meggie had changed towards her. She had done nothing wrong, as far as she knew, yet the housekeeper was picking on her for the least little thing, and she was getting so nervous that she was dropping dishes and breaking them, which brought more trouble down on her head. Besides that, she was made to work on until sometimes eleven o'clock at night, tasks which she used to do only occasionally but had to do almost daily now. This meant that she couldn't go out in the evenings, not even on Thursdays, because the housekeeper always left her long lists of things to do.

After being cooped up inside for some weeks, and in a state bordering on nervous exhaustion, Lizann decided to take a risk one night when Meggie left to visit her friend. She had to get out, if only for ten minutes to shift her pounding headache, then she'd feel more able to do her chores.

Waiting a short time in case Meggie came back for something, Lizann opened the back door and took a few deep breaths of the honeysuckle-scented air. Then she set off, but was only halfway down the path to the burn when a triumphant voice cried, 'I ken't it! I ken't you'd sneak out as soon as my back was turned, you two-faced besom!'

It was so unexpected, and so shameful to be caught, that Lizann burst into tears. 'I wasn't doing anything wrong. I was just . . .'

'I ken fine what you were doing, but you're not getting away wi' it. You're not getting your claws into Mr Fordyce.'

'But I wasn't . . .'

'You needna think I've been blind to what's been going on. Making up to him, and maybe sneaking into his bed, for all I ken.'

'No, no!' Lizann was bitterly hurt that the woman could even think such things.

'It maybe hasna reached that stage yet, and it never will now. I'll make damned sure you never get him!' Meggie grabbed Lizann's arm and shoved her roughly towards the open door, and one last vicious push sent her sprawling on the kitchen floor.

Coming out of the sitting-room on his way to bed, Dan almost fell over Lizann, who was on her knees in the hallway, her head bent over a pail. 'God Almighty!' he exclaimed. 'I could have broken my neck, and yours, too. Why in God's name are you scrubbing the floor at this hour of the night?' It struck him suddenly that she hadn't lifted her head, and his tone softened. 'What's wrong, Lizann? Are you sick.'

'No,' she mumbled, her hand going up to her eyes.

'Look at me,' he ordered, 'and tell me what's wrong.'

She still didn't look up. 'Nothing's wrong.'

Bending, he hoisted her to her feet and turned her to face him, her swollen eyes making him long to kiss away her troubles, whatever they were. Not yet sure of how she felt about him, he put an arm round her waist and led her into the room he had just left. Closing the door, he said, gently, 'Tell me, Lizann.'

'It's nothing,' she gulped.

'You wouldn't be crying for nothing. Come on, my dear, tell me.'

'It's nothing,' she repeated, but his sympathy was too much for her, and the tears she'd tried to keep him from seeing flooded out again.

She leaned against him gratefully as his arms went round her. 'My dear sweet girl,' he murmured, patting her shoulder, 'it surely can't be as bad as that.'

'It's Meggie,' she sobbed. 'She's being awful to me.'

'You should have told me. I'd have put a stop to it.'

'I thought I could put up with her, but I can't, not any longer.'

Now she had started, it all came hiccupping out. 'She must have seen us ... that last night you came walking with me.'

He looked bewildered. 'There was nothing to see.'

'You kissed my cheek ... and called me your dear, sweet Lizann because I'd told you ... your lady friend might marry you if you asked her.'

'I have no lady friend,' he said, quietly.

She was too fraught to take this in. 'It all started the morning after that ... so she must have seen you.'

'What started?'

His voice was so harsh that she knew Meggie was in for more than just a telling-off, but she could do nothing except carry on; she would have to leave the farm anyway. She told him that the housekeeper made her pay for the things she broke, and made her work late every night, at which he said, 'So that's why I haven't seen you for so many Thursdays.'

She went on to tell him about the one time she had gone out and the housekeeper had been waiting for her. 'She started accusing me . . . Dan, it was awful.'

'What exactly did she accuse you of doing?'

'She said I'd been . . .' Lizann couldn't bring herself to repeat the vile thing the old woman had suspected. 'She said I'd been making up to you, and I wasn't, Dan. I wasn't!'

Dan's anger at his housekeeper was building up, but he kept his voice gentle. 'Go on, my dear.'

'She gave me such a shove when we were coming in, I fell on the floor and skinned my knees. And I knocked against the table, and the willow pattern tureen I'd washed after dinner fell off and smashed. She said it was your mother's favourite dish, and she lifted the ladle and hit me on the face. I'd the mark for weeks.'

'She actually hit you . . . with the ladle?' He was boiling with fury at Meggie, but tried to keep it under control so that he wouldn't distress Lizann any further.

'And she's been punching my back every time she goes past me . . . and I'm all black and blue.'

'Oh, my dear Lizann,' he burst out, 'I never dreamt that she was ill-treating you.'

'I thought she'd get tired of it . . . but it's been months and . . .'

She looked into his face now, so pathetically that he just had to kiss her trembling mouth, and having kissed her, he was lost. 'Oh, my darling girl,' he moaned, 'I'll make sure that she doesn't hurt you again.'

Fully believing that he was still consoling her, she gulped, 'But you can't sack her. She's been here a lot longer than me, so it's me that'll have to leave. How much notice will I have to work?'

'You are not going to leave. I want you to marry me, my darling.' His grey eyes searched hers for some sign of affection, even gratitude, but she stared back at him in dismay.

'You can't marry me to stop Meggie hitting me. She'd think I made you do it, and she'd be nastier to me than ever.'

'You don't understand, my dear. It has nothing to do with Meggie. I'm asking you to marry me because . . . I love you. I've loved you since the very first time I saw you – selling fish at my door.'

She gave a horrified gasp. 'No, I don't believe that. I was an awful mess. You're just saying that to make me feel better, but I can't . . .'

His lips stopped her, and he tried to let his long tender kisses tell her that his declaration of love was genuine. 'Now do you believe me?' he asked, when he let her go. 'I love you with all my heart, and I'll go on asking you to be my wife until you say yes.'

'No, Dan,' she protested, when his arms went round her again, but he kissed her until her senses reeled.

At that moment, the housekeeper walked in, coming to a dumbstruck halt when she saw the loving tableau. She soon found her tongue, however, her brows going down as she sneered, 'So! She's got you at last, has she? I'm surprised you let her take you in, Mr Fordyce. And whatever she's been telling you, it's just a pack o' lies, for I never touched her.'

Still holding Lizann although she was struggling to get away from him, Dan said coldly, 'Were you wanting something, Meggie?'

'I wondered where she was.'

'If you mean Lizann, I took her in here because she was so upset, and I'd be grateful if you would leave us. I shall talk to you later.'

Meggie was not easily intimidated, but she had never

423

seen his eyes so icy before. 'Oh ... well ...' she stammered, backing away, 'just mind what I said, for she's trying to get you ...'

'Lizann has no need to try to get me,' Dan said, firmly. 'She got me long ago without trying. Now, shut the door behind you.'

He waited until Meggie had gone. 'I'm sorry about the interruption. I asked you to marry me, Lizann, and I'm still waiting for an answer.'

'I can't,' she whispered. 'I don't ... love you. I like you an awful lot, as a friend, but it's not the same. I'm sorry.'

'I have enough love for two,' he persisted. 'I gave you this job in the hope that you would come to feel as I do, and I was prepared to wait until you did. I've spoiled it by springing it on you too quickly.'

She looked at him in deep distress, hating having to hurt him. 'It wouldn't have mattered how long you waited, Dan, my answer would have still been the same.' She stroked his cheek to show how badly she felt about it. 'It seems awful to refuse you when you've been so good to me, but I can't pretend to love you.'

His searching eyes gave up their quest for a sign of something more than liking. 'No, my dear, I wouldn't want you to pretend, and you don't need to leave.'

'I was going anyway, and I couldn't stay after this.'

'What will you do? Where will you go?' The words were torn from him.

Recalling how she had felt when she and George had parted in Yarmouth, her heart went out to Dan, but she couldn't marry a man she didn't love, no matter how much she liked him, how sorry she felt for him. 'I was thinking of going to Aberdeen,' she said gently. 'I couldn't go before, when I'd no money of my own, but with you giving me a paid job ...'

He gave a rather ironic smile. 'I made it possible for

you to leave? When all I wanted was for you to be here as my wife.'

'I'm sorry, Dan.'

'It's my own fault for taking things for granted. Will you let me do one last thing for you? Let me ask my sister to give you a room . . .'

'Oh, I couldn't . . .'

'Aberdeen is a big city. You would never find lodgings on your own. If you don't want to live with Ella permanently, she would help you to find somewhere else. She might even help you to find a job.'

Lizann gave in. 'All right, but just till I get other lodgings.'

He moved away from her. 'I had better go and deal with Meggie.'

'Please don't sack her, Dan. I think she was scared she'd lose her job if you took a wife. She was just trying to get rid of me.'

'And she succeeded,' he said dryly. 'I feel like throwing her out for what she did, but she's more to be pitied than punished.'

'You're a good man, Dan, I wish I . . .'

'I'll write to Ella in the morning, but if you don't feel up to facing Meggie again, you can stay up in your room until you go.'

'She won't do anything to me when she knows I'm going away.'

'Lizann, my dear, are you quite sure you . . . ?'

'Yes, Dan, quite sure.'

His deep sigh showed his despondent acceptance of her decision. 'Wait here until I come back.' He swung round and went out.

In the kitchen, Meggie looked at him apprehensively. 'I suppose you've come to tell me to get out, Mr Fordyce?'

'I should send you packing,' he said grimly, but the fear in her old eyes made him hasten to add, 'but Lizann pleaded with me not to. We both understand why you treated her so badly, so you will be relieved to know she has not accepted my proposal.'

'She's refused you?'

He smiled sadly. The old woman obviously could not believe that any girl in her right mind would turn down his offer of marriage – a man who owned a large thriving farm. 'So you see, Meggie, she wasn't out to get me. In fact, she is leaving in a few days and I doubt if I shall ever see her again. In the meantime, she is willing to keep working alongside you, but I must make it clear that you treat her properly, otherwise . . .'

He left the sentence unfinished, and Meggie muttered, 'I ken I did wrong, Mr Fordyce, but I was that feared for my job . . .'

'Yes, I know, but . . . well, I'll say no more. I will see about getting a replacement for Lizann . . . as a maid. She is the only woman I have ever wanted . . . will ever want, as a wife.'

As he went out, Meggie said, 'I'm awful sorry, Mr Fordyce.'

And so she should be, he thought. If it hadn't been for her, he would not have revealed his feelings to Lizann until he was sure of her, but it was too late now. Going back to the sitting-room, he said, 'You will have no more trouble from Meggie, my dear. She knows her job is safe.'

Lizann sighed. 'I could have told her she'd nothing to fear from me. I'd better go and finish scrubbing the hall.'

'It's all right as it is. Just empty the pail and go to bed.'

He sat down and picked up his pipe when she left him. It pained him to think of all the menial jobs she'd had to do, might still have to do in her next job. If only she wasn't so stubborn. She had admitted to liking him quite a lot, and given more time, he could have made her love him.

* * *

Three days later, Lizann bade goodbye to Meggie Thow then went into the dining-room to take her leave of Dan. He jumped up from the table and took her in his arms. 'I'll be thinking of you every day,' he murmured, running his rough forefinger down her cheek. 'And if you don't get a job in Aberdeen, or if you don't like it there, please come back. Meggie has got over everything.'

'I know, she broke down when she apologized to me the day after . . .'

His kiss prevented her saying more, and when he released her, she turned away, unable to tell him that it wasn't the housekeeper who made return to Easter Duncairn impossible, it was his proposal.

Walking towards the main road to catch a bus, she recalled how she had felt when she made the journey from Buckie to Pennan. She hadn't nearly so far to walk this time, and she was in far better health than she had been at that time, but she had the same sense of not knowing what lay ahead. Her spirits lifted when she remembered that the money she had saved was in her pocket, plus what Dan had insisted on giving her. She also had his sister's address, so at least she would have a home. But Ella Reith, a countrywoman married to the headmaster of a city school, would know nothing about the fish houses which would be the only places offering the kind of work she could do.

Despite having kept house for the Laings for the best part of eighteen months, and working as housemaid at the farm for nearly a year, it did not occur to Lizann to look for domestic work. She had been born by the sea, her roots were by the sea, and it seemed to her that her place was by the sea. Besides, gutting fish would help her to remember her meeting with poor George.

PART THREE

1942–1944

Chapter Thirty

Dan opened Ella's letter with apprehension, but its contents made him smile.

> Dear Dan,
> I wasn't too sure about having Lizann when you wrote and asked me, and I only agreed because you sounded so smitten with her. Now I've met her, I can see why. She's a very nice girl, maybe a bit young for you, which is likely why she turned you down, but John and I will work on her and try to make her understand she's right for you – for she is right for you, Dan, I'm positive of that. John's quite taken with her too, but you needn't worry – I'll keep my eye on him, ha, ha.
> I don't think she's done anything about looking for a job yet, she's been too busy exploring the Gt. Western Road area. It will take her a wee while to settle down, I suppose, and I'll try to put her off looking for anywhere else to live. We'd be happy to have her for as long as she wants – till she decides to become Mrs Daniel Fordyce? You should wait a few months before you come to see her, though. I've the feeling she'd shy off if she thought you were pestering her.
> I'll keep you posted.
> Yours, Ella.

Slipping the letter back into the envelope, Dan felt grateful that his sister was taking an interest in the girl he loved. She would be able to persuade Lizann to marry him, if anyone could. As for waiting, he would wait a whole year if he thought she would say yes at the end of it.

From the time she arrived, Lizann had felt quite at home in the Reiths' house in Great Western Road. It was part of a lovely stretch of tall, well-built granite houses on this long west end street which ran out of the city towards Deeside. There was only a small garden at the front, but a large one at the rear, which Ella's husband John had lovingly tended for the ten years they had been there. Since the outbreak of war, of course, he'd had to trim down the size of his lawn – now just enough to hold his wife's four clothes poles – and convert all his flower beds into vegetable patches, as instructed by the Min. of Ag. and Fish, as he scathingly called this special Ministry.

From the street the house looked smaller than the farmhouse at Easter Duncairn. But, having more depth than width, there were almost as many rooms, although they were perhaps not quite so big. Downstairs there were the usual dining-room, living-room and sitting-room (for visitors), plus what Lizann thought at first was a library, but Ella called 'John's den', which was lined with books of all descriptions. Being a teacher of English, John Reith had collected hundreds of classics from Ancient Rome right down to those of the early twentieth century, as well as novels by popular modern writers and even some which he laughingly admitted were lurid romances. 'I may look an old fuddy-duddy,' he told Lizann, 'but I still like a little light relief from the daily grind.' The kitchen was also on the ground floor, a well-equipped, airy room which the Reiths had obviously converted to their liking bit by bit.

The bathroom was upstairs. 'Still late Victorian,' Ella had laughed, when she first showed her lodger round. 'We'll get round to changing it when we can afford it.

The bath's too big and though we're always being told just to use five inches of water, it takes ages to run. Don't be alarmed at the noise the lavatory makes when you flush it. You'll get used to it . . . in fact, I'm quite fond of it myself.'

There were three bedrooms on the same floor, two facing the street and the third, like the bathroom, at the back. 'I hope you don't mind me putting you in here,' Ella said. 'It is actually quieter than the other two, even if it is next door to the lav.'

'I don't mind where I am,' Lizann murmured. 'I'm really grateful to you for taking me in.'

She would have been happy to stay there but for one thing: she was afraid that Dan might come to see how she was getting on. She suspected that Ella and John knew she had turned him down, and they might not be so friendly towards her if she refused him again under their roof.

Deciding that finding somewhere else to live was her first priority, she did nothing about looking for a job and devoured the Accommodation Vacant column in the *Evening Express* every day. Most of them stipulated 'men sharing', and she had been in Aberdeen ten days before she saw an item offering, 'Room suitable for one or two women, non-smokers', with an address in Rosemount Place. After looking it up in a street map, she set out to walk there the next morning, hoping it was a decent district. She found that Rosemount Place was another long street of sparkling granite buildings – not private houses like Great Western Road, but shops at ground level and tenements above. That was the only difference, because it was every bit as clean and tidy.

When she came to the number she was looking for, she went up to the first floor to ask about the room. The landlady was a small, stoutish woman with hair which looked as if it might have been red at one time but had faded to a sandy-grey. She introduced herself as Mrs Melville and took Lizann into a back room looking down on a long narrow stretch of grass. The rest of the view was constricted to the rears of other tenements, with their drying greens back to back with Mrs Melville's, and it all looked very peaceful.

On learning that the rent was thirty shillings a week with breakfast and an evening meal, she explained to Mrs Melville that she was out of work meantime, but hoped to find a job in one of the fish houses. 'Will the smell of fish bother you?' she asked, warily.

The woman smiled. 'Not me. My father was a trawlerman.'

After arranging to take up residence the next day, Lizann paid a week in advance, and returned to Great Western Road to tell Ella Reith that she would be leaving.

'I'm sorry to hear that. Dan did say you might be looking for digs, but I thought you were happy here.'

'I am, but . . . I'm trying to get work in the fish, and you wouldn't like the smell.'

Astonished that such a lovely young woman would want to work amongst fish, Ella sighed. 'I don't think I would. Well, I'm glad you've found somewhere to your liking. Where will you be?'

Afraid that Ella might pass her new address to Dan, Lizann said, 'In a tenement, and the landlady seems really nice.'

She packed her clothes in the evening – still those which had belonged to Adam Laing's daughter Margaret, but which she hoped to supplement from her wages when she found a job. Next morning she had a glance at the newspaper and saw that a firm in Sinclair Road was looking for experienced fish workers. Not wanting to ask Ella, she waited until she went to her new lodgings, and Mrs Melville gave her detailed directions. 'We used to have buses and trams both coming down past here – the buses went to the Bay of Nigg and would have taken you almost to the door – but·after the war started the Corporation Transport just made them do a shuttle service to Mile End, so we've only trams now, and they just go to the Castlegate. You'll have to come off in Union Street, opposite Woollies, walk down Market Street and carry on past the harbour till you come to Victoria Bridge. That takes you over the Dee into Torry, and I think Sinclair Road's first on the left.'

Not even stopping to unpack her case, Lizann went out and had only about five minutes to wait for a tramcar. The journey was short and quite pleasant, but when the rails turned into Union Street, she kept her eyes peeled for Woolworth's store. When she got off she crossed over into Market Street, her spirits lifting as her nose picked up a whiff of the sea, which grew stronger as she went down the hill. She was fascinated to see that the harbour was fenced off by high metal railings – to prevent spies getting anywhere near, she supposed – and she carried on along the outside of the barrier, passing coal boats unloading on the quay and having to watch her feet on the goods railway lines. Wondering if she would be safer on the other side of the street where there was a pavement, she decided against it. She would have to cross back again later and the traffic was quite fierce, with horse-drawn carts holding up impatient lorry drivers who put a spurt on once they managed to get past.

The bustle of the Fish Market amazed her, but she would learn that it was much busier in the early mornings. Coming to another of the docks, thronged with trawlers, she saw a bridge ahead and realized that she had not far to go now. There were several fish houses on Sinclair Road, and as she walked along searching for the one she wanted, and trying not to skid on the brine seeping from the wooden boxes piled up outside them, a nostalgic ache started inside her. Most people would turn up their noses at this awful stink, she thought in amusement, but it was like coming home for her.

There were other applicants for the jobs, but when the manager saw how expertly she gutted what he gave as a test, she was amongst those told to start at eight the following Monday morning. 'It's piece-work,' he explained, 'so the harder you work, the more wages you'll get.'

Jenny had been at her lowest ebb ever since the delivery of the telegram from the War Office. She had recovered fairly quickly from the deaths of her mother and father, but she'd had Mick to lean on at the time. She had coped with Hannah's death although she had given birth just a few hours before, but again, Mick had been there for her. She had seen Elsie Tait breathe her last, which had been something of an anti-climax after the shock of learning how her mother-in-law had met her end. She had thought Mick would help her to get over that, too, when he came home, but he would never come home again . . . and who would help her to get over losing him?

The Berrys had done their best. Babsie, close on seventy, had stayed with her night and day for over a week, had fed Georgie and wee Lizann when their mother was too grief-stricken to think about their needs, and had even kept them amused to save them bothering her. Jake had appointed himself as messenger, shopping from the lists his wife wrote out and carefully noting the prices so she wouldn't query the change he brought back. All the neighbours had been good, popping in every day to see if she needed anything, though mainly to check that she was all right.

And she was gradually coming round, Jenny thought, one fine morning. Little pieces of the ice that had imprisoned her heart for so long were beginning to break off. She could actually smile occasionally, speak to people about the war without a spasm of sorrow for her husband making her stop in confused embarrassment. Time *was* a healer, but not long enough had elapsed yet. Her emotions still seized up when Georgie asked when Daddy would be coming, but, thankfully, she could confine her tears to the solitude of the double bed now.

Someone giving a sharp rap on her door, she went to see which of her neighbours had called, and was quite taken aback to see a stranger, a tall elderly man with silver hair and a fresh complexion that told he wasn't a seaman of any kind. His clear blue eyes were looking at her apologetically. 'Yes?' she asked, wondering what had brought him there.

'I'm sorry to bother you, but does Willie Alec Jappy still live here?'

This astonished Jenny even more. 'No, he died years and years ago.'

His face fell. 'I was hoping to ... but I have left it too long. What about Hannah ... his wife? Is she still alive?'

'No, I'm afraid she's dead, too. Did you know them?'

'I did. I was quite close to them at one time.'

Detecting tears in his eyes, Jenny felt a sudden rush of sympathy for him. 'You'd better come in, Mr ... ?'

'Chapman. Robbie Chapman.' He followed her inside and took the seat she indicated. 'You are very kind, Mrs ... ?'

'Jappy.' She gave a slight smile. 'I'm Jenny, Mick's wife ... his widow. His ship was blown up earlier this year. Did you know him?'

'He was only about a year old last time I was here, but I'm so sorry, Mrs ... um, Jenny. How are you coping? Have you any children?'

Robbie Chapman had the knack of establishing instant rapport and Jenny didn't feel that she was talking to a stranger. 'Two, a boy and a girl. Lizann, after Mick's young sister – she hadn't been born when you were here before – George after her man. He was lost at sea before the war.'

Robbie nodded. 'Yes, the sea is a cruel master. Was that how Willie Alec died, too?'

'No, he'd a heart attack, and Hannah never got over it.'

'Did she have a heart attack, as well?'

Jenny hesitated then said quietly, 'Yes, her heart stopped suddenly.' It was the only thing she could say, and it wasn't a lie. 'I'll make a pot of tea, Mr Chapman. You look like you need cheering up.'

He raised grateful eyes. 'Thank you, my dear, it's been quite a shock. I was so looking forward to seeing . . .' Pausing briefly, he gave a tight smile. 'Please call me Robbie. Not many people do nowadays.'

He studied the fire until Jenny made the tea, and when she handed him a cup he said, 'I'd better tell you my story, but first, did Hannah ever show you a sketch of her as a fishwife with a creel on her back?'

About to say no, Jenny recalled the picture which had hung over the kitchen fire at Freuchny Road, though Lizann had never said it was her mother. 'I've seen it,' she murmured, guardedly, for she couldn't think what it had to do with anything.

'I'd known Willie Alec for years, though we were never what you would call pals, and when I heard he'd married a lassie from Portessie, I was pleased for him. He knew I was interested in sketching folk, so when he asked if I'd draw his wife, I thought it would be good practice for me. Besides, I wanted to see the kind of girl he'd chosen. Hannah wasn't at all happy about being drawn as a fishwife, but Willie Alec insisted that he wanted a permanent reminder of how she looked the first time he saw her, and she agreed to pose for me.'

Jenny sat enthralled as he told her how he had gone to the Yardie on week nights – as Willie Alec had instructed because he didn't want to see the sketch until it was finished – how he had fallen in love with his friend's wife and how he had repressed his feelings in the belief that she was only being friendly with him to please her husband.

'Of course,' Robbie continued, 'something had to give. I was spinning the drawing out as much as I could, and I was pretending to change a few bits one night when Hannah came over and stood close beside me. Well, that finished me. I grabbed hold of her and . . .'

When he broke off, Jenny had to contain her curiosity. She couldn't believe that prim Hannah – who according to all sources had never had eyes for anyone but Willie Alec – had let another man kiss her . . . maybe more? At last she had to ask, 'Didn't she tell you to stop?'

'I think she was too surprised at first. Anyway, her kisses were all the sweeter to me for being forbidden fruit . . . and then, all of a sudden, she jumped away and started to cry. I apologized for upsetting her and left.'

He regarded Jenny anxiously. 'That would have been that – I'd have kept away from her – if Willie Alec . . . he loved the picture, and he asked me to supper every Saturday as a way of paying me. Hannah looked guilty every time I went in, and I don't know if that's what made him jealous, or if he could see how I felt about her. Anyway, he managed to hide it till she told him she was going to have another child. He was waiting outside for me when I turned up the next night, and accused me of being the father.'

His listener looked at him as if he had led her up the garden path before, but his smile was frank as he continued, 'He wouldn't listen to my denials at first, but I got through to him at last, and I think it made him love her all the more to know she was still so innocent as to believe kisses would make her pregnant. I can only think that my last few kisses had been too passionate for her.'

He grinned now. 'I suppose you know the kind I mean, Jenny?'

Colouring, she gave a small nod. The first time Mick had given her a French kiss she had worried herself sick till her period started . . . but Hannah had been a married woman, and according to what Robbie had said, she'd already had Mick. She must have known how babies were made.

Robbie gave a long sigh. 'Upon my oath, I was never intimate with her. I did manage to convince Willie Alec I was speaking the truth, but he said it would be best if I stopped going to the Yardie. I thought things over long and hard and decided to leave Buckie altogether. I had often fancied my chances as an artist in London so I just packed up and went.'

'Didn't you try to get in touch with Hannah again? To explain?'

'No, though I sometimes thought of coming home to ask her forgiveness for the trouble I caused. I should have known I was playing with fire by being alone with her for an hour or so five nights a week.'

His mournful eyes cleared suddenly, and giving a low chuckle, he said, 'Ach, you'll think I'm in my dotage telling you about things that were over and done with more than thirty years ago. I've had a good life. I did get married and I loved Dora, but sadly, we had no children.'

Just then, Jake Berry gave a tap and walked in, stopping in dismay when he saw Jenny was not alone. 'I'm sorry lass. I didna ken you'd a visitor, but Babsie sent me to tell you she's giving your bairns their dinner. She wanted me to ask you and all, but you'll . . .'

'Tell her thanks, but I've got dinner made here, and maybe Robbie'll help me to eat it.' Not wanting to be drawn into long explanations as to who Robbie was and perhaps make the Berrys delve into their memories and come up with two and two making five, she said that he had been a friend of her father's, and Jake went away pleased that she had company.

She turned to Robbie again and prompted, 'Is your wife . . . ?'

'She died nearly six years ago, and I tried not to give myself time to brood about her. I've kept busy, and I don't miss her as much as I did.'

'I'll never stop missing Mick,' Jenny said, bursting into tears.

'Oh, my dear, I'm so sorry. I'm an insensitive brute, but let me pass on some advice I got. I had been a widower for over three months when I met someone I hadn't seen for a while. He knew of my bereavement but was shocked to see me looking so haggard, and even more shocked that I had shown nothing in the recent art exhibitions. "Get out of the Slough of Despond, Rob," he scolded me. "Stop feeling sorry for yourself, it does no good. If you can't face sugary sympathy from friends, however well-meant, look for people who are also needing help. You may find it beneficial for you, too." What he said made sense, so I offered my services to a club for youngsters in the East End, and I got as much pleasure out of coaching the boys in football as they did.'

He eyed Jenny uncertainly. 'You are not in the same position as I was, you have two young children to look after, but I think you, too, have sunk into the Slough of Despond. Have you no friends?'

'Just neighbours,' Jenny sniffed, 'and they're all ancient.'

'As am I,' he grinned. 'But you're an attractive young woman, Jenny, and there must be another man out there who will . . .'

'There couldn't be another man like Mick.' She stood up resolutely now. 'But you're right, I'll have to give myself a shake and get out and about more. You're my first new friend, so you'd better help me eat what I made for the dinner.'

'I'll be delighted,' he grinned.

During the meal he told her more about the work he had done with the youngsters, and finally admitted that a heart attack had forced him to give it up. 'The doctor warned me to take things easy, and it was while I was resting one afternoon that I got this deep urge to come home and spend some time with my older sister.'

Jenny couldn't help noticing that he was still referring to Buckie as home, but she did not remark on it as she stood up to clear away the dirty dishes.

Robbie insisted on drying them and it wasn't until she was laying them past that he said, 'I was trying not to ask this in case you think I did have something to do with it, but it's nothing more than curiosity. You said Mick had a young sister. Was she the baby Willie Alec thought . . . ?'

Jenny shook her head. 'Lizann was five years younger than Mick.'

'So she's not . . . wasn't there one in between? Perhaps a year and a half younger than Mick?'

'There was just the two of them that I know of . . . no! Wait a minute! I nearly forgot! Lizann once said her Auntie Lou told her there was a baby between her and Mick, but I think it was still-born.'

'Oh, how sad,' Robbie murmured. 'You know, when I'd had time to think about it properly, I realized Hannah was just a touch . . . what should I say? Unstable? Little things I connected long afterwards that showed . . . but I shouldn't be saying things like that to you.'

'You're right, though. Her sister had always looked out for her, so there must have been something unstable about her all along, and she turned funny when Willie Alec died. Poor Lizann had an awful time with her.' Jenny paused, recalling the years of suffering she'd had herself.

'Mick's sister will have been a great comfort to you since he . . .'

This was too much for Jenny. Throwing herself into his arms, she wept quietly on his shoulder for some time, and when at last she drew away, embarrassed and ashamed, he said gently, 'I think you should tell me, my dear. Mick's death wasn't the only thing to have upset you. It had been the last straw, the worst of all . . . yes?'

'Yes,' she whispered.

'Whenever you like,' he coaxed, 'take your time. You'll feel better when you've got it out in the open. It's easier talking to a stranger, someone who isn't involved.'

It was easier. Nevertheless, Jenny still took quite a time to tell him – a complicated story going back many years, involving people and events which, although it did not appear so at first, did have some bearing on what happened later. Lizann's engagement to Peter; her fight to marry George and how she lost both him and their baby on the same day; her mysterious disappearance; Lenny Fyfe's infatuation with Elsie Tait and the subsequent tragedy.

'Poor Lenny,' she murmured here. 'His mother didn't know it was his fault Elsie died, and she wrote and told him about it. His commanding officer sent a letter the very next week saying he'd been killed in an accident during his training, but I'm near sure there hadn't been any accident. I think he committed suicide.'

Jenny told Robbie everything except what Elsie had done to Hannah – that was something she could never divulge to anyone – but he seemed to be most taken up with the subject of the missing Lizann. 'You should have reported it to the police. They would have done everything in their power to find her.'

'She gave up her house and took all her belongings with her, and Lou was sure she didn't want to be found. It wasn't till Peter's wife told me what she'd threatened

443

that I realized that's what had made her run away, and there was what I said as well, though I wasn't hitting at her at all. She must have been nearly out of her mind.'

'How long is it since you saw her?'

'Over three years. Mick always said she must be happy where she was, and nothing bad could have happened to her or else we'd have heard.'

Robbie nodded slowly. 'Yes, I suppose you will have to draw comfort from that. Now, Jenny, I have thoroughly enjoyed talking to you, but I had better go, otherwise my sister will think I've dropped down dead somewhere. I am rather tired – resurrecting dormant emotions can't be too good for a man in my condition, but I don't regret it.' He stood up and held out his hand. 'Would you mind if I kept in touch? I want to know how you get on, and if you ever hear from Lizann.'

When both his smooth hands clasped hers, Jenny's heart ached for him. He was obviously a lonely man and living hundreds of miles away from the place he still considered home. 'I'd like if we kept in touch,' she assured him, 'and, remember, you're welcome back any time, Robbie.'

She went inside thoughtfully. It had come across quite clearly that he had no real friends down in London, which was most surprising, for he was such a nice man. Maybe he'd been too taken up with his wife and his painting to bother with outsiders. Maybe he'd never really got over what the Jappys had done to him – fancy him still loving Hannah after all these years and coming all this way in the hope of seeing her again. It was very sad. Well, apart from Georgie and wee Lizann, she herself was the only Jappy left, and it was up to her to make things up to him. Once he let her know his address, she would write to him every week.

* * *

As Robbie walked away, he couldn't get over how little the kitchen had changed. He could picture Hannah with the creel on her back standing on the clootie rug in front of the fire to let him sketch her. He had not been entirely truthful with Jenny. After leaving he had sent a letter to Hannah, a letter of hopeful apology, but she hadn't replied. He had been convinced that Willie Alec had destroyed it without her ever seeing it, but it was possible that she hadn't wanted to answer. And he should be thankful for that. After all, if she had run away with him to conduct an illicit affair, which is what he had hoped, he would never have left home, would never have made his name as an artist.

Robbie smiled suddenly. The head of a publishing firm had asked him some years ago if he had thought of writing his autobiography. He had said no at the time, but having had the memories of his young manhood so vividly recalled – he had actually felt again the see-sawing of his love for Hannah and his hopes that she might love him, the heartbreak of her rejection which had made him run off to London, the misery of living in poverty until people with influence took notice of his paintings – he realized that the first part of a book was waiting to be written and he was itching to get started. Hannah's childlike belief that kissing would make her pregnant, even though she had already conceived and given birth to one child, would not be the only element which would make his book different from run-of-the-mill life stories. There was his seafaring background. He would describe how, over the course of two years, his mother had lost her husband and two of her sons to the sea, which was why she had encouraged him in his ambition to be an artist and had kept his early sketches of family and friends. Most of them were still in the attic, according to his sister, who had given up a good job in a Glasgow hospital to nurse their mother in her last illness and now lived in the family home in Cliff Terrace, a spinster, but neither lonely nor sourly old. Unfortunately, the only sketch that would be of any value, the one he still considered his finest because of the love he had felt for his subject, was lost to him. Probably Willie Alec had burnt it to save Hannah being reminded of her folly . . . poor, naive Hannah!

He had never stopped loving her . . . but perhaps it had not been love, just nostalgia for his youth. He had loved his Dora as a man, though he had been disappointed that she had not borne him a son to perpetuate his line. Not that he would have cared if it hadn't been a son . . .

The next thought to enter Robbie's mind made him stop with his hand on his heart. A strong pulse was beating in his throat, but he came to the conclusion that it was too momentous a decision to rush. He would have to take time to think it over properly. In fact he might be better not even to mention it to Pearl when he got back, but wait until he had settled down in London again before giving it his full consideration. There was no fool like an old fool, as they said, and having been such a fool in his youth, he had no wish to repeat the degradation of rebuttal.

'Are you all right?' Pearl asked anxiously when he went in. 'I was beginning to worry with you being away so long.'

'I'm fine, just a bit tired.' Wondering how much he should tell her, he plumped for absolute honesty. He would go over everything that had been said, however much it might shock her, but there was no need to mention what he had been thinking just before he arrived home.

Having suspected at the time how he had felt about Hannah, Pearl was not shocked at that. It saddened her that Hannah and Willie Alec had died while she was in Glasgow, and George Buchan and Mick Jappy, though she hadn't known them. She was intrigued by Lizann's

446

disappearance, and the shock only came when Robbie told her about Elsie Tait's life and death. 'I hope Jenny's not like her?' she asked, afraid for her brother.

'Jenny's a lovely young woman,' he assured her. 'A real gem!'

Before her first day was finished, Lizann was on Christian name terms with most of the gutters, who ranged in age from fifteen to sixty. Quite a few had husbands in the forces, and the majority of single girls were younger than she was, but age and marital status made no difference to them. The girl who worked next to her was soon talking to her as if they were old friends. Gladys Wright, red-haired and as thin as a rake, could not be described as pretty, but her bright blue eyes, pert nose and wide mouth gave her an appealing attractiveness.

On the Saturday morning, their half-day, Gladys remarked, 'You've got a wedding ring on. Is your hubby in the services?'

Lizann shook her head. 'I'm a widow.'

'I wondered why you never spoke about him. Mine's a prisoner of war, so God knows how long it'll be till I see him again. What about coming to the pictures with me tonight?'

'I'd better wait to see if I can afford it,' Lizann smiled. 'I've my board to pay before I do anything else.'

When the wages were given out, she was pleasantly surprised. After paying Mrs Melville and laying past what she needed for bus fares, she would have enough to save something for clothes and still have a few shillings to spend. Gladys was delighted when she said she'd love to go to the pictures, and they arranged to meet outside the Capitol.

This was the beginning of a close friendship, and the two young women discovered that they both liked the same kind of films, often coming out of a cinema and walking down the street singing a song from the musical they had just seen. Other people smiled at their infectious gaiety, and the servicemen who tried to date them were turned down nicely.

'I'm glad to see you so happy,' Mrs Melville said, when Lizann went in one Saturday night. 'Have you found a lad?'

'Gladys and me don't need lads,' Lizann smiled. 'We've enough fun on our own.'

'Aye, but she'll have her man coming back after the war,' Mrs Melville pointed out, 'and you'll have nobody.'

'I don't need anybody. I loved George so much, no other man would do.'

'You're still young, though. I've just been a widow for five years and I know how lonely it can be. Just think how you'll feel by the time you reach sixty, with nobody to bother about you. I've got two lassies, but they're both in England and can't come to see me very often. That's why I always take female lodgers.'

'Gladys'll still be my friend after her man comes back, and anyway I'll always have you.'

'I'll not last for ever.'

'Nobody lasts for ever,' Lizann said sadly.

Sorry now at having pricked Lizann's happy bubble, her landlady gave a little laugh. 'Ach, I'll maybe live till I'm a hundred.'

His hand trembling, Peter laid the letter from his mother-in-law down on the counterpane. Elsie was dead! Mrs Slater had been very careful not to desecrate her daughter's memory, but he could read between the lines. Why had his wife stayed two nights in Elgin, if not to be with some man or other? She'd been up to her old tricks again, and he felt no sorrow, no jealousy, only relief that he was free of her. She would have left him in any case when he was sent home, a useless wreck with just one leg. But . . .

maybe she'd been notified about that and had walked out on him before he returned. That could be why she left their children with her parents. She had told her mother it was only for two days, but she could lie like a trooper. He had years of experience of that.

Leaning back, he closed his eyes wearily. He had known from the time he went into the Navy that he wouldn't have her to depend on if he was invalided out, but he'd never thought he would be incapacitated to this extent. Oh, the doctors told him he'd be able to walk again when he had the prosthesis fitted, but he had his doubts about that, so what would happen when he was finally discharged? Would they send him to some home for cripples, where he would be confined until he died of old age?

It would have been better if he'd been lost, like most of his shipmates. He would never forget the agonies of the night the torpedoes hit them. He had been speaking to Mick just minutes before the first one struck, and he'd been horrified at the thought of all the engineers trapped below decks. Then the ship had been blown to pieces by a second, taking half his leg with it. He had still been conscious, just, hanging on grimly to a bunk attached to its wooden surround when the survivors were picked up. He didn't remember anything after that, not until he came to in a hospital in Gib. The first thing he did was to ask about Mick, and when he learned that his old friend had gone, he nearly went out of his mind and they'd had to keep him under sedation.

Next day the surgeons had amputated a bit more of his leg, and after giving him some time to recover from the shock, he had been sent to this naval hospital in Plymouth. He'd been here for weeks now, but his mail had only just caught up with him: a few letters from Elsie which didn't tell him anything, and one from her mother – the fateful one.

That night, with everything fresh in his mind, Peter had

a fearsome dream, in which Elsie was bobbing around him in the sea and laughing her head off at his attempts to reach a big double bed behind her. Then an aircraft carrier ran them down and her head was floating past him with the eye sockets empty. Screaming and thrashing about, he woke up to find two sick-berth attendants holding him down.

'Good God, Tait,' one of them exclaimed, releasing him and wiping the sweat from his own brow. 'You nearly had my head off then, throwing your arms about like that.'

Peter recoiled at the reference to a head, and muttered, 'I'm sorry. I'd a nightmare.'

Having to settle some poor devil every night, the other orderly said, 'That's okay, pal. We're used to it.' He flexed his aching arm muscles.

When the two men walked away, Peter remembered what he and Mick had been talking about in those last few minutes. His dreams of searching for Lizann after the war had gone down with his ship, but at least he could keep the promise he'd made to his best friend . . . his late friend. Whatever happened, however he would manage to get there, supposing it was in a wheelchair, he would have to go to Buckie to make sure that Jenny was coping without her husband.

With a purpose to his existence now, he was more co-operative with the doctors and attendants, who couldn't understand what had brought about the change in him.

The afternoon bombing of the harbour area was really frightening, and Lizann was glad that her fellow workers were so used to having to run to an air-raid shelter that they could make fun of it. She certainly didn't find it funny hearing explosions coming closer and closer, and praying they wouldn't be killed by a direct hit. But at last the danger was over and they went back to work.

Mrs Melville was full of it that evening. 'Was anywhere near you hit this time? I was worried with you working so near the docks.'

Lizann tried to allay her fears. 'We've to go to the shelter when the sirens blow, so we're quite safe.'

'But there was a good few bombers today, and I mind June 1940, when there was only one, and by gum, he didn't half do a lot of damage. He hit Hall Russell's yard, you know, the shipbuilders, and killed over thirty men in the boiler room. Then he started dropping bombs all over the place, till the Spitfires got after him and shot him down at the new skating rink. There was a lot of sore hearts in Aberdeen that day.'

'I never thought it would be anything like that,' Lizann murmured. 'It was awful hearing the explosions, and we were all huddled together. We cheered when the noise died down, for we just thought of ourselves, not the poor people that got it.'

'You know,' Mrs Melville said, thoughtfully, 'you're not safe working there, Lizann. The Nazis have bases in Norway now, that's nearer here, so they'll likely come a lot oftener, and they'll always be after the harbour.'

'They're not scaring me into giving up my job,' Lizann declared. 'I'll take my chances, the same as everybody else there.'

'Aye, and I suppose it doesn't really matter where you are, we're all in the front line now.'

Each time he heard of a raid on Aberdeen, Dan wished that he had tried harder to stop Lizann from going there. If he had known where she lived he would have taken her back to Easter Duncairn by force, if necessary. Ella's letters, however, made him realize that most of the rumours going round of wholesale damage to the city every day had little foundation, or were greatly exaggerated.

Never completely free of worry for the girl he loved, he did his best to concentrate on the work of the farm, which was much easier since he got the Ferguson tractor, even with several of his men off to the war. He was showing a higher profit than ever before. Most of the vegetables he grew now were sold to shops in the larger towns, and he'd needed some sort of vehicle to make deliveries, but with buying the tractor, all he could afford was a rattly old Ford lorry. Still, it did the job.

Dan was dreading the harvest, but when the time came, all the farmers in the area rallied round to help each other. He thought it strange that it took a war for this to happen, though he felt guilty that it was so. Young Alice, the daughter of his cattleman whom he had hired after Lizann left, had proved her worth by ferrying out what old Meggie and the cooks from the Mains and Wester Duncairn made for the workers, although she and the other maids flirted shamelessly with old men and young boys alike.

Having waited impatiently for months for his artificial limb, Peter was delighted to be told on 20 November that he should have it the next morning, and he pictured himself being on his feet by Christmas.

The reality, however, was a bitter disappointment. The fitting was agony, and when he put his weight on his leg, an excruciating pain shot right up through his body forcing him to sit down again, sweat beading on his brow. 'I'll never cope with this,' he gasped.

The specialist looked at him sympathetically. 'It'll take time, but it *will* get easier. But we'll leave it today, and the therapist will start working with you tomorrow.' Kneeling down, he unstrapped the metal leg.

Left alone again, Peter thought it had all been a waste of time and money. He would never walk on that thing. How could anybody expect him to suffer like that for the rest of his life? Then Mick came into his mind. Poor dead

Mick. At least he was alive and had a duty to do. He must keep his promise to his friend.

The therapist persevered with him for an hour a day, and in just over a week he mastered the art of taking a few steps using crutches. It took another fortnight of grim persistence, and many falls, for him to hobble about slowly with just one crutch, and he eventually cast that aside, determined to arrive at Jenny's door under his own steam. He could sort out his own life after he'd sorted out hers.

Chapter Thirty-one

There had been an alert every night for over a week, and apart from about three hours on the Saturday, when she and Gladys had been in the Majestic cinema, Lizann had sat with her landlady in the kitchen. They didn't want to take shelter in the cellar, where some of the residents of the tenement had taken to going, or even in the common lobby, because there would be more masonry to fall on them if the building was hit and they might never be found.

Lack of sleep was making them increasingly edgy, but at seven every morning Lizann washed, put on fresh clothes, had breakfast, then set off for work whether or not the all clear had gone, as did all the other citizens who had a job to do.

'You might be going right into the middle of it,' Mrs Melville said, one day. 'You should wait till it's past.'

'Nothing's been happening for a while,' Lizann reminded her. 'I think the bombers are away already. See, I told you,' she smiled, as the long-awaited signal rent the air.

There seemed to be excitement in the yard when she arrived, the men nodding and smiling to each other in a most secretive manner. 'What's going on?' she asked Gladys.

Her friend grinned. 'You know Timmy Fraser, the young cooper? Well, he's getting married tomorrow.'

There were only a few young men who had not yet been called up – the majority of males in the yard, coopers or overseers or whatever, were older, although they were still ready for a bit of a lark. Lizann still didn't understand. 'Are they going to do something to him?'

'The usual thing.' Gladys laughed at Lizann's puzzled expression, but didn't satisfy her curiosity. 'Wait and see.'

When the hooter went at five o'clock, everyone stopped work, the men rushing outside and the women, still in their rubber aprons and boots, following behind, not wanting to miss any of the fun. In a few minutes, two coopers dragged Timmy out, and amid loud hilarity, he was stripped down to his underpants and made to sit on a stool. The noise from his fellow workers reached a crescendo when his foreman produced a tin of shoe polish and, with the help of two others, blackened every inch of his exposed body, from face to feet.

'Why are they doing that?' Lizann whispered.

'You'll find out in a minute,' Gladys giggled.

After an initial feeble struggle, Timmy let them carry on. It was a ritual carried out on every bridegroom on the eve of his wedding and, having known it would come, he was enjoying it as much as anyone. When he was completely covered, the same three men carried him to one of the lorries, lifted him on and climbed up beside him. Another ten or so men jumped on as the driver let off the handbrake, some with handbells, some with old pans and lids, and the vehicle moved out on to the street with a great clamour of metal clanging against metal, combined with the more melodic ringing of the bells.

Those left behind ran out to watch as the lorry went slowly along the cobbled street, waiting until it was out of sight before going inside to make ready to go home.

Putting on her shoes, Lizann asked, 'Where are they taking him?'

'Round about to let folk see him.' Gladys shoved her boots under the bench and straightened up. 'It's called the feet washing, for it started with just blacking their feet, but you know men, they weren't content with that.'

'He'll have to wash more than his feet when he does get home,' Lizann giggled. 'He'll have an awful job getting that lot off.'

'I've heard some of them saying their faces still had black streaks when they were standing in front of the minister. Still, it's all good clean fun.'

This unintentional witticism made them both howl with laughter.

The journey from Plymouth to London was bad enough, but on the train to Aberdeen, Peter thought his stamina would never hold out. Luckily he had a few hours to wait in the Joint Station, which gave him the chance to walk around, to relieve the stiffness of his good leg and persevere with his artificial one. When he eventually arrived in Buckie, he was surprised by the wave of homesickness which swept over him; he hadn't felt like that once while he was away.

Slinging his kitbag over his shoulder – it did help to steady him – he set off towards the Yardie. He had decided to go there first, before he went to see his in-laws, because he was afraid that the sight of his three children might knock him back a bit. His nerves were still quite dodgy. He hesitated when he came to Jenny's door, wondering if she would be upset at seeing him, if she would resent the fact that he was alive when Mick was gone, then, bracing himself, he lifted his hand and gave three gentle taps.

'Peter!' Jenny cried, when she saw him. 'Oh, it's good to see you!'

Limping over to the fire, he sat down and looked at her anxiously. 'How are you, Jenny?'

'Not too bad now. It was an awful shock, and I don't think I'll ever get over it, but I had to keep going for the kids.'

'Aye, of course.' He said nothing more, and guessed that she too was lost for words.

'You'll have a cup of tea?' she asked suddenly.

'Thanks, I wouldn't mind.' He watched her as she filled the kettle and set out cups and saucers. She had always been a bonnie girl, with red hair and rosy cheeks, and she had hardly changed at all – maybe a little paler. There was a deep sadness in her eyes, which was only natural, but she also had a peace about her, as though she had accepted her fate and was getting on with her life as best she could.

It occurred to Peter that this might be a good time to speak about his wife, when he didn't have to look at Jenny and see the pity he might not manage to handle. 'Elsie's mother wrote and told me what happened,' he began, staring into the heart of the fire and so missing her alarm.

'I'm awful sorry, Peter,' she murmured.

'There's no need to be sorry for me,' he said. 'Maybe you'll think I'm a callous blighter, but we were never suited, and I knew she had other men. Her mother tried to play it down, but I'm sure she'd been up to no good in Elgin.'

'I don't know what to say, Peter,' Jenny said sadly.

'I wasn't expecting you to say anything, or tell me anything. You were chums with her, so you likely knew what was going on, but I don't want to know. I don't care, it's as simple as that.'

Jenny filled the cups, and waited until she sat down again before she said, 'I couldn't help noticing you were crippled. Was that at the same time as Mick . . . ?'

He heaved a deep sigh now and turned towards her. 'Yes, Jenny, I lost a leg, and I often wished I'd . . .'

'No, Peter, don't say that! You're walking quite well. Did you get an artificial leg?'

'I didn't want it. I didn't want to be able to walk. But

. . . will I tell you something, Jenny? It was remembering I'd promised Mick to see you were all right if anything happened to him that made me fight back.'

'I'm glad, but you don't need to bother about me, I'm fine. It's you I'm worried about. Are you going to live with the Slaters? Have you seen them yet?'

He shook his head. 'I don't know what I'm going to do. I can't seem to plan ahead. I want to see my kids, but that's as far as I can think.'

Jenny laid her cup into her saucer. 'Things'll get clearer to you once you've seen them again.'

'Maybe.' He twirled his empty cup by the handle. 'Jenny, can you tell me how you kept going when you must have thought there was nothing worth living for?'

'It was different for me. There was nobody else to look after Georgie and little Lizann. Besides, I'd my health, and you still haven't got over what's happened to you.'

'It's the boys and Norma . . . I can't see how I can be father and mother to them if I take them back to Main Street.'

'The Slaters'll maybe not let you take them back, and there's nothing coming over them, they're being well looked after. And maybe you'll be asked to move in there with them.'

'It wouldn't work. I've still got my dark times . . . you know, when I wonder what I'm good for like this.'

'Don't let it get you down, Peter. Think things over properly before you come to any decisions.'

He put his cup and saucer down and stood up. 'You amaze me, Jenny, you're always so . . . sensible.'

'Not always. There's times I give way and have a good cry. Besides, it's easy for me to give you advice, I'm an outsider.'

'You'll never be an outsider to me, Jenny. Mick and you have been the best friends I ever had. No, don't get up, I'll see myself out.'

'You'll let me know what you decide on?'
'I'll do that.'

Peter would have been horrified to know how his visit affected Jenny. She burst into tears when he left her, tears of pity for him and of longing for the husband she had loved so dearly, and she went to bed that night wishing that Peter had never come. She wasn't sensible, as he had said, she was living a lie, pretending she was coping when she often felt like taking her two children by the hands and walking into the sea with them. Walking, walking, walking . . . until they were swallowed up.

Her morbid thoughts came to an abrupt end as she pictured two small faces distorted from long immersion in the water. She couldn't do that to them; they had a right to live, whatever the future held for them. And she wasn't as bad as Peter. At least she had her health, and two good legs. Mick wouldn't have wanted her to give up. She would manage without him. She had to manage.

In the morning, Jenny rose determined not to slip back into the Slough of Despond which had nearly claimed her again. At thirty-three she had many years ahead of her, years she would devote to Georgie and Lizann. She was blessed compared to those widows who had nobody; she had a son and a daughter to buck her up when she was tired, to care for her when she grew old.

For the first time in months, Jenny whistled blithely as she made the breakfast.

It was two weeks before Peter returned to the Yardie. He shrugged when Jenny asked him if he had made up his mind yet. 'The kids don't want to leave the Slaters,' he said, mournfully, 'and the Slaters want to keep them. I've been sleeping on a camp bed in the same room as the boys, but I'm about round the bend with Chae and his jokes, for he keeps on till I feel like throttling him. Pattie and Tommy think he's great, and Norma clings to her grandma like she was terrified of me.'

'She won't remember you,' Jenny soothed. 'And the boys'll feel strange with you, they haven't seen you for so long.'

'No, it's me, Jenny. I can't summon up any fatherly feelings for them. Oh, don't get me wrong, I still love them and I want them back, but to tell the truth, I'm quite glad they won't come.'

'You're still all mixed up, Peter. You've been through an awful lot, and it's going to take you time to get over it.'

'The thing is, sometimes I feel so down I don't think I'll ever get up again, and I can't expect folk to put up with that. No, I'd be best to live in Main Street on my own. Would you think it was awful cheek if I asked you to come and help me to sort out Elsie's things?'

The thought of him sitting night after night by himself, and getting more and more depressed made Jenny burst out, 'Sell your house, Peter, and come and live here with us. We'd be company for one another.'

His eyes brightened a little. 'Do you mean that?'

'Yes, I do. I'll help you to clear it out, and you can take whatever you want with you ... within reason.'

'Have you room for me, though?'

'Well, I shifted downstairs to give my two a room each, but you can have my bed, that'll save you having to climb the stairs, and I'll go in with little Lizann.'

'Will she not mind?'

'She's easy-going. Now that's settled, so go and tell the Slaters, and I'll move my things upstairs. We can start on your house tomorrow.'

Peter shook his head. 'I was supposed to look after you, Jenny, not the other way round.'

'We'll look after each other. Besides, I could be doing

460

with an extra bob or two, so I'll expect you to pay something for your keep.'

'Yes, of course.' They stood up at the same time and at the door he clasped her hand. 'Oh Jenny, you've taken a weight off my mind.'

Going inside, she thought wryly that the weight was on her mind now. She had offered him a home on the spur of the moment and she couldn't back down, but what would people say about a widow and a widower in the same house with only two young children as chaperones? The more Jenny thought about it, however, the less she worried. Her neighbours all knew he had been Mick's pal, and it should seem as natural to them as it did to her that she should take him in. Robbie Chapman had told her to share someone else's troubles and who better than a disabled ex-serviceman who deserved a decent place to live and decent food to eat?

Next morning, when Peter arrived with his kitbag, Jenny went along to Main Street with him, and while he packed his civilian clothes into a case, she took Elsie's things out of the wardrobe and chest of drawers, her eyes widening when she came across the provocative nighties. Her cheeks were deep scarlet when she asked, 'What do you want me to do with . . . this lot?'

He too coloured, with mortification as well as embarrassment. 'I'll burn them. I . . . I don't suppose you want any of her other clothes?'

'They're not the kind of things I'd wear.' Pity for him welled up in her again. He was such a nice man, it was awful to think that his wife had set herself out to attract other men with these short skirts and low-necked blouses.

Peter made a big bonfire on the shore, starting with Elsie's clothes and piling on other items Jenny said he should dispose of. While he was thus occupied, she inspected all the cupboards, and finding them clean and tidy, she guessed that Mrs Slater had been busy. She had likely been appalled at the state of things when she came to collect the children's clothes after their mother died. It suddenly crossed Jenny's mind that there must be quite a few young couples who would be glad to walk into a fully-equipped house like this – there were only 'utility' furniture and bedding to be had now, and some household items weren't available at all – so before beginning on the mammoth task of packing Peter's belongings into boxes to be sold, she went out to talk to him.

He seemed relieved when she made the suggestion that he should rent out his house as it stood, and promised to see about it the following day. She left him tending to the fire and went home to prepare a meal. Babsie Berry was looking after Georgie and wee Lizann to leave her free to help Peter – at least her nearest neighbour hadn't been shocked by her taking in a lodger. Recalling how black Georgie had got from just standing beside a fire, Jenny boiled kettles and pans of water ready for Peter, but when he came in and she said she would fill the enamel bath for him, he shook his head. 'I couldn't . . . not in front of you and the kids.'

'Why not? Mick often did.'

'That was different,' he mumbled, uncomfortably.

It *was* different, she realized suddenly. Mick had been her husband, the children's father. Noticing her confusion, Peter said, 'I'll wash my face and hands just now, and change my clothes, and I'll have the bath when you're all in bed.'

'That's a good idea.' While she set the table, she realized that it wasn't going to be easy living in the same house as a man she had known practically since the day she learned to walk. Her house had been across the street from his, and they had played together even before they went to school. But they were man and woman now, not bairns. She couldn't come down in the mornings in her nightie like she'd done with Mick. She would have to be more circumspect.

In spite of the blackout and the frequent air raids, Lizann was happier than she had ever been before. Even when she was married to George, she had always had the worry of him being at sea, and her mother to contend with. She was in charge of her own life for the very first time. There was a camaraderie amongst her fellow fish workers that made her set off for Sinclair Road every morning looking forward to the day ahead. The men teased her light-heartedly, as they did to everyone, and the other women couldn't be more friendly, though Gladys Wright was still her closest pal. They swapped lipsticks and powder compacts, they went to each other's homes and tried out the latest hairstyles, Gladys settling on the long page boy bob with up-swept sides which she found easier to manage than the slinky, one-eye-covered hairdo which film star Veronica Lake had made popular. Lizann, however, found that the metal curlers just made her black curls frizzy, and she ended up like a golliwog.

At work, all the females wore headsquares knotted so that their hair was completely hidden. As Gladys observed one Saturday afternoon, while Lizann wielded a pair of curling tongs on her, 'Goodness knows why I suffer this torture. Nobody sees what our hair's like under our turbans. Oucha! Watch what you're doing, Lizann, you burnt my scalp just now.'

At this, Mrs Melville, who had been watching in silent amusement, let out a loud roar of laughter. 'What you lassies'll go through to look beautiful!'

'I'll never be beautiful with my nose,' Gladys said, rue-fully, 'but that's not to say I shouldn't try.'

'That's it, then.' Lizann laid down the tongs. 'Should we paint our legs, as well? All my stockings have ladders in them.'

'We might as well. I'll do yours and you can do mine.'

When Mrs Melville saw the tan going on her lodger's legs, she shook her head. 'I hope that stuff doesn't come off on the sheets.'

Gladys pointed to the instructions. 'It says there it won't.'

The older woman gave a sigh of resignation. 'If it does, you can wash them yourself, Lizann.'

The task completed, Gladys dived into her handbag and brought out the pencil she used on her plucked eyebrows, a fad Lizann had always refused to follow. 'I'll use this to mark a seam down the back.'

'What next?' Mrs Melville exclaimed, but she followed the procedure with interest.

'Now then,' Gladys said, when her legs were done. 'We look like we've got fully-fashioned silk stockings on, don't we?'

'And we can't get rips in them,' Lizann added.

'I don't know why you bother. You've been wearing slacks to your work for months now.' The trousers had shocked the elderly woman when Lizann bought them, but she had come round – nearly every girl she saw going to work was wearing them nowadays.

'We put skirts on to go out,' Gladys reminded her, 'and we're going to see *Gone With the Wind* tonight. It's the third time I'll have seen it, but I just love Clark Gable.'

'He'll not be there to see your legs,' Mrs Melville said, dryly. 'Now, if you two are finished making yourselves into something you're not, are you ready for your tea?'

At first Jenny thought nothing of Peter sitting in the kitchen all day. She knew it must be difficult for him to walk much, and did her best to spare a little time to talk to him every morning and afternoon. It was when she noticed how much brighter he was when Georgie came home from school that the answer dawned on her. He was missing his sons. He had gone to North Pringle Street once and was quiet and withdrawn for hours after he came back; she had thought his stump was hurting him, but it hadn't been just that. A day or two later she had what she thought was a brilliant idea, but she waited until her children were in bed before mentioning it.

'I was thinking, Peter. Why don't you ask Pattie and Tommy and Norma here for their dinner and supper every Sunday? Just on their own, so you wouldn't have Mr and Mrs Slater breathing down your neck.'

'That's very thoughtful of you, Jenny, but would you not mind having so many kids in the house?'

'My two would be glad to have somebody else to play with.'

'Well, if you're sure, I'll see what the Slaters say tomorrow.'

His face was etched with pain when he returned the following day, and Jenny's heart ached for him. It must be agony for him to walk so far, and it was no wonder he hardly ever went out. When her children were in bed that night, they sat comfortably by the fire as usual, she doing a bit of make-do-and-mend (adding false hems to her son's shorts and her daughter's skirts), he reading. They never said much, but Mick hadn't been one for saying much either, and it showed that Peter felt at home. Her sewing finished, she laid it down and rose to fill the kettle.

He looked up now. 'That time already?'

'Peter,' she said timidly, 'is your leg very sore?'

'It's throbbing like the devil,' he admitted. 'But I'm used to it.'

'Would you let me take a look at it? Maybe it needs bathing . . .'

'I couldn't let you do it, Jenny.'

'I wouldn't mind. I used to give my father and mother all-over washes every day. Come on, take your artificial leg off and let me see.'

He pulled up his trousers and his hands fumbled so much at the straps that she knelt down to help him. When she saw that the puckered skin of his stump was raw, she exclaimed, 'Oh, why didn't you tell me, Peter?'

'I didn't like.'

'I don't know how you could bear to wear that thing.' She stood up and poured some warm water into a basin, carried it over to the fireside and went to get cotton wool, disinfectant and the tin of ointment from the press. She dabbed slowly and gently, looking up into his face now and then to make sure that she wasn't hurting him too much, and patted the area dry with a soft towel.

'I'll put on some of this Germolene,' she smiled then. 'Georgie says it makes his scraped knees better.'

When she had emptied the basin and was laying past the other items, Peter said sadly, 'I came here to help you, and I've ended up giving you a lot of extra work. You're the strong one. My life's not worth a damn any more.'

She felt like throwing her arms round him and cuddling him like she cuddled her son when he hurt himself, but she busied herself making a pot of tea and said without looking round, 'That's not true, Peter. You used to be a draughtsman, and I'm sure Jones would take you back if you asked. If you'd a job, you'd feel different.'

'Jones wouldn't employ a cripple, and besides, I'm not fit to walk so far every day. I'm not fit to work. I'm not fit for anything.'

Longing to dispel his misery, she knew that sympathy would only make him worse, so she laid the teapot down and stood in front of him. 'Stop feeling sorry for yourself, Peter Tait. You can do anything if you set your mind to it. Give your stump a few days to heal, then go to the yard.

466

With so many men away, they'll be glad of somebody experienced. And if they don't want you, try Herd and McKenzie.'

She could tell that he was wavering, although his face bore deep hurt at her reprimand. At last he muttered, 'You're just trying to get me out from under your feet.'

She bent over and grasped his hands. 'You know I'm not. I hate seeing you like this, that's all. Now, we'll drink our tea and get to bed.'

Lying alongside her daughter, Jenny wondered if she had been too harsh with him. Maybe she was the cause of his depression. He had arrived here primed with the idea of helping her to get over Mick's death and she had made him believe she didn't need his help, when her so-called bravery was really bravado. Her heart was crying out for Mick, and she couldn't count the nights she had lain awake since she got the telegram, sobbing until her head was pounding and her pillow was soaking. If she admitted that, it might let Peter see she wasn't as strong as he thought. She was as weak as any other woman, and would have given way altogether if she hadn't kept a tight grip on herself.

The next day being Sunday, Chae Slater arrived just after twelve with his three grandchildren – his own idea, to save Peter the walk. 'I'll come back for them at seven,' he said.

To give Peter a few minutes alone with his family, she went out to see Mr Slater off. 'He looks a bit better now,' Chae remarked. 'You've taken on more than I'd like to have tackled, so how do you get on with him? Is he still as moody?'

'It's sitting about feeling useless that gets him down,' she smiled, 'so I've told him to go to Jones and ask for his old job back.'

'D'you think he's up to it, lass? He'd be a lot worse if he'd to give it up after he started.'

'He'll manage the job, it's the walking he'll have to get used to. But I'm sure he will.'

'Ach well, they'll maybe nae take him back.'

'We'll have to wait and see.'

'Aye, so we will. Well, see you at seven, lass, and I hope the nickums behave themselves.'

When Jenny went back to her kitchen, she was delighted to see Peter's eyes shining. Norma had climbed on to his knee, and Pattie and Tommy were engrossed in the comics Georgie had left on the table before going to Sunday school with his sister. Occasionally, however, they flung a question at their father, which told that they accepted him as a friend, if nothing else.

The dinner was quite hectic, with three shrill voices wanting to speak at once, and Jenny was thankful that at least the two little girls were quiet and got on together. In the afternoon the boys wanted to hear about the corvette and Peter willingly obliged, glossing over how he had lost his leg, which was really what they wanted to know.

Supper was a repeat of the earlier meal, and before they knew it, Chae Slater was back. When Peter went out with his children, Georgie turned a puzzled face to his mother. 'Peter's Pattie and Tommy's dad, isn't he? Why doesn't he live with them?'

'Do you not like him being here?' she countered.

'I don't mind, he's all right.'

Relieved, she shooed him and his sister up to bed, but when Peter came in he looked so tired that she said, 'Was it too much for you?'

'I enjoyed having them, but you're right, I am tired.'

'So'm I,' she smiled.

'Should I tell Chae to stop bringing them?'

'No, no. We'll get used to all the commotion. A body can get used to anything . . .' Hesitating, she added, 'I haven't got used to not seeing Mick, though. I still miss him.'

He looked at her sadly. 'Aye, you're bound to, I miss him myself. It doesn't seem right for me to be here with you . . .'

Tears were prickling her eyes now. 'I'm sorry, I don't like letting anybody see me crying,' she gulped.

'Jenny, whenever you feel like crying for Mick, don't let me stop you. I know how much you loved him, and losing him must feel like losing a part of yourself . . . like me losing my leg.'

'Oh, Peter.' She was sobbing now, deep shuddering sobs that shook her whole body, and in a moment she jumped to her feet and ran upstairs. She hadn't meant this to happen. She had only mentioned missing Mick to let Peter see that she wasn't made of iron, and now he must think she was a proper weakling.

He gave her an anxious look in the morning, but said, 'I think I'll go to Jones's after breakfast.'

'Good.' But she couldn't leave things like that. 'I'm sorry about last night, Peter. I don't know what came over me.'

'My grannie used to say a good greet's the best way to get over what's bothering you. I just wish I could have been some comfort to you.'

'You were a comfort just being here. Seeing you, I can remember Mick better and how the two of you were always together when you were boys.'

Peter smiled. 'Aye, we were always good pals.' He changed the subject in case she got upset again. 'I'm a bit scared of going to the yard. If they do take me back, I just hope I haven't forgotten . . .'

'It'll soon come back to you.'

Her two children appearing just then, she concentrated on seeing they had enough to eat. When Georgie was ready to go out, Peter said, 'I suppose I'd better get going as well.'

'I'll keep my fingers crossed for you,' she assured him.

It was over an hour before he returned, his gaunt face wreathed in smiles. 'The manager said they were falling behind with orders for the Navy, and he nearly flung his arms round me.'

'I told you,' she grinned.

'I've to start tomorrow, how's that for speed? Oh Jenny, I feel like I've been born again. I'm floating on air.'

'Anchor yourself to that chair,' she laughed, 'and we'll have a cup of tea ... with a wee drop of Mick's whisky in it to celebrate.'

At first the walk to and from the yard made Peter's metal leg chafe against his stump, and Jenny had to attend to it every evening after her children were in bed. 'I don't know how you can walk at all,' she said, one night.

'It's not as bad as it looks. It is sore, but I can put up with it.'

When she thought of applying a soft pad between metal and flesh, it did reduce the rubbing, so this became another daily task. Jenny didn't mind the extra work, although there were times, lying beside her daughter, when she wished that it had been Mick who came home. But after a little weep she felt deeply ashamed. Peter's marriage had been nothing like hers. He deserved peace now, contentment, and maybe some day, when he got over what had happened to him, he would meet a nice girl and find true happiness at last.

Robbie Chapman's letter arrived when Jenny thought he had forgotten his promise to keep in touch. 'He's sold up his house in London and he'll be arriving in Buckie the day after tomorrow,' she told Peter when she was carrying out her nursing duty that night. 'That's why he's been so long in writing, and he says he'll come and see me

470

once he's settled in with his sister. You'll like him, he's . . .'

'But who is he?' Peter asked. 'Is he a relation? I never heard Mick speaking about him.'

She couldn't help laughing at his astonished expression when she gave him Robbie's story. 'Hannah?' he gasped. 'Oh, no, I can't believe that!'

'I know how you feel,' Jenny giggled, 'and he swore Hannah thought his kisses made her pregnant. He said he had never . . . you know, but he was awful anxious to find out about a baby he thinks was born between Mick and Lizann.'

'Mick never said anything about that, either.'

'He'd have been too young to know.'

Robbie appeared after dinnertime just five days later, and laughed at her embarrassment when he kissed her on the cheek. 'It's the normal greeting down south, my dear, and I forgot people were less outgoing up here. My, but you're looking well, much better than last time I saw you. Is there any particular reason for that?'

His roguish eyes told her what he was thinking, and she hurriedly told him why she had offered Peter Tait a home.

'Peter Tait?' Robbie said, reflectively. 'Yes, I remember you telling me about him.'

'He lost a leg when . . .'

'Ah, so you feel he needs you . . . as much as you need his support?'

Jenny smiled now. 'That's what you told me to do, but he doesn't need me so much now. He's got his old job back.'

Robbie had been grinning, but his features sobered abruptly. 'Shall I tell you why I gave up my house in London and disposed of my furniture et cetera, my dear? When I told my sister about you, she could see that I thought a lot of you . . .' He broke off for a moment then said, 'This is very difficult, and I hope you won't think I am out of order by what I am about to suggest.'

'No, I'm sure I won't.' In spite of her denial, Jenny felt uneasy . . . surely he wasn't going to ask her to marry him?

'I had no children, and at the time this came into my head, you had no one to turn to when you needed help . . .' He stopped and drew a long deep breath. 'I had hoped you would allow me to adopt you and your family, so that I could be a father to you and grandfather to your children, but now you have Peter. He might not like me interfering.'

'Peter's got no claim on us,' Jenny said, a little shakily because of the relief she felt. 'He's only a lodger, and no doubt he'll get married again some day . . . I hope he does. Yes, Robbie, I'd love you to be part of my family. My bairns never knew any of their grand-fathers.'

He rubbed his hands gleefully. 'Pearl will be delighted about this. It was her idea that I should come home, but I'd never have had the nerve to ask you that if she hadn't pushed me into it.'

'How would she like to be their grandmother?' Jenny surprised herself as much as Robbie with her unexpected offer.

He caught her hand and brought it up to his lips. 'My dear, she'll be beside herself with joy. You will have made two old fogeys very happy.'

Blushing, Jenny laughed. 'You're not old, Robbie, and certainly not a fogey, and you'll have to bring your sister here as soon as you can.'

Just then, Babsie Berry, who took Georgie and little Lizann for a walk most afternoons, brought them back. Seeing the man, she asked, 'Will I keep them for a while yet?'

'No, no,' Jenny smiled. 'This is Robbie Chapman, an old friend of my father's, and he'd like to get to know my bairns.'

'Well, I'll away then.' She nodded to Robbie. 'Nice to meet you.'

Noticing Georgie eyeing the stranger doubtfully, Jenny knelt down and put her arms round both her children. 'This is Robbie. He'd like to be your granda, if that's all right with you two?'

The little girl took only a second to make up her mind, running over and climbing up on his knee to kiss him. 'Will you be a real granda and take us out walks sometimes, like Josie May Yule's granda?'

'I'll take you wherever you want to go,' he grinned.

Jenny, however, could hear the trembly catch in his voice and gave her son a wee push. 'Are you not going to say anything to him?'

He looked round at her, his face a study in perplexity. 'He can't be our granda. A granda is either your mother's father or your father's father and he isn't . . .'

'He'll be a pretend granda,' Jenny explained, hoping the boy wasn't going to be difficult. 'He didn't have any children of his own, so he hasn't any real grandchildren, and . . .'

'But if he's only a pretend granda, he might want to stop pretending after a while. He might want to get new grandchildren.'

Quickly handing wee Lizann to her mother, Robbie held his hand out to Georgie. 'Come here, son.' When the boy moved closer, he went on, 'If a man pretends something hard enough, he begins to believe it's true, and that's what's going to happen with us. That is . . . if you want it to.'

Flattered at being classed as a man, Georgie held out his hand with a shy smile. 'Maybe it'll be all right.'

'You bet your boots it will,' Robbie laughed, 'and you're going to have a grandma, too. Would you like that?'

Both children assuring him that they would, he gave them his full attention for the next hour, but at quarter past five he stood up. 'I'd best be off before Peter . . .'

'I want you to meet him, and you can't go away without some supper.'

Peter had been prepared to dislike Robbie Chapman, a feeling that deepened when he was told what had happened, but he found that there was something about the man that he couldn't help but respond to. Soon he was talking easily to him, and while Jenny was engaged in getting her children to bed, he told Robbie more about the night the corvette was torpedoed and his spells in hospitals than he had ever told her.

Later, when she came in from seeing her caller out, she said, 'I want you to understand why I agreed with what Robbie wanted.'

'You don't have to explain anything to me,' Peter said quickly.

'Just listen,' she smiled. 'The first time he was here I could tell he was a lonely man and I wanted to do something for him. And he's so nice, I knew my bairns would like him. I really want him and his sister to be part of my family, even if you think I'm stupid.'

'I don't think that. I think he's a genuine man, but . . . you'll have to watch he doesn't take you over altogether. He looks as though he wasn't short of a few bob, and he'll likely want to throw his money around to impress your kids . . .'

Jenny frowned. 'No, I won't let him do that. I'll let him give them birthday and Christmas presents, but nothing big.'

*　　*　　*

After telling Pearl the good news and having a short discussion on what it would mean to them, Robbie went to bed. Steeped once again in the atmosphere of the Yardie, he turned his mind to the night Willie Alec had told him to stop visiting. He had come home, asked for a loan of his mother's writing pad, and come up to this same room. He had written from the heart, his torment almost unbearable, and could still remember every word of the letter which had gone unanswered.

My darling,

My heart is breaking at not being able to see you, for I love you more than I could ever tell you. I do assure you that nothing I did could have had the effect you thought, so you had no need to worry. I have the feeling that you had begun to love me, and if this is the case, I would gladly take you away from Buckie and look after you and HIS child, when it is born. Let me have your answer right away, my beloved, so that I can make the arrangements. If I do not hear from you within two days, I might kill myself. Meantime, I will live in hope.

He had mentioned no names, not even his own, and thinking about it now, coming up for seventy, what he had written seemed melodramatic and childish. He had always believed that her husband had kept the letter from her, but now he wasn't so sure. Jenny had said that Hannah never got over Willie Alec's death, so she must have loved him very much, and she had wanted to forget the impudent young artist.

But he had made a start at reparation now, Robbie mused. He had offered himself, and been accepted, as a substitute grandfather to a young boy and girl who were in fact Hannah's grandchildren. He wished he could take her real daughter under his wing, too, the older Lizann who had vanished in such peculiar circumstances, but that seemed to be an impossible dream – she wouldn't turn up again after being away for so long. All he could do was to make life easy for Jenny, who was, after all, the widow of his dear Hannah's son.

Chapter Thirty-two

❦

Aberdeen had suffered many air-raids since the war started, mostly what became known as tip-and-run. It was in fact the most frequently bombed city in Scotland, but not the most severely – that dubious honour went to the Clydebank area of Glasgow – and Aberdonians had begun to think that the Luftwaffe had no intention of unleashing a large attack on them. On the night of 21 April 1943, however, their complacency was rudely shaken. Twenty-five Dorniers came sweeping in from the north just after nine o'clock, as dusk was falling, and wreaked mayhem on the city.

When the first explosion came, Mrs Melville and Lizann were sitting in their nightdresses having a last cup of tea before going to bed. 'Oh, my goodness!' the older woman exclaimed in dismay. 'That sounded awful like a bomb, but I never heard the siren, did you?'

'No, I'm sure it didn't go.'

The vacillating wailing of the alert sounded a few minutes too late, accompanied by a series of crr...rumps from, it seemed, all around them. 'Will we go down to the lobby?' Mrs Melville asked, nervously. 'We'd be safer there.'

'We can't go down like this,' Lizann pointed out.

'We could put our coats on.'

'It'll likely all be over before we get down the stairs.'

'Aye, it sometimes doesn't last very long.'

But they were both wrong. The bombs kept falling, and when Lizann rose and edged open the curtains, the sky was blood-red with reflections from dozens of burning buildings. 'Come away from that window,' her landlady burst out, 'it's not safe standing there. And put out the light, just in case.'

They pulled their chairs together and held hands as the house shook. Neither of them dared to say anything now, each believing that her last moment would come at any time. In spite of, or perhaps because of, her fear, Lizann found herself thinking of her mother and brother, of her Auntie Lou and Uncle Jockie, of Jenny Cowie, of Peter Tait. If she was killed, none of them would know. They didn't know she was in Aberdeen. Nobody knew ... except Dan Fordyce. But she didn't want to think about him and concentrated on George. Was he looking down from above and waiting for her to join him? This should have been a comforting thought, but it was anything but.

An extra-loud blast made the two women grip hands more tightly – they could not see each other's faces in the darkness – and when the fearsome reverberation died down, Mrs Melville whispered, 'That was a close one.'

Lizann's agreement was drowned by another exceptional bang. It was quite some time before the terrifying sounds faded and eventually died away, and some time after that before the sirens gave the sustained tone of the all-clear. The fear-bred silence of the people in the tenement between the apparent end of the raid and the official signal that it was over was broken now, as feet tramped up the stairs and voices chattered in a somewhat hysterical manner.

'They've all been down in the lobby,' Mrs Melville whispered. 'I told you we should have gone down as well.'

Lizann rose to switch on the light. 'Yes, I suppose we should, but we were lucky.'

'We mightn't be so lucky another time, though.'

Aware of this, yet thinking that the short passageway from the outside door wouldn't be much safer, Lizann just said, 'I feel like another cup of tea. How about you?'

The only topic of conversation in Aberdeen the following morning was of course the air-raid, and Lizann was horrified to learn that there was hardly a part of the city that hadn't been affected, some areas very badly. Two schools had been set alight and one got a direct hit. Vast damage was done to the Gordon Highlanders barracks, the Royal Mental Hospital and its nurses' home. Rows of houses were flattened, and both a Presbyterian and an Episcopal church were bombed – the Luftwaffe could not be accused of religious discrimination. The final tally showed a hundred fatalities, nearly a hundred seriously injured and 141 minor injuries. It was the worst night the city had suffered.

Details of the raid reached Easter Duncairn in bits and pieces, the van drivers who called relating what they had heard, people who had gone to Aberdeen to see for themselves coming back with horrific stories, and Dan Fordyce soon realized that these were not idle rumours. Never free of fear for Lizann's safety, he was now frantic with anxiety. He had no idea where she lived, but it seemed that all the city had got it, and he couldn't bear to think that she had been killed or maimed in any way. On Saturday morning he decided to go to his sister.

He wished now that he hadn't been so taken up with his studies when he was at university. He had never explored the city and, being concerned solely with agricultural matters, he had not gone near the harbour area nor across the river to Torry. But Ella would tell him where to find the fish houses and curing yards and he would go round every last one of them. He had to find Lizann and persuade her to leave Aberdeen, even if she refused to return to the farm with him. Then he remembered that all these workplaces would be closed from Saturday lunchtime, and he spent a miserable weekend champing at the bit.

Only taking time on Monday to give instructions to

his grieve as to the work to be done, he set off in his lorry, filling the tank at the nearest garage with the pink petrol issued to commercial vehicles.

Ella was astonished when he told her what he meant to do. 'We'll make a list from the Post Office Directory, and I'll put them in order for you, but we'd better have lunch first.'

Dan was annoyed that the journey – over fifty miles in an antiquated vehicle – had taken so long, for it was almost three in the afternoon before Ella leaned back. 'That's it, but there's an awful lot of them.'

'I could be lucky at the first place I try,' Dan said, hopefully.

'I doubt it. Take the map with you, so you can find all the different streets. The lorry would just be a hindrance, so leave it here and get the tram to Market Street. You'll have to walk the rest.'

Dan studied the map on his way to the centre of the city, and when he came off the tram, he hurried down Market Street and along South Market Street until he came to Palmerston Road, the first on his list, where he had to pass several warehouses before finding any fish houses.

At each place he tried – going on to Poynernook Road, Raik Road and Stell Road – and only after having to wait to see this one or that one, he was told that they had never heard of Lizann Buchan, and it seemed no time at all until his watch told him that he need go no farther – work would have stopped for the day.

'No luck?' Ella asked sympathetically when he went back. 'Never mind, there's always tomorrow.'

'I have to go back tonight. I'm short-staffed, and I don't know when I'll manage to get away again.' Dan contemplated asking her to carry on the search, but decided against it. He wanted to find Lizann himself.

*　　*　　*

If not exactly deliriously happy, Jenny was quite content with her life nowadays. Robbie and Pearl visited every Saturday afternoon, and because Jenny had asked them not to spoil her children, they brought only small gifts. Of course, with sweets being on ration, Georgie and Lizann were thrilled to get little pokes bought with their surrogate grandparents' coupons, and their mother made sure they kept some to share with the three Taits on Sunday.

On the Saturday evenings, while Jenny got to know Pearl Chapman, Robbie talked to Peter and after a few weeks was satisfied with what he learned of him. He brought up the subject with his sister. 'You know, they're right for each other, that two.'

'Don't you dare poke your nose in,' she warned. 'You want a fairy-tale ending, you old romantic, but it's not as simple as that. They've a lot to think over first. She has two children already, he has three, and if they fall in love and get married, they'd likely have more. That house wouldn't be big enough, and with all those mouths to feed, I shouldn't think Peter could afford to buy anything bigger. And they'd likely be offended if you offered them money.'

'It's too late to say "if they fall in love", Pearl. Didn't you see the way he looks at her?'

Pearl clicked her tongue and then sighed. 'Maybe he's fallen, but not Jenny. She likes him, but nothing more than that, and I hope he doesn't say anything yet; he might scare her off.'

'So you do think they're made for each other?' Robbie's button-bright blue eyes twinkled mischievously. 'You're a bit of a romantic yourself.'

Jenny would have gone on regarding Peter as a very dear friend as well as a lodger if two-and-a-half-year-old Lizann hadn't set the cat amongst the pigeons. Putting on her coat to go to Sunday School with Georgie, she said, 'Mummy, can I have my room to myself again? You used to sleep with Daddy, so why don't you sleep with Peter?'

Sure that she was crimson from head to toe, Jenny avoided looking at Peter as studiously as she evaded the question. 'Remember, Pattie and Tommy and Norma'll be here for their dinner, so come straight home.'

Georgie grinned. 'Oh, great! I love when they're here.'

When they went out Jenny rose to clear the table, and after a moment Peter said, 'I'll give you a hand.'

As she filled the basin to wash the dishes, she felt surprised that he was ignoring her daughter's innocent remark, but assumed that he was as uncomfortable about it as she was. Bairns had a habit of coming out with the most embarrassing questions, she thought, swishing the bar of yellow soap through the hot water to get a good lather.

The kitchen was spotless again by the time Chae Slater took the young Taits in, only a few minutes before her own two appeared. As usual, the boys did all the talking during the meal, Jenny and Peter smiling at the noise they were making. By the time they finished eating the rain had come on, and Peter suggested that they play some games, so the rest of the afternoon was punctuated by cries of delight or disappointment, depending on who had won at Ludo, snakes and ladders or draughts. When Lizann and Peter sat down after washing up, they were persuaded to take part and made a point of losing every game. They were soon twigged by Pattie, who by now was an intelligent, serious boy, very like his father. 'You don't need to cheat to lose,' he objected. 'We'd beat you anyway.'

'Nothing gets past you, does it, lad?' Peter laughed, ruffling his son's fair head.

When Chae came for his grandchildren, he hung back to speak to Jenny while the others were at the door. 'Nell and me was wondering . . .' He stopped and winked. 'You ken.'

'No, I don't.' She did know what he meant, however, and was dismayed to feel her cheeks burning.

'It's quite a while you've bade together . . . it would be natural if you . . .' He gave another suggestive wink.

'There's nothing like that between me and Peter.' She was astonished at how her heart had speeded up, though it was likely just because she hadn't thought of Peter in that way before.

'Well, just mind, me and the wife'll be happy to see him wed again, if things ever get that far. He's a good man.'

That night, when Jenny went to fill the basin to bathe Peter's leg, he said, 'Leave that and come and sit down. I want to speak to you.'

Warily, she took the chair at the opposite side of the fire, and he smiled as he said, 'Don't look so worried. I've been thinking about what your Lizann said this morning.'

'I'm sorry about that, Peter. She's not old enough to . . .'

'I'm glad she said it. She made me think, and I've made up my mind to look for other lodgings.'

'Oh no, Peter,' she gasped, hurt that he could even think about it. 'There's no need, unless . . . are you not happy here?'

'I'm maybe too happy. Oh, Jenny, I'm trying to tell you I can't go on like this.' To cover his embarrassment, he ran his fingers through his hair, the blond waves simply springing back into place again. 'I didn't want to say anything yet. I know how much you loved Mick, but . . . is there any chance you could come to care for me . . . just a wee bit?'

She dropped her eyes, confused by her own feelings. 'I've always been fond of you,' she murmured, 'and I've felt a lot closer to you since . . . I thought it was . . .' She looked at him apologetically. 'I thought it was pity, but it's . . . more than that.'

'I shouldn't have said anything yet. You won't feel easy with me now.'

She slipped off her chair to kneel on the floor beside him. 'Peter,' she said, softly, 'I have to ask you. What about Lizann?'

His surprise was clearly genuine. 'Lizann?' He leaned down and lifted her hand to his lips. 'I can't pretend she never mattered to me. I still think about her sometimes. To tell the truth, when Mick . . . just before the torpedoes hit us, he made me promise to look after you if anything happened to him, and I made him promise to tell Lizann, if she ever came back, that I'd never stop loving her. I did love her, and when George Buchan was lost I thought it was still love I felt for her, but I know now it wasn't. That was pity, and I've kidded myself for years. Anyway, she never loved me and I truly hope she's found somebody else. Suppose she was to walk through that door right now, Jenny, it's still you I'd want. I'd be pleased to see her, to know she was all right. Nothing more than that.'

'You're sure?'

'Absolutely positive. It's you I love. I always told Mick he was lucky having you, and if you ever say you'll be my wife, I'll consider myself the luckiest man in the world.'

'All right, Peter,' she murmured, 'consider yourself the luckiest man in the world.'

'You'll marry me?' he gasped.

'You've made me see what I should have seen for myself. I love you and all, Peter.'

His face was a study in uncertainty now. 'You're not just saying that to save me thinking I've made a fool of myself?'

'We've both been fools, but Chae must have guessed how the wind was blowing. He said they wouldn't mind if you got wed again.'

'Thank goodness! I thought they'd be annoyed, that's why I waited so long before I said anything. Oh, Jenny, I can't believe this.'

'Is that why you haven't kissed me yet?' she smiled.

He took her face in his hands, his lips hesitant at first, as if he were doubtful of her, but her eager response told him there was nothing to worry about.

After a few moments, she drew away with a sigh. 'I'd better make one thing clear, Peter. I'll never stop loving Mick, but not in the same way as I used to.'

'I didn't expect you to stop loving him, Jenny, and we've other things to talk over, Elsie for one, but not now. Now's for us, for showing how much we love each other. If you want to wait a while before you marry me, I'll understand, but we can discuss that another time, as well.' His mouth came down tenderly on hers again.

Jenny broached the subject of Elsie three days later. 'I wasn't going to tell you, Peter, but I don't want any secrets between us and I can't keep it to myself any longer.'

She looked so serious that Peter said apprehensively, 'What d'you want to say, my darling?'

'Elsie asked to see me before she died. I was taken to the hospital and . . . she confessed something to me.'

'If it's about her making Lizann run away, she told me herself.'

'That was one of the things, but there was more.'

'And she said she told Hannah long before the midwife let it out.'

'More than that,' Jenny whispered, unable to look at him now. 'She said she smothered Hannah with a pillow.'

'Oh Jenny,' Peter groaned. 'Don't look so guilty at telling me. I knew that and all . . . well, I was nearly sure, and like you I kept it to myself. I couldn't hurt Mick by telling him, and I couldn't report her to the police. They'd have locked her up, maybe hanged her, and with me in the Navy, my kids would've been left with nobody.' He gave a harsh laugh. 'They were left with nobody at the end, anyway.'

'They'd their grandma and granda, and that's another thing I meant to speak to you about. I'm willing to take them when we're married, if the Slaters let them go. If they argue about it, you'll have to remind them they're your children.'

'Jenny my dearest, much as I love my kids, I can't expect you to take them on. They'd drive you up the wall if you had them all the time.'

'They're not that bad, and the Slaters manage to put up with them.'

He leaned back with a satisfied smile. 'You know this, Jenny, you're a woman in a million, and I'm happier now than I've ever been in my life.'

'I'm an ordinary woman, Peter, don't put me on a pedestal. The boys are bound to squabble, and maybe the girls, but I'll try not to make any more of my two . . .'

'I know you won't make any difference between them.' He looked at her and grinned, his eyes twinkling. 'Yours, mine . . . and ours, come time?'

Colouring, she smiled. 'They'll all be ours. The thing is, we'll have to look for a bigger house before we fix a date for the wedding.'

'You're not getting cold feet, are you?'

'No, I'm just being practical. We'd better go to bed now, though, or we won't feel like getting up in the morning.'

Going upstairs, she thought that it shouldn't be long until they were sharing the same bed, and she wondered if he was thinking the same. The new life ahead of them would not be a bed of roses, with five children to feed and clothe and keep in order, but surely their love was strong enough to overcome anything.

On the following night Peter was a little late in coming

home. 'I went to tell the Slaters we're getting married, and when I said we wanted my kids with us, Nell went on her high horse.'

'Oh,' Jenny exclaimed in dismay. 'Will she not give them up?'

'She said I'd been damned glad of her looking after them for so long, but good old Chae reminded her she wasn't getting any younger and they were always getting older, and she climbed down.'

'Are Pattie and Tommy going to be staying with us?'

The adults had forgotten that Georgie would be listening, and Jenny was relieved when Peter sat down and drew the boy beside him. 'Your mum and I are getting married, and we'll all be one big, happy family. Will you like that?'

'Can me and Pattie and Tommy all sleep in the same room?'

'If that's what you want. They've always slept together, so they won't mind sharing.'

Quiet little Lizann had also been taking everything in. 'What about me? If you're sleeping with Peter, Mummy, can Norma come in with me?'

Jenny turned to Peter with a laugh. 'They've sorted everything out between them, so as soon as the minister can manage . . .'

Immediately he arrived, Robbie Chapman could sense that something had changed. Jenny's eyes were absolutely starry and Peter couldn't keep his off her. About to voice his pleasure, he glanced at his sister who, by only the merest descent of her brows, made him think better of it.

When the visitors were seated, Peter drew Jenny towards him and put an arm round her waist. His eyes on Robbie, he made his announcement. 'I've asked this beautiful young lady to marry me, and she's said yes.'

'Well, well!' Robbie boomed. 'What a surprise!'

'Never heed him,' Pearl chuckled. 'He's been waiting for it.'

'You guessed?' Jenny gasped.

'I wondered how long it would take. Oh my dear, dear girl, I'm truly happy for you.' Standing up, he gave her a quick hug and then turned to Peter. 'As for you, young fella-me-lad, see you look after her properly . . . but I don't suppose I need to tell you that.'

Getting to her feet too, Pearl gave her brother a small push. 'Would you stop hogging the stage?' When he stood aside, she put her arms round both young people. 'Do the bairns know? All of them?'

Lizann nodded and Peter said, 'They've got the sleeping arrangements worked out already, and I think we'll all fit in here nicely . . . for a year or so, anyway, unless we start fighting.'

Hearing this as she came in from playing on the shore, little Lizann said, 'Norma and me won't fight, Grandma Pearl.'

She smiled fondly. 'I'm sure you won't, my wee lamb; it's the boys that'll have to behave themselves.'

The wedding was, literally, very quiet . . . most of the time. The Reverend Lawrie had agreed to perform the ceremony in the house, and the children seemed to be overawed by his presence, even the boys. Robbie and Pearl were best man and matron of honour, the only other guests were Chae and Nell Slater – whom Jenny had insisted on inviting although Peter had not been altogether easy about it – and Jake and Babsie Berry – whom no one thought of not inviting – and merriment was the order of the day. As Mr Lawrie was to say to his sister when he went home, 'Remembering that Jenny and Peter had both been afflicted by several tragedies in their lives, it did my heart good to see how happy they were today . . . how happy they all were. There's a resilience in the fishing community that we ordinary mortals would be wise to strive to emulate.'

The three boys did get a bit noisy once it was past their normal bedtime, and Mrs Slater eventually whispered to Jenny, 'I'd better take our lot home before they get out of hand. But before we go, I want to thank you for what you've done for Peter. I never saw him like this before, so proud ... and his love for you's shining out of his face for everybody to see. I'm really delighted for him.'

Jenny understood the meaning behind this. Mrs Slater must have known that Peter hadn't loved Elsie and couldn't have been proud of her, and she was, in her own way, giving her blessing on his second marriage. 'He did a lot for me, and all,' she murmured, 'and I love him just as much.'

The three Tait children were to be spending another night with their grandparents, and Robbie and Pearl, who lived not far from the Slaters, said they might as well all go along the road together. Babsie made Georgie go upstairs for the bag with his and Lizann's night clothes, because they were to sleep at the Berrys' house for this one night ... and at long last, the newly-weds were alone.

Peter was strangely silent as he turned from the door and went to sit by the fire, and Jenny, who had expected him to take her in his arms as soon as he had the chance, took the seat at the opposite side, trying to hide her disappointment. Presently she asked, 'What's the matter?'

'I can't help thinking this is all wrong,' he mumbled. 'I can't stop thinking about Mick. I can't ... touch you ... you're his wife.'

'No, Peter, I've been his widow for quite a while now, and Mr Lawrie made me your wife this afternoon.'

'But what would Mick think about it?'

Standing up, she crossed to sit on the arm of his chair. 'I couldn't sleep last night for worrying about that myself, but when you put the ring on my finger, a calmness came over me. I'm sure Mick was letting me know he approves.' She slipped an arm round Peter's shoulder. 'But he wouldn't want us to spoil our wedding night thinking about him.'

He turned towards her now, and after only a few kisses, pulled her to her feet and took her through to their bedroom, where a new double bed – Robbie's wedding gift – was waiting to be tested.

Waiting for the kettle to boil for a last cup of tea one night a few weeks later, Pearl could see by her brother's face that he was up to something. 'What are you hatching up now?' she asked, sharply.

'You're worse than a wife,' he grinned. 'I haven't reached a definite conclusion yet, but I might as well tell you what I was thinking. D'you remember that letter I got this morning? It was from Perry Fry, the art dealer. When I was getting my London house ready for selling, I showed him all the drawings and sketches I had lying about, and he offered to try and sell them for me. I didn't think he'd get much for any of them, not with a war on and everybody having to tighten their belts, but the crafty beggar got an American army colonel to take them to New York.'

'Did he manage to get some of them sold?'

'Some of them?' Robbie gave a loud guffaw. 'Apparently they could have sold fifty times as many. The Americans were clamouring for them, and he's asking if I've any more, but that was the lot, worse luck.'

'The sketches you did before are still in a tea chest in the attic.'

'None of them were much good. If only I had the one I did of Hannah Jappy. Of all the drawings I ever did, even after my training, that was my masterpiece. It would probably fetch a fortune if I knew where to lay my hands on it, though I wouldn't sell it, even if it were mine to sell, which it isn't.'

'You might as well send that dealer the ones upstairs, though.'

'I suppose so. I could always tell him to destroy them if he doesn't think they're worth anything. Now, I'm going to tell you what I was planning. He sent me a cheque for ten thousand pounds, and what am I needing with that kind of money . . . or you? We've both got enough already to see us out comfortably.'

'Jenny and Peter won't take any of it,' she pointed out.

Robbie gave a sly smile. 'There are ways and means of . . . that wee house is bursting at the seams already with seven of them in it, and I don't think it'll be long till they need something a lot bigger . . . like this.'

'Peter couldn't afford anything as big as this.'

'That's where my plan comes in. I'll say it's too big for us, and we want to buy a small house but we don't like the idea of strangers being here. Then I'll ask if they would do us a favour and move in.'

'Well,' Pearl said, thoughtfully, 'that might work, but for any sake, don't say anything for a while yet.'

'Not till they mention the overcrowding themselves,' he nodded. 'By the way, have you made out a will?'

'I've left everything to you, and this house is yours, anyway.'

'And I left everything to you, but I'm going to change it. I'm going to leave it to Jenny and Peter . . . on condition that they divide it with Lizann if she ever turns up. That way, I'll feel I've done something for Hannah Jappy at last.'

Pearl looked shocked. 'But it was through her you left home and . . .'

'. . . and made my fortune in London,' Robbie smiled. 'I do owe her and her family something, Pearl. And by the time they learn about it I'll be dead, and they can't refuse to accept it.'

Pressure of work at the farm made it impossible for Dan to get away as often as he would have liked, and he had only managed to get to Aberdeen three times in the past three months. Every morning at breakfast, cooked and served by Alice because Meggie Thow was growing increasingly frail, he glanced at the front page of the *Press and Journal* to see if there had been any more raids on the city. For security purposes, all that appeared in the headlines day after day was 'Raid on North East town', which told him nothing. He did hear that Peterhead had got it on such-and-such a night, or Fraserburgh, or Aberdeen, but nothing more than that, and his sister's letters gave few details. He supposed that she was taking heed of the slogan: 'Careless talk costs lives'.

Knowing that he would not have another chance until after the harvest, he set off early one morning at the beginning of August, and took up his search from where he had left off on his list. He had combed the various quays in previous weeks, so he started on North Esplanade East. Meeting with no success there, he tried North Esplanade West, and once again, although there were yards on only one side of the road – the River Dee being on the other – time caught up with him, and he had to leave Torry for another time.

'Don't you feel like giving up?' Ella asked him when he went back to pick up his lorry.

He shook his head. 'I'll never give up.'

She smiled affectionately. 'You've got it bad.'

'I love her,' he said, simply.

'She's the first girl you've ever had, isn't she?'

'The first and last.'

As he drove home, he began to wonder if he should give up. Even if he did find Lizann, would she want to leave the friends she must have made, the new life she had spun for herself? It could be that she was in love with another man. It could be that she was already married. This last thought, although it turned a knife somewhere deep inside his breast, made him determined to keep on with his search. He had to find out, no matter how unpalatable the truth turned out to be.

Chapter Thirty-three

❦

'You're mad,' Ella told her brother, when next he appeared, one stormy day in November. 'Why don't you leave it till after the winter? It's an awful strain on you, driving two ways in this weather.'

'I can't leave it,' Dan admitted. 'I can't sleep or concentrate on anything for worrying about her, but I've been so tied up, today was the only opportunity I had.'

She touched his cheek fondly. 'Oh, Danny boy, I don't know what I'm going to do with you. You'll make yourself ill if you don't stop.'

'I'll be worse if I can't find her. You've no idea how much I love her, Ella.' Putting on his coat and cap again, and drawing his leather gloves over his fingers, not yet thawed out from the long drive in the draughty lorry, he went out to catch the tramcar to Market Street. He had tried every fish house and fish-curing yard on this side of the Dee, so he would go over the bridge into Torry today. If he still didn't find Lizann, he would ask Ella to make a list of all the fish shops for him to start on. He wouldn't give up, however long it took him.

It had been dull and overcast when he left the farm, and the sleety rain which had kept the sky dark had become huge flakes of snow, but he marched along his chosen route doggedly, slithering on the iced rail tracks and cursing when he actually fell. Picking himself up, he brushed the knees of his trousers, but with the snow falling like a blanket now, it made little difference. Despite the weather there was the usual activity of coal boats being unloaded along the harbour, but there were more trawlers in the Albert Dock, probably moored up because of the bad weather and packed like sardines, he thought, amused.

Just over the bridge now, and here was Sinclair Road, a long curving street which, according to the map he'd looked at before he left Great Western Road, went towards the Bay of Nigg. At the first yard he came to he didn't bother asking any of the workers if they knew Lizann; he had found it better to go straight to the office, although there was often no one there and he had to wait some time before the clerkess or manager came hurrying in from an errand to the fish house.

A small man was perched on a high stool at a sloping desk, a paddy hat sitting at the back of his head, a cigarette dangling from his mouth. Looking up from the papers he was turning over, he muttered, 'If you want to buy some fish, you'll have to ask at . . .'

'No, I don't want any fish, thank you. I was wondering, if it's not too much trouble . . . can you tell me if Lizann Buchan works here?'

The little man slid back a panel in the glass partition in front of him and shouted, 'Hey, Sandy! Have we got a Lizann Buchan here?'

A burly elderly man came forward, his sleeves rolled up, a rubber apron covering him from neck to feet. 'Nae Lizanns here.'

'Sorry.' The little man on the stool bent his head to the papers once again, and saying a quick 'Thank you,' Dan went out.

He had no more luck at the next place, but at the third the middle-aged clerkess, a tall, scraggy woman, answered his question positively. 'Yes, that name rings a bell.'

Dan's throat tightened with excitement and he had trouble saying, 'Where can I find her?'

'Wait till I look up . . .' She lifted a ledger marked 'Wages' and after flicking through some pages she said,

'She's in the gutting shed, but you'll have to wait till she's finished work if you want to speak to her. The boss is real strict about that.'

It was hardly four o'clock, a whole hour from stopping time, but Dan didn't care. 'I'll wait.'

'You can't wait here,' the woman snapped indignantly.

Dan was ecstatic at finding Lizann at last, but after standing out on the street for five minutes in the blinding snow, he realized that he would have to keep moving. For the next three quarters of an hour, he walked up and down, his heart beating at twice its normal speed, the rest of his body, especially his nose, numb with the cold.

To be sure that he wouldn't miss her, he took up his position outside the yard again, stamping his feet and thumping himself with crossed arms to keep up his circulation. When the hooter blew, he tried to watch each exit, stepping back as a horde of men, women and girls surged out.

'Lizann!' he called, desperately, because he couldn't see her and was afraid that she would go past without him noticing. 'Lizann! Lizann!'

The throng reduced to a trickle, the trickle came to an end and still there was no sign of the girl he loved, but he kept standing, refusing to admit defeat, although bitter, bewildering disappointment was making him feel sick.

In the first aid room, Gladys looked at Lizann. 'Off you go, there's no need for you to wait. It's just a wee cut.'

'It looks more than a wee cut to me, and I'm not in any hurry.'

Gladys let out a sharp squeal as the nurse dabbed at her finger with cotton wool soaked in iodine. 'It's not as bad as it looks,' the woman pronounced as she rolled on a bandage. 'It'll sting for a while, but it'll soon heal. Don't let any salt into it tomorrow, though, or you'll know about it.'

'Thanks, Mrs Martin,' Gladys murmured, slipping her uninjured hand through Lizann's arm.

The big doors were already closed, and they were forced to separate to get through the narrow opening left for stragglers. 'Oh, look, Lizann!' Gladys exclaimed as they emerged into the street and linked arms again. 'Somebody's built a life-size snowman along there.'

The sound made the snowman move forward stiffly, and both girls were alarmed as it approached them. 'Lizann?' it croaked. 'Oh, thank God I've found you!'

Terrified, she clung to Gladys and recoiled when it tried to touch her elbow. 'Don't be scared,' the apparition soothed, 'it's Dan Fordyce.'

'Dan?' she gasped.

'Do you know him?' Gladys looked from one to the other.

'I used to work for him,' Lizann murmured.

'D'you want me to get rid of him for you?' Gladys whispered.

'No, it's all right. What are you doing here, Dan?'

'I've been looking for you for months. Oh Lizann, I can't tell you how glad I am to find you.'

Gladys blew into her hands. 'Is it okay if I leave you with him? I'm blooming perishing.'

'No, I'm coming with you.'

She grabbed her friend's arm again, and Dan had no option but to walk alongside them. Not one word was spoken until they reached Union Street, where Gladys said sotto voce, 'Will I wait with you till your tram comes?'

But Dan had heard. 'I'll see her home.'

Come to her senses now, Lizann nodded her head. 'It's all right, I'll be safe with him.'

When Gladys walked away, Dan said, 'I thought I'd never get a chance to speak to you on your own.'

There was a long queue at the stop for the Rosemount

tram, and they had to stand most of the way, so it was only when they came off that they were alone, and it was too cold to hang about talking. Noticing for the first time how wet Dan was, and how badly he was shivering, Lizann said, 'I can't take you upstairs, I don't know what my landlady would say, but you'd better come into the lobby.'

In the dim light from a small electric bulb, he looked at her sadly. 'I've imagined seeing you again for so long, but not like this.'

'If you've come to propose again, Dan, the answer's still no.'

'I didn't come to propose, I came to take you away from the bombing.'

'But I don't want to get away. I like my work, I like my digs and I've got friends here.'

'Will you let me see you occasionally? So I'll know you're all right?'

'You won't get me to change my mind ... about anything.'

'I won't try, I promise. I've always come to Aberdeen on weekdays, but I could make it Sundays when you don't have to go to work. I don't want to lose touch with you again. Please, Lizann?'

He started to sneeze now, and she felt affection for him stirring in her. 'I hope you haven't caught your death of cold.'

'I wouldn't care if I had. At least I've found you.'

'Oh, Dan, it's good to see you ... and I would like to see you again ... but just as friends.'

'That's all I want, too, my dear.'

'All right, I'll meet you at two at ... where would be best for you?'

'Anywhere. I leave my lorry at Ella's.'

'Have you to drive back to Easter Duncairn tonight?'

Her obvious horror at this warmed his heart. 'Yes, but

498

I'll take care, I promise. So where will I meet you on Sunday?'

'At the top of Market Street? Do you know where that is?'

'Yes, and that's fine. I'll say goodnight now, Lizann.'

'Goodnight, Dan. See you on Sunday.'

She went upstairs thoughtfully. She shouldn't have agreed to meet him at all. She knew how he felt about her, and if he thought he could talk her into marrying him, he was going to be hurt.

'You're awful late tonight,' Mrs Melville remarked when she went in.

'Gladys cut her finger, and I waited with her till the nurse bandaged it.' She couldn't speak about Dan yet, not until she had got used to the idea of seeing him again.

'Good God, Dan!' Ella exclaimed. 'You're soaking wet!'

'Soaking wet and walking on air,' he grinned.

'Don't tell me you found her . . . after all this time?'

'Yes, I found her and I'm meeting her again on Sunday.'

'You won't be meeting anybody on Sunday if you don't change out of those wet clothes. You can have some of John's things, but will you be fit to drive home?'

'I'm fit for anything. Lizann says she just wants us to be friends, but it's early days and at least she did agree to see me again. I'll get her to come round.'

Ella grinned. 'Knowing you, I'm sure you will. You're like a cat with a mouse, you never give up.'

'That's not a very nice comparison,' he laughed.

'You know what I mean.'

Gladys kept on at her so much about Dan the following day that Lizann told her who and what he was, and that he had already proposed to her.

Her friend was amazed. 'He has his own farm and he loves you, and you turned him down?'

499

'I don't love him.'

'But you like him, I know by the way you speak about him.'

'Yes, I do like him, but marriage needs to be based on love.'

On Sunday, Dan's streaming cold made Lizann so sorry for him that she wondered if it was just affection she felt for him. It was flattering to think that he'd been searching for her for months, even in weather that had him soaked to the skin and frozen to the marrow. 'You shouldn't have come today,' she told him. 'You should be in bed with a cold like that.'

'I couldn't leave you standing waiting,' he grinned, 'and I'll soon get over it. I'm as strong as a horse.'

'You'll get a worse dose after this. It's still freezing.'

'At least it's dry. Now, where can we go to talk?'

'Nowhere's open on a Sunday.'

'Ella said I could take you there, and she'd let us have the lounge to ourselves.'

'You've got Ella on your side?' she smiled.

'It's nothing like that. She knows we didn't get much of a chance to speak on Tuesday, and I want to hear what you've done since you came to Aberdeen. I promise I won't say anything you don't want me to say.'

Lizann gave in. 'I don't want you to be ill, either, so we'd better go to Great Western Road.'

Ella was pleased to see her again, and after giving them a cup of tea she sent them through to her lounge. Lizann sat down in one of the deep leather armchairs, but Dan stood up in front of the fire, his hands held out to the flames.

'Are you still cold?' she asked anxiously.

'A wee bit, but I'll soon thaw out.' He took the other seat and leaned forward. 'Now, are you going to tell me how you found that job, and who told you about the lodgings?'

Lizann explained everything, then asked about the farm, and they were soon chatting away easily, recalling the days she had gone round with her creel, the time she had lived with the Laings, the months she had worked at Easter Duncairn. 'Did you find another maid?' she asked.

He told her about Alice, then said hesitantly, 'Meggie hasn't been keeping too well lately.'

'Oh, I'm sorry to hear that. I don't bear her any grudge for what she did to me – she was only trying to protect her job.'

'I felt like killing her,' Dan admitted, 'though I'm glad I didn't.'

'So'm I,' Lizann burst out. 'You might have been hung for it.'

'I was only joking,' he smiled, then looked away. 'Would you really have cared if I was hanged?'

'You know I would.'

He lifted his eyes to hers again. 'I'd break my heart if anything ... that's why I want you to leave Aberdeen.'

'But I don't want to leave Aberdeen, Dan.'

When Ella came through to tell them a meal was on the table, they were sitting silently, and she said brightly, 'You won't have to be too late if you're taking Lizann back to her lodgings before you go home ...'

Lizann stood up. 'No, I'll be all right myself.'

'I'll drop you off on my way,' Dan assured her, also rising.

'Not yet,' his sister laughed. 'Have your dinner first.'

John, Ella's husband, was already seated in the dining-room, and he jumped up to shake Lizann's hand vigorously. 'I'm pleased you two have got back together again.'

'But ...' Lizann began, looking helplessly at Dan, who said, 'Nobody's more pleased than I am, John.'

Later, on their way to Rosemount Place in the old lorry, Lizann said, accusingly, 'Dan, why didn't you correct

John? We're not back together. We've never been together, not really.'

'What would you call this, then?' he smiled.

She paused for only a few seconds. 'Together,' she giggled, a warmth sweeping through her in spite of the icy blasts of wind coming through the ill-fitting window of the ancient Ford.

Chapter Thirty-four

❦

Over the winter, with less work to be done on the farm, Lizann had seen quite a lot of Dan and was well aware of how deeply he loved her. It was in his eyes, in his soft, caressing voice, but ... At Christmas, Ella and John had clearly thought marriage was imminent, and Mrs Melville also seemed to think so, but she herself was still not sure.

The realization came for her one Sunday in March. She had been lying in bed looking forward to seeing him in a few hours, when it dawned on her it wasn't just pleasure she felt. Her heart was beating faster at the thought of him, her inside was behaving in a way that only being in love could explain. It wasn't the sharp aching love she had felt for George – which she had been waiting for – it was a warm, comforting sort of love, a mature love, a thirty-year-old woman's love, and she had been last to recognize it.

Dan had respected her wish by not proposing again, and she couldn't bring the subject up herself. Anyway, she couldn't go back to the farm as his wife with Meggie Thow still there. The housekeeper would think she'd been right in what she thought before.

This problem was resolved at the end of April, when Dan told her that Meggie had died. 'Poor lonely woman,' she said. 'Easter Duncairn was her whole world, and she was terrified you'd take a wife and put her out.'

'Dear Lizann,' he murmured, 'you have a heart of gold.'

The moment was too sweet to let slip, and she whispered shyly, 'It's all yours, Dan.'

There was a quick intake of breath before he said, 'Do you mean that?'

'It's been all yours for weeks. I was waiting for you to . . .'

'And I've been waiting for some sign . . .' He took a step towards her, then hesitated. 'I'd like to kiss you . . . but . . .'

Knowing that he was afraid she might object to being kissed in such a public place, she smiled, 'What's stopping you?'

And so, standing on Union Street's wide pavement, thronged with men, women and children out for a Sunday stroll on this sunny spring afternoon, he kissed her. 'You'll marry me now?' he asked, presently.

'As soon as you want.'

They took the tramcar to Great Western Road, where one look at their rapturous faces was enough to make Ella rise to hug Lizann. 'Oh, thank goodness! I was beginning to think I'd have to hit the pair of you over the head with a hammer to knock some sense into you.'

Her husband rose to shake Dan's hand. 'So you managed to propose at long last?'

Chuckling, Dan said, 'It was more of a combined effort.'

In a few minutes they were all sitting with a glass of the champagne John had managed to buy somewhere in readiness, and after toasting the happiness of the couple, Ella said, 'Have you decided when and where the wedding's to be?'

'As soon as possible.' Dan glanced at Lizann who said, 'I'd like it to be here in Aberdeen.'

'Wherever you want, my sweet,' he smiled.

'You can see my minister if you like, Dan,' Ella suggested. 'Stay over tonight, and you can arrange everything tomorrow.'

'I want a quiet wedding,' Lizann said, timidly, 'with a

wee do for my friends afterwards . . . if it wouldn't cost too much.'

Dan smiled adoringly. 'I don't care what it costs if you're happy.'

Ella raised her eyebrows to her husband and stood up. 'I think we're superfluous at the moment, John.'

'I think you're right,' he grinned, rising to follow her out.

Lizann gave a long, happy sigh. 'This doesn't seem real.'

'You're not having second thoughts, I hope?'

'No, it's just . . . now we've come right out and said we love each other, everything's happening so quickly.'

'Would you rather we waited? It's up to you, my darling.'

'No, I don't want to wait. We've wasted enough time as it is, and it's all my fault. I should have accepted when you proposed before.'

'You didn't love me then.'

'I must have, I just didn't know it. I was in a bit of a state at that time, don't forget.'

He stood up and pulled her to her feet, tilting her face up to kiss her. 'I'll make you happy, my sweet, sweet Lizann. I'll do everything in my power to please you.'

When Dan took her back to her lodgings, Mrs Melville was delighted at what they had to tell her. 'I'll be sorry to lose the best lodger I ever had,' she said, then added mischievously, 'even though my house always reeked of fish.'

In bed, Lizann wondered how she would shape as a farmer's wife. Would Dan's workers resent him marrying the girl who had once been his maid? Would some of them remember that she had once sold fish at their doors? Whatever happened, she would never regret marrying him, and she would give him the love he'd been starved of for so long.

* * *

'I wondered how long it would be before you saw sense,' Gladys grinned, when Lizann told her she was going to marry Dan.

'I wasn't sure I loved him,' Lizann explained.

'I knew you loved him, right from the day he turned up here.'

'Liar,' Lizann laughed.

'Honest, and if you'd dithered about much longer, I'd have told you to pull your socks up. When's the wedding?'

'Dan's going to try to make it three weeks from Saturday. His sister's going to arrange everything else – I'm too excited. It's to be in Ella's kirk, and I wanted you to be matron-of-honour, but when Dan said he was having John as best man, I felt obliged to ask Ella. You're invited to the Douglas Hotel after, though – you and whoever else wants to come.'

Gladys turned round and shouted, 'D'you hear that? We're all invited to the Douglas after Lizann's wedding.'

Lizann was swamped with congratulations, plus a few remarks and jokes rather too near the knuckle for her liking, though she took them all in good part. As she observed to Gladys later, 'What a great lot they are. The best set of friends I could wish for.'

'You'll maybe not be saying that when they let their hair down in the Douglas. Are Dan's folk easy offended?'

'I don't think so.' Lizann's face grew anxious as a new thought struck her. 'I won't get a feet-washing, will I?'

'No, it's just men that get that,' Gladys assured her.

Having taken Gladys at her word, Lizann had a shock when the hooter blew on the evening before the great day and she was whisked to the cloakroom and draped in an old lace curtain which someone had taken in. 'What's going on?' she gasped.

'We're dressing the bride,' she was informed, as some-one put a garland of newspaper roses round her head.

'Don't be scared,' Gladys whispered. 'They won't blacken you.'

The last embellishment was a large feather duster stuck into her hand as a bouquet, and then she was carried into the yard and hoisted on to a lorry. This time it was girls and women who jumped on with handbells and pans held aloft. She knew what to expect, and covered her ears as the lorry moved out slowly into the street. The din made the workers who were coming out of the neighbouring yards join in the cheering, and as they went over Victoria Bridge and along South Market Street, everyone they passed shouted out their good wishes. The fun became frenetic when they went up the steep hill of Market Street itself – the floor of the 'wedding carriage' was awash with brine and bits of fish, and it was all the 'bride' and her 'attendants' could do to keep their feet.

'How're you doing?' Gladys yelled, as they turned into Union Street, seething with people bound for home.

'I'm surviving,' Lizann yelled back, 'but what'll folk think?'

'They'll think we're mad! No,' Gladys added, seeing her friend's look of shame, 'they've seen this lots of times. All the yards and factories do it.'

The lorry sailed majestically up the main thoroughfare, often having to stop behind a tram when it picked up or deposited passengers, and Lizann soon saw that the onlookers were enjoying the spectacle. When a group of workmen shouted, 'Give's a smile, lass,' she grinned, waving her brightly-coloured 'bouquet', and was rewarded by cries of 'Good luck', and one ribald, 'Watch you dinna land wi' a honeymoon bairn.'

At the end of Union Street they turned left into Holburn Street, just as long but not quite so busy. The crowds had dwindled to an odd person here and there by the time they reached the Bridge of Dee, where the driver made another left turn to go along North Esplanade West. All the yards here had emptied long before, so he put on a little spurt and in only minutes they were back at Sinclair Road and his cargo of women all jumped off.

'That's something for you to remember,' he joked to Lizann as she was extricating herself from her 'bridal' accoutrements.

'Yes,' she laughed. 'I'll never forget it, and thanks, Davey.'

'Nae bother,' he grinned.

'You'll come to the Douglas tomorrow?'

'We'll all be there.'

'Great! Well, I'd better go and get on my coat, for my landlady'll be wondering why I'm so late.'

When she went into her digs, Mrs Melville said, 'I thought they'd get up to something. I've seen brides being taken round before.'

'I wish you'd told me. I didn't know what was happening, but it was good fun. I'll miss them.'

'You'll have your man to keep you occupied,' her landlady smiled. 'Is he coming to see you tonight?'

'He's coming to collect the case with all my clothes, and he'll only stay a wee while. You know, I can't believe everything's going so well for us – even the war's taken a turn for the better. It'll all be over soon.'

The newspapers were jubilant over the Allied advance into France in the four days since D-Day. Mrs Melville was sure that the situation was not as rosy as some reports would have it, but kept her misgivings to herself.

Dan was very amused by Lizann's account of her 'wedding' parade. When he was leaving she went down to the street entrance with him, her eyes popping when she saw the shining black car instead of the rickety lorry. 'What . . . ?' she gasped, as he laid the suitcase on the back seat.

'I couldn't take my bride home in an old Ford,' he grinned. 'And I can't get away from the farm long enough to give you a honeymoon, so I hired the car as the next best thing.'

She flung her arms round his neck. 'Oh Dan, I love you.'

'I should hope so. You'll be Mrs Fordyce by this time tomorrow.'

Remembering that they would probably be going to bed about this time the next night, Lizann was too embarrassed to say anything, which was just as well because Dan couldn't have waited any longer to kiss her.

When she went upstairs, her face was so radiant that Mrs Melville gave a deep sigh. 'Oh lassie, I'm happy for you. You're getting a good man, a gentleman, and I know you'll never regret it.'

'There's just one thing I regret,' Lizann smiled. 'I wish I'd said yes the first time he proposed. I've wasted so much time . . . but if I'd never come to Aberdeen I wouldn't have met you.'

'And that's another thing,' her landlady said, a little tearfully now. 'You've done me a great honour asking me to give you away.'

'I'm honoured that you agreed. You've been like a mother to me, Mrs Melville, and there's nobody I'd rather have to give me away.'

'We'd better get to bed. We'll need all our beauty sleep if we're to look our best tomorrow. I just hope it's a fine day.'

It was more than fine, it was a perfect June day, the sun streaming through the window as, one after the other, they washed at the kitchen sink. Fully dressed, Lizann took one last look in the wardrobe mirror, and smiled in satisfaction. The straw picture hat was the same shade as the powder-blue two-piece. She hadn't been too sure in the shop under the electric light, but in daylight it matched exactly. Looking at her reflection from every angle, she was positive that the costume made her look slimmer, or maybe it was the cuban heels of her court shoes, which certainly made her taller. Picking up the navy clutch bag, she went into the kitchen.

'Oh, Lizann, lass, you're a perfect picture,' Mrs Melville breathed.

'You're very elegant yourself,' Lizann smiled.

The grey coat-dress was very smart, and the silk, swathed turban sat on the silver hair – permed and blue-rinsed for this occasion – as if it had been specially fitted. 'I'll not need a coat, will I?' her landlady asked, anxiously. 'I've only the one I wear every day.' After buying her own dress, Mrs Melville had handed over all the coupons she had left, which had enabled Lizann to buy a decent trousseau . . . not flimsy nightdresses and lingerie this time, though. She was older now, more sensible.

'It's too warm for a coat.' And when Lizann stepped out of the taxi at the church, she was thankful that she had chosen something lightweight to wear; she would have melted in the heat if it had been any heavier.

Ella came forward when they went through the door and walked behind them up the aisle to where Dan and John were waiting, and the ceremony began. After placing Lizann's hand in Dan's, Mrs Melville stood back, fishing her handkerchief out of her sleeve to wipe away the tears which persisted in edging out.

The ceremony did not take long, and the bride and groom walked out hand in hand, to be whisked off in a taxi to the Douglas Hotel, where, as only the fish workers knew how, the real celebrations took off. Even with food on ration, the hotel – helped by items provided by Ella, Dan and Mrs Melville – had laid on an appetizing meal, which was eaten amid a joyful hum of voices and loud cackles of laughter at obviously risqué jokes. Dan had been disappointed at not being able to get more whisky and other drinks for the toasts, but looking around,

Lizann couldn't help smiling at the amount of bottles on the tables. Most of the men must have taken something in with them – bought on the black market, more than likely – so it promised to be a very convivial affair.

It was hilarious, everyone determined to have a good time and to make sure everyone else did, too. Eventually it came time for the cake to be cut. It was more Madeira than wedding cake – Mrs Melville having made it from an egg-less, fruit-less recipe in the *Gert and Daisy Cook Book* – but Dan guided Lizann's hand on the knife as if it were a three-tiered confection par excellence. Cries of 'Speech! Speech!' made him blush, but he kept standing when Lizann sat down.

'First of all,' he began, letting his eyes rove round the now hushed assembly, 'on behalf of my wife and myself . . .' He had to wait until the foot-stamping died down before he could carry on. '. . . I'd like to thank you for making our wedding day one we shall never forget. I would also like to thank the matron-of-honour and the best man for executing their duties so well . . .' more cheering '. . . and last, but by no means least, my undying thanks to Mrs Melville for giving Lizann to me.'

He sat down to thunderous applause, and when it died away, John stood up. 'Now it's my turn,' he smiled. 'I didn't realize until Gladys told me that the best man has to read out all the telegrams, but here goes.'

Lifting the papers in front of him, which he had already arranged in what he thought would be the most suitable order, he went through the straightforward good wishes from some of Dan's workers and the women who had worked with Lizann, then he said, 'Now we come to the more colourful messages. First, "To Lizann and Dan – May all your troubles be little ones – Davey."'

'He drove the lorry yesterday,' Lizann whispered to Dan. 'That's him sitting at the far end of the table on the left.'

'Next,' John went on, once the clapping stopped, '"May your joys be as deep as the snow in the glen, and your troubles as few as the teeth of a hen." That's from Mr Birnie.'

'He's the manager,' Lizann whispered. 'His wife's ill so he couldn't come, but it was nice of him to send a telegram, wasn't it?'

John was grinning broadly as he held up a hand for silence. 'There are two more, gems from the pens of poets who prefer to remain anonymous.' Taking up an orator's stance, he recited:

> 'We all fell in love with Lizann,
> We were sure she was needing a man,
> But now she is leaving,
> And leaving us grieving,
> For the man she has chosen is Dan.'

The tumultuous applause increased when an apprentice admitted proudly that he and the other mechanics had taken their whole half-hour off one dinnertime to make this up, and John had to bang the table before he could read out the final item.

> 'We'll look for the sun, we'll look for the rain,
> We'll look for Lizann, but all in vain.
> She's left us for love, for a farmhouse so nice –
> She'll gut no bloody fish now she's Mrs Fordyce.'

John looked up and, doing his best to make himself heard above the gales of laughter, shouted, 'It just says "From all the coopers".'

'Stand up and take a bow, Runcie,' came a yell. 'We ken it was you.'

To everyone's delight, a small, middle-aged man rose

to his feet and looked across at Lizann. 'I hope it didna offend you?'

'No, no,' she assured him. 'We'll treasure it . . . all of them.'

John sat down to a sustained round of applause, and for the next ten minutes there was great activity as the men helped to dismantle and move all the tables to make way for the dancing. The floor cleared, the three-piece band supplied by the hotel came in and struck up a swingy quickstep. Every male, it seemed, wanted to dance with the bride, and Lizann thoroughly enjoyed her popularity for the next couple of hours. At last, however, she knew it was time for more serious matters, and taking her life in her hands, she mingled amongst the friends she had made and was now on the brink of leaving, to bid them goodbye. Knowing that she would break down when she came to Gladys Wright, she left her until last, and they stood in a corner amid all the uproar clasping hands tearfully. 'You'll write?' Gladys asked.

'Yes, and you too? I want to get all the news.'

Both were aware that they would have less and less in common as time went past – Lizann would have only the farm to write about; Gladys would give up work when her husband was released from the prison camp – but they meant what they said at that moment.

Most of the men, and some of the women, were what was euphemistically termed 'merry' by this time, a few even more than that. The cackles of laughter had become screeches, the jokes bordered on the obscene, and Lizann was quite relieved when some of them began to make a move towards the door. Before leaving, everyone shook hands with the bride and groom, said how much they had enjoyed the 'do' and wished them health and happiness. Mrs Melville had only time to give her lodger a tearful hug before she was swept away by the woman with whom she was to share a taxi home, but it was perhaps a good thing, Lizann thought. She couldn't have coped with a long-drawn-out parting from her just then. She would write to her in a day or two.

At last only the bride and groom and their matron-of-honour and best man were left. John leaned back in his chair. 'I've attended quite a few weddings in my time, but I've never enjoyed one so much before, not even my own.'

'The same goes for me,' his wife smiled, 'but don't settle yourself down. These two have a long journey ahead of them.'

Lizann stood up. 'Yes, we'd better be going, or it'll be all hours of the night before we . . .'

She came to a halt when Dan pulled her back into her seat. 'We're not going anywhere tonight, my sweet. I booked a room here. It isn't much of a honeymoon, but I thought . . .'

'Oh, Dan,' she said, her eyes brimming, 'you're an absolute darling.'

'I do my best,' he beamed.

'In that case . . .' John began, leaning back, but Ella fixed his lapel. 'In that case, nothing! Dan and his wife want to be alone.'

'Oh, of course. Sorry!' He rose rather unsteadily. 'I hope you have a good journey home, Mr and Mrs Fordyce . . .'

'Come on!' Ella urged, adding to Lizann, 'He'll be like a bear with a sore head in the morning.'

'He's all right,' Dan told her. 'He didn't have a lot to drink.'

'Enough. Cheerio, Lizann.'

'Thanks for all you did . . . both of you.'

'I thought they'd never go,' Dan sighed when they went out.

Lizann looked apologetically at her groom. 'You'll have to get my case out of the car before we go to our room.'

'I did all that earlier,' he smiled.

When they went upstairs he turned to her with a peculiar expression. 'I hope you don't expect too much of me, my sweet. I've never been with a woman before, and I'd hate to think you were comparing me with . . .' He broke off, his face suffusing with colour.

'With George, you mean?' She laughed at that. 'He was so drunk on our wedding night, he fell asleep with all his clothes on.'

'But he must have . . . you had other nights . . .'

'Stop worrying, Dan my darling. I'll never forget George altogether, but I'd never dream of comparing the two of you. You're my husband now, and I'll love you whatever you do . . . or don't do.'

She was not disappointed in him.

Chapter Thirty-five

❧❧❧

Over breakfast, Lizann said, 'Booking a room here was a lovely surprise, Dan. It's made me love you more than ever.'

He beamed with pleasure. 'I'm pleased to hear it, and I've got another surprise up my sleeve ... no, two surprises, but I'm not going to tell you anything. I don't want to spoil them.'

'Just a wee hint?' she coaxed.

'No, my sweet, you'll have to wait and see.'

'Oh, Dan,' she sighed, then smiled. 'Whatever they are, they can't be as good as this.'

His eyes twinkling, he wagged his finger at her. 'Don't be too sure.'

She wondered if he was going to give her a piece of jewellery when they were in the car, but when they went outside he settled her into the passenger seat and drove off. 'Thank goodness the weather's kept up,' he observed.

Although bursting with curiosity, she asked no further questions and relaxed to enjoy the scenery. It didn't cross her mind to wonder why he kept to the coast road when he could cut off the north-east corner of Aberdeenshire – the scenery was probably more interesting – but she began to feel uneasy when they passed the road which would have taken them to Easter Duncairn. Nevertheless, she waited until they had left Banff behind before venturing, 'I hope you're not going where I think you're going, Dan.'

His smile irritated her, and her unease turned to alarm when they went through Cullen. 'Dan! If this is your idea of a surprise, I can tell you right now, I don't want to go to Buckie!'

He let his hand rest on her knee for a second. 'Lizann, you must face up to your past before we can have a decent future.'

'No, Dan! Please don't make me go!'

'I know it'll be difficult for you, at least to begin with, but you'll end up thanking me.'

'I won't! Oh Dan, please!'

'If you don't go, you'll always have it at the back of your mind that you turned your back on your family. They'll probably be so glad to see you they'll forgive you anything.' Her growing agitation, however, made him slow down and stop. 'I didn't mean to hurt you, my dearest. If you think it'll be too much for you, we'll go home instead.'

After a short, meditative silence, she murmured, 'I suppose you're right, Dan, but if things get out of hand, promise you'll take me away.'

'I promise, and I'll be at your side all the time.'

Her stomach churned as they drove through Portessie, and she was barely able to direct him to the Yardie, she was so filled with dread. 'Here,' she told him at last. 'Stop here.'

He came round and opened the car door for her, and she clung to his hand as they walked to the house where she had been born. 'You knock,' she whispered, sure that she wouldn't have the courage to walk through the door when it was opened . . . if they were asked in.

Lifting the brass knocker, he gave two loud raps which were answered too quickly for Lizann, but when she saw the young woman who was looking questioningly at Dan, she burst out, 'Jenny!'

Jenny's face paled, but there was no hesitation as she took a step forward and flung her arms round her sister-in-law. 'Oh, Lizann! Is it really you?'

Watching them weeping together, Dan found himself striving to keep back his own tears, but Lizann held out her hand and pulled him to her. 'This is Dan Fordyce,' she said, proudly. 'We were married yesterday.'

Emotionally, Jenny flung her arms round Dan now, then said, still with a catch in her voice, 'Come into the house, for goodness' sake.'

When Lizann noticed the man sitting in the shadows in his shirtsleeves and slippers with his back to the light, she assumed, quite naturally, that it was Mick and started forward eagerly, but when he turned his head she drew up abruptly. 'Peter!' she gasped, blanching.

Jenny held Dan from going forward as Peter stood up, his face ashen. 'Lizann!' he croaked, holding out his hand and then changing his mind and embracing her with a fervour which she hoped wouldn't end in a kiss. To prevent it she said, 'Peter, I'd like you to meet my husband.'

As the two men shook hands, Jenny said, 'They were married yesterday.'

Grinning, Peter put his arm round his wife. 'So we beat them to it.'

Lizann was puzzled. 'Beat us to it? What d'you mean?'

'Jenny and I were married months ago.'

'But . . . what about Mick?' she exclaimed in bewilderment. 'Did you not marry him, Jenny?'

Peter's face sobered. 'Yes, she married him, but he was lost two years ago.'

Dan gripped Lizann's elbow, but she went on a trifle unsteadily, 'And Elsie?'

'You'd better sit down,' Jenny murmured, 'and I'll make a pot of tea. We've an awful lot to speak about.'

Aware that hearing about her brother's death had distressed his bride, Dan sat on the arm of her chair while Jenny filled the teapot, and not a word was said until

518

Lizann remembered something that had been knocked completely out of her head by what she had learned so far. 'My mother? How's my mother?'

Jenny looked at her in dismay. 'I forgot you didn't know about that, either. I'm sorry, Lizann, your mother died . . . over three years ago.'

There was a brief pause. 'Was it because . . . I went away?'

'No, no! We never told her that. We said you couldn't get over losing George and the baby . . .' Jenny halted, not knowing if Dan had been told about either of these tragedies.

As she handed round the cups, Peter said, 'I often wondered how you were, Lizann, but you were looking well when you came in.'

'I couldn't have been better.' She gave Dan a watery smile.

They had not even touched on the mammoth task of filling in the five-year-gap when the door was flung open and five children rushed in. Jenny smiled fondly. 'Here's our scallywags home from Sunday School. Pattie, Tommy, Norma . . .' she paused and added somewhat apprehensively, 'and Georgie and little Lizann.'

The first three were obviously Peter's, with the same blondness and bright hazel eyes, but the small boy and girl bringing up the rear had Mick's dark eyes and Jenny's colouring. 'It was nice of you calling them that,' Lizann said, a little huskily. Then, afraid that Dan might not be so pleased, she cast a wary eye on him, but he was nodding in agreement.

'It was a lovely idea,' he smiled.

'We'll have two sittings for dinner,' Jenny observed, 'seeing there's nine of us. Adults first.'

Lizann got quickly to her feet. 'No, no, we're not staying.'

'Of course you're staying. Sit down, you can't leave

without something to eat – as long as you're prepared to muck in.'

Lizann glanced at Dan, who grinned. 'Thanks, Jenny, we'll be happy to muck in.'

After the meal, at Dan's suggestion, he and Peter took the children for a walk to leave the women to talk freely. Going over past events and what had led up to them was a painful process for both Jenny and Lizann, but each tried to play down the agonies they had suffered. To save Jenny's feelings, Lizann laid the blame for her sudden flight squarely on Elsie's visit, and made light of her spell as a fishwife, and when it was Jenny's turn, she played down Hannah's mental deterioration and the hell her own life had been while she nursed the old woman. She also said that Elsie had been killed in a road accident without mentioning how and where, and kept the dying confession to herself – that was something she would never divulge again. Only then did Lou's death come up, and Jockie Flett's – he had died five months earlier from cirrhosis of the liver.

More or less up-to-date with all each other's news now, Lizann said, 'I'm glad you and Peter got together, Jenny.'

'So'm I . . . he lost a leg, you know . . . when the ship he and Mick were on was torpedoed.'

'Oh, no! Poor Peter. I thought he was crippling just now, but I never dreamt he'd . . .'

'He was in a bit of a state when he came back first, that's why I took him in and told him to rent out his house. His bairns were with Elsie's mother and father and they didn't want to . . . I think his artificial leg scared them.'

'I can't feel sorry about Elsie,' Lizann said shamefacedly.

Because she felt it was too dangerous to dwell on Elsie, Jenny changed the subject. 'Will you and Dan be living at his farm?'

'Yes. I thought that's where we were going this morning and when I realized he was making for Buckie, I was angry ... well, not angry, more scared, for I thought Mother wouldn't want to see me. I should have come home before, Jenny. It shouldn't have been left to you to nurse her. Did she ever speak about me?'

'All the time,' Jenny said to make her sister-in-law feel better, and purposely not referring to Hannah's confusion.

'I wish I could have seen her and Mick again.'

She sat pensively for some moments, then Jenny said quietly, 'I'll never forget Mick, Lizann. I told Peter that when he asked me to marry him, and he said he didn't expect me to. But I'm his wife now, and I do love him, and I'm going to do my best to make him happy.'

'Peter's a good man, I always thought a lot of him. You know, Jenny, we're really lucky, you and me. I had George and now I've got Dan, and you had Mick and now you've got Peter – all fine men.'

This went some way towards dispelling the doubt which had arisen in Jenny's mind when Peter took Lizann in his arms, but a little niggle persisted – the love had been mostly on his side before.

It was after four when the others came back. 'I think we should be making tracks, Lizann,' Dan told his wife. 'I've to start work early tomorrow, and I've some things to ... do first.'

'You'll come to see us at Easter Duncairn?' Lizann begged Peter.

'It's a bit difficult without transport,' he pointed out, 'but who knows, I might be able to afford a secondhand car after the war, though it's a bus we'd need for all this gang.'

Outside, Jenny said, 'You two'll come back here, though?'

'I'm afraid this is only a hired car,' Dan said, as he

opened the passenger door, 'but I do have an old lorry, if my wife doesn't object to coming in that.'

'I'd come on a bike, if that's all we had,' she laughed.

Arms round each other's waists, Peter and Jenny stood until the car disappeared round the bend. 'Did you tell her Robbie wanted to know if she still had that picture?' he asked, when they turned to go inside.

Her hand flew to her mouth. 'Oh, I forgot, but she said she'd to sell all her things when she left Buckie. I can't get over me forgetting to tell her about Robbie, though. Still, it'll be something to speak about next time they come. You know, I nearly dropped dead on the spot when I saw her.' Jenny hesitated, then added, 'How did you feel?'

'I was pleased . . .' His voice strengthened suddenly. 'Of course I was pleased to see her, damned pleased, and she'd hardly changed a bit.' He looked at Jenny, his eyes entreating her to believe him. 'But it was just like an old, very dear friend had turned up again. That's all.'

Jenny was satisfied now. She had needed to hear him say it.

Sitting beside her husband-of-a-day, Lizann sighed blissfully. 'Oh, I'm glad you made me come, Dan.'

'I was sure it would be all right,' he smiled, 'and I must say Jenny and Peter make a lovely couple.'

'But it's sad to think it's because Mick's dead they've . . .'

'Look at it this way, my sweet. They both lost their partners in very tragic circumstances . . .'

'I don't think Elsie's death would have bothered Peter,' Lizann said, a little sharply.

'Perhaps it wouldn't have affected him as much as Jenny was affected by losing Mick, but he must have felt something for his wife.'

'You wouldn't say that if you'd known her.' Lizann paused, then said, repentantly, 'I shouldn't say things like that when she's dead. You must think I'm callous and hard-hearted.'

'I know you're not, and you're perfectly right, I shouldn't criticize you when I knew nothing about the woman.'

'I really am pleased they've got together, though. Peter deserves some happiness. I was engaged to him at one time, you know, and I broke it off because of George . . .'

Dan turned to smile at her. 'I had the feeling that you had been more than just friends.'

'Don't be jealous. I never really loved him, not enough anyway, but he was a very good friend to me when George was drowned, and so was Jenny.'

'I'm not jealous, my dearest. In fact, I'm happy that you have what is more or less a family again. I felt guilty at having a sister while you had nobody. Unfortunately, my hope of reuniting you with your mother and brother proved impossible, but even if Jenny is not a blood relative you do have a niece and nephew who are.'

Lizann brightened now. 'Yes, George and Lizann. You weren't put out by their names, were you?'

'Not in the least. It showed me how thoughtful Jenny was . . . and Mick.'

'Dan, would you like us to have children?'

'Only if you want them.'

'I'd like two, close together, so they'll be company for each other.'

Approaching Easter Duncairn, Lizann gave a little chuckle. 'The second surprise turned out well, after all, so what about the last one? When do I get it?'

'Any time now.'

They entered the farmhouse by the kitchen, and when she saw that most of the old items had been replaced and that a refrigerator had been installed, she turned and gave

523

her husband a bear hug. 'Oh, Dan, this is another lovely surprise.'

She broke away to inspect everything and didn't notice the contained excitement on his face. When at last she went back to him, he said, 'I had the whole house done up. Come and see the rest.'

The dining-room made her exclaim in delight. With wallpaper having disappeared from the shops during the war, Dan had painted over the dingy paper she remembered and stippled on a pattern to decorate it. The room seemed much lighter and airier, this impression being helped by a new table and chairs, with a long sideboard to match. 'They're not new,' Dan said, apologetically. 'Nothing was new, not even the refrigerator. I got everything at a roup in a big house outside Rothienorman, all good quality. What do you think?'

'I'm speechless,' she murmured.

Taking her elbow, he led her into the sitting-room, watching her face as he opened the door, but when she spotted what he had been waiting for her to notice, he had as big a surprise as she did, because she just stood and stared. He couldn't tell by her expression whether she was angry or pleased, and started to babble an explanation. 'I saw it in a second-hand shop in Aberdeen one Sunday on my way to meet you. It had something very special about it, and it reminded me of the first time I saw you. The shop was closed, of course, but I got Ella to go next day and buy it for me.' He was very much taken aback when she started to weep; it was the last thing he had expected. 'I'm sorry, my dear, maybe you don't want to be reminded. If you don't like it . . .'

Her tear-filled eyes were fixed on a spot above the fireplace, on the gold-framed drawing of a girl with a creel. 'I love it,' she whispered. 'I've always loved it.'

'I loved it, too, as soon as I saw it, but I don't understand . . .'

'Dan, it's the most wonderful, wonderful surprise you could ever have given me. I thought I'd never see it again. It's my good luck token, so I know we'll always be happy together.'

She slid into his arms, still weeping softly, and having no experience of women he couldn't understand why she was crying when she professed to be pleased, but he deemed it best not to tell her about the letter just yet. Wanting his gift to her to be perfect, he had bought a new frame, and when he removed the brown backing paper to take out the actual sketch, he had found the love note. He had no doubt that she would be just as intrigued by it as he had been, and they could have some fun making up suggestions as to who had hidden it and why, also imagining the story behind the writing of the billet-doux in the first place. They might try asking in as many fishing communities as they could if anyone had any information, though it would be difficult with no names to give ... unless someone could identify the girl. Of course, the truth might turn out to be disappointingly unromantic.

Dropping a kiss on Lizann's head – now with a few white hairs through the curly black – Dan was sure that she would tell him in her own time why the picture meant so much to her, and why it had come to be lying in the window of a rag and bone merchant amongst a lot of old junk.

Chapter Thirty-six

❧

'We'd better get up,' Dan said, regretfully. 'Alice'll be here soon.'

'I don't really need anybody,' Lizann smiled. 'I could easily manage.'

'I want you to take things easy.' He kissed the point of her nose then swung his feet to the floor. 'She worked like a slave when Meggie was ill, and I wouldn't like to sack her.'

'Oh no, you can't sack her, but we're bound to feel awkward with each other. Even if she doesn't remember me coming round with the creel, her mother and all the other cottar wives will.'

'They'll respect you for having had to work hard.'

By the time her maid appeared – at seventeen, a tall robust girl with bright blue eyes and fair hair covered by a checked blue duster – Lizann had set the table in the kitchen and was supervising the toast under the grill while a pan of eggs was boiling on top of the stove. 'You're nae eating in here?' the girl asked, her lips pursing in disapproval.

'It'll save dirtying the dining-room,' Lizann smiled. 'And I lit the boiler nearly an hour ago, so you can start on the washing when . . .' This sounding too much like an order, she started again. 'Look, Alice, maybe you'll think I'm making out you didn't do things right before, but I'm only trying to help. If we share the work, we'll soon get used to each other's ways.'

The girl's scowl vanished. 'Aye, Mrs Fordyce, I suppose so.'

Once Dan had eaten and gone out, Lizann cleared the table, washed up the dishes and swept the floor, by which time Alice had finished the first load of washing. 'Look at this, Mrs Fordyce,' she said, holding up a linen sheet they had just put through the mangle. 'You could read the morning paper through this, it's that thin.'

Lizann's heart sank. 'Are they all like that?'

'Most of them. It took me a while to find a decent pair to put on for you coming. I didna worry when it was just Mr Fordyce, for men never see that kind of thing, but a woman's different.'

'I'll go up in the afternoon and see what's to be replaced.'

While Alice was scrubbing Dan's grimy shirt collars on the corrugated washing board, Lizann pegged out the whites, sighing when she saw that the pillowcases were as thin as the sheets, the towels were on their last legs and the tablecloths had already been darned several times. Then she remembered Meggie telling her, with a touch of pride, that they had all belonged to Dan's mother. They'd given good service, Lizann thought as she went back inside, and the same quality wasn't available nowadays – just cotton, with the wartime utility mark on.

'I dinna ken what we'll have for our dinner,' Alice observed. 'It's a good job the master never comes in for anything on washing days, for there's nae left-overs to be eaten up.'

'Of course, he was away over the weekend. Well, it doesn't matter to me. I'd be quite happy with a cup of tea and an oatcake and cheese. What about you?'

'Aye, that'll do me and all.'

After they had finished their snack, Lizann went to check on the linen and Alice took in those items dry enough for ironing. She was covering the table with an old blanket when there was a sharp knock on the back door. It turned out to be an elderly man and someone she took to be his daughter. 'Is Mrs Fordyce in?' he smiled.

'She's upstairs, but if you come into the sitting-room, I'll go and tell her you're here.'

She led them through the kitchen and across a wide hall, and, holding open a door, asked, 'Who'll I say?'

'If you don't mind, we'd like to surprise her.'

Jenny walked into the large, welcoming room, and was about to take a seat when she was startled by a painful gasp from behind her. Looking round, she saw that Robbie was pointing to something, and following his trembling finger, her eyes widened when they came to rest on a familiar picture. Fearful for his heart, she turned back to him, to find him regarding her in deep entreaty.

'Tell me I'm not dreaming,' he begged.

'You're not dreaming,' she assured him, going over and putting her arm round his shoulder. 'Are you all right? You're awful white.'

'It's my Hannah,' he murmured, his hand going to his chest as if to still the inner turmoil. 'I thought I'd got over her, but it just took one glimpse of that picture to bring it all back.'

Just then the door opened and Lizann walked in, her brow wrinkling in puzzlement when she saw the two people standing with their backs to her, and clearing when the woman turned her head. 'Jenny! What on earth are you doing here?'

'I asked her to come with me.' Rather unsteadily, Robbie stepped away from Jenny to face the woman he had been longing to see.

The next few minutes were something of a blur to him. In his mind it was Hannah who had come in, looking no older than he remembered her, her near-black eyes holding no recognition but filling with concern for him. But there should be love there as well as concern, he thought sadly, as gentle hands guided him to a comfortable chair. He wanted to speak to her, to ask why she ignored his note, but there was an agonizing pain in his chest. He became conscious of Jenny's soft voice soothing him while she slackened his tie and opened his front stud to ease the pressure of the starched collar on his throat. 'You'll be fine,' she was murmuring. 'You got a shock seeing the picture, and seeing Lizann on top of that ... I should have warned you.'

Lizann? he wondered. But it had been Hannah ... hadn't it? No, what was he thinking? Jenny had said Hannah died years ago, and even if she had still been alive, she'd have been quite old now, the same as he was. There would have been more than a sprinkling of silver through the jet black hair. He should have known, but her daughter was so like her, so heart-stoppingly like her. He moved his lips now and found himself able to croak a squeaky, 'I'm sorry, Jenny.'

'It was my fault.'

Still ignorant as to who he was and why he was there, Lizann said, 'I'll go and ask Alice to make some tea.'

When she came back, Jenny said, 'I haven't introduced you yet. Lizann, this is Robbie Chapman.'

The name did sound vaguely familiar to her, but before she had time to think where she had heard it, he rose and embraced her tightly. 'You're so like your mother, I can hardly believe you're not really her.'

'You knew my mother?'

'He's the one that drew the picture,' Jenny was explaining when Dan walked in, giving a peculiar smile when he murmured, 'So you're the artist, Mr ... um ... ?'

'Chapman's the name.'

'Not Rob Chapman?' Dan gasped. 'The famous portrait painter?'

'The very same,' Robbie laughed, 'but a raw unknown when I sketched Hannah Jappy. So raw that I fell in love with her, but she wouldn't let herself love me.'

Having delved into the recesses of her past, Lizann

had recalled what her Auntie Lou had told her after her mother's astonishing denial that 'it wasn't Robbie's baby!' She didn't want to dwell on what those few words suggested, so she said coldly, 'I was led to believe that she was already married to my father when you drew her.'

'That didn't stop some women from running off with another man,' he retorted, then his shoulders sagged. 'I'm sorry. It's your parents we're speaking about, of course. But you must understand, Hannah wasn't like other women. She was so innocent . . .'

He broke off, overcome by memories, and Jenny had to relate the story of why he had been banned from the Yardie, making it quite clear that nothing actually sinful had happened between Hannah and him, except in her childlike mind. Then Robbie took up the reins once more. 'It nearly broke my heart not to be allowed to see her, so I left home and went to London to try my luck as an artist.'

'You wrote her a letter first.' Dan's expression was enigmatic now.

Robbie turned pale again. 'I did, but I didn't get a reply.'

Lizann looked indignantly at her husband. 'How did you know there was a letter? You didn't say anything about it to me last night.'

'My dear girl, I didn't get much chance. I saw you were knocked off balance by the picture, and I didn't want to make you any worse. I was going to tell you tonight.'

It was Jenny who persisted. 'How did you know, Dan? And Lizann sold the picture with the rest of her stuff, so where did you find it?'

'I'd better start at the beginning,' he smiled. 'I saw it in a secondhand shop in Aberdeen . . .'

'Goodness knows how it got there,' Lizann butted in.

'. . . and the girl was so like Lizann as I saw her first, I had to buy it. When I was replacing the damaged frame, I found a letter behind the backing paper.' He walked across to the old mahogany bureau and took out a grubby envelope. 'It's not addressed, so I think she had destroyed the original one.'

Robbie shook his head when it was held out to him. 'I can remember every word as if I'd newly written it. Let Lizann read it, then maybe she'll understand how I felt about her mother.'

The two young women put their heads together to read it, and Lizann's expression was softer when she looked at Robbie again. 'You really did love her, didn't you?'

'With all my heart, and I tried to tell myself she didn't answer that because she didn't get it, but it seems she did get it.'

His deep sigh and his stricken face made Lizann say impulsively, 'She must have thought a lot of you before she kept it.'

He had been biting his bottom lip, but this thought cheered him. 'You think so? She did the right thing, I know that now. She was better with him . . . she couldn't have depended on me. I nearly starved for years . . .' He broke off, sighing again.

Lizann looked at Dan with her eyebrows raised, and when he nodded, she said, 'Robbie, I'd like you to have the picture as a reminder of her.'

'Oh, no! It's yours, you can't give it away!' He hesitated briefly, then said, hopefully, 'But if you didn't mind, I'd quite like to borrow it for a couple of weeks. A London art dealer has been pestering me to send something down for an exhibition he's putting on, and I've only some of my first attempts at sketching, amateurish compared with this. It's the best thing I ever did, and I'd take it in the railway carriage with me and guard it with my life . . .

and I'd make Perry put on a sticker to show it's not for sale. What d'you say?'

She was grateful that he had refused to accept the picture as a gift; she hadn't wanted to lose it again. 'Yes, I'm quite agreeable to that.'

'I promise to bring it back when the exhibition closes, for I don't need a reminder of your mother. For one thing, every time I look at you I'll see her.' His eyes twinkled now. 'If Fate hadn't decreed otherwise, my dear, you might have been my daughter.'

Noticing the tray which Alice had taken in some time ago, and glad to change the subject, she said, 'I'll make some fresh tea.'

Over the refreshment, Robbie did some more explaining. 'When Jenny came to tell us you'd come back, I couldn't wait to meet you. So I hired a van for the afternoon, and . . . we'd better be going, Jenny, or the bairns'll be home from school.' He had left his sister at the Yardie to be there for the children, but he was eager to tell her the miraculous result of his mission.

Dan having wrapped the picture in sacking and placed it on Jenny's knee in the van, he stood with his arm round Lizann, waving until their visitors were out of sight. He said nothing as they went through the kitchen – Alice was a bit of a gossip – but back in the sitting-room he asked, 'How do you feel after all that?'

She snuggled up to him. 'Still hardly able to believe what he said. I'm glad you were with me . . . but how did you know they were here?'

'Alice came and told me, and I wouldn't have missed it for anything.' He eyed her anxiously now. 'Are you sure you want to go to Buckie again this Saturday? You likely hadn't wanted to refuse when Jenny asked, but isn't it a bit soon?'

Lizann gave a trilling laugh. 'If you think I'll feel jealous because Peter married Jenny, I won't! I could see yesterday they were absolutely right for each other. But so are we, Dan my darling. Not just right, perfect! Don't you think so?'

His answer was to kiss her, so passionately that neither of them saw Alice when she looked round the door to ask when they wanted to eat, and she withdrew without a sound.

Back in the kitchen, a broad grin spread across her face. All the folk round about said it was a marriage of convenience, a lonely old bachelor needing company and an ex-fishwife looking for security, but it hadn't looked like that from where their maid had been standing. It was a real love match, no doubt about it, and she'd be as well turning off the oven and going home.

That two wouldn't be needing any supper tonight!